The Best
AMERICAN
SHORT
STORIES
2003

GUEST EDITORS OF
THE BEST AMERICAN SHORT STORIES

The Best AMERICAN SHORT STORIES® 2003

Selected from
U.S. and Canadian Magazines
by WALTER MOSLEY
with KATRINA KENISON

With an Introduction by Walter Mosley

HOUGHTON MIFFLIN COMPANY
BOSTON • NEW YORK 2003

Visit our Web site: www.houghtonmifflinbooks.com.

ISSN 0067-6233
ISBN 0-618-19732-X
ISBN 0-618-19733-8 (pbk.)

Printed in the United States of America

MP 10 9 8 7 6 5 4 3 2 1

"Compassion" by Dorothy Allison. First published in *Tin House,* No. 13. Copyright © 2002 by Dorothy Allison. Reprinted from *Trash* by permission of Plume, an
imprint of Penguin Group (USA) Inc.

"Space" by Kevin Brockmeier. First published in *The Georgia Review,* Vol. 61,
No. 2. Copyright © 2002 by Kevin Brockmeier. Reprinted from *Things That Fall from
the Sky* by permission of Pantheon Books, a division of Random House, Inc.

"The Bees" by Dan Chaon. First published in *McSweeney's,* No. 10. Copyright ©
2002 by Dan Chaon. Reprinted by permission of the author.

"Johnny Hamburger" by Rand Richards Cooper. First published in *Esquire,*
March 2002. Copyright © 2002 by Rand Richards Cooper. Reprinted by permission
of the author and Watkins Loomis Agency. Lyrics to Rick Astley's "Together Forever" by Mike Stock, Matt Aitken, and Pete Waterman (Stock Aitken Waterman).

"Night Talkers" by Edwidge Danticat. First published in *Callaloo,* Vol. 25, No. 4.
Copyright © 2002 by Edwidge Danticat. Reprinted by permission of the author and
Aragi, Inc.

"Baby Wilson" by E. L. Doctorow. First published in *The New Yorker,* March 25,
2002. Copyright © 2002 by E. L. Doctorow. Reprinted by permission of International Creative Management, Inc. Lyrics from "Sweet Dreams of You" by Abel Baer
and Murray Ross copyright 1953, copyright © renewed 1981. Used by permission.
All rights reserved.

Contents

Foreword

MY SON JACK, a fourth-grader, was having a hard time getting interested in an assigned book recently, so I offered to read the first few chapters to him. In the early pages of *Incident at Hawk Hill,* a quiet little boy has an extraordinary encounter with a female badger. Soon after, another badger is caught in a steel leg trap, and the author describes in graphic detail the searing pain and blind terror of an animal literally struggling to its death. We meet the cruel redneck hunter and his mean cur of a dog; we see the badger being skinned by the boy's unwilling father; and we experience the child's bewilderment when his father, manipulated by the trapper, lashes out in fury and hits his son. Pretty heavy going for ten-year-olds, I thought.

Last night I returned from a weekend away to find that Jack had finished the book on his own. "It was really, really good, and sad, and violent," he reported. "There was a lot more killing."

"Were there any happy parts?" I asked.

"The boy's life was saved by the badger, so that was good, but then that badger got caught in a trap, and at the end it's dying too," Jack said. "It was so sad that I almost cried."

I told him that many books have made me cry, beginning with *Heidi,* when I was just his age, right on up to the novel I finished last week.

"Well," he admitted then, "I actually did cry. Reading that book just reminded me of all the sadness in the world, and it made me feel sad too."

So, I thought, now he has been through this rite of passage, the discovery that words on a printed page can give rise to such intense emotion — that a *book,* of all things, can move you right out of your own comfortable little self and into someone else's pain. Don't we all remember how it was, as a child, to enter a story innocently, only to emerge at the other end utterly wrung out, red-eyed, and in some intangible way transformed? Thus we come to realize that if we are to remain fully engaged in life, open to its mysteries and compassionate toward its suffering, we indeed need stories to grab us by the scruff of the neck and remind us of the sadness in the world that is not our own.

Reading again through Walter Mosley's selections for *The Best American Short Stories 2003,* I'm struck by the exquisite balance he has found between pain and exultation, pathos and humor. In Dorothy Allison's deathbed saga, "Compassion," four sisters hold vigil through their mama's last days, scrapping over ancient family history, rock 'n' roll, and reincarnation ("What I think is, if you were good to the people in your life, well then, you come back as a big dog. And if you were some evil son of a bitch, then you gonna come back some nasty little Pekingese"). There's nothing wrong, Allison reminds us, with laughing through the tears.

Kevin Brockmeier's "Space" also deals with those left behind after a death, in this case a father and son tentatively beginning to reconstruct a family of two after the loss of a beloved wife and mother. Bound only by grief, but separated by it too, man and boy slowly dance, at arm's length, through a new landscape, stumbling with every step but not quite giving up on each other. It is a moving, ultimately hopeful portrait of the heart's resilience.

Death is also a theme in Edwidge Danticat's "Night Talkers," but this time it is a death well timed, preceded by the reunion of an embattled young man and his wise, blind old aunt, who had raised him from childhood and then waited patiently for his return to his native Haiti before passing away peacefully in her sleep, all the important words having been spoken, all the essential stories told. "Perhaps she had summoned him here so he could at last witness a peaceful death and see how it was meant to be mourned," he muses, grateful at last to have been in the right place at the right time.

While death is inevitable — and thus irresistible to writers — other stories in this richly textured collection stand out as celebrations of life in all its strange complexity. Suffering, these stories seem to suggest, is simply a fact of our daily existence, as necessary to the processes of growth and transformation as breath is to life. Having professed at the outset a penchant for stories that "have something to say," Walter Mosley has proven as good as his word. There are no transparent coming-of-age tales here, no character sketches passing themselves off as short stories, no memoirs thinly disguised as fiction. Instead, Mosley offers bold forays into the realms of dream and fantasy, artificial intelligence and mental illness, terrorism and heroism, passionate love and platonic passion.

We meet a desperate young kidnapper and her sympathetic boyfriend, and in the hands of master storyteller E. L. Doctorow, they arrive at an ending that is as blissful as it is unexpected. Newcomer Sharon Pomerantz brings us into the heart and soul of a woman willing to risk everything for sex in public places with a married politician, only to realize that she's the one with nothing to lose; Adam Haslett disturbs the well-burnished peace between an elderly woman and her brother by introducing the complication of a former paramour. In "Rationing," a young Japanese man's deeply felt admiration for his self-sufficient father inhibits him from ever expressing his true feelings, until it is too late. Anthony Doerr's shell collector, a self-exiled blind naturalist, finds his well-ordered universe upended when he accidentally discovers the healing powers of the deadly cone snail.

There is not a character in these pages who escapes suffering altogether, but not one of these stories can be judged as humorless or overly sentimental, either. Good fiction lifts the heart even as it reminds us of the sadness in the world — for who among us leads a charmed life? Taken as a whole, this collection is a vibrant affirmation of the power of love and human connection, be it a young boy's attraction to a compelling mechanical doll in the eerie "Moriya," an immigrant nanny's love for the child entrusted to her care in Mona Simpson's "Coins," or an amputee blues musician's passion for his pious, cross-eyed nurse in ZZ Packer's deliciously unlikely love story, "Every Tongue Shall Confess."

Chosen as they were with Mosley's unerring eye for writers with an original approach to the genre, all twenty of the stories gathered here reward us with the deep satisfaction of art that is fully alive, nourishing to the soul and enlivening to the imagination. Describing the wild playing of a venerable Ojibwa fiddler in "Shamengwa," Louise Erdrich writes, "The sound connected instantly with something deep and joyous. Those powerful moments of true knowledge which we paper over with daily life. The music tapped our terrors, too. Things we'd lived through and never wanted to repeat. Shredded imaginings, unadmitted longings, fear, and also surprising pleasures. We can't live at that pitch. But, every so often, something shatters like ice, and we fall into the river of our own existence. We are aware."

Such is the power of fiction. May the stories of 2003 bring you into the river of your own existence, reminding you of all the sadness in the world, and all the grace as well.

The stories chosen for this anthology were originally published between January 2002 and January 2003. The qualifications for selection are (1) original publication in nationally distributed American or Canadian periodicals; (2) publication in English by writers who are American or Canadian, or who have made the United States or Canada their home; (3) original publication as short stories (excerpts of novels are not knowingly considered). A list of magazines consulted for this volume appears at the back of the book. Editors who wish their short fiction to be considered for next year's edition should send their publications to Katrina Kenison, c/o The Best American Short Stories, Houghton Mifflin Company, 222 Berkeley Street, Boston, MA 02116.

K. K.

Introduction: Americans Dreaming

WHENEVER ANYONE ASKS my opinion about the difference between novels and short stories, I tell them that there is no distinction between the genres. *They are essentially the same thing,* I always reply.

How can you say that? the fiction lover asks. *Stories are small gems, perfectly cut to expose every facet of an idea, which is in turn illuminated by ten thousand tiny shafts of light.*

But I hold my ground, answering the metaphor with a simile. A novel, I say, is like a mountain — superior, vast, and immense. Its apex is in the clouds and it appears to us as a higher being — a divinity. Mountains loom and challenge; they contain myriad life forms and cannot be seen by anyone attempting the climb. Mountains can be understood only by years of negotiating their trails and sheer faces. They contain a wide variety of atmospheres and are complex and immortal.

You cannot approach a mountain unless you are completely prepared for the challenge. In much the same way, you can't begin to read (or write) a novel without attempting to embrace a life much larger than the range of any singular human experience.

Thinking in this way, I understand the mountain and the novel to be impossible in everyday human terms. Both emerge from a distance that can be approached only by faith. And when you get there, all you find is yourself. The beauty or terror you experience is your understanding of how far you've come, your being stretched further than is humanly possible.

The fiction lover agrees. She says, *Yes, of course. The novel is a large thing. The novel stands against the backdrop of human existence just as mountains dominate the landscape. But stories are simple things, small aspects of human foibles and quirks. A story can be held in a glance or a half-remembered dream.*

It's a good argument, and I wouldn't refute it. But I will say that if novels are mountains, then stories are far-flung islands that one comes upon in the limitless horizon of the sea. Not big islands like Hawaii, but small, craggy atolls inhabited by eclectic and nomadic life forms that found their way there in spite of tremendous odds. One of these small islets can be fully explored in a few hours. There's a grotto, a sandy beach, a new species of wolf spider, and maybe the remnants of an ancient culture that came here and moved on or, possibly, just died out.

These geologic comparisons would seem to support the fiction reader's claim that novels and short stories are different categories, distant cousins in the linguistic universe. But where did those wolf spiders come from? And who were the people who came here and died? And why, when I walk around this footprint of land, do I feel that something new arises with each day? I eat fish that live in the caves below the waves. I see dark shadows down there. I dream of the firmament that lies below the ocean, the mountain that holds up that small span of land.

I cannot climb the mountain that sits in the sea, but from where I stand it comes to me in detritus and dreams.

Short story writers must be confident of that suboceanic mountain in order to place their tale in the world. After all, fiction mostly resides in the imagination of the reader. All the writer can do is hint at a world that calls forth the dream, telling the story that exhorts us to call the possibility into being.

The writers represented in this collection have told stories that suggest much larger ideas. I found myself presented with the challenge of simple human love contrasted against structures as large as religion and death. The desire to be loved or to be seen, represented on a canvas so broad that it would take years to explain all the roots that bring us to the resolution.

In many of the stories we find exiles, people who have lost their loved ones, their homelands, their way. These stories are simple and exquisite, but they aren't merely tales of personal loss. Mothers have left us long before the mountains were shifted by southward-moving ice floes. Men have been broken by their dreams for almost as long as the continents have been drifting. And every day someone opens her eyes and sees a world that she never expected could be there.

These short stories are vast structures existing mostly in the subconscious of our cultural history. They will live with the reader long after the words have been translated into ideas and dreams. That's because a good short story crosses the borders of our nations and our prejudices and our beliefs. A good short story asks a question that can't be answered in simple terms. And even if we come up with some understanding, years later, while glancing out of a window, the story still has the potential to return, to alter right there in our mind and change everything.

WALTER MOSLEY

The Best
AMERICAN
SHORT
STORIES
2003

MARY YUKARI WATERS

Rationing

FROM MISSOURI REVIEW

SABURO'S FATHER belonged to that generation which, having survived the war, rebuilt Japan from ashes, distilling defeat and loss into a single-minded focus with which they erected cities and industries and personal lives. Reflecting on this as an adult, Saburo felt it accounted at least partially for his father's stoicism. This was conjecture, of course. When Japan surrendered he had been only six, too young to remember what his father had been like in peacetime.

Saburo's memories of the surrender included his uncle Kotai being brought home, delirious with hepatitic fever, from Micronesia. He lived only a few weeks, unconscious the entire time and nursed round the clock by Saburo's parents. One of the visitors to their home was Uncle Kotai's sweetheart, a pretty girl of nineteen on whom Saburo had a crush. She wiped away her tears with a handkerchief patterned with cherry blossoms and announced brokenly that her life was now over. Saburo was impressed. "Big Sister really loves Uncle, ne!" he said later that day to his parents at dinner.

"The grief didn't hurt her appetite," his mother said curtly. She was referring to the rationed tea she had served at lunch as well as to a certain fish cake that had been purchased, after two hours of waiting in line, for their own family dinner.

In a dispassionate voice, Saburo's father explained that the amount of energy you have is limited, just like your food, and that when you love a sick person you have to make the choice of either using up that energy on tears or else saving it for constructive actions such as changing bedpans and spoon-feeding and giving sponge baths. "In the long run, which would help your uncle more?" he asked.

Saburo supposed the constructive actions would.

"That's right," his father said.

Saburo's father had not fought in the war. He was barred from service because of his glaucoma, which was discovered for the first time during his military recruiting exam. So he stayed home while the war claimed the lives of his best friend, then his cousin, and last of all his brother-in-law Kotai. Growing up, all Saburo understood of glaucoma was that it consisted of some sort of elevated pressure within the eye. "Your father has to keep calm" was his mother's constant refrain. "Don't you dare upset him, or his eye pressure will go up." It seemed to young Saburo that this condition was in some insidious way a result of the war, not unlike those radioactive poisons pulsing within survivors from Hiroshima.

At Uncle Kotai's funeral Saburo had overheard a woman say, "At least in his short life he was never thwarted." He understood later that Uncle, the babied youngest son of a wealthy family, had had no profession save that of martial arts champion and dandy. He drank too often, laughed too loudly, used too much hair pomade. Saburo had very few memories of him or of their former wealth, which had been lost in the Tenkan bombing, forcing Saburo's family to move into the merchant district. He did recall that once when he had gotten a nosebleed as a little boy, Uncle Kotai stopped it instantly by giving a hard chop with the side of his hand to a specific vertebra on his nape. "Aaa, be careful!" Saburo's mother had wailed, watching with both hands pressed to her mouth. Uncle Kotai used another trick when Saburo tried to tag along on one of his outings. "Let me come; I want to go too!" he had demanded, squatting at his uncle's feet and clutching fistfuls of his long yukata. With a rumble of amusement, Uncle Kotai reached down to press some secret nerve between thumb and forefinger, and Saburo's fists miraculously unclenched.

Seen across the gulf of the war that separated them, this lost uncle held for young Saburo all the magic of a lost era, a magic emanating from throwaway details: a photograph of Uncle and his well-dressed friends sitting around a heavily laden banquet table, heads thrown back in laughter; or his mother's nostalgic recounting of Uncle's outrageous pranks. The aura of careless abundance often wafted up around him, faint and nebulous as spirit incense. Yet running through this wonder was a hard thread of moral disapproval. Uncle had had it coming. Saburo had overheard his mother telling a neighbor that Uncle Kotai had been born in the year of the rooster. Roosters, as Saburo knew, finished their crowing early in the day.

When Saburo joined the track and field team in his first year at Bukkyo High School, the sport was enjoying a popularity it had not known before the war. At the time, few schools could afford baseball bats or gymnastic equipment. And there was something in the simplicity of the sport — the straight path to the goal, the dramatic finish line — that stirred the community to yells and often tears. On Sundays entire families came outdoors to cheer, Thermoses of cold wheat tea slung across their chests. They sat on woven mats and munched on rice balls, roasted potatoes, hard-boiled eggs, and pickled shoots of fuki gathered up in the hills.

"So what distance are you running?" Saburo's father asked at the dinner table.

"Eight hundred meters," Saburo said. He would have preferred a long-distance event, which commanded the most respect. But he had watched those runners stagger toward the finish line, eyes rolling back in their heads, some even vomiting in the grass afterward, and he had been afraid. Sprints came next in popularity, but Saburo was not particularly fast. Two laps around the track seemed the most appropriate distance.

"Eight hundred meters? Is that all?"

"I just want to focus on one," Saburo said, "and perfect it."

His father nodded in approval.

Saburo's father was old, much older than his mother. His gray hair, ascetic cheekbones, and scholarly decorum (he was professor of astronomy at Nangyo University) commanded both respect and distance. When sitting down beside his father at the low dining table, Saburo had moments of readjustment similar to entering a temple from a busy street. Dinner table conversations, more often than not, were monologues on the moons of Jupiter, the Andromeda nebulae, or various theories on cosmogony. Chewing his food slowly — a habit from rationing days, when the rule had been one hundred times — Saburo let the academic words flow through him like water through a net. What he heard was his father's voice: a voice like the universe, regulated and unknowable, with the endurance of silent planets rotating in their endless, solitary orbits.

Something about the running must have struck a chord with his father, although as far as Saburo knew, he had not been a track man in his youth. At any rate, the following evening at dinner his father made an announcement.

"On the days you don't have practice," he told Saburo, "I'll be taking you out to Kaigane Station to clock your runs."

Saburo's mother looked up from ladling rice into a bowl. "Maa, Father, what an excellent idea!" she said. She then turned to her son, surprise and pleasure still in her face. "Saburo, thank your father," she said. Saburo was not altogether happy with the actual arrangement; his devotion to running was not that strong. Nonetheless, he was suffused with a quiet, manly pride that he tried to mask with an expression of nonchalance. "So nice, ne — a father and son, doing things together!" sang Saburo's mother, expecting no reply and getting none besides a good-willed "That's right" from her husband. Dinner that night felt very much like a rite of passage, and Saburo's mother served up the mackerel with a gravity reserved for celebratory red snappers.

Saburo's father never attended Saburo's track competitions; he left that to his wife. But he always inquired after the results at dinner, showing more interest in his son's times than in his rankings — a good thing, since Saburo never placed especially high. The boy never thought to question his father's absences or to complain. His father was simply different. He was old. He was an academic, whereas Saburo's friends' fathers were grocers and merchants. If he got excited, his eye pressure would go up.

But from that evening on, each time Saburo came home on nonpractice days, his father was waiting, still dressed in his Western-style lecture clothes: white short-sleeved shirt and gray trousers, creased and starched. They sat gingerly side by side in the streetcar as it bumped and clattered through the bustling fish vendors' district, the smells and raucous vendor calls floating in through the windows. It was awkward and silent in the streetcar, just the two of them. Saburo's mother, with her cheerful chatter, so often served as their buffer. Saburo stole a glance at his father, who was carefully holding both their tickets ready in one hand, even though there were still a dozen stops left to go. He wished his father were like his friends' fathers: sun-browned, guffawing men who ruffled children's hair with affectionate ease.

The streetcar rattled on until there was no more open-air market, only an asphalt road slicing through kilometer after kilometer of rice paddies. Kaigane Train Station was the final stop on the route. Because of postwar cutbacks the train came through only once a day now, so in the evenings the station was deserted.

Only here, with silence stretching over the open fields like an extension of his father, did Saburo feel complete harmony between them.

Saburo took his place at the makeshift starting line exactly 800 meters south of the platform (they had measured it out on the first day, using a 100-meter ball of string). His father waited back at the platform, a slight, gaunt figure next to the metal station billboard. As he peered at his wristwatch, clutched in both hands, Saburo raced toward him on the asphalt. A sea of rice plants, dyed red from the sunset, undulated on either side. On those spring evenings, the sharp green smell of growing things stung Saburo's nostrils as he sucked it in and pierced his lungs like frosty air. His elongated shadow floated beside him with effortless strides, like a long, fluid ghost. If he suddenly stopped running, his shadow might have kept on going.

"Two forty-nine," his father said. Saburo panted, leaning over with hands on knees, waiting to regain his wind so he could run it again. Somewhere in the paddies, frogs were croaking.

"Are you pacing yourself?" his father asked. "Remember, it doesn't matter who's in front of you. Beating your own time's all that matters. You can do that with practice. So don't be affected by those other runners. You just keep on improving, slow and steady." Everything his father did was slow and steady. Saburo pictured how he might run: rationing each breath, timing each footfall, looking neither left nor right at anything else around him.

Saburo quit the team after one year in order to devote his second and third years to tutoring sessions for college entrance examinations. His father said gravely that it sounded like a fine idea. Despite his relief — he had never really liked the running or its accompanying pressures — Saburo felt guilty over ending their sessions, which he sensed his father had enjoyed and wished to continue. He had the sad premonition that they would never again have a similar experience. As it turned out, the sessions could not have continued anyway; within a year, Kaigane Station's activity increased, along with the upswing in Japan's economy, and the surrounding fields gave way to construction sites for future buildings.

Over the next few years prosperity continued, bringing with it an increase in motorbikes and automobiles — menaces in the cluttered, swarming alleyways of the merchant district. Saburo's mother was a casualty of one such motorbike as it made a sharp turn around the corner near the seaweed grocer's. She died several hours later on the hospital operating table.

Saburo was nineteen at the time, home from the university for New Year's vacation. He and his father took a taxi to Shin-jin Municipal Hospital as soon as they heard of the accident. Mutely they waited on a bench in the hallway, faces blanched from the blue fluorescent light. The doctor finally arrived, told them "nothing could be done to save her," lingered a respectable interval, then hurried away to his duties.

Saburo turned to his father. He was hunched forward with his elbows on his knees, gazing down into his dangling hands, which showed the beginnings of liver spots. He seemed to have forgotten his son's presence. "Father —" Saburo said. There was no response. The awkward streetcar rides flashed into his mind, and in that moment of panic he understood himself to be on the verge of something he had feared, subconsciously, all his life. Lifting his hand, Saburo rested it on the middle of his father's back. Despite the gravity of the situation, his gesture felt ill-timed and melodramatic. There was no response through the scratchy wool of his father's sweater. Saburo lowered his hand to his side.

When they got home from the hospital, Saburo's father stopped before the calendar hanging above the kitchen counter, above a bowl of water in which kelp strips were still soaking for that night's dinner. With a black ballpoint pen, his father drew a big firm X over the box for the twenty-eighth day. "December twenty-eighth," he said, retracing the X over and over with growing force. "This was a bad, bad day." Each time Saburo passed the calendar, that black X jumped out at him from an otherwise empty month, the tips of four neat triangles curling outward from where the ballpoint pen had sliced through the paper.

In the ensuing weeks, Saburo had a recurring dream about high school track. In this dream two runners were ahead of him but not by much, and it was only the first lap; he was positioned right where he wanted to be. But wait. The crowd was cheering too much for just the first lap. Then he knew, as one does in dreams, that he had made a mistake. This was not the 800. This was the 400.

Eventually, however, he was rescued by the memory of one long-ago Mother's Day when he had presented his mother with a necklace he had woven from sweet peas and clover. She had exclaimed over it, then added, "But the best present you can give me is good grades so that someday you'll do well at the university and make your country proud." What a letdown that had been at the time. But now her words glowed hot in his brain, and for the first time Saburo understood how loss could resolve itself through complex transfers of emotion. Back at school, subdued but focused, he immersed himself in his engineering studies.

His father, meanwhile, altered his domestic routine: each night at six he strolled to the o-den cookery, where he chewed his dinner, calm and controlled as always; on Friday evenings he dropped off his clothes at the launderer's. The rhythm of this new schedule suggested years of familiarity, as if no prior way of life had existed. Saburo remembered with a pang the seamless way his father had replaced their running sessions with paperwork. Over the next few months, when Saburo came home on his increasingly brief visits, he noted the gradual disappearance of his mother's effects — with the exception of one framed photograph beside the family altar — leaving the house monkish and austere, a mirror of his father.

Saburo pondered the fact of his parents' arranged marriage. Did that lessen the heartbreak? Once, his father, while turning down the volume of a *Madama Butterfly* aria swelling forth from the radio (he was not a fan of Italian opera, which was "full of ego"), had muttered, "True love, true love . . . who even knows what that means?" Saburo could not tell if a response was expected.

Yet years after his wife might have faded from memory, Saburo's father mentioned her, if only in passing, each time his son came visiting: "Now your mother, on a day like this she would have loved sitting out here in the garden." Saburo thought how much easier it would have been if their emotions — his and his father's — could have been realized, apportioned, and spent, in their entirety, over his mother's lifetime.

At thirty, Saburo was doing well for himself. He held a respected position at a civil engineering firm. After years of saving he had purchased a Western-style condominium in the up-and-coming Kiji district, built over those fields where he had once run. A handsome man, with something of his Uncle Kotai lurking about the lips, Saburo attracted women with an ease he did not fully understand. It required little effort: some lighthearted banter, which came easily in adulthood, and on occasion a calculatedly mischievous grin. Given his unremarkable past, this was gratifying to his self-esteem. "Takes after Kotai-san," said one elderly woman from his old neighborhood. But unlike his uncle, Saburo did nothing in excess, not even banter. Perhaps it was this restraint that attracted the women. At any rate, Saburo was in no rush to marry; there was plenty of time. Life was pleasant and under control. On weekends he swam laps with sure, unhurried strokes.

Around this time his father's glaucoma began giving him trouble. Over the decades its pressure had increased steadily despite medication, and several years ago a severe migraine had required that his right eye be replaced with a glass one whose chestnut hue was a close, but not exact, match with the more faded brown of his left eye. Now his peripheral vision in the remaining eye had disappeared to the point that he could see only what was directly before him, as if looking at the world through a narrow pipe. During one of his sporadic visits, Saburo saw how his father patted the air around him like a blind man. He proposed — in the same quiet way his father had once announced the running sessions — that he visit his father every Sunday, at which time he would take care of all grocery shopping and outside errands. Afterward he would escort his father on a walk through the neighborhood streets, which were too dangerous now for a frail, half-blind man in his seventies. His father's ready acquiescence, in contrast to his usual self-sufficiency, indicated how grave the situation must have been.

And so a new routine began. They strolled in the afternoons, through narrow alleyways where morning glory vines, their blooms shrunk to purple matchsticks in the afternoon sun, cascaded over old-fashioned bamboo lattices. It became second nature for Saburo to walk two steps ahead on flat surfaces; otherwise his father, with his tunnel vision, would lose track of him entirely. Occasionally in the alley they met a housewife who stopped her sweeping to bow watchfully as the pair passed: the younger man taking slow, tiny steps, the distinguished-looking old gentleman shuffling close behind him.

Now that Saburo was an adult, their conversations were no longer awkward. Any conversational opening inevitably led to a lecture on astronomy; thus, little was required on Saburo's part. He felt relaxed, self-assured in the knowledge of all he was doing for his father. At appropriate pauses, he made a comment over his shoulder ("That kind of magnitude is hard to grasp") or asked a question ("And how was that discovery received by the scientific community?"). His father, he realized, had a passionate side. At rare intervals, when caught up in some obscure detail, the old man's voice rose with fervor, and he came to a full stop in order to make his point. Saburo pictured his father as a student in some university teahouse, robed in good-quality silks and ardently discussing science, ideals, the future of the world. It was a brief, fragrant whiff of that prewar world of which Saburo had never been a part.

Sometimes he discussed his own work — the new railroad they were currently building through the Hiei pass — or else he inquired after his father's routine, which seemed to consist largely of scientific reading interspersed with eye exercises, radio news programs, and long sitting sessions in the garden. But as time passed Saburo dwelled less and less on such mundane topics. He began looking forward to his father's monologues, which at first he had tolerated out of filial duty. They filled him now with a sense of wonder, of vast sweeps of time and space and human endeavors and intellectual possibilities. It reminded him somehow of those open fields of his childhood. On his way home after these visits, riding the bus through the open-air market — which at that hour was cluttered and bustling in the warm red glow of paper lanterns — Saburo was keenly, inarticulately aware of the sky beyond, purpling and darkening.

An exception to this companionable routine came several days after a quarterly eye checkup. His father's range of vision had dropped, not by 0.5 to one point as expected, but by two points and a quarter. "If I go blind now, at my age," he remarked gravely as they shuffled their way along the alley, "I plan to end my life."

Saburo froze. With anyone else he would have said all the right things: "Don't be silly! There's always something to live for! I love you and I'm here for you!" He was good at such gestures, especially with women. But someone like his father must not be insulted by such clichés. This was not a cry for pity but a nonnegotiable decision related out of courtesy. Saburo knew his father must have pondered this alone for months, weighing the pros and cons in his academic fashion.

After a few minutes Saburo asked, "How would you do it?"

"With a gun. Very simple, just hold it to your ear and pull the trigger."

"Not something easier," he asked tentatively, "like gas or sleeping pills?"

"Those don't work right away. Someone finds you halfway through, then they've got you in the hospital, making a big fuss. You come out of it half paralyzed, brain-damaged."

Saburo said nothing. They walked silently. The alley was deserted, and the early autumn sunlight slanted down, reddish, at a low angle. They approached the Sunemuras' olive tree; its branches leaned out over the old-fashioned adobe wall of their garden and shaded the alley. Waiting for his father to reach his side, Saburo cupped his hand behind his father's sweatered elbow as they passed beneath the olive branches, steering him around the slippery black pulp of overripe olives that had dropped onto the cement. He did this every time they passed the olive tree, although his father's refusal to lean on him, to physically acknowledge the assistance in any way, made Saburo remove his hand the moment they were in the clear.

"That's life, Saburo." His father's voice was grave and modulated as ever. "And your time will free up. There's nothing wrong with that. You need more than a busy job and a sick parent."

They walked. From somewhere in the distance came a faint smell of burning leaves.

Then his father launched easily, noncommittally, into a deploring commentary on this week's radio series on Mars. "Life . . . on . . . Mars!" he said dryly, mimicking the radio host's dramatic tone. "Hehh, they can't even present simple facts without dramatizing them all out of proportion."

Only now did Saburo notice that the underarms of his own imported linen shirt were damp with sweat. He thought he had outgrown this terror from the day of his mother's death, when he had reached over to touch his father's back. His mother would have known what to do. Mother . . . Once when Saburo was in the first grade, she had gripped his face between her hands and, driven by some intense private emotion, kissed the top of his shaved head with furious pecks.

After the visit with his father, on the bus ride home, Saburo reviewed the situation realistically. Outsiders would not understand their exchange. They would not see that his father, far from begging for sympathy, would have considered it out of place. The truth was that there was an understanding; they had no need for embarrassing displays. Saburo thought of the railroad they were drafting at work, its parallel ties never touching, yet exquisitely synchronized, committed in their separateness as they curved through hill and valley. That, he was comfortable with. That, he could do.

His father's cancer, a year later, came as a complete surprise. The possibility of another disease had never occurred to Saburo; there was simply no room for it. It began when his father telephoned him early one morning, his voice fainter than usual yet admirably steady, to say he had terrible stomach cramps and could Saburo escort him to the emergency room? Never before had his father called him at home. "No need to bother you," he always said. "It can wait till Sunday."

Doctors sedated his father for the rest of the day; they took X-rays and informed Saburo that a large tumor was obstructing his colon. An emergency colostomy was performed. "Terrible!" said one doctor around Saburo's age, shaking his bristly head and peeling off his rubber gloves. "The cancer's spread all over the place. Maa, the white cell count is incredible! Why wasn't it caught before?"

"My father doesn't like doctors," Saburo said.

The young doctor made a knowing grimace. "That generation, well," he said.

Waiting for his father to regain consciousness after the operation, Saburo stood before the window in the little hospital room, alternately peering back over his shoulder at his father's bed and gazing out at the city below. The landscape had changed since he had been here last. In his youth, dusk would have melted those distant

hills to smooth lines like folded wings. Tonight, against a fading sky
of pink and gray, the sharp black silhouette of the hills bristled with
crooked telephone poles. The hills themselves were spattered with
mismatched lights. *The rate of progress,* he recalled someone, somewhere, saying.

"What happened?" his father murmured within the first few minutes of coming to. Saburo had to bend over to hear him. He was attached to an oxygen tube, an IV, and an ancient machine with
rather grimy indicator knobs. The machine filled the room with a
soft, continuous roar.

"Everything's taken care of, Father," Saburo said. He explained
about the colostomy.

"I don't have to use this bag for the rest of my life, do I?"

The truth was his father had only a few months left to live. That
news could wait till tomorrow. "I'm afraid you will, Father," Saburo
said.

"Sohh . . ." A sigh like a deflating balloon, then silence.

The following day Saburo had no chance to break the news; spe-
cialists were performing tests most of the day. For lunch Saburo ate
a plate of rice curry in the hospital cafeteria. Through the glass
wall, he watched nurses striding by in the hall, clipboards pressed
against their chests. The sight of them — the very smell of this
place — stirred up memories of his mother's death; he was conscious now, as he had been then, of his utter uselessness. From now
on, it was the nurses and doctors who would do everything, to
whom his father would turn for help. Which would help your uncle
more? he remembered his father saying.

"One of them told me the results," his father reported that evening. "Quiet fellow, very nice." Sipping miso soup from a Styro-
foam cup, his father recounted the details of the cancer that had
already metastasized to his stomach, lymph nodes, and lungs.
"The doctor recommends," his father said, "a small place in Fuji-no
with round-the-clock medical staff . . ." He was tiring now, taking
short, shallow breaths. ". . . and dietitians. That'll work out best for
everybody. It won't be for long."

If only he could have broken the news to his father. If only he
could have caught the spontaneous reaction, however minute! He
saw ahead to how his father would die, as courteous and restrained
in his final hours as he had been in his life. Saburo had expected

more: a brush fire to drive some vague, crouching thing out of hiding. He had dreaded an onset of naked emotion, had pushed it off to the future when he would be better prepared, but never, he realized now, had he considered the possibility of its not happening.

That night Saburo dreamed he came across his mother in the alley, playing jump-rope in her apron with some neighborhood girls. Strands had come loose from her bun, and she was flushed, laughing. She noticed him and said brightly, "Ara, ara! Is it time already?"

"Mama! There you are!" Saburo cried out. Such relief surged through him that it lifted him out of sleep. Lying awake in the dark, it took him several moments to comprehend that his mother had been gone for years.

Saburo did what he could. He ate well, three meals a day. He cut back drastically on his work hours. He curtailed his social life, although on occasion he lightened his routine by inviting a girl to accompany him to the movie theater. He deliberately chose comedy: Teppan-gumi or foreign films featuring Charlie Chaplin.

Nonetheless, the situation took its toll. The old track and field nightmare returned. Unable to fall back asleep, Saburo tossed and turned, seeing before him his father's glass eye crusted over with yellow mucus, as it had once looked when a nurse forgot to wash it out with eyedrops. Or he saw him wearily close his eyes and whisper "Thank you" after a nurse changed his colostomy bag.

By now his father was installed in the recommended Fuji-no hospital for terminally ill patients. He had little strength — he had never quite recovered from the operation — and he fought to sit up, even to shift position on the bed. Still, he courteously attempted conversation. "How are you holding up, Saburo?" he asked each evening, as if his son were the ailing one. To save his father's energy, Saburo did most of the talking. Then, running out of topics, he took to reading *History of the Cosmos,* a book he had found on his father's desk at home. There was something soothing about reading aloud; all meaning dropped away, and he was borne along on a cadence reminiscent of boyhood, when his father's voice had washed over him at the dinner table.

One evening the reading lulled his father to sleep. Saburo gazed at the drawn, wasted face. The hospital was silent — it might have been midnight instead of seven o'clock. If Saburo stared long enough in the eerie fluorescence of overhead lights, the pallid face with its sunken eye sockets became that of a corpse.

Above the blanket, his father's hand twitched in sleep. It was the surreal quality of this moment — a tenuous balance of his father's unconsciousness, the temporary absence of night nurses, the lingering effects of reading about an impersonal cosmos — that made Saburo reach out with one finger and touch his father's hand. Its folds were cold and surprisingly loose, like sea cucumbers he had once poked as a boy in the open-air market. The forearm was warmer, but so much smaller, so much more frail between Saburo's fingertips, than eyesight had prepared him for. Saburo went on to trace the bony blade of a gowned shoulder. This felt like a violation, and it made him nervous: was his father really asleep? Maybe he was conscious behind those closed lids. Maybe the touching bothered him but he was too polite, or too weak, to react. But Saburo couldn't stop. He couldn't help himself.

The physical contact dissolved some hard center of logic within him. And Saburo wondered, with sudden urgency, whether his father was really as self-sufficient as he had always assumed him to be. Might his father have hoped for a different reaction the day he talked of suicide? Might he have longed for closeness but not known how to go about it? Unlikely, but still . . . dangerous thoughts.

Saburo had made the best decisions he could, as his father had, surely, with all his careful ways. But warped by circumstance and changing worlds, compounded by time and habit, the results had come up short. It was inevitable. The longer one's life, the more room it left for errors of calculation.

If things had been different he might have told his father, as other sons surely did, "I admire you more than anyone I've ever known. For your intellect, for your great dignity." If such words were possible, he would have felt only the clean, sharp arrows of pain; there would have been a rightness to it all, a bittersweet perfection of a setting sun. What Saburo felt now bordered on nausea, which had always terrified him. He had thrown up only two or three times as a child, but he still remembered that instant of panic when it all came rising up, unstoppable.

His father's eyes opened. "Saburo?" he whispered.

"I'm here, Father," Saburo said. He stilled his hand, keeping it over his father's icy hand. It occurred to him that his father would not be able to feel this. Poor circulation in the extremities, the nurse had told him, causes numbness.

"Aaa, it's you . . ." his father said.

"Father," Saburo began. He stopped. His Adam's apple was constricting, shot through with the ache, long forgotten yet familiar, of impending tears. He waited until it subsided.

"Father," he said in a rush, "I'm not good at saying fancy things." His throat closed up again, and he sat helpless.

His father's good eye had turned toward his son's voice, the pupil shrunken to pinpoint from glaucoma medication. Saburo felt a great mute pain open out in his chest. It reminded him of track days: anguish escalating unbearably in oxygen-deprived lungs, the blind rush down the home stretch on legs that were too slow.

SUSAN STRAIGHT

Mines

FROM ZOETROPE

THEY CAN'T SHAVE their heads every day like they wish they could, so their tattoos show through stubble. Little black hairs like iron filings stuck on magnets. Big roundhead fool magnets.

The Chicano fools have gang names on the sides of their skulls. The white fools have swastikas. The Vietnamese fools have writing I can't read. And the black fools — if they're too dark, they can't have anything on their heads. Maybe on the lighter skin at their chest, or the inside of the arm.

Where I sit for the morning shift at my window, I can see my nephew in his line, heading to the library. Square-head light-skinned fool like my brother. Little dragon on his skull. Nothing in his skull. Told me it was cause he could breathe fire if he had to. ALFONSO tattooed on his arm.

"What, he too gotdamn stupid to remember his own name?" my godfather said when he saw it. "Gotta look down by his elbow every few minutes to check?"

Two names on his collarbone: twins. Girls. EGYPT and MOROCCO. Seventeen and he's got kids. He's in here for eight years. Riding in the car when somebody did a drive-by. Back seat. Law say same as pulling the trigger.

Ten o'clock. They line up for shift between classes and voc ed. Dark blue backs like fool dominoes. Shuffling boots. Fred and I stand in the doorway, hands on our belts, watching. From here, seeing all those heads with all those blue-green marks like bruises, looks like everybody got beat up big-time. Reyes and Michaels and the other officers lead their lines past the central guard station, and when the wards get closer, you can see all the other tattoos. Names over their eyebrows, teardrops on their cheeks, words on their necks, letters on their fingers.

One Chicano kid has PERDÓNEME MI ABUELITA in fancy cursive on the back of his neck. Sorry my little grandma. I bet that makes her feel much better.

When my nephew shuffles by, he grins and says softly, "Hey, Auntie Clarette."

I want to slap the dragon off the side of his stupid skull.

Fred says, "How's your fine friend Tika? The one with green eyes?"

I roll my brown eyes. "Contacts, okay?"

I didn't tell him I saw Tika last night, at Lincoln Elementary. "How can you work at the youth prison? All those young brothers incarcerated by the system?" That's what Tika said to me at Back-to-School Night. "Doesn't it hurt you to be there?"

"Y'all went to college together, right?" Fred says.

"Mmm-hmm." Except she's teaching African-American studies there now, and I married Ray. He quit football and started drywalling with his uncle.

"Ray went with y'all too, didn't he? Played ball till he blew out his knee?"

The wind's been steady for three days now, hot fall blowing all the tumbleweeds across the empty fields out here, piling them up against the chain-link until it looks like hundreds of heads to me. Big-ass naturals from the seventies, when I squint and look toward the east. Two wards come around the building and I'm up. "Where you going?"

The Chicano kid grins. "TB test."

"Pass."

He flashes it, and I see the nurse's signature. The blister on his forearm looks like a quarter somebody slid under the skin. Whole place has TB so bad we gotta get tested every week. My forearm's dotted with marks like I'm a junkie.

I lift up my chin. I feel like a guy when I do it, but it's easier than talking sometimes. I don't want to open my mouth. "Go ahead," Fred calls out to them.

"Like you got up and looked."

Fred lifts his eyebrows at me. "Okay, Miss Thang."

It's like a piece of hot link burning in my throat. "Shut the fuck up, Fred." That's what Michaels and Reyes always say to him. I hear it come out like that, and I close my eyes. When I get home now, and the kids start their homework, I have to stand at the sink and wash my hands and change my mouth. My spit, everything, I think. Not a prayer. More like when you cool down after you run. I watch the water on my knuckles and think: No TB, no cussing, no meds. Because a couple months after I started at Youth Authority, I would holler at the kids, "Take your meds."

Flintstones, Mama, Danae would say.

Fred looks up at the security videos. "Tika still single, huh?"

"Yeah."

She has a gallery downtown, and she was at the school to show African art. She said to me, "Doesn't it hurt your soul? How can you stand it?"

I didn't say anything at first. I was watching Ray Jr. talk to his teacher. He's tall now, fourth grade, and he smells different to me when he wakes up in the morning.

I told Tika, "I work seven to three. I'm home when the kids get off the bus. I have bennies."

She just looked at me.

"Benefits." I didn't say the rest. Most of the time now Ray stays at his cousin Lafayette's house. He hasn't worked for a year. He and Lafayette say construction is way down, and when somebody is building, Mexican drywallers get all the business in Rio Seco.

When I got this job, Ray got funny. He broke dishes, washing them. He wrecked clothes, washing them. He said, "That ain't a man — that's a man's job." He started staying out with Lafayette.

Tika said, "Doesn't it hurt you inside to see the young brothers?"

For my New Year's resolution I told myself: Silence is golden. At work, cause me talking just reminds them I'm a woman. With Ray and my mother and everyone else except my kids. I looked at Tika's lipstick, and I shouted in my head: I make thirty-five grand a year! I've got bennies now! Ray never had health care, and Danae's got asthma. I don't get to worry about big stuff like you do, cause I'm worrying about big stuff like I do. Pay the bills, put gas in the van, buy groceries. Ray Jr. eats three boxes of Cheerios every week, okay?

"Fred Harris works there. And J.C. and Marcus and Beverly."

Tika says, "Prison is the biggest growth industry in California. They're determined to put everyone of color behind a wall."

Five days a week, I was thinking, I drive past the chain-link fence and past J.C. at the guard gate. Then Danae ran up to me with a book. They had a book sale at Back-to-School Night. Danae wanted an American Girl story. Four ninety-five.

Tika walked away. I went to the cash register. Five days a week, I park my van and walk into the walls. But they're fences with barbed wire and us watching. Everything. Every face.

"Nobody in the laundry?" I ask, and Fred shakes his head. Laundry is where they've been fighting this week. Black kid got his head busted open Friday in there, and we're supposed to watch the screens. The bell rings, and we get up to stand in the courtyard for period change. We can hear them coming from the classrooms, doors slamming and all those boots thumping on the asphalt. The wind moving their stiff pants around their ankles, it's so hard right now. I watch their heads. Every day it's a scuffle out here, and we're supposed to listen to who's yelling, or worse, talking that quiet shit that sets it off.

All the damn heads look the same to me, when I'm out here with my stick down by my side. Light ones like Alfonso and the Chicano kids and the Vietnamese, all golden brown. Dark little guys, some Filipino, even, and then the white kids, almost green they're so pale. But all the tattoos like scabs. Numbers over their eyebrows and FUCK YOU inside their lips when they pull them down like clowns.

The wind whips through them and they all squint but don't move. My head is hurting at the temples, from the dust and wind and no sleep. Laundry. The wards stay in formation, stop and wait, boots shining like dark foreheads. I hear muttering and answers and shit-talking in the back, but nobody starts punching. Then the bell rings and they march off.

"Youngblood. Stop the mouth," Fred calls from behind me. He talks to the wards all the time. Old school. Luther Vandross–loving and hair fading back like the tide at the beach — only forty-two, but acts like he's a grandpa from the South. "Son, if you'da thought about what you were doing last year, you wouldn't be stepping past me this year." They look at him like they want to spit in his face. "Son, sometimes what the old people say is the gospel truth, but you wasn't in church to hear." They would knock him in the head if they could. "Son, you're only sixteen, but you're gonna have to go across the street before you know it, you keep up that attitude."

Across the street is Chino. Men's Correctional Facility. The wards laugh and sing back to Fred like they're Snoop Doggy Dogg: "I'm on my way to Chino, I see no reason to cry . . ."

He says, "Lord knows Mr. Dogg ain't gonna be there when you are."

The Chicano kids talk Spanish to Reyes, and he looks back at them like a statue wearing shades. The big guy, Michaels, used to play football with Ray. He has never looked into my face since I got here. My nephew knows who he is. He says, "Come on, Michaels, show a brotha love, Michaels. Lemme have a cigarette. You can't do that for a brotha, man? Brothaman?"

Alfonso thinks this is a big joke. A vacation. Training for life. His country club.

I don't say a damn thing when he winks at me. I watch them walk domino lines to class and to the kitchen and the laundry and the field. SLEEPY and SPOOKY and DRE DOG and SCOOBY and G DOG and MONSTER all tattooed on their arms and heads and necks. Like a damn kennel. Nazis with spider webs on their elbows, which is supposed to mean they killed somebody dark. Asians with spidery writing on their arms, and I don't know what that means.

"I'ma get mines, all I gotta say, Auntie Clarette," my nephew always said when he was ten or eleven. "I ain't workin all my life for some shitty car and a house. I'ma get mines now."

I can't help it. Not supposed to look out for him, but when they change, when they're in the cafeteria, I watch him. I don't say anything to him. But I keep seeing my brother in his fool forehead, my brother and his girlfriend in their apartment, nothing but a couch and a TV. Always got something to drink, though, and plenty weed.

Swear Alfonso might think he's better off here. Three hots and a cot, the boys say.

We watch the laundry screens, the classrooms, and I don't say anything to Fred for a long time. I keep thinking about Danae's reading tonight, takes twenty minutes, and then I can wash a load of jeans and pay the bills.

"Chow time, baby," Fred says, pushing it. Walking behind me when we line everybody up. They all mumbling, like a hundred lit-

tle air conditioners, talking shit to each other. Alfonso's lined up
with his new homeys, lips moving steady as a cartoon. I know the
words are brushing the back of the heads in line, the Chicano kids
from the other side of Rio Seco, and I walk over with my stick.
"Move," I say, and the sweaty foreheads go shining past like wind-
shields in a traffic jam.

"Keep moving," I say louder.

Alfonso grins. My brother said, Take care my boy, Clarette. It's
on you.

No, I want to holler back at him. You had seventeen years to take
care of him. Why I gotta do your job? How am I supposed to make
sure he don't get killed? I feel all the feet pounding the asphalt
around me and I stand in the shade next to Fred, tell him "Shut
up" real soft, soft as Alfonso still talking yang in the line.

I have a buzzing in my head. Since I got up at five to do two loads of
laundry and make a hot breakfast and get the kids ready for school.
When I get home, I start folding the towels and see the bus stop at
the corner. I wait for the kids to come busting in, but all the voices
fade away down the street like little radios. Where are these kids? I
go out on the porch and the sidewalk's empty, and my throat fills
up again like that spicy meat's caught. Ray Jr. knows to meet Danae
at her classroom. The teacher's supposed to make sure they're on
the bus. Where the hell are they?

I get back in the van and head toward the school, and on Palm
Avenue I swear I see Danae standing outside the barbershop, waving at me when I'm stopped at the light.

"Mama!" she calls, holding a cone from the Dairy Queen next
door. "Mama!"

The smell of aftershave coats my teeth. And Ray Jr.'s in the chair,
his hair's on the tile floor like rain clouds.

My son. His head naked, a little nick on the back of his skull,
when he sees me and ducks down. Where someone hit him with a
rock last year in third grade. The barber rubs his palms over Ray
Jr.'s skin and it shines.

"Wax him up, man," Ray says, and I move on him fast. His hair
under my feet too, I see now, lighter and straighter. Brown clouds.
The ones with no rain.

"How could you?" I try to whisper, but I can't whisper. Not after
all day of hollering, not stepping on all that hair.

The barber, old guy I remember from football games, said, "Mmm-mmm-mmm."

"The look, baby. Everybody wants the look. You always working on Danae's hair, and Ray-Ray's was looking ragged." Ray lifts both hands, fingers out, like he always does. Like it's a damn sports movie and he's the ref. Exaggerated. "Hey, I thought I was helping you out."

I heard the laughing in his mouth. "Like Mike, baby. Like Ice Cube. The look. He said some punks was messin with him at school."

I go outside and look at Ray Jr.'s head through the grimy glass. I can't touch his skull. Naked. How did it get that naked means tough? Naked like when they were born. When I was laying there, his head laced with blood and wax.

My head pounding when I put it against the glass, and I feel Danae's sticky fingers on my elbow. "Mama, I got another book at school today. *Sheep in a Jeep.*"

When we were done reading, she fell asleep. My head hurt like a tight swim cap. I went into Ray Jr.'s room and felt the slickness of the wax.

In the morning I'm so tired my hands are shaking when I comb Danae's hair. "Pocahontas braids," she says, and I feel my thumbs stiff when I twist the ties on the ends. I stare at my own forehead, all the new hair growing out, little explosions at my temples. Bald. Ray's bald now. We do braids and curls or Bone Strait and half the day in the salon, and they don't even comb theirs? Big boulder heads and dents all in the bone, and that's supposed to look good?

I gotta watch all these wards dressed in dark blue work outfits, baggy-ass pants, big old shirts, and then get home and all the kids in the neighborhood are wearing dark blue Dickies; Ray is wearing dark blue Dickies and a Big Dog shirt.

Like my friend Saronn says, "They wear that, and I'm supposed to wear stretch pants and a sports bra and high heels? Give me a break."

Buzzing in my head. Grandmere said we all got the pressure, in-herited. Says I can't have salt or coffee, but she doesn't have to eat lunch here or stay awake looking at screens. Get my braids done this weekend, feels like my scalp has stubbles and they're turned in-side poking my brain.

Here sits Fred across from me, still combs his hair even though it looks like a black cap pushed way too far back on his head. He's telling me I need to come out to the Old School club with him and J.C. and Beverly sometime. They play Cameo and the Bar-Kays. "Your Love Is Like the Holy Ghost."

"What you do for Veterans Day? Kids had the day off, right?" he says.

"I worked an extra shift. My grandmere took the kids to the cemetery." I drink my coffee. Metal like the pot. Not like my grandmere's coffee, creole style with chicory. She took the kids to see her husband's grave, in the military cemetery. She told Danae about World War II and all the men that died, and Danae came home crying about all the bodies under the ground where they'd walked.

Six — they cry over everything. Everything is scary. I worked the extra shift to pay off my dishwasher. Four hundred dollars at Circuit City. Plus installation.

I told Ray Jr., "Oh, yeah, you gonna load this thing. Knives go in like this. Plates like this."

He said, "Why you yelling, Mama? I see how to do it. I did it at Grandmere's before. Ain't no big thing. I like the way they get loaded in exactly the same every time. I just don't let Daddy know."

He grinned. I wanted to cry.

"Used piano in the paper cost $500. Upright."

"What the hell is that?" Ray said on the phone. Hadn't come by since the barber.

I tried to think. "The kind against the wall, I guess. Baby grand is real high."

"For you?"

"For Ray Jr. Fooled around on the piano at school, and now he wants to play like his grandpere did in Baton Rouge."

Ray's voice got loud. "Uh-uh. You on your own there. Punks hear he play the piano, they gon kick his ass. Damn, Clarette."

I can get louder now, since YA. "Oh, yeah. He looks like Ice Cube, nobody's gonna mess with him. All better, right? Damn you, Ray."

I slam the phone down so hard the back cracks. Cheap purple Target cordless. Fifteen ninety-nine.

Next day I open the classifieds on the desk across from Fred and start looking. Uprights. Finish my iron coffee. Then I hear one of the wards singing, "Three strikes you're out, tell me what you gonna do?"

Nate Dogg. That song. "Never Leave Me Alone."

This ward has a shaved black head like a bowling ball, a voice like church. "Tell my son all about me, tell him his daddy's sorry . . ."

Shows us his pass at the door. "Yeah, you sorry all right," Fred says.

The ward's face changes all up. "Not really, man. Not really."

Mamere used to say, "Old days, the men go off to the army. Hard time, let me tell you. They go off to die, or they come back. But if they die, we get some money from the army. If they come back, they get a job on the base. Now them little boys, they go off to the prison just like the army. Like they have to. To be a man. They go off to die, or come back. But they ain't got nothin. Nothin either way."

Wards in formation now. The wind is still pushing, school papers cartwheeling across the courtyard past the boots. I check Alfonso, in the back again, like every day, like a big damn Candyland game with Danae and it's never over cause we keep picking the same damn cards over and over cause it's only two of us playing.

I breathe in all the dust from the fields. Hay fields all dry and turned when I drive past, the dirt skimming over my windshield. Two more hours today. Wards go back to class. Alfonso lifts his chin at me, and I stare him down. Fred humming something. What is it?

"If this world were mine, I'd make you my queen . . ." Old Luther songs. "Shut up, Fred," I tell him. I don't know if he's trying to rap or not. He keeps asking me about Ray.

"All them braids look like a crown," he says, smiling like a player.

"A bun," I say. He knows we have to wear our hair tight back for security. And Esther just did my braids Sunday. That's gotta be why my temples ache now.

"They went at it in the laundry room again Sunday," Fred says, looking at the screens.

I stare at the prison laundry, the huge washers and dryers like an old cemetery my grandmere took me to in Louisiana once, when I was a kid. All those dead people in white stone chambers, with white stone doors. I see the wards sorting laundry and talking, see J.C. in there with them.

"Can't keep them out of there," I say, staring at their hands on the white T-shirts. "Cause everybody's gotta have clean clothes."

At home I stand in front of my washer, dropping in Danae's pink T-shirt, her Old Navy capris. One trip to Old Navy in spring, one in fall all I can afford. And her legs getting longer. Jeans and jeans. Sometimes they take so long to dry I just sit down on the floor in front of the dryer and read the paper, cause I'm too tired to go back out to the couch. If I sit down on something soft, I'll fall asleep, and the jeans will be all wrinkled in the morning.

Even the wards have pressed jeans.

In the morning, my forehead feels like it's full of hot sand. Gotta be the flu. I don't have time for this shit. I do my hair first, before I wake up Danae and Ray Jr. I pull the braids back and it hurts, so I put a softer scrunchie around the bun.

Seen a woman at Esther's Sunday. She says, "You got all that pretty hair, why you scrape it back so sharp?"

"Where I work."

"You cookin somewhere?"

"Nope. Sittin. Lookin at fools."

She pinched up her eyes. "At the jail?"

"YA."

Then she pulls in her chin. "They got my son. Two years. He wasn't even doin nothin. Wrong place, wrong time."

"YA wrong place, sure."

She get up and spit off Esther's porch. "I come back later, Esther."

Esther says, "Don't trip on Sisia. She always mad at somebody."

Shouldn't be mad at me. "I didn't got her son. I'm just tryin to make sure he comes home. Whenever."

Esther nodded and pulled those little hairs at my temple. I always touch that part when I'm at work. The body is thy temple. My temple. Where the blood pound when something goes wrong.

The laundry's like people landed from a tornado. Jean legs and shirtsleeves all tangled up on my bed.

"You foldin?" I say. Ray Jr. pulling out his jeans and lay them in a pile like logs. Then he slaps them down with his big hand.

"They my clothes."

"Don't tell your daddy."

"I don't tell him much."

His hair growing back on his skull. Not like iron filings. Like
curly feathers. Still soft.

Next day Fred put his comb away and say, "Give a brotha some
time."

"I gave him three years."

"That's all Ray get? He goin through some changes, right?"

"We have to eat. Kids got field trips and books to buy."

Three years. The laundry piled on my bed like a mound over a
grave. On the side where Ray used to sleep. The homework. Now
piano lessons.

Fred says, "So you done?"

"With Ray?" I look right at him. "Nope. I'm just done."

"Oh, come on, Clarette. You ain't but thirty-five. You ain't done."

"You ain't Miss Cleo."

"You need to come out to the Comedy Club. No, now, I ain't
sayin with me. We could meet up there. Listen to some Earth,
Wind, and Fire. Elements of life, girl."

Water. They missed water. Elements of life: bottled water cause I
don't want the kids drinking tap. Water pouring out the washing
machine. Water inside the new dishwasher — I can hear it sloshing
around in there.

I look out at the courtyard. Rogue tumbleweed, a small one, rolling across the black.

"Know what, Clarette? You just need to get yours. I know I get
mines. I have me some fun, after workin here all day. Have a drink,
talk to some people, meet a fine lady. Like you."

"Shut up, Fred. Here they come."

Reyes leading in his line and I see two boys go down, start punching. I run into the courtyard with my stick out and can't get to
them, cause their crews are working now. The noise — it's like the
crows in the pecan grove by Grandmere's, all the yelling, but not
lifting up to the sky. All around me. I pull off shirts, Reyes next to
me throwing kids out to Michaels and Fred. Shoving them back,
and one shoves me hard in the side. I feel elbows and hands. Got to
get to the kid down, and I push with my stick.

Alfonso. His face bobbing over them like a puppet. "Get out of
here!" I yell at him, and he's grinning. I swear. I reach down and
the Chicano kid is on top, black kid under him, and I see a boot. I

pull the top kid and hear Reyes hollering next to me, voice deep as a car stereo in my ear.

Circle's opening now. Chicano kid is down, he's thin, bony wrists green-laced with writing. The black kid is softer, neck shining, and he rolls over. But then he throws himself at the Chicano kid again, and I catch him with my boot. Both down. Reyes kicks the Chicano kid over onto his belly and holds him. I have to do the same thing. His lip split like a pomegranate. Oozing red. Some mother's son. It's hard not to feel the sting in my belly. Reyes's boy yelling at me in Spanish. I kick him one more time, in the side.

I bend down to turn mine over, get out my cuffs, and one braid pulls loose. Falls by my eyes. Bead silver like a raindrop. I see a dark hand reach for it, feel spit spray my forehead. Bitch. My hair pulled from my temple. My temple.

My stick. Blood on my stick. Michaels and Reyes take the wards. I keep my face away from all the rest, and a bubble of air or blood or something throbs next to my eyebrow. Where my skin pulled from my skull, for a minute. Burning now, but I know it's gon turn black like a scab, underneath my hair. I have to stand up. The sky turns black, then gray, like always. They're all heading to lockdown. I make sure they all see me spit on the cement before I go back inside. Fred stands outside talking to the shift supervisor, Williams, and I know he's coming in here in a minute, so I open the classifieds again and put my finger on Upright.

MONA SIMPSON

Coins

FROM HARPER'S MAGAZINE

I ALWAYS SAY, We are the second oldest profession. That is because we serve the needs of women. And what we do is harder. Because we are giving more than only our bodies. Our bodies too — I carry him, he is now already forty pounds.

We may be selling our time — we are here in America for the money, that is our purpose — but still we give our love.

Dee told me, when I first came here, I don't need to teach you children. You have been a mother to five, she said, you know. Children, they are not hard.

But most you need to think about the mother. Here, the mothers are the ones who throw the tantrums.

You may have had nannies, but you have not before been a nanny.

Dee has always been my teacher, of America. I was never the only one learning. No, in the house of Dee there is always a crowd. After only one month, I was no longer even the newest. But I understood that I was the teacher's favorite pupil. I had never before been the favorite of any teacher; I used to be the favorite of the class. When the teacher turned around to the blackboard, I stood up and made the face that caused everyone to laugh. Dee believed I had the talent for baby-sitting, because of the schools my children attend in Manila. Even in the provinces, people know the names of our best colleges. I was the only one Dee ever asked for a job from her employer. "The others, they are not for Beverly Hills," she said, quiet because that is Dee's way of talking.

*

I hold my hands open in front of me to take away whatever my employer is beginning. If she starts to sew a button, I finish. If she runs water to rinse a lettuce, I say, I will be the one. When the husband spills something and pounds a wet napkin at the spot, I reach out my hands and say, Give it to me. I will make it clean.

All the while with a smile. It is not hard. No. Not when you have a purpose. And I have five purposes, the youngest seventeen, entering medicine.

But I have a good job. The parents of Ricardo get him in the morning, while they eat their breakfast. I fix their bed, take the glass of water from the side table, pick up Kleenexes.

Always the parents first, Dee said. A kid cannot fire you. Even here. They can love you but they cannot pay you. And anyway, they will forgive.

When I started with Richard, Dee said, I'm not going to tell you how to love, because either that will happen or it won't. And in six jobs, twenty-five years, she said, only once it did not happen to her. And then you need to quit. Because you cannot do the job if you do not love the baby.

But children, they are easy to love. Especially if you have them from a baby. Ricardo, they put him in my hands the first day at the hospital. They gave him to me.

Call me Lola, I whispered. That will be my name for you. (I was two years in America, I had been only a housekeeper. He is my first baby here.)

For me it is the parents who are more hard to love.

No, Dee said, at the beginning, I will not tell you how to love. I wouldn't if I could, because what I would tell you if I knew would be how not to so much. Because you will love him the same as your own and he never will. They love you, but it is not the same.

"I know, I *know*," I told her then. "I am a mother too."

But now I think, if you can keep them until they are five, then they will not forget you. I ask Ricardo, "Will you remember your Lola?"

"Why? You are not going away," he says.

"Someday," I tell him, "I will return to my place."

"And what will you do there?"

I will just sit in my house. Look at my kids' diplomas.

"Comeon comeon comeon comeon comeon. CometoLola. I have something for you," I say. Because he is very angry.

Usually it is the dad. But today it was the mother he was hitting. She has her hand on her eye and I dab ice, the way I do with his boo-boos. My employer when she is hurt she sounds like an animal.

So I take him in my arms, away. We turn on ground now in the yard and he is strong, three years old, I cannot so easily hold him. And Lola told a lie. I do not have anything for him. So I make promises.

"Someday," I whisper, "I am going to take you home with me. And there we will make the ice candy."

He lies still in my arms, not any longer fighting. His bones they feel different now, not pushing to get out. They fall in a pattern, like the veins of a leaf.

"I will put you in my pocket and I will feed you one candy every day. And you will be happy. Because the ocean at our place it is very blue. The sky, higher than here. And the fruits that grow on trees, very sweet. Durians, mangos, atis."

His head hangs down between his knees, but he is listening.

"In my pocket I will give you one lichee. You can bounce it for a ball."

"If you were a kangaroo you would have a pouch," he grumbles. He is better now, slower his heart.

Through the window I see my employer on the telephone. She holds the ice to her eye and thumps around the kitchen talking to her friend, long distance, a woman who reads many books about the raising of children. When my employer becomes upset she calls this friend, the full-time mother.

My employer works and she has the American problem of being guilty. But you should not be guilty to your children. It is for them that you are working. I am here for my own, to pay for their professional education.

He is better now. Only his mouth smears outside the edges. He will come with me. I lift him into the stroller and promise candy, not the ice candy, just candy we can buy here. "But-ah, do not tell your mother." I call, "Excuse but, we are going now."

"Is that okay? Thanks, Lola." This is how my employer believes she cannot live without me. She is telling her friend who reads the books that he is better with me than with her.

And her friend will say to her that it is perfectly normal.

"Play date," she says into the phone cross-country. "I can't even stand the word."

"Smell," I say. "Do you have a poo-poo?" I pull his diaper back. I am paid to smell that. By the time I change him and we are ready to leave, the mother is going too.

Claire walks out into the world, away from us, holding keys in front of her, ready to start her car.

With a child small small it is a little like a ball and chain. You are never free. Not even sleeping. So with her it is a prance almost, an escape. She can walk under the old pines of the university, talking about an even older book.

But what she said to her friend on the phone is true. With me, he is no problem. When she takes him with her, it is not the same for me. Some weight is lifted off my lap. I have no purpose. For me alone here, I am too light.

My employer she says, When a baby comes home from the hospital, a Filipina should arrive with him. That, for her, would make a perfect world.

I take Ricardo to the store to show him our place on the map.

I say, Where is Lola from, and he points.

Very good.

I told my employers already, When they go to Europe to celebrate their tenth anniversary, I will take Ricardo to the Philippines. We are already saving for the tickets. I have one hundred twenty-five put away. I cannot save much because every month I have many tuitions. I even wrote in a letter to my husband that I will bring Ricardo home. Only my kids, they do not yet know. They are a little jealous, especially BongBong, my son, who has two children. And it is true. I am closer to Richard than I am to my own grandchildren. Because I see him every day. He is my albino grandson.

We are just alone. This neighborhood is ours, during the daytime. You do not see the white mothers walking. Only sliding in and out of cars, carrying shopping bags. In my place, I was at one time one of these ladies. Now that I see from afar, it looks like a lot of work.

I push him in the stroller and he sits. That is the good of fighting: it makes them very tired. The sun is solid, like many small weights on our arms. We pass the park, and in the distance we see baby-sitters and children, so I roll him under the tall trees.

All the while, I keep talking to him. Dee told me, You have always to talk to him. Even a baby, it is very important that they hear words. And I always talked to him, more than to my kids, because my kids I had one after the other, five in ten years. But with Richard, I talk and talk, I tell him everything, and see, now, he is very *madaldal*. He understands more than one hundred words Tagalog.

In the class of 2020, at Harvard University, which is where the parents of Ricardo would like him to go, there will be six Santa Monica boys saying to the cooks in the cafeteria, Excuse, where is my adobo?

Lola by then will be swaying in a hammock, back in the Philippines.

"What for?" he says to me.

He is young. He does not yet understand the importance of rest.

"They change when they move to the big house," Rita says, kneeling in the sandbox, holding a sieve, "they really change."

For your salary, I am thinking, let them change! Rita gets one hundred dollars a day. Six months ago, her employers transferred to a fourteen-room mansion they had custom-built for themselves. My employer's house is the smallest. We compare jobs, the same as women will compare their husbands. Usually you would trade a part of what you have, but not all. If you are wanting to trade all, then there is trouble.

"But-ah, your employers, they are good," I say. I am always the one telling baby-sitters to stay in their jobs. Because too much change, it is bad for children. I look at the two little girls in the sandbox. Of all of our kids, those two of Rita are the best behaved. Maybe because they are Asian (Chinese, adopted).

"They don't think I will leave but I can leave," Rita says. "Lot of people they are looking Filipinos."

"The richest people all want Filipinos," Kitkat says.

"Like a BMW," I say. "We are status symbols." With only women, I can make them laugh.

"No, you know why? You know what Prudence told me?" Rita whispers. "It is because we are quiet. Prudence told me in the hospital they have a joke: What does *yes* mean in Tagalog? *Yes* means fuck you."

"That is right. Fuck you," Kitkat says out loud.

"Shhh," I say. Ricardo is a mynah bird, and sure enough the head springs up.

"What?" he says. Always, What? He is very intelligent.

I have never said out loud but I have thought before, I am not the same as other baby-sitters. A part of me, I want to be known for what I can do. I want to be seen alone. At a few certain things, maybe I am the best.

The baby-sitters stand and brush sand off their laps, ready to go. "Tomorrow at the house of Rita," Kitkat calls, hitting me in the stomach.

"I want to go there now," Ricardo says. "To Ritahouse."

In their voices, that is the only time it is our house.

Back home, I have ready a project. We put into cardboard all the coins we can find. His mother told us we could have the pennies for the choo-choo bank, our place to save for tickets to the Philippines.

We also find nickels, dimes, and quarters, and I have brown tubes from the bank for those too. There is always money in this house, little puddles, where people empty their pockets. "It is a hunt," I tell Ricardo, and we discover nests in the carpet, piles on counters, little dishes filled. If someone came to the door with a pizza and I needed ten dollars, I could always collect, in coat pockets and cups, next to little slips of paper with writing. My house in the Philippines is like this too. I leave money places I forget. That way if I become very low I can dig.

That is what Lola calls her secret garden. People who too much like order, they do not have this security, the many seeds.

Richard is a very good worker. We pile the tubes of coins. We build with them an American log cabin, using Richard's Play-Doh for the mortar. If we can also keep the quarters and dimes and nickels, we will have a lot. The pennies they are ours already. But the rest I will have to call and ask.

Claire answers her office phone, "Hey."

"We are wanting," I explain. "Can we have the money also for the silver coins we find?"

"Sure, Lola," she says. Usually she will say to me, "Sure, Lola." There are certain people in life, you know, they will always say to you yes.

At the bank, we wait in line a long time. Then when we go to the front, the lady acts all business, making a total of the rolled dimes. I say to her, "This little man rolled the nickels by himself."

While she finishes the silver coins, I lift a bag of pennies from his wagon. It is very heavy. We have many pennies. We took apart the fort and the log cabin. We counted forty dollars from nickels, twenty-seven dollars from dimes, and one hundred and three dollars from pennies. I lift Ricardo up so he can see.

But the lady pushes our tubes out of the cage. "We cannot take pennies," she says.

Richard picks one roll in his hand, to give it back to her. I remember this moment, again and again. It is like the giving of a flower. He does not yet understand.

"We don't take these," she says.

For a second then his face changes, what his mother calls berry-with-a-frown. Cartoon looks, they are really true on children. The upside-down smile, an open mouth, then he is bawling. And he throws the roll of pennies at the lady's face.

Her hand goes to a place above her eye. "I cannot help you," she says, setting the teeth. She has already given us the paper money for the other coins. She looks at me with hate. I have seen real hate only a few times in my life. The shape of diamonds, it is shocking. But she is hurt above the eye and I am not white.

"Come, Ricardo." I fight him down into the wagon. I will have to pull all the rolls of pennies and him. "We will make our getaway."

But he runs dragging pennies to a garbage can and begins dumping the tubes in the open top. Still crying but he is mad now. Also mad. I have to stop him. This is not right. All our effort. With him what I do is almost tackle. Lola is not a big person. But I get on the floor and hold him until the fight is out. Then I tell him a story, keeping him in my lap.

"Once upon a time," I say, "I work in Beverly Hills. In a house that is very fancy. Three layers. Floors like a checkerboard. All marble.

"When I was first here, new, the lady she open the door and

saw me and right away she said, You are hired. She told me, she knew like that — and when she said that she snap her fingers — you will never guess from why. She said, because of the way I tie my sneakers."

"How did you, Lola?"

"She thought Lola was a tidy person. But Lola is not so very tidy, not really. I can be. If I have to. And for her I was neat. I clean everything. But that is not the way I live my life. It is too much time, always straightening. I would rather see people, taste some part of life.

"The lady's husband, he had an office, and she wanted that to be neat too. She hired me extra to go on the Saturday and straighten. He was there working while I clean. And he had one jar like this, up to my waist, full with pennies. I asked him did he want me to get tubes from the bank. And he said, 'You can take the pennies.' But I could not lift.

"And so I came back Sunday, my day off, and I sat on the floor out of his way and put all the pennies into tubes. He stepped around me when he went down the hall to use the restroom or the machines. He'd ask me how much money it was as he went by, and I'd tell him the total so far.

"'Thirty-six dollars,' I said.

"'Good job, Lola.'

"The next time it was ninety-two.

"By the last time he passed, I was at two hundred and six. That time his face looked strange, like two lines cross over it. He went down the hall and I heard xeroxing.

"On his way back, he stopped over my legs and said, 'Maybe you better leave the pennies.'

"'Whatever you say. It is up to you.'

"When he was back in his office, on the phone, I stood and left it all there, the rolled pennies, the pile on the floor, the jar turned over. I took the bus to the place of Dee, and I never went back to that house. That was the end of my career for a Beverly Hills nanny."

"Is that when you came to me?"

"That is before," I say. "You were not yet born. Still I had to wait one year more. But-ah, when the husband took the pennies I rolled to the bank, you know what they are telling him? They are telling him too what they are telling us. 'We cannot help you.' And you know what he will do then?"

"He shouldn't have taken your pennies, Lola. He is a bad man."

"A little bad. Listen, you know what he will do? He will throw the pennies in the garbage and walk away in a hurry, he is always in a hurry. He is too busy, see?"

Now I fish with my arm in the garbage, feeling among wet things for our tubes, the ones Ricardo threw.

"But we will do something else. Come. You watch Lola." I pull him in the wagon out of the bank into the bright air. We go to the five-and-dime. And then the candy shop. And then the Discovery Store, where we study the globe. Each place, I count out the money in pennies. I put in piles of ten on the counter, so it is easy for the register clerk.

My father always told me, Spend your small money first. He remembered in our place when money became light, the smaller denominations would not buy anymore. And still at that time, he told me, there was so much wealth.

In the wagon, Ricardo is eating long orange and green candy worms.

"See, in the bank it is nothing, but out here in the world it is money. Not for the Philippines, but we can still buy. Every day a little. It is our own private fund. Our trust fund. I trust you and you trust me. You have your candy. Now, we will use some pennies to buy Lola her cup of coffee."

That is what my kids and Ricardo, they will remember. That Lola loved her coffee.

When we return home, the hallways round to caves, warm, dark already. I hear the mother of Richard making dinner in the kitchen.

I take the tomatoes from my employer. "I will be the one," I say. That is our way. My employer did not grow up living with helpers. She cannot easily ask. Also, my employer is a very good cook. I am happy to chop chop, while Ricardo plays on the floor with his action figures.

Tonight, Claire's eye, where he hit, shines black and blue, there is yellow also. Over it she has applied makeup.

"Now he's fine," she sighs when I bend to look closer. "I don't know what I'm doing wrong."

"It is the age too," I say. But my children, they were not like this, not even my boy. Here in America, they are different. They are also taller.

My employer whispers, "Maybe I should find a psychologist for him. Do you think this is all still normal?"

Really, I do not know. The hitting too, I worry. I cannot tell her the woman at the bank. "You are talking to the wrong person," I say. "Because-ah, I like naughty boys."

She sighs, but she is better. We are like magicians. With us too there is what the employer sees and there is sleight of hand.

I feed him his dinner because that is easier for the baby-sitter.

Then, when Ricardo has eaten enough, I get out of the way and let the family sit together. My employer gives me my plate, covered with a napkin, and I carry it back to my own place.

At first they used to ask me to eat with them, but I always said no.

Dee advised me, Don't, even if they ask. Americans do not know what they want. They will invite you, and then later on they will pine for their privacy. Americans need very much privacy. Because it is a big big land.

And the parents of Richard work all day, it is their only time together. Also, if I was eating with them, when Ricardo needed more milk or the salt was not on the table, I would be the one getting up and down. I like to put my feet up, watch the TV. It is important to have hours in the day when you are comfortable.

Later on, he can come back to my place, but then it is not my job anymore, he is a visitor, my buddy-buddy. And he is very good in my house. He never breaks anything. He looks at my pictures, he knows the names of my children, and we study the map.

We will save for the globe, on a layaway plan. Each day we will give the man fifty pennies. It will help teach Ricardo counting.

The parents do not come out here. My work is done. They leave the dishes, I do them in the morning. My money is earned. I can sit. That is my day.

So, some people across the Pacific, they had better be studying.

JESS ROW

Heaven Lake

FROM THE HARVARD REVIEW

My DAUGHTERS are almost grown: sixteen and twelve. Mei-ling, the elder, makes her own cup of coffee, and twists her hair into a careless rope at the breakfast table; Mei-po, tall and slender as a rice shoot, carries a backpack that weighs thirty pounds, as if at any moment she could be summoned to climb Mount Everest. They move through the apartment beginning at dawn: I open my eyes to the sound of the shower running, bare heels knocking along the hallway, a burst of music, a door slammed shut. When I walk into the kitchen, their eyes slide from the table to the floor to the television without looking up. *Zao,* I say, Morning, and they stiffen, as if I've dropped a glass, or scraped my nails against a chalkboard. Sometimes I imagine I've stumbled into an opera at the pause between the overture and the aria, and at any moment their voices will twine together in lament. *Our father keeps us captive in his castle,* I can hear them sing. *Rescue us!*

Of course there's nothing wrong with them. They are sensitive, untouchable things — like butterflies that have just broken their cocoons. If their mother were alive, she would say, *Let them be. Enjoy the silence.* And perhaps I should. In the six years since she left this world I've learned to make French braids and instant noodles, and memorized the names of a hundred pop singers. I imagine I am the only teacher of comparative philosophy who has ever shaken hands with the Backstreet Boys. How hard can it be, after all that, to learn to be ignored? But when I sit next to them, bent over a cup of tea and the *Ming Pao,* and no one says a word, I have a feeling I can't easily describe. It's as if my heart has puffed up inside my chest like a balloon, and every beat presses against my ribs, like the thump of a muffled drum. It's nothing, my doctor says, but he's wrong. That beat is the sound of time passing. I stare down at my newspaper and think, *No, it's not so easy. Silence is not a luxury for me.*

Look, Mei-ling tells her sister, flipping the pages of a fashion magazine. In July she will go to Paris, to finish her last year of high school at the American University there. She stabs a finger at a picture. It's where all the models live, she says. In the fifth arrondissement.

Mei-po looks curiously over her shoulder. I thought you said Monaco, she says.

That's for the *winter.* In the spring you have to be in Paris. Everyone knows that.

I raise my head. Don't get any ideas, I say. You're going there to study. Not to have men taking pictures of you.

I know that, she says. I *know.* Her eyes flicker across my face and she turns her head away. Old man, I hear her thinking, what more do you have to say to me? Tell me something I haven't heard before.

And I have an answer for her, too. That's the worst of it.

After they've left, in the pale morning light, I put on my favorite CD — Rostropovich, the Bach unaccompanied cello suites — and pace the floor in my socks, soundless. Outside my windows the March sun burns away the mist, and if I wanted to, I could look out all the way across Tolo Harbour to the eight peaks, the Eight Immortals, their broad green slopes dappled with cloud shadows. But I don't. I've lived in Hong Kong for thirteen years, and it has always seemed unreal to me, so clean and bright, like a picture postcard some clever photographer has retouched. In my study there are stacks of papers to grade, books I should have read and reviewed months ago, but I have no concentration: the time slips through my fingers like water. I whisper my daughters' names to the air and say, *Listen. Listen to me.*

When I was your age, I was just like you. I thought that everything in my life had happened by accident. I decided that when I was old enough I'd go to the other side of the world. Everyone said that it was impossible, but I worked hard, and waited, and finally my chance came. And then —

And then?

Why should it be so difficult to explain?

*

In the fall of 1982, when I was nineteen, I went to New York City, from Wuhan, China; I had won a government competition and received a special scholarship to study at Columbia University. It's hard for me to imagine now how innocent I was. New York then was not like those television shows my daughters watch, where young people stroll the streets, laughing and making jokes. At that time muggings were so common that no one went outside unless they had to, even during the day. After sunset the shop owners pulled grates over their storefronts to keep robbers from breaking the windows; even in the dormitories we locked ourselves into our rooms three times over. On warm nights that September I stuck my head out of my window in the International House and looked up and down Claremont Avenue, searching for a single person in the street. The buildings were as faceless as prisons. I knew New York was the biggest city in the world, that there were twelve million people hidden behind those walls, and yet I felt as if I had been locked in an isolation chamber. I thought, *Either I'll go insane in here or I'll be killed by a madman on the street. How can anyone live this way?*

The problem was that I had to make money. Even with my tuition and my books and my room paid for I didn't have enough to eat three meals a day. Though it rained all through that first October I couldn't buy an umbrella, or new shoes to replace the ones I'd brought with me from home. I wore the same ragged suit to class every day, and the other students stared at me. I was humiliated. In China my family was not poor; my father had survived the Cultural Revolution, and had been reinstated to his post in the history department at Huazhong University. But then, of course, in China everyone wore the same clothes day after day, unless they were fabulously wealthy. There were many times that term when I looked out the windows of my classroom at the American students in their fashionable ragged shirts and jeans worn through at the knees, and wished I could go to the scholarship office and ask for a ticket back to Beijing, where at least they didn't make promises they couldn't keep.

But the answer was much closer at hand. One day on the bulletin board in the International House lobby I saw an index card of scribbled characters. "Make Money Now Without a Work Visa. Just Call Wu," it said, and gave a telephone number.

You're a student? he asked in Chinese, as soon as he heard my voice.

I live in the International House —

Come to Fifty-sixth and Broadway, he said. Look for the Lucky Dragon.

Yes —

He slammed down the phone.

The Lucky Dragon was a Chinese restaurant on a busy corner in midtown, with enormous dark windows that reflected the street. I stood on the sidewalk for a moment, trying to comb my hair with my fingers, and then cupped my hands to the glass. I was astonished. There were no Chinese there, only Americans, whites and blacks and Latinos, eating on enormous American plates, with forks and knives, drinking cocktails and Coca-Cola. The woman at the register saw me and shouted something, and an enormously fat man came out of the kitchen and opened the door. He wore a white jacket that looked as if someone had vomited on it. Speak English? he barked at me in Mandarin, with a thick Cantonese accent.

Yes.

Do sums without an abacus?

Of course.

Ride a bicycle?

I burst out laughing, despite myself. Asking a person from China whether he can ride a bicycle is like asking a fish if he can swim. Only in Hong Kong do Chinese people ride bicycles for exercise.

Good, Wu said. I'll give you a map. The bicycle is down in the basement.

Uncle, I said, what will I be doing?

Chinese food delivery! he shouted at me in English, his eyes nearly popping out of his head. Twenty minutes or less! What did you think, Mr. Peking Duck?

At first I was always afraid. I studied the map that Wu gave me until I could reproduce every cross street in my mind, so that I'd never have to stop, never ask directions. I rode with the heavy bicycle chain looped around my shoulder, the lock undone; if someone grabbed me from behind, I told myself, I would swing it around and strike. Another delivery boy showed me how to tie a white cloth across my forehead, so I would look like the *gongfu* actor Bruce Lee. If someone tries to mug you, he said, just wave your arms and make a face and shout a lot. They'll leave you alone. But really I knew I'd never have the courage to fight. I was a fast bicycle-rider, and that was what I relied on. Each delivery was like a mission into enemy territory, and I returned at the edge of panic, whipping between delivery trucks and taxis, as if fox ghosts and ox demons pursued me.

For a month I worked this way, four nights a week; then I relaxed a little and began to look around, reading the signs as I rode. Jake's Deli. The Floral Arcade. Columbus Circle. The Sherry-Netherland. In the theater district I learned the network of alleys and side streets where the stage doors were, where men in black clothes snatched the bags and thrust wads of money into my hand: some-times twenty dollars for a fifteen-dollar order, sometimes ten for thirteen-fifty. On Central Park West, the doormen waved me in-side impatiently, and old women living alone lectured me on stay-ing warm and keeping safe. I interrupted arguments, let cats es-cape past my ankles, and held crying babies while their mothers counted out the last penny of their order, nothing extra.

The money was terrible — I know that now. But at the time it seemed like a fortune: enough for a winter coat and a pair of boots at Woolworth's and five shirts for fifty cents each at the Salva-tion Army. And when I glided into the alley behind the Lucky Dragon I felt very happy. To me it was a great adventure, the kind of thing I had never imagined in my parents' apartment in Wuhan. Who would have thought that I would move freely and alone through the streets of New York City, speaking the language, handling the money, as if I belonged there, and it was nothing ex-traordinary at all?

I wish that were the end of the story. I'd give anything for that.

At eleven o'clock on a Thursday night in late October, one last or-der came in from Tenth Avenue. Two bags of food, so heavy the kitchen boy grunted as he carried them out the door. I looked at the receipt — three orange chicken, two moo shu pork, six egg rolls — and raised my eyebrows when I came to the bottom. Forty-three dollars. Who had that kind of money to spend on Chinese food?

They said it's a birthday party, Wu shouted at me from the door-way. He had a cleaver in one hand and a scalded chicken by the neck in the other; blood ran down the edge of the blade and dripped onto his shoes. Promised a big tip. Don't worry.

I thought we didn't deliver past Eighth Avenue at night.

If you don't want it, anyone else will take it. *Daak m'daak a?*

Daak, I said. Fine. I pushed away from the curb carelessly, balancing on one pedal, as I'd seen the other delivery boys do. But when I passed the last lit bodega at the corner of Fifty-second and Ninth, I cursed my bravado. It was a neighborhood where the warehouses and garages didn't even have windows, only blank walls and steel doors bolted shut. Most of the streetlights were broken: I sped from one small pool of light to the next, sometimes half a block away. When I turned onto Tenth I could feel the sweat pooling under my arms, on my chest, at the base of my throat. But here at last there was a light: a storefront, its windows covered with brown paper, glowing like a lantern at the Moon Festival. I checked the number: this was the place. There were no sounds coming from inside, but still, I was relieved. As long as the address was right — as long as no one stepped out of the shadows and brained me with a brick — the delivery was all right. By that time I had made hundreds of trips from the Lucky Dragon; perhaps I thought I was invincible.

The door opened a few inches when I knocked, and a face appeared in the crack: a nose, a thin mustache, and lips, the eyes hidden from view.

Who is it?

You order Chinese food?

The face disappeared, and the door swung wide open. I took a step forward and all at once the lights switched off and two hands pushed me to the side; I dropped one of the bags and swung the other in front of me. It struck nothing, and flew from my fingers, and I heard it hit the floor with a heavy thud. The door slammed shut; I was sealed in darkness. The hands pushed me again, and my shoulders bumped against a wall. Hold still! the voice said. I got a gun! Hold still!

OK! I said. OK! No problem! I put my hands up in the air. What you want?

Shut up for a second. A flashlight beam swept across the floor and into my face; I winced, and closed my eyes. Where's the money?

I reached under my shirt and unbuckled the belt we used to carry change. I don't see you, I said, holding it out. I don't see you, you let me go, OK?

The light dropped from my face. I heard the pouch unzipping,

coins tinkling on the floor. Fuck! he hissed. Fuck! This all you got?
Ten bucks?

Delivery only carry ten.

Where's your wallet?

I took it from my front pocket and held it out. I have nothing, I
said. I am poor.

I heard it slap against the floor, on the other side of the room.
My wallet, I thought. It was the first thing I bought in America, at
Krieger's Stationery on 112th and Broadway; to keep my new student ID card and a copy of my visa, a picture of my parents and
my brother and sister. The room smelled of spilled Chinese food:
garlic and ginger and the too-sweet orange sauce that Americans
liked. If I have to die, I thought, let it be here. Don't let him take
me away from my parents' faces and the smell of my own food.

I don't see you, I said, more loudly this time. I won't say anything. You let me go.

There was no answer. I opened my eyes. The flashlight was lying
on the floor, throwing a dim half-moon against the front wall. He
was crouched down with his back to the door: a small, pale man,
hardly bigger than me, wearing an open-necked shirt and black
polyester pants, holding his head in his hands. Beside him on the
ground was a tiny silver pistol, shining like a child's toy.

You got to help me, Chinaman, he said, his voice muffled by his
palms. I got ten minutes to get seventy bucks.

But I have no money.

Yeah, no shit, he said. You got friends? There's a phone in the
back. You got family here? Someone with a car?

All my family in China.

You sure? He dropped his hands and looked at me: a handsome
face, I thought, thin and angular, except for a long pink scar de-
scending from the corner of his mouth. You got no cousins in Chi-
natown? Aren't you supposed to all be cousins? Chin, Chong,
Wong, like that?

My name is Liu.

Shit. He gave a sudden high-pitched laugh, like a small dog barking. My damn luck. Me and the loneliest gook in New York.

Why you need this seventy buck?

He looked at me incredulously, as if I'd asked him why the sun
went down at night. I got debts, man. Serious debts.

You don't have job? Don't make money?

Yeah, I got a job. I run the numbers. You know what that means?

I nodded, though I had no idea.

I work for Ronnie Francis, he said, as if it were a name that everyone knew, like Nixon, or Colonel Sanders. Ronnie don't mess
around. Last time I took a little extra off the top, this is what he did.
He held up his hand in front of him, the fingers splayed. I squinted
in the half-light and saw that his little finger was a stump, cut off at
the knuckle.

This time I'm dead, he said. Ronnie promised me. I only get one
warning.

I cannot help you, I said again, in my loudest, most American
voice. I am only delivery man. I don't come home, my roommate
calls police.

He stared at me for a moment without speaking. Chinaman, he
said, you don't get it. Time the police get here we'll both be gone.

I felt a tingling sensation rise from my toes, as if I'd just stepped
into a freezing bath. *I'm his ransom,* I thought. *I'm his way out. He'll
never let me go.* And then I thought, *Give him something. He's desperate
— he'll believe you.*

Why stay here? I asked. You hide somewhere else.

He picked up the pistol and stood, wrapping his arms around his
chest and shaking from side to side, as if he were freezing cold.
Can't, he said. Ronnie's got spotters everywhere. I couldn't even
get a bus out of Port Authority.

I call my boss, I said. He find someone take you to New Jersey.
Easy. You pay him later.

After I kidnap his delivery boy?

He don't care about me, I said. Only about money. You tell him
you pay one hundred dollars, he take you anywhere.

He didn't answer, but walked to the window and peeled away a
scrap of paper so that he could look out at the street.

Chinese delivery van, I said. No windows. No one see you. You
want me to call?

I got a cousin in Newark, he said. His voice had grown raspy, as if
something was swollen in his throat. My sister's in Philly. He looked
down at the tiny gun, and out the window again. Would you do that
for me?

Give me the light, I said. He tossed it over. I picked my way to the back of the room, stepping over a pile of broken bricks, batting cobwebs and loose wires from my face. The telephone was on the floor in one corner, connected to a raw copper wire. I squatted next to it and dialed the only number I knew: the office of my department at Columbia. I covered the mouthpiece and spoke loudly in Chinese. Father, I said, using his proper name, I hope you can hear me. I am about to do a terrible thing. You must forgive me. And then I said yes a few times, *hao, hao,* to make it seem like an agreement, and slammed down the phone.

We walk around the corner, I said. I turned and saw my wallet lying against the wall, a few feet away; I picked it up and put it back in my pocket, my fingers trembling. Hide behind dumpster, I said. He meet us there.

When I was a child in Wuhan, during the Cultural Revolution, the Red Guards that ruled our city split into factions and fought battles in the streets, with sticks and knives, with machine guns and hand grenades. In those years I learned that a small pistol can be fired accurately only from a few feet away. If I was able to get away from this man and run, I was sure that he would miss. This is what was in my mind as we left the building and walked along Tenth Avenue, toward Fifty-second; as soon as we turned the corner, I thought, I would sprint away, zigzagging from side to side to make it harder for him to aim.

Can't believe it, he said as we walked. He seemed even smaller than he had inside, hunched over, darting glances up and down the street. His voice was almost tearful. Once I get out, that's it, he said. Can't ever come back to the Apple. Ronnie Francis, man, even I showed up after he was dead, his ghost would track me down and get me.

I said nothing. My eyes were locked on the corner, estimating the number of steps it would take and wondering whether I should simply run or shove him aside first, to give myself an extra second or two.

My name's William, he said. My friends call me Willie. What's your name, man?

Liu, I said. My name is Liu.

What the hell kind of a name is that? Loo? That's a girl's name, man. Like Lucinda, or Lulu, or something. No, I got a name for you. You're from the Lucky Dragon, right? So you're Mr. Lucky. You're my luck, man.

OK. Mr. Lucky, I said, barely hearing him.

I got a bad feeling. He took a long, trembling breath and wrapped his arms around his chest again, although it was a warm, humid night for October. I feel like I'm going to die, man, he said. I'm scared.

You not going to die, I said. Everything fine. Soon the van come.

Tell me a story, he said. Would you do that? Just to get my mind off it.

We were twenty feet from the corner now, six or seven paces, and my body was tingling, sizzling, as if I'd jammed my finger into an electric socket. I was tempted to leap onto him and wrestle the gun away, although I knew that that, more than anything, could easily get me killed. I clenched my fists so hard the nails tore my skin. I don't know any stories, I said. I'm sorry.

Come on! He was breathing so hard I thought he might have a heart attack. Everybody knows a story. Gimme a break, man!

All right. I closed my eyes for a moment, and heard a string of Chinese words out of nowhere; at first I didn't recognize them at all. There was a fish, I said. A giant fish in the northern ocean. And it changed to a bird — a bird big as the whole sky. This bird flew to the Heaven Lake.

William nodded vigorously. That's cool, he said. I like it. The Heaven Lake. So where's that? Where's Heaven Lake?

We had almost reached the corner, and the muscles in my legs were tensed to run; I felt as if I were walking on stilts. A taxi rounded the corner and sped up Tenth Avenue. I looked over my shoulder to make sure it didn't stop and saw a blue car coming slowly down the street from the opposite direction. It was a Chevrolet, I think, and one door was a different color, as if it had been replaced. It was driving with its lights off. Two men were sitting in the front, and I could see their arms and chests in the glow of the streetlights, their faces hidden in shadow.

Come on, man, William said. Heaven Lake! Don't stop now.

The car sped up and pulled alongside us, the driver's door opening as it moved.

Hey, Willie. Where you going, Willie?

William stopped, and his mouth sagged open, like a child caught sneaking a piece of candy. He turned around, and I stepped away from him. I wanted to run, but my legs locked at the knees; instead, I folded my arms in front of my chest, as if that would protect me.

Hey, William said, his voice cracking. Curt. It's OK, man. I was just waiting for you.

Curt stepped out of the car and stared over William's shoulder at me. He was tall, dressed in a tan leather coat, and his eyes were the palest blue I'd ever seen, like a cat's. I squeezed my arms tight around my chest; my ribs felt ready to crack.

This is Mr. Loo, William said. He's going to get me a little loan. I'll have it for Ronnie tomorrow. I swear.

That true?

I swallowed hard; my mouth tasted as if it were coated with dirt. I looked at Curt's face, and his hands hanging open at his sides, and I thought, *He'll know. He'll know if you're lying.* I shook my head slowly.

Get in the car, Curt said to William.

What? Why? I just said I was —

Curt grabbed William's wrist and bent his arm back, took his shirt by the collar, and swung him around, banging him against the side of the car. William turned his head and stared at me. Call the police! he shouted. The rear door swung open, as if by magic, and Curt pushed him inside and slammed it. Then he turned to me and took out his wallet. Charlie, he said. Hey. Charlie. Here's fifty bucks. He threw the bills in front of him, and they scattered on the sidewalk like loose napkins, bits of trash. Everything's OK, he said. Get down on the ground. Don't look up. Please. You understand me?

I understand, I said.

Then get down there. And count to a hundred.

I did what he said. I pressed my face to the sidewalk until the car rounded the corner, and then raised my head. There were no shouts, no sirens; only the echo of my own breathing. I stood up slowly, leaning forward, my hands on my knees. After a minute I broke into a run. I unlocked my bicycle and pedaled furiously away, taking a long, circling route, and when I finally reached the Lucky Dragon I left the bicycle and chain at the back door.

I am a teacher of philosophy. My gods, if I have gods, are ancient, dry-lipped men who stay awake in the small hours worrying over the substitution of one word for another. *Yi,* for example, which means righteousness. *Ren,* which means benevolence: the love of a father for his children, the love of one man for all men. I speak of these things in my seminars, and often my young students, who are the same age that I was in 1982, say, *There are no exceptions. Kant was right. Mencius was right.* I look at them and I think of myself lying in bed in the International House that night, rolling over and over, the sheet coiled around me like a rope. There was a telephone next to my bed, and a white sticker on the side that said EMERGENCY CALL 911. I could see William's face, twisted in pain, and then I thought of my father and how the police nearly beat him to death in 1968, when he dared to report the murder of his friend. I think of these things, and I look at my students and say, *No. It's not our job to decide.*

In the *Nicomachean Ethics,* Aristotle says, *In some cases there is no praise, but there is pardon, whenever someone does a wrong action because of conditions that no one would endure.* Sometimes I take great comfort from this. Not because I feel guilty for saving my own life. No, because I know there are people who would say that William deserved to suffer, and that I was brave, like an action hero. Even my own daughters, I think, would look at me with new admiration, as if I were like Schwarzenegger, who always rolls away from the cliff or turns so that the knife strikes the other man instead. This is why I like the word *pardon.* A pardon is a little space, an opening, where the world stands back and leaves you alone. It is the door I walk through every day when I open my eyes.

Here is my problem, again: *I* understand perfectly. But a pardon isn't an explanation; it isn't something to pass on to your children. A pardon is the opposite of a story.

The CD is finished: its fourth repetition. The sun pours through my windows, and the water of the harbor has turned a bright blue-green, the color of laundry soap. It strikes me now how foolish I am to think this way. Another man would be able to say, *This is what I've learned from my life.* And he would include everything I haven't: the woman named An Yi I met later that year in the International House cafeteria, and how we struggled for five years in New York while I finished my degree, how Mei-ling was born one night in the Columbia Presbyterian Hospital during a driving rainstorm in June. How we came here, to Hong Kong, and how the cancer in An

Yi's breast took her and left me alone with two small children and a heart as hollow as a Buddhist's wooden drum. I try to hold it all in my mind at once, and it slips away from me, like my shadow, as if I'd raised my hands to cup the light that falls across the floor.

Where is Heaven Lake?

In the ancient tale, it was the home of the Immortals, a place we humans could never reach. But this is what I think: in this world there are no more Immortals. We cross the oceans in a matter of hours; we talk to people thousands of miles away; we even visit the moon. So if Heaven Lake exists, it is wherever we are, right in front of us. Even here, in this strange city, where I so often wake up and wonder if I am still dreaming. And it may be that stories do not have to have endings we understand, any more than human lives do. Perhaps beginnings are enough.

It is four o'clock. My daughters are on their way home, standing together in a crowded subway car, rolling up the sleeves of their uniforms, loosening their Peter Pan collars. Mei-ling is listening to her Walkman and reading a fashion magazine; Mei-po pages quickly through a Japanese comic book she's borrowed from a friend, the kind I won't let her read. If my wife were alive, I would ask her: *Is this what it means to have children? To be able to see them so clearly, and never know what to say?* I am not any kind of storyteller, but my daughters are coming to my door, in these precious last days, and I have to give them something. They come in, and let their heavy bags drop with a thud that shakes the apartment, and turn to see an old man standing with his arms open, and his mouth is open, as if he is about to sing.

EMILY ISHEM RABOTEAU

Kavita Through Glass

FROM TIN HOUSE

Now that he had won a lifetime supply of colored glass, Hassan Hagihossein felt he could endure the vagaries of Ramadan and Kavita Paltooram's moods. He was no longer tempted by Pete's Pancake House. He was no longer kneeling at his wife's feet offering her mango chutney and almond gelato and other mouth-watering things he could not touch until the sun went down. He was content simply to sit in the rattan chair, turning the pieces of glass over and over in his hands, loosely pondering his dissertation or the arc of Kavita's distended belly or nothing at all.

It was the ninth month of the Islamic lunar calendar as well as the ninth month of Kavita's pregnancy. It was also nine days since Kavita had stopped talking to him. None of the significance of this was lost on Hassan, who was a mathematician as well as a loosely practicing Muslim.

The pieces of colored glass were smooth and flattish and oblong, shaped like teardrops roughly the size of robins' eggs. They fit in his palms perfectly. Each piece was punctured with a delicate hole at one end. It had crossed Hassan's mind that these were designed to be craft items, that he ought to make a chandelier out of them, or bead curtains or something of that nature. But he was positive Kavita would find a colored glass chandelier or bead curtains tacky, and he wasn't sure he would find them beautiful himself anymore if he had to look at them all clustered together in one aggregate form.

Kavita was an architect and didn't like "things," which is to say that she didn't like clutter. She preferred open space, negative space, and the color white. She had decorated their apartment sparely. The little furniture there was was white. So were the appliances, the dishes, the bedspread, the towels, and the sheets. Hassan was made to keep his library in a closet fitted with shelves so as not to break up the whiteness of the walls with the colored spines of his books.

Kavita added to the sparseness of the place by lolling about in the nude. She cooked and cleaned this way as well, brown and lithe and utterly naked. This made him blush. Hassan regarded her body as a perfect arrangement of spheres, a planetary form, a heavenly thing, a thing that might turn his eyeballs to salt if he looked too long, and so he tried not to.

During the first few months of their marriage, he had found the apartment antiseptic and cold. He found himself afraid of breaking things, although there really was nothing to break. He felt like he was stuck on the set of a movie about the future. Because of these feelings, he was childishly insistent that Kavita let him keep his rattan chair from college. He knew that the chair was an eyesore. He knew that it pained Kavita to have it in the living room, but for a long time it was the only thing he found comfortable about their home.

Later he began to find the apartment peaceful. He understood Kavita's design sense more when he found himself opting to work at home rather than in his tiny office over at the math department. It was like living in a tabula rasa. White is a color without depth, he thought, or a thing without depth, since it is not a color at all, but a thing that makes depth possible. Ideas like this came to him, and new ways of solving problems.

One afternoon, as he sat quadrilating aspect ratios at the kitchen table, he was struck by the slow movement of a rectangle of soft not-yellow afternoon sunlight sliding across the white wall opposite him. It was moving infinitesimally. It was shifting its shape. He perceived its path, and it was telling him something about the basic probability of time that he could not put into numbers or words. Then a cloud crossed the sun and the shape was suddenly not there. The wall appeared to be a different shade of white than it was before. He was surprised to find his eyes stung with tears.

In that moment he felt he understood Kavita Paltooram more than he ever had and more than he ever would. And later that week when he skulked home from a disappointing multivariable calculus section in which he realized he was not transferring his passion for gradient functions to a group of stunningly disinterested undergraduates, he wasn't even upset to find that the rattan chair had been painted white as a bleached bone. He was simply glad to be home.

Once in a while he would find arabesque strands of his wife's black hair shed on the white furniture or the white bathroom tiles and he would read them like calligraphy. Today she wants me to pay the electric bill, he would figure, or today she wants me to bring home a cantaloupe. Almost always he was right.

That was before Kavita became pregnant. That was before she locked herself in the bathroom to urinate on a magic stick and refused to come out for two hours while Hassan paced the white rooms like a tiger on eggshells, wanting to pound down the door but not daring even to knock. Not daring even to tap. That was before she finally came out of the bathroom wielding the little magic stick with two pink lines, looking like a decidedly different person. Like a person with pointed edges instead of round ones. That was before she became impossible to read, left to right or right to left.

"I'm going for a walk," she had said, "and I don't want to be followed." As if he was a stalker and not her husband of three years. That night he divided the time it took for her to come home into nanoseconds, suffered an outrageous hollow craving for pancakes, and neglected to praise Allah for his blessings. When three hours passed without a sign of her, Hassan reached for the phone and dialed his father long-distance in Rasht to ask if this was normal behavior for women who've just discovered they are pregnant.

"It most certainly is not, my son, and don't say I didn't warn you. What did you expect? You married a Hindu from New Jersey."

"Don't start with that. I should think you'd be happy. You're going to be a grandfather."

"Of what?"

"Of a baby."

"That's not what I meant."

"I know what you meant."

"You know everything, Ph.D. So why consult with your father at all?"

"I don't want to argue."

"Why not consult me before the marriage? Why not marry Khaled's daughter instead as we arranged?"

"Khaled's daughter was twelve."

"Khaled's daughter was more beautiful than the moon!"

"I didn't call to argue."

"And she knew how to respect men. Now she's married to Zaid's idiot son. The one who drives his motorcycle like a maniac. It's a shame."

"I told you I don't want to argue. I'm just not sure what to do."

"You do what they all do in that godless country. You go buy a box of cigars and smoke them all."

It was true that Gulmuhammed Hagihossein had warned his son. He had opposed Kavita Paltooram from the moment he first laid eyes on her, which was the first time Hassan had seen her as well. Afterward it astonished Hassan that in his four years at Columbia he had never once noticed her, and it struck him as fateful rather than random that they should meet on graduation day before almost separating paths forever. It was fate that brought the Paltoorams to sit for their celebration supper at the round lacquered table in Lucky Cheng's Four Star Halal No Pork Chinese Restaurant next to the very one where Hassan sat glumly between his father and his square black graduation cap.

"Avert your eyes from her flesh," Gulmuhammed insisted in Farsi, even as he stared with his son at the indescribable midriff of Kavita, bedecked in her blood-red sari.

Hassan's mother had worn a hijab up until the day she swelled like a cresting wave after being stung on the tongue by a wasp in the kitchen while preparing a khaviar. After that she was wrapped in a shroud by a brood of shrieking neighbor women and covered with two thick yards of Iranian earth. Watching Kavita at Lucky Cheng's, it occurred to Hassan that he could not remember his mother's hair. Kavita's hair reached to her waist. It was oiled in a blue-black braid that snaked over her shoulder like a question mark. The Hagihosseins stared at her impossible curves.

"That woman is wicked. Completely shameless. It is clear that she will break a man's heart one day for sport with her wiles," Hassan's father intoned.

She wore the sari exclusively to please her parents. That much was clear. Hassan understood this because he was wearing a starched galabiya for the exact same reason. He also recognized the customary apologetic look that first-generation offspring wear in public with their mothers. As Mrs. Paltooram sat weeping like a camel over her vegetable lo mein (not from sadness, but from joy because her daughter was going to be successful), as Gulmu-hammed sat pontificating over his kung pao chicken about per-forming ablutions (and chastising his son for becoming too Amer-ican), Hassan's eyes locked with Kavita's. They rolled their eyes and smiled.

That was the beginning. On the streets of New York, where they started their courtship, she was approached by Mexicans and re-sponded in halting Spanish, while he more often than not was mis-taken for a light-skinned black man on account of his woolly hair. This amused them. They pondered how confusing their children would be, if they ever had any.

When she became pregnant, he was himself confused. When she became pregnant and started the night walks, he became strangely bewildered by language. It wasn't that he had lost his grip on Eng-lish so much as that he couldn't connect signifiers and signified anymore. He would falter in the middle of a sentence even though he knew the string of words coming out of his mouth was correct.

Is this thing really called an elbow? he thought. And if so, is my knuckle the elbow of my finger? Is my wrist an elbow? Is Kavita's waist an ankle? They are both slender and they both bend and they are both the color of cinnamon. Is a joint on the body an angle or the possibility of an angle? Is Kavita's little finger a cinnamon stick? No, a cinnamon stick does not bend like an elbow.

He worked furiously on his dissertation, *On Finsler Geometric Man-ifolds and Their Applications to Teichmueller Spaces,* to rid himself of his vicious thought cycles. This failed to work. He just found himself thinking about his wife in elementary mathematical terms. For ex-ample, he imagined Kavita and himself as the axis on a graph plot-ting the growth of their child. He also tried using Kavita and the baby as the set of coordinates and tried to design an algorithm to classify the shape of their future as a family. He thought of them as a triangle, of course, but one whose boundaries he could not begin to measure.

Kavita's night walks became regular. He assumed she had taken a lover. He doubted his paternity. He doubted his doubt. Every time

she left she would admonish him not to follow her. Of course the
night came when he decided to do just that.

She was walking very fast. Hassan kept three quarters of a block
behind her, trying to move in the shadows and keep cover behind
parked cars. He felt ridiculous. His shirt was sweat-stuck to his back
like a postage stamp. Kavita crossed a street. The wind lifted her
hair so that several thick strands of it pointed backward in his direction like accusing fingers, but she did not turn her head. He realized she was making a beeline for the campus. At one point she
leaned against a tree and brought one foot up against the trunk to
adjust her sandal strap. The gesture hurt him physically. He realized Kavita was monumentally graceful. She began walking again.
He let himself lag farther behind. From a distance he watched his
wife stop in front of the university's Art and Architecture Building,
a gray monstrosity of a structure. She pushed through the revolving
door and was gone. Hassan began to breathe again.

She is taking a class, he thought, straightening his tie. That's all.
She is continuing her education. Still, he was nagged by the fact
that this should be kept secret from him, and he was left with the
troubling image of Kavita being swallowed up by the building, like
a tiny sea horse in the striated mouth of a humpback whale. Then
he thought of their child growing in her. A pearl in the belly of
a sea horse in the belly of a whale. A pearl. A precious thing.
The night was heavy and wet. "Allah Akbar," he said to no one
in particular. He kept saying it as he followed Kavita's trajectory
backward to their white home. "Allah Akbar, Allah Akbar." God
is great.

In the third month of her pregnancy, Hassan drove Kavita to the
Corning glass factory. He picked the factory because he'd noticed
her reading a library book on stained glass windows and thought it
might be of interest. She was growing more distant from him every
day, and he hoped an excursion might draw them together.

Upstate, the leaves were blazing, almost radioactive tones of red
and yellow somersaulting to the road. Kavita was silent in the car.
Veiled without a veil. She had the window rolled down on the passenger side and her hair was whipping around like a system of angry black vectors, hiding her face and revealing it in turn. An equation came to Hassan as he took in the simultaneous motion of the

leaves falling down and her hair lifting up. He understood these things to be linked. The equation was this:

$$Distance \div Longing = Desire$$

Hassan quickly dismissed the equation as nonsensical. Longing and desire were too close in meaning to be considered separate variables. There wasn't a word in the English language to describe the cause and effect of Kavita Paltooram's remoteness on his heart. He was very hungry.

"Would you like a tunafish sandwich?" he asked her. He'd packed them an elaborate lunch. "An éclair?"

"Where are you taking me, Hassan?" she answered. Her voice was tired.

"It's a surprise. I can keep a secret just as well as you."

Kavita gathered her heavy hair, tied it in a knot at the nape of her neck, and closed her eyes.

"Would you like some cashew nuts?"

"No."

"Would you like a pickle?"

"No. I'm going to take a nap." Her eyelashes cast long elliptical shadows down her cheekbones. While she slept, Hassan wound up eating everything, both her portion and his own.

Inside the factory, they watched a man blow a tiny glass sparrow from a long spinning pipe. Hassan watched Kavita watching the beak and the wings harden out of liquid glass. On her face was the trace of a smile.

She carefully chose a set of wineglasses from the gift shop. Before they left, Hassan entered a contest. He wrote three words on a slip of paper: *Delicate, Durable, Divine.* It was supposed to be a new slogan for the cover of the CorningWare catalog. He had been trying to describe his wife. On the car ride home he thought about how none of the words was right.

The second time Hassan followed Kavita to the Art and Architecture Building, he waited until she came out. He chose a bench near Stanhope Hall because it afforded him a view of the revolving door while obscuring him slightly behind the Rockefeller statue. While he waited he ate through the large bag of jelly beans Kavita had turned down because they hurt her teeth, and he thought about what he could say to her to make her love him. He had a lot of things he wanted to tell her. Whenever he tried his tongue got tied.

"Kavita," he wanted to say, "in my country, a bowl of goldfish on the table means an auspicious new year. A sturgeon fish can live a hundred years. My grandfather was a fisherman. He couldn't spell his own name. My grandmother was a poet. She wove her verse into Persian rugs and traded them to an Englishman. One rug for two lambs. Her loom was lost in the war. My grandmother's name was Khadijah. Her mother's name was Khadijah. Khadijah was the first wife of the Prophet. Khadijah was also my mother's name. My mother wore a hijab from her head to her toes. I do not remember the color of her hair. Every woman in my family has named her daughter Khadijah for the past two thousand years."

Before she became pregnant, Hassan didn't think like this. Before she became pregnant, he thought of himself primarily as a mathematician and, as such, a citizen of the world. The roster of names in his department read like a litany of united nations: Imran Abbaspour, Antonio Cavaricci, Saul Diamond, Ricardo González de los Santos, Hank Hansell, N'gugi Obioha, Nicolas Paraskavopolous, Olga Rasvanovic, Hoc Sung, Almamy Suri-Tunis, Li Wang, Toshio Yamamoto. Three quarters of the members of the Applied Probability Research Group could barely speak enough English to ask what time it was, yet they were understood just so long as their equations were sound. Yet here he sat, gorged on gourmet jelly beans, not knowing how to talk to his wife.

After exactly two hours, Kavita emerged in a thin wave of students. She was noticeably pregnant. She was talking to a very tall man. Hassan watched in horror as this man stooped over his wife and picked something from her shoulder. Was it a hair? Were this man's fingers touching Kavita's hair? He watched her say goodbye. He waited until she turned a corner to tail the man. He followed the man across the quad and underground to the all-night library, where he noticed under fluorescent lights that the man was blond and blue-eyed and had a mustache that resembled a baby caterpillar crawling on his upper lip.

This was the night Hassan unraveled. He dreamed Kavita gave birth to a moth with blue eyes and wings that extended to the roof. He called his father in Rasht. He let the phone ring twenty-seven times. Gulmuhammed was not at home. On another night he dreamed he asked Kavita why she had married him.

"Out of kindness," she replied, "so that you could get your green card."

He had to ask Toshio to cover his multivariable calculus section two weeks in a row because he feared he wouldn't be able to hold a piece of chalk without dropping it. In one week he ate five Hungryman breakfasts at Pete's Pancake House. When he weighed himself on the white bathroom scale, he discovered to his dismay that he'd gained nearly twenty pounds.

The third time Hassan followed Kavita to the Art and Architecture Building was Lailat-ut Qadr. It was raining, and he'd been fasting. For Ramadan, for clarity. He waited a half-hour and went inside. He'd never set foot in the building before, but as if guided by instinct, as if making a hajj of doom, he found the classroom without really trying. It smelled of turpentine. A dozen students sat like a solar system in a semicircle with paintbrushes clutched in their hands or held between their teeth. In front of each student was a canvas. On each canvas was a naked Kavita. Kavita herself was sprawled out at the semicircle's center on a filthy couch, her belly rounder than the sun and twice as painful for him to look at.

Hassan reached for the closest thing he could grab. Later he would remember the gesture with embarrassment. His hand found a thing. It was a coffee can full of soaking brushes. He flung it as hard as he could without aiming at anything and not knowing why. A woman gasped. The can grazed the corner of one of the canvases, knocking it to the floor and splashing turpentine on at least three people. One of them was the blond-haired blue-eyed man. Hassan fixated on him.

"What is your name?" he demanded. His voice didn't sound like his voice.

"Excuse me? What's going on here?" asked the man, rising to his feet.

"What is your name?" repeated Hassan.

"I'm Burt. Burt Larson." He came toward Hassan with his arms held out in a placating way that reminded Hassan of a jellyfish. "We don't want any trouble here, man."

Hassan spun on his heels and fled through the rain. His socks were wet. It was Lailat-ut Qadr, the night of power, and his socks were soaking wet. When he got home he had to breathe into a paper bag because he was hiccupping violently. He rewrote the scene so that he broke a canvas over the blond man's head, threw a blanket over Kavita, and led her out of the Art and Architecture Building by the hand.

That was the day Kavita Paltooram stopped talking to him altogether. Which at first was fine, because he didn't want to talk to her either. She had shared her body with a circle of strangers. She was just as far away as before. The difference now was that she seemed far away and *dirty*. He busied himself in Finsler Manifolds and stayed away from the apartment. He made astonishing progress with his dissertation. He attributed this clarity to his fast and also to Kavita's imperfection.

Then he dreamed again about the moth. This time it was gargantuan, with feelers as long as trees and wings as shaggy as a llama's fur. In the dream, Kavita was mounted on the moth and carried away into the blue sky. She was naked, of course, but small as a dot on the back of the moth. In the dream, as the moth carried his wife toward the sun, he was filled with longing. Hassan woke up gut-wrenchingly hungry.

On the ninth day of her silent treatment, the glass arrived. "Congratulations, Mr. Hagihossein," read the card. "Your slogan was chosen for our catalog! We send you these timeless treasures with gratitude. Sincerely, Peter Simpkin, Executive President, Corning, Inc."

There were dozens of pieces. Hassan sat in the rattan chair turning them over in his hands. He held up a blue piece over one eye and watched Kavita through it. She had just taken a shower and was wearing her white bathrobe. Through the glass, her body was distorted. Her edges were running. She looked like she was under water, a drowning angel. It occurred to Hassan that he didn't know how to make her happy. He didn't know how to speak her language. Kavita did not think in the terms of water. Kavita, who had grown up in Teaneck and taken perhaps one desultory trip to the Jersey shore every other summer, could not understand what it had meant to grow up on the rim of the Caspian Sea. This is why the glass pieces, which put his mind at rest, did not mean the same thing to her. She didn't know what it was to hunt a beach for sea glass.

Hassan fished in his toolbox for some wire. He moved to the kitchen table and began sketching a design.

"Kavita," he called.

She came.

"Do you see? I am making a mobile to hang above the baby's crib."

She was silent.

He looked up at her and saw that her eyes were bloodshot. He steadied his voice. "If it's a girl, I want to name her Khadijah."

Kavita fingered an orange piece of glass.

"It was my mother's name," he explained, placing his hand gingerly on her hip.

"I know," she said. "It's beautiful."

"Yes. And it sounds like yours."

She moved his hand to her navel and held it in place with her own. A riptide tore his stomach like a hunger pang. Her body gave him gooseflesh. She opened her mouth to speak, then shut it, as if reconsidering.

"Yes? You were going to say something?" he begged.

Kavita spoke slowly. "Do you realize you never look at me?" Her voice was soft like sand under bare feet. "I can't remember the last time you touched me."

Hassan stood. He swallowed. He didn't know the name for the way his wife's hair smelled. He gathered it in his fists and combed his fingers through to its snarling ends. Then, with the wet tips of Kavita's hair, he painted concentric circles on his face. Over his eyebrows, temples, cheekbones. By which he meant to say, "You are all I look at. You are all I see."

SHARON POMERANTZ

Ghost Knife

FROM PLOUGHSHARES

DIMITRI AND I are half naked when the woman shows up with the dogs. He is sitting up and I am astride him, my dress around my waist. What we had thought to be a secluded park looking out on an all-but-abandoned pond is actually someone's back yard.

"We're clean-living people here," the woman says. Then the low constant growling of the two dogs straining their leashes. Pit bulls, she tells us as we grab for our scattered belongings. She lets the dogs get a little closer. One bares his teeth not far from my shoulder. The other is at Dimitri's ankles. "This is a family neighborhood. I mean, I don't know where you people come from, but . . ."

"I understand, ma'am, I understand," Dimitri says, reaching for his shirt, which I had removed moments before and tossed onto a bush. "We're terribly sorry." He has a deep voice, a sexy, midnight-radio kind of voice. This does our case no good. The woman lets the leash out a little more.

"The filth," she says. "The filth that comes into this neighborhood."

We stand up. "Don't give it another thought, ma'am," Dimitri says. "Please don't give it another thought."

"Don't what!" she asks. One of the dogs has a perfect stream of saliva hanging from its hot pink tongue.

"Don't give it another thought," he repeats, taking my hand, and we run for the parking lot and his car, fueled by adrenaline and shame. She doesn't come after us. There is some barking, but that's all. We sit in his car, silent and breathing hard. Not far away, children are singing the jump-rope song. *Mary Mary Bobary, Banana Fanna Fofana . . .*

I lean my head against the back of the seat.

"What time is it?" he asks, shaking his wrist and frowning.

"Two o'clock," I tell him. "Has your watch stopped?"

"My father's Rolex," he says, taking the watch off and holding it up to his ear. "It's one of the few things I have from him." His voice gets shaky and his eyes tear a little whenever he mentions his father, who died six years ago, suddenly and from a heart attack. No time to say goodbye. On this and many other things, Dimitri is a man who lacks closure.

"I hope that woman doesn't remember you," I say. Dimitri is planning to run for a judgeship in this district, just as his father once did. Family court. To be considered for the nomination, he recently changed his party affiliation to Republican.

"Don't worry," Dimitri says. "It's not like she knows my name or anything."

I am surprised he's so calm — usually he's obsessed with what others think of him. Guilt, he was raised on it. Pays his taxes early, cries if he can't make his daughter's dance recital, does not understand, even scorns, sex without love. As a lawyer, he takes on more than the requisite pro bono work; he prosecutes deadbeat dads and has gotten large alimonies out of rich wife-beaters. His one weakness: sex in dangerous places, often outdoors. He is never more potent than when he fears public humiliation. This time is no different. I reach over and unzip his pants.

"It shouldn't take long," he whispers, knowing I have a train to catch.

I first met Dimitrius Quaid three years ago on an Amtrak train bound for Buffalo. I was going to a suburb of Albany for the weekend to visit my college roommate, Debra, married with a new baby. When the train pulled out of Penn Station, the early spring afternoon was sunny and cloudless, but the farther we got from Manhattan, the darker everything became. By the time the train pulled into Poughkeepsie, around five o'clock, the sky was the color of midnight. Then the storm came all at once, and a wind so powerful it flung the rain against the windows in violent sheets.

Dimitri sat in front of me. We were each alone in our row, me by the window and he by the aisle. I'd noticed him when I got on. His long legs were spread out, and he'd had to move them for me to pass. He looked up, and we smiled at each other for a moment —

long enough for me to note that he was almost but not quite handsome, with blue-black hair and very pale skin. There was something
shocking about his face, dramatic and off-putting: the thick, heavy
arch of his eyebrows, long, dominant nose, full lips. We spoke not a
word to each other until just outside Hudson, when the train came
to a grinding halt and all the lights went out.

"My cell isn't working," he said. In the shadows I could make out
his face leaning toward me. He smelled of vanilla aftershave and
Ivory soap. "Could I borrow yours?" he asked.

Neither of us had service.

"Well," he said. "At least no one will yell at me for a little while."

"Do people often yell at you?" I asked.

"Clearly you're not married," he said.

"No."

"And you're not an attorney."

"Also no."

A man entered our car just then; the intercom was out. We were
waiting for the storm to pass, he said. There was a tornado in Massachusetts, just hours away. No telling how long we'd be. Then he
left, amid moans of frustration, and threats, as there always were
such threats, to sue Amtrak.

Our conversation started haltingly, then moved at a rapid pace,
from his ambition to pursue a career in politics to my job as a book
publicist; from his interest in tropical fish (he claimed that staring
into the tank calmed his nerves before court) to our shared love of
movies from the 1940s. Our lives were a series of almost intersect-
ing coincidences. We both loved Delphyn's, a Greek restaurant in
Manhattan on 85th and Columbus. Dimitri lived upstate but had a
few big clients in the city, kept an apartment on the Upper West
Side, blocks from mine, and ate at Delphyn's on Wednesdays; I usually went there on Tuesdays. My mother and his father went to the
same high school in Atlantic City, New Jersey. We were born on the
same day in June, four years apart.

By then, he had long since moved to my row. He told me his full
name, Dimitrius Quaid. Half Greek and half Irish. I have always
been attracted to halfbreeds, to the mixing of cultures. Perhaps it's
because my own large extended family, the Liebermans, are ridicu-
lously inbred. Too many cousins with cousins even now, and in Po-
land, generations back, an uncle with a niece. We look alike and

are all nearsighted. Though an only child, I am also the baby of the family — grew up encircled by older relatives — so that the faces I looked into always reflected a little too much of my own expression back at me. First chance I got, I ran to Manhattan, in search of the freedom that comes from being surrounded by millions of strangers. There can be such a thing, I told him, as too much intimacy.

I know exactly what you mean, he said, but would not elaborate.

Strangely, our opposite antecedents had produced similar characteristics: dark, dramatic features; feuding families; a tendency toward careless behavior; insanity; guilt. There was one particularly curious difference between our families, though: whereas mine, whose gene pool was weak and overbred, should have been rife with chronic diseases, we in fact were blessed with tremendous longevity. And his family — which should have been healthy and strong from combining and recombining with a variety of outside influences — contained not one male who lived past the age of sixty-five. "Heart disease," he said, and was silent.

I asked him then how long he'd been married. "Ten years," he replied. He and his wife, Beth, had met in law school. They had a daughter, Lucy.

"How old is she?"

"Ten," he said.

Months later, I realized how odd it was that he told me the story so quickly in our acquaintance, admitted straight away that he and Beth weren't married when they conceived Lucy. Usually he lied and said they'd been married the extra year, for whose business was it? He was not a sharer of his own secrets. But for some reason he told me the rest that night.

They were both at NYU. When Beth realized she was pregnant, a friend told her about that abortion place in the Thirties on Park. Every woman in Manhattan knows the address, advertised on the subways. I've gone with several girlfriends over the years, women who still got a little too drunk at parties and occasionally went off with the wrong man, or the condom broke, or they were married but just couldn't afford another child. The abortions were legal, safe, and cheap, the women desperate and grateful. But there was a rushed carelessness about the place, how they put you all together in a big room, like a classroom, like high school health, with a podium in front, about thirty pregnant women and the people accompanying them. Almost always, women showed up with other women. Few men came along.

He had been, that day, one of the few. Beth was miserable, biting her nails to the bleeding cuticles, hadn't slept in days. He could hardly bear to look at her face, the lower lids red from sleeplessness and crying. Roman Catholic, she was, European parents, parochial school upbringing. She couldn't even say the word *abortion*. But she might have gone through with it, he'd asked it of her and she was willing to comply, were it not for that room where they kept you sitting for so long, then a receptionist came out and called your name in front of everyone. Every time Beth heard a name, she winced. After an hour, Dimitri couldn't take it anymore. He leaned over and whispered in her ear that if she wanted to change her mind, they could go.

She was up and heading to the door before he finished his sentence. They walked up Park Avenue and then drifted west, toward the diamond district in the Forties. He claimed it hadn't been his intention at all, but that walk more or less cinched their future. Her face, he said, when she saw the rings in the windows. What she'd wanted of him all along. They were engaged by the end of the day, married two months later. He told himself, on the wedding day, that it was good for a man with his family history, a man who would likely not reach seventy, to marry young, reproduce quickly. Leave someone behind.

This seemed to me a morbid approach to marriage, but I didn't realize then the extent to which mortality hung over Dimitri Quaid. He clung to assumed knowledge of his own lifespan, believing he had to squeeze everything — from passionate love to stellar professional standing, from devoted husband to remarkable father — into fewer years than most people. He assumed he would die young of a heart attack, he told me, like his father and grandfather, just as I assumed I had, always, time to burn.

"Is it a happy ending? Your marriage?" I asked, knowing full well the answer. A man doesn't tell a woman a story like that on a darkened train if he's happy, if he has someone to confide in, if he hasn't thought a million times of what might have happened ten years ago if he'd walked toward the Village instead of uptown.

In the dark, his hand brushed my shoulder and gave me a shock. "So what about you?" he asked. "Tell me more about yourself."

Before I could say a word about visiting Debra from college, or how I wanted to leave my firm and strike out on my own but didn't have the courage, not to mention my string of unsuccessful, casual, or careless relationships — in short, before I could lay out my whole life for him like a banquet of indecision and ambivalence — a giant lightning bolt flashed in the distance, long and perfect, glowing silver.

Our car was silent as the sky crashed and sizzled. Several smaller lightning bolts followed, momentarily illuminating his face close to mine. Then he leaned over and kissed me. His lips were soft and full, a bit cold.

The lights came on in the train.

We retreated, startled, to our respective corners. I was squeezing the armrest so tightly that my hand hurt. He ran his fingers through his hair. We took sidelong, embarrassed glances at each other as if looking at strangers. We were strangers. I reviewed his face and found it kinder this time. The eyebrows were strong, but his large gray-blue eyes were soft, with tiny laugh lines in the corners. A voice came over the intercom. "We will be moving shortly. We apologize for any inconvenience . . ."

"What's your final destination?" he whispered. The rain slowed, was not coming down in hard sheets now, but instead beat rhythmically against the roof.

"Rensselaer," I said. "The last name's Gessup. Tom and Debra Gessup."

The train began to move.

"I'm just outside Schenectady," he said. "Niskayuna. Not so far from there. I get off first."

We said nothing else until his stop.

"I hope you don't think I do this sort of thing often," he said, getting up.

"What sort of thing?" I asked. "Talk?"

"Pour out my troubles to . . ."

He never got to finish. The doors opened, people pushed for the exit — ours was the only one for several cars — and he had no choice but to go with them, carried away by the tide.

For the next two days of that trip, my friend Debra sang the virtues of upstate living.

"Everyone here is fat," she told me. "It's wonderful. You can gain sixty pounds in a pregnancy and no one notices."

Is that a reason to leave Manhattan? I asked her.

In the city, Debra had been an ad copywriter at a big midtown agency. Then she became an account exec, and was about to make VP when she met Tom, an architect from Accord, New York. The Debra I knew then got $200 haircuts, had a personal trainer and a guy at the New York Look who picked out all her clothes. She never ate dessert. The woman who sat in front of me, nursing her baby, was round and puffy and relaxed, her face broken out, her hair overgrown and askew.

"People stay married here," she said. "You can buy a house for what a studio costs in the city. Nobody gets Botox injections; they embrace their wrinkles. It's the real America."

The baby had stopped nursing, and Debra eased her nipple away, buttoned up her bra, and told me that she couldn't wait to get a nanny. "I love her," she said, glancing down at Claire, four months, two weeks. "But I feel like I haven't been out of this house in years."

This was the lament of all my nursing friends: time stopped. They wondered who and where they were, as if living in a dream, locked with their newborn in a mysterious, powerful dance. Watching them filled me with a combination of fascination and repulsion, horror and awe.

"It's worth it," Debra told me, holding Claire up in front of her, then slinging her over her shoulder and patting her on the back. "The problem with you, Annie," she said. "Do you mind me telling you what your problem is?"

"Go right ahead." From the time I passed thirty, I'd begun to get a lot of advice from my married women friends. I didn't mind so much. Most of them had put their careers on hold and were now at home with small children and Elmo videos. On the whole they no longer had love affairs, which take up a lot of thought and energy. They saw fixing my life as a challenge. It kept their minds sharp, like doing the *Times* crossword puzzle.

"The problem is that you back into everything. I've never seen you really go after a man or a job or even an apartment. You just take what's offered to you and live with the consequences until you get sick of them, then you take the next thing offered to you. The path of least resistance."

"It's a strategy," I said.

"For disaster," she said. "You think you're going to be young forever?"

Claire gave a loud, aggressive burp. "Let me hold her," I said, and put out my arms. She smelled of baby shampoo and pure sweet baby smell. I kissed the edge of her ear.

"Do you want kids?" Debra asked. "You've never talked about that."

"I don't know," I said, leaning Claire on the crook of my arm. She grasped my finger hard and pulled. I wanted to tell Debra that I didn't think a baby was one of those things you could aggressively go after. Like an apartment or a job or a share in the Hamptons. I wanted to tell her that for two days I'd thought of nothing but the married man who'd kissed me on the train. And so, if I went to our favorite restaurant on 85th and Columbus on a Wednesday, when I knew he'd be there, instead of on the Tuesday when I usually went, was that backing into life, or going after something I wanted? Did I want what I thought I wanted? In waiting for life to come to me, I was also, in a certain way, in control. I could say yes or no to what came my way and take no responsibility for failure, because I did not actively court disaster. I courted nothing. I wanted to ask her about all those things, but I didn't, because I knew exactly what she'd say. She'd say, Take a risk, for God's sake, but not with a married man. Taking a relationship risk with a married man is like taking no risk at all. Then the baby started to shriek, and I handed her back.

He only likes to take chances upstate.

Two weeks have passed since the incident with the woman and the dogs. He zips up his trousers and hands me a handkerchief. "This is getting crazy," I whisper into the darkness. "You are about to run for public office. In a conservative district."

He is silent.

"If you're so unhappy, then ask for a divorce, don't bring one upon yourself," I say. "Like this."

"There's Lucy," he whispers. "She's too young. I can't do that to her. There are no children of divorce in her class."

"What year is this?" I ask him. "Where am I?"

I hear a faint shushing noise in front of us.

"Even if I could do that to Lucy," he says, "Beth would never want a divorce. She'd make my life a living hell." He pauses. "You and I are like Spencer Tracy and Katharine Hepburn."

"You're no Spencer Tracy," I say. "And I'm sure no Katharine Hepburn."

"True," he whispers. "She'd never give me a blowjob in theater four at the Schenectady Octaplex."

Downstate, he never wants to take risks. Central Park is too urban, the landscape doesn't appeal to him. The subways are too dirty, he says, the movie theaters too small and crowded. Here's what I think is the real reason: in Manhattan, if you're discovered having sex in public, there's a big chance no one will give a damn.

In Manhattan we're free. For three years we've been free. We see each other Wednesday nights, and usually he stays over until Thursday. Sometimes when he can swing it, he takes the train down on a Friday and stays until Saturday. Mostly we stay at his place, sometimes at mine. We always go to excellent restaurants, sometimes meet my friends — my single friends — for dinner. Sometimes he can't stay — birthdays, in-laws, or, most often, a court appearance upstate. Countless times he's left me dateless for openings at the Whitney, Broadway shows, and other things that require planning. So I long ago stopped planning. He's always gone for New Year's but never for our shared birthday. Somehow, then he manages to get away. My mother thinks I haven't had a date in three years. Sometimes she gets choked up when I talk to her on the phone. She told my aunt I'm probably a lesbian.

Still, after all this time, when he walks through the door, my heart is bursting. I can feel it in there, expanding with each beat. At night in bed, he measures the length of me, running his index finger along my spine until I'm shaking. Some nights we attack each other, hungry from our endured separation. Other times I slide into his arms and inhale, ready for the most dreamless and wonderful of sleeps. His hair is thick and black, his beard always scratchy, but his skin is pale and fragrant, soft as a woman's.

When he wins a case, which is most of the time, he'll call from the courthouse, or his car or office, to tell me the size of the settlement. Often he'll go into the details, leaving out the names of the clients. There's the twenty-year-old stripper who married her sixty-year-old boss; in the first year of marriage, he broke so many of her bones that she's now suing him for divorce and workers' comp.

There are the parents, rich enough to hire teams of expensive lawyers, who lose custody for trying to force-feed their children drugs, or for accidentally leaving them outside the supermarket and driving away. And then my favorites, the marriages of upstanding citizens — kindergarten teachers, church organists, social workers — that end over someone refusing to be urinated on, beaten with a metal paddle, or included in a threesome with a sibling. Bondage — it's amazing how many marriages end because of bondage.

Once he calls from his car and is quiet, sniffles as if holding back tears, and must pull over to the side of the road. He has lost the case. Such times are rare. I know then that there must be custody involved, a decent father is going to be restricted from seeing a child, for only these cases push him to the brink, haunt and obsess him. I utter words of comfort about how hard he works, about how he hasn't slept in weeks, preparing, and what else could he do? I sound so banal, and yet after I repeat myself a few times, he seems calmer, perhaps because I know, without his having to say it, the real roots of his emotion: Lucy.

He gets back on the road, thanking me, saying he loves me, and then the line crackles and goes out for a moment, the connection suddenly tenuous.

"Listen, baby," he says. "I'm pulling into the driveway now. I'm home. Gotta go." I hear a child's voice in the background, loud and rhythmic. You promised, Dad, she says. You promised to take me for ice cream. Then the empty click of the receiver.

I hang up, look around at the four walls of my studio apartment, then remember what Dimitri said once, about how we are like Katharine Hepburn and Spencer Tracy. I have always loved the famous story about the proud and independent Hepburn — fearless wearer of men's trousers, determined controller of her film roles — kneeling at Tracy's feet to remove his shoes after a long day on the set. It occurs to me just then that there must have been days not mentioned in her biography, days when, expecting him as usual, there was no knock on her trailer door. And what about the evenings when she placed her hands on the smooth leather and pulled — revealing his socks, then the soft and vulnerable instep that only she was allowed so close to — and was told that he had to go home. Home, the word reserved for the place you don't take your mistress.

*

Dimitri wins the nomination and has to spend even more time in Albany preparing for his campaign. He calls often and begs me to visit. He needs me, he says, to help him get through the stress of this election. I remind him, yet again, that my presence upstate is dangerous for him, then review the many cautionary tales of politicians brought down by affairs, but he refuses to acknowledge that anything bad could come of our love. Oh, how I want to believe him, yet I feel a sense of impending doom. And fear, there is always fear — mixed more than I like to admit with fantasy and desire — that I will be the one, without meaning to, who brings down his house, and maybe even his upstate career. Leaving him with no alternative but to choose me, and move.

I stay at a small hotel in Schenectady, a bed-and-breakfast owned by an elderly couple, Jane and Howard Winter, who allow their cat her own seat at the kitchen table. My room is old and dark and smells like my grandmother's closet. Someone in Dimitri's office recommended this place. He likely wanted something that felt more like a home than a hotel. When we're not being completely careless, he worries about dignity, about how best to treat me well. He knows this is a tricky business.

There are doilies on the bureau, and black-and-white photos of Albany at the turn of the century line the walls in dust-encrusted frames. Friday morning I sit up, completely awake at seven A.M. with no idea what to do until one, when I'm meeting Dimitri for lunch. The shades on the windows throw a dull brown light across the bed, and I catch a glimpse of myself in an oak-framed mirror with a big crack down the center. My hair is standing up at odd angles, and I look tired and old, scowling, aware of every line and crease pulling me toward middle age. Looking around the room, I feel like I've woken up in an Edith Wharton novel. Am I becoming one of those women about whom everyone says, What a waste?

I show up at Debra's house two hours later, having told her that the dust at the B&B is aggravating my allergies and can I have breakfast with her and stay for a few hours?

"No lectures, please," I say, crossing the threshold with my overnight bag. Debra stands in the doorway of her contemporary split-level, her arms folded across her chest. She is five months pregnant, and her belly peeks out from under her folded arms. Claire, who is now walking and talking, about to begin preschool, sits in front of the television watching Barney.

Tom is not home, she tells me. He never seems to be home, as people are building and building in this part of the state, the great migration from Manhattan. For a moment I comfort myself: How is Debra's life any different from mine? She sees her husband for an hour in the morning and an hour at night, and then, when does she have his attention? But then I look around the living room at the plush white bears and piles of children's books, the overstuffed couches and groupings of pictures on the wall: Debra and Tom's wedding, Claire's first step, a family vacation to the Grand Canyon. And it occurs to me how much my life resembles that of a clever spy, a good criminal, an amnesia victim: there is no clutter and no documentation.

We sit down to tea in the kitchen, and Debra offers me a croissant but declines to take one herself. She looks annoyed, slams her mug down on the table, and I wonder if I'd have been better off eating breakfast with Mr. and Mrs. Winter and the cat, who sits up on her hind legs and waits for her omelet with remarkable deportment. Claire comes into the kitchen asking for a cookie. I hand her one from the tin on the table, and she nibbles on it for a moment, then puts her arms up, wanting to be lifted into my lap. I pull her onto me. Older now, she smells of bubblegum and fabric softener. She sucks her cookie and asks me if I like Teletubbies. Before I can answer she slithers off. Her love comes in flashes, then she's gone, on to her next task. My own parents had one child, and I too had only to put my arms out to dip into their constant, hovering attention, like an embarrassment of riches. They had been married for seven years when I was born. A biblical number. And they saw me as a kind of miracle, their lives focused on my every movement and expression. Debra's parents divorced when she was three; her mother moved her across the country, away from her father. Where I have feared commitment, loss of freedom, she has sought stability, continuity. And then there's Dimitri, seeking a little bit of both. What exactly, I wonder, was going on in his house?

"No matter how many books I read Claire, she's way too caught up with videos and product branding," says Debra, sounding like she did back in her advertising days. "I think my child is bored."

"I think her mother is bored," I say.

"No one told me motherhood could be so boring," she says. "And lonely."

"But you're having another one?"

"I want her to have someone," she says, her glance a little too penetrating. "She's already too comfortable playing alone."

I do not reply.

"Are you tired of all this yet?" Debra asks. "All this running around, pretending. For God's sake, you're thirty-six. How much more time do you have to waste?"

"I love him," I tell her. "Honestly, when I met him on the train that time, I never imagined I'd feel this way." I try to explain how easily Dimitri and I can talk, the effortlessness of our connection. "Plus we can't keep our hands off each other."

Debra sighs. "I remember when Tom and I were like that," she says. "Before Claire was born. Before he started working six days a week."

I can see on her sad face, as she can see in mine, the following question: Why is there no perfect way? Why is a secure marriage so little like a romantic, passionate affair? Why does a romantic, passionate affair so rarely lead to the security of marriage?

I stand in Dimitri's upstate office, waiting for him to take me to lunch. Against the back wall is his tank of tropical fish. I look at the Tiger Barbs and a strange-looking black blob, his favorite, the Ghost Knife. Blind and dependent on sonar, it moves slowly, hesitantly, and mostly travels backward. Last summer Dimitri started out with three of them in the tank, but he is now down to one. Even my fish, he'd joked, have a short lifespan.

"I'm sorry, are you starving?" he asks, looking over some papers. He sits in a wide leather desk chair. 'I'll be finished in a moment, I promise." But then the intercom buzzes again, and he takes the call, leans back and stares out the window.

"I told you, if I don't see those discovery documents by four," he says. "You're lucky I don't haul you in front of Judge Dunbar! Now you know I'm right and you're trying to fuck me up the ass and you also know I'm not going to let you . . ."

Dimitri goes on like this, loud and menacing. I have heard this side of him before, seen him in the courtroom, confident, brash, taking up space and height, but still the tone shocks me a little. The lawyer is aggressive and domineering, the man docile, solicitous. When we sleep together, he wraps his arms and legs around me as if he's drowning; sometimes while dreaming he will call out the words "I don't know" over and over again, like a chant. Here in this room, though, he is altogether different. I wonder what he is like at home. He plans to make one of those local TV commercials for his campaign. I imagine him and Beth and Lucy in front of their three-story house, holding hands. "Albany's families matter," he says, and the camera pans into a closeup.

I pick up a school picture of Lucy on the desk. She is a small feminine version of Dimitri, pretty with huge gray-blue eyes and thick eyebrows. She is not happy about having to be on television, Dimitri has told me. Perhaps because she looks so much like her father, or perhaps because Lucy too is an only daughter, her life spliced between the disappointments and desires of her two parents, I feel a rush of love for her. I think of that day Dimitri told me about in the abortion clinic and how back then having a child felt to him like the ruination of his life. And I suddenly fear, putting Lucy's picture back on the desk, that there will come a time for me when not having a child will feel exactly the same way.

At lunch he tells me about all the people who are sure he can win. He wishes Albany were like Manhattan, where family court judges are appointed by the mayor and that's that, but I can tell he's excited for a fight. He's taken up golf and now plays with various public officials, committeemen, higher court judges. He tries to tell me how he'll manage, with his practice and the judgeship. How he'll divide up the time. Suddenly he sounds uncertain, even a little sad.

"What's the matter?" I ask.

"I'm a damned good lawyer, and maybe I won't be such a good judge," he says, leans across the table, takes my hand. "If I get this I'll have less time in the city," he says. "That's the biggest thing that makes me feel . . . reluctant."

I tell him we'll figure something out. He wants this so much, and so I want it for him.

"Maybe you could move up here," he says.

"What would I do?" I imagine myself in this land of married forever, minor league baseball, and pastel fabrics. The lone single woman in Niskayuna, New York.

"I'm sure they'd let you work from home," he says. "Or you can start your own company. You always talk about that, you know it's what you want."

"If I go off on my own," I say, "then I really have to be in Manhattan."

"That's ridiculous," he says. "Don't you think there are publicists up here?"

Then he tells me a story. Finally, a story of his own childhood, for he rarely refers to it in any real way. About his now dead father, whose secretary lived with them when Dimitri was growing up. She had an apartment above the garage.

"Your father's secretary lived in your house?"

"Yes," he says. "She sometimes baby-sat for us when my parents went out. Other times she and my father went on long business trips, and we were alone with my mother. Her name was Ellen. We loved her. She was enormous fun and very beautiful. She taught me to play chess." He pauses. "She never married."

"Did this upset her?" I ask, starting to feel a little sick.

"No, she was a very happy person. She was remembered," he says. "In the will."

"How about your mother, how did she feel about all this?"

He is momentarily quiet. I see him thinking of his father, and of the sudden heart attack that claimed him on the golf course. His dad was with two men he barely knew, Dimitri tells me, business acquaintances. Neither of the women he loved was close by, neither of them was able to hold the dying man's hand or say goodbye. Dimitri looks at me and adds, "I think my mother came to understand."

Suddenly I am old and bitter and living over someone else's drafty garage in a room full of doilies and cracked mirrors and brown shades. Nothing is my own, everything belongs to someone else. This isn't Edith Wharton, I think. This is Stephen King.

"You all right?" he asks. "You don't look so good."

I nod, but all I want is to get back to Manhattan. I want to wake up in my dark, cramped apartment and go to my annoying office.

There's a train at three, I tell him, can he drop me off?

"Forget what I said before, about Ellen, about moving up here. Just forget it," he says, taking out his gold card. "I thought, somehow, the idea would make you happy."

"Only if I lived in Utah." I get up without him, walk toward the door.

On the way to the station, he frowns and looks miserable.

"I hate when you stop talking and get all moody," he says. I see my face reflected momentarily in the car mirror. My hair is a mess, my lipstick smeared. How could he let me walk around like this? I take out a compact and begin to fix myself up. Dimitri pulls into a parking lot across from the station, then leans over the steering wheel and puts his face in his hands. His voice escapes from between his fingers in low gasps. "I've made a mess of my life," he says. "And there's nothing to be done about it."

I feel sympathy for him, even as I'm still angry. He really thinks it's best to try and please all of us a little bit, even if he can't please any one of us completely. He really thinks that by doing nothing he is doing something. He has no idea why he keeps tempting fate in parks and movie theaters, endangering his family, reputation, and career, or why, six years later, he is still mourning his father as if the man died yesterday. He told me recently that he's thinking about calling one of those people who contact the dead. So he can know where his father is, and if he's all right. But now I understand that Dimitri really wants to ask his father what to do about us, how to handle it, how to live his life loving two women at the same time. We are alike, he and I, hoping time or circumstance or other people will decide for us what we can't decide for ourselves.

"It's all right, baby," I say, and put my fingers on his, pull his hands away from his face. His eyes are wet, his skin even paler than usual.

"I can't lose us," he whispers. I draw his face toward me, and we kiss and kiss, hungry and afraid. There are forty minutes before your train, he says. He starts the engine and mentions the park we were looking for weeks ago, when we got lost and met up with the woman and the dogs. "It's five minutes from here," he says. "Come on, I can find it this time. Come on, Annie."

He looks optimistic again, full of energy. His old deluded self. When he gets like this, I can't refuse him. For even angry and annoyed, confused, afraid, I still want to make him happy. That is love, after all. We set off for the park and are there in minutes, standing at the edge of a large pond enclosed by rows of trees and bushes. It's fully spring now, warm and sunny, though there's been some rain. No one is in sight, not even another car in the parking lot. Dimitri takes off his raincoat and lays it on the grass. In moments we are rolling around on his coat and then on the wet earth, tugging at each other's clothes.

We are back to where we started, yet again, back to where we always begin. I inhale Dimitri's smell of vanilla and soap, feel the rhythm of his breath on my neck, look into his eyes turning just then from gray to pale blue. Time stops, I don't know if a minute or an hour passes. I close my eyes, and when I open them, a man is staring down at us, his face fleshy, expressionless.

"Baby," I whisper in Dimitri's ear. "A policeman. You better get up." The policeman looks extremely tall from this angle, with a chunk of blond hair falling in his narrow blue eyes. His nostrils are flared, his lips thin. A stick is fastened to his belt. I think of a retort we used in high school — *What are you, the morality police?*

Dimitri rolls off me, his face pink, his fingers fumbling with his zipper. I cover myself in his coat, reaching behind to rehook my bra and quickly rearrange my clothes.

"Dimitri?" the policeman asks. "Dimitri Quaid? Counselor?"

Dimitri tries to get the whole thing forgotten, smiles, brings up a captain they both know. But there is no budging; this guy is a rookie and all business. "I'm sorry," the policeman says. "I won't cuff you, but you'll both have to come to the station." Someone not far from here filed a complaint, he tells us. A cop's wife, and she's been raising a fuss. Two naked people copulating on her lawn, and we fit the description. "We take public nudity very seriously here," he says. "No offense or anything."

Disregard for public standards of decency, obscene behavior in an area trafficked by minors. Something like that; I'm not paying attention because the policeman is leading me to a squad car. He opens the door, and I duck tentatively, awkwardly inside. I hear Debra's words in my mind: *You back into everything.* Even breaking the law. I look through the smudged window at the abandoned factories and gray office buildings, the narrow, congested row homes of downtown Albany. The state capital looks barren, hopeless, and depressed.

In minutes the squad car pulls into a driveway and stops. We are only blocks from the park, the train station, Dimitri's office. You can't go too far in this town, everything is connected, close. I look across the seat at Dimitri, sure that he will be distraught, pale, biting his fingernails, his lips, all his worst displays of anxiety, but he looks calmer than I've ever seen him. There is color in his cheeks, and he turns, looks me in the eye, and smiles. Finally, his face says, a verdict will be pronounced, public and irrevocable. He will suffer and be forgiven, or he will be abandoned, shamed, and left for me to love, but either way, I realize, I am the fallback, and either way, once again, neither of us has made a decision, only waited for one to come to us.

But of course it's not too late. Dimitri is removed from his side of the car, and I watch the policeman walk him around, both of them coming to get me. When, I wonder, did my life become somebody else's morality tale? When did I learn to ask for so little? The doors open, and the policeman reaches down to pull me up, push me forward. In his disapproving expression I can see the future: the station house, where everyone knows Dimitri; our names in the papers; his opponent's certain victory in the election; the disappointed little girl who will see me forever as the woman who ruined her life. And her father, stripped of everything he loves but me. Here's the thing about married mistresses — they too can become resented wives. Standing on the sidewalk, just blocks from the train station, finally, finally, I know what I must do. But just as I take a step toward the sidewalk, preparing to run for it, Dimitri reaches out and grabs my wrist, his fingers tightening, like a handcuff, around my pulse.

MARILENE PHIPPS

Marie-Ange's Ginen

FROM CALLALOO

MY NAME IS Marie-Ange Saint-Jacques and I got on that boat November third with my heart open and my eyes closed. My mother, Venante Saint-Jacques, also got on the boat. She too did this with an open heart since she got on that boat only because of me, but, unlike mine, her eyes were open — they had to, you see, because she had come to watch over me. So that Sunday morning she faced the ocean, dropped on her seventy-year-old knees, took the scarf off her head. It flapped softly like a flag in the early breeze before she could lay its white square flat on the gray sand of Balanye beach.

The others were startled when they saw her kneel, bare her head from its cotton-cloth protection, expose her white hair and the vulnerability of old age — offer it all, whatever its worth, whatever the cost, with such a simple gesture as that of pressing the white square into the sand, neatly, and with both her bare hands, as if to say, "This is all I have and take it — my head and all the images stored in it." I knew more than they did, so I did not have to be startled and imagine what she'd be thinking. I knew her heart. What was going on in it at that moment would have sounded like "Take all that my head has kept safe all this while — take my father's smile when he last saw me, take my mother putting cushions on her old chair to make me comfortable near her, take the trees, the friends, the old folks, the luster of leaves at the rainy season, my *demanbre*, my whole life, here! I am going up that boat because I know you are hungry — death is always hungry. More, give more! So here I am to feed you with my body — you can bite it, chew it, maul it, disperse it, erase it and erase all that my body ever meant to me or to anyone else, just so you don't take her standing behind me. Don't take her! Change your plans, don't take my baby, my daughter who sees no other way out of her misery than to sell that bit of land we had so she can pay our way onto this boat and jump into your mouth. Take my life and all the good I ever did and remember I served you well — this has real weight. Dismiss the bad — there is no power in the bad."

They were startled and scared because they could see that she had no hope. She had no hope and that is why she was going up that boat. No hope for the boat's fate, no hope for them, no hope for her daughter on that boat unless she came and bargained with death — traded herself. They knew too that she could have lit a candle. She hadn't. She could have lit three, seven, nine, twenty-one candles! She hadn't. She could have deposited flowers on that scarf. She hadn't. She could have offered an egg, white flour, white rice, and even meat — chicken meat, goat meat, cow meat, any or all meat. She hadn't. The simplicity of that white scarf bare of everything else besides itself was more powerful and frightening than if she had loaded it with gifts. These would have been palliatives. Straw men! They knew it. With the determination of complete abandon, she had reached for the double knot behind her head, untied it slowly as if she were thus undoing any resistance in her or any desire to live. She slid the scarf off her head as one exposes the ridiculous simplicity and flimsiness of the self, and laid it all down.

They waited for her to finish and she, the most hopeless, was the first one to get up the plank to the boat and lead the way to the journey at sea they had all paid so dearly to make. Each one of us here had paid our fare with all we had left that we could call our own. In some ways, we had also paid with the whole of our lives and of our parents' lives before us, because it took the slow unfolding of all these life stories in order for fate to have brought us to that point, that day, to go up that boat. What they saw my mother do was familiar. Disturbingly familiar — her desperate deal was understandable to their anxieties, to their cramping, empty stomachs, their restless sleep, their dying children, their dying lives. Everyone here had made the same desperate deal. But my mother had one less thing than anyone here had — hope for herself. My mother's hope was that when all of us, the boat people of Balanye, when we get lost at sea and get engulfed by the ocean, when fate would have it that there'd only be one survivor, one survivor to make it alive to the land of promise — America — that it'd be me. No one smiled at what she was doing, no one smirked, and no one stepped on that scarf on their way up the boat. Each one skirted it carefully, paying it the kind of respect they wished death at least would give them, if life never did.

By the time we had all gotten into the boat, the tide had risen and reached for the scarf. The same Chenèl I grew up with and who sat on the deck most of the first day said the scarf followed us for a long while, undulating like the water's surface until something below pulled it down abruptly. Chenèl says that then his heart sank with the scarf too — he didn't know if what he had just seen meant the bargain old Venante made was accepted or if it was a symbol of the coming fate of the people of Balanye — all of us as one.

I had never imagined that Chenèl had a heart that could sink. Chenèl's step was always light on the way and to the usual *"Kouman w ye?"* he'd answer, "Doing fine, after God." I could never have imagined I'd be on this kind of a boat with Chenèl, who repeatedly said about himself, "I was born in Balanye, I'll die in Balanye." I too was born and lived in Balanye most of my life. Except when I lived for a while in Port-au-Prince with my mother and Jo, her husband. She then worked as a cook so she could raise me and put me through school. I became an elementary school teacher. People in Balanye say that my luck in life eventually turned around because I did not follow the ancestral command and become a *saj fam* — a woman of wisdom, a midwife. My mother had been a midwife like her mother, her mother's mother, her grandmother's mother, and all the way back to the days of the plantations, when the women of my family were feared because they knew spirits who gave them knowledge in dreams and assisted them in their work. Everyone in Balanye knew my mother, and she, being what we call in Haiti a *pèsonaj* — an old person — knew them too. Hell! She brought most of them into this world. They call her *Grann* Venante — the way we call great woman spirits in Vodou — meaning she has knowledge passed straight down from *Ginen* — Guinea, the mythical Africa, the mystical place of origin, the dwelling place of spirits, the one to which we must return, in death.

Tony was a *djaspora* — someone who had left Haiti and emigrated to America. He had been gone for ten years when he turned up in Balanye with enough money to build the kind of boat we call *kanntè,* and to sell passage to Miami on it. Ever since he was a kid, Tony was always on a hustle to strike some mysterious deal, and we knew that as soon as he got half a chance he'd be out of Balanye. One by one, he managed to send for his family — his father and his two brothers. All except for his baby half-sister, Claudine. We had heard he got citizenship by marrying an American woman in Miami and that's how he got everybody their green card. It was taking longer for Claudine.

That *kanntè* took shape in no time on the Balanye beach, and it seemed just the right place for it to happen. This had been the playground for all our childhood games as far back as any one of us could remember. It was the site of our adolescent dreams and first loves. The beach had marked us — it was such a part of all the significant events of our lives that it seemed part of the very fabric of our cells. And we had marked it as well — with hopscotch, ball games, Mardi Gras festivities, community meetings, Sunday meetings, and private evening prayers muttered in the wind while one stood on its grainy stage. And the sea kept having to wash our markings, tide after tide — our countless footprints overlapping each other in all directions, witness to how busy we were doing nothing, how busy we are just staying alive. And for the tide to wash over as well, there was body waste, human and animal, and this because the beach was also the adult world thoroughfare — this one taking his cow to some grassy patch at the other end, that one with his goats, this one with her donkey loaded with cooking coal on her way to the market, that dog sniffing garbage pails from one beach hut to the next.

Tony had come back with all sorts of ideas and new language like "Take it or leave it," "Time is money," "No money, no deal." We were baffled and disturbed. The news went up and down the beach like bush fire. That was all everyone was now sleepless about. We had grown accustomed to a life of utter and hopeless destitution. We wore our resignation as a kind of badge justified and redeemed through the daily injunction of proverbial wisdom in which all that happens to us is attributed to God's will. Now the surface wisdom had easily been blown off and replaced by a state of continuous agitation. Tony's *kanntè* had awakened our despair because he showed something we wanted and could perhaps grab. The new footprints on the beach overlapping each other in all directions were all of people who had the one and same thing in mind.

He wanted five hundred dollars a head and said the boat was going to take as many people as wanted to go in for what he boasted was a "direct flight." "Just give me the money and your seat waits for you."

That's how he spoke. But we watched that boat go up, and no one saw any seat being built. No bed either, and no bath, no toilet, no kitchen.

"Tony! Just how many days is it gonna take for us to get to Miami?" we'd ask him.

"No time! No time at all!"

And we were satisfied with that answer, because the timelessness of time was a familiar notion. Time did not take time when there was nothing for us to do. Our own lifetime had taken "no time." So OK, we'll be there in no time. But by the time the boat was ready, most of us still had yet to find the money to buy this "timeless" passage. When we realized that we had so little time to gather a sum of money most of us could neither add nor count, we quickly understood the meaning of "time." Tony had said it — "Time is money." With that, he also taught us the power of words — words like "deadline," which he flung at us as if with a swing, a word with hooks that caught and pulled in our throats. Where does one go? Whom do you ask? What can I sell? Trade? Promise? Steal? Where? When? How? From whom? To whom do I pray? How far should I walk on my knees? Oh God! I'd rather die than not be on Tony's *kanntè!*

Tony's wallet was getting so full that three days before the date set to leave, he gave their money back to people who had their "seats waiting," saying, "The fare is now seven hundred." People went crazy. Since yelling at Tony didn't change anything, they started yelling at each other and were once again wasting what had become a precious commodity: time. And then Claudine decided she was going to be on that boat — she was tired of waiting for papers that never arrived, tired of being here when her family was over there, tired of seeing the Balanye beach. It's on Miami Beach that she wanted to walk.

"Hey? Why not?" we said.

And everyone got distracted by the idea — direct flight! No time! No time! Why should she wait?

"Hey, Tony! Why not let your sister go? She'll be with us — she'll be fine. We're all gonna walk on Miami Beach!"

It was Tony's turn to panic, and we should have worried about that — why didn't Tony want Claudine on the *kanntè*? But we got distracted again when Tony announced the price was back to five hundred and that since there were too many requests for space on the boat anyway, there would be no room for Claudine. Besides, he added, this was a business deal and he could not afford to lose one space on a girl's whim — he had a family to feed, important commitments in Miami, life is expensive there, so he declared, "Claudine is not going!" And instead of worrying about Tony's shifting back and forth, we were just happy he decided we were all back on, including those who had only given him part of the money just to hold the seat until the rest could spring from God-knows-where.

We had all gathered silently on Saturday night. Only those taking the boat knew the date. Many faces turned out to be unfamiliar. Some of us came from as far as Fort-Royal. We had kept the departure date a secret so we could evade the police, who obviously had seen that a *kanntè* was going up at Balanye — hard to hide such a big thing on a public beach — but until you are caught on the boat and ready to leave there isn't much they can do about it. It wasn't until Sunday morning at five o'clock that we left the shore of Balanye beach. Either the police were asleep or they didn't think we would dare launch the boat once daylight started. And Claudine had gotten on. No one saw her walk up the plank, and yet there she was, down in the hold with us, sitting next to my mother, her bundle on her lap, wearing a pink dress and a grin. Tony was nowhere on the boat to be seen and Claudine said he didn't know she was on it.

There was wind in the sail from the onset but we thought it was good. First because the wind-swollen sail looked lovely against the light ultramarine of the sky, which we could see from the opening leading up and down the hold where we sat, crowded next to each other. And then we were grateful for the wind because it did not take long for the boat to run out of gas. It became obvious that just enough had been put into the boat to get us far enough into the middle of the ocean and let God take over, if he would. Though we had grown up by the sea, none of us besides Chenèl, who was a fisherman, had ever been in the middle of it. We were taking turns to go onto the deck — first to relieve ourselves overboard, and then, when we ran out of gas, to evaluate the situation and argue about it as if we could do anything besides be thankful to the wind pushing us toward La Gonave Island.

We were islanders, but we had never seen a whole island all at once. La Gonave is part of every Haitian's memory — from the shore or from the mountains, it's always there in the distance. And seeing it from so close was a thrill — we could witness the miracle of it — this piece of earth, this bouquet like a gift emerging out of nowhere at sea. We came out of the hold and sat calmly on the deck in an orderly way, next to each other like schoolchildren at recess. Though La Gonave seemed as familiar and comforting as an old parent who had come to embrace us, we were slowly becoming aware that, only halfway through the first day, we already were people lost at sea, that we had nothing to return to since we had bargained everything we could in order to pay the way, and that our destination might be unreachable even if it were to exist. The voyage was indeed a passage, but one turning into an ordeal — a rite of passage. Those of us who had thought of bringing food were taking quick little snippets of it so as not to attract attention and jealousy. No one had thought of water. We were hungry and thirsty when the boat docked at Latanye Point, but the island of La Gonave revealed itself to be a barren rock. Chenèl had started a collection to raise money to buy gas. We had enough for twenty gallons if there was any to be bought on that small island in the middle of the ocean and — as we could plainly see — the middle of nowhere.

Tuesday morning, we packed ourselves back into the hold and left Latanye Point. People at La Gonave had not been happy to see us turn up with the wind, literally, on Sunday night. We traded clothes for bread. For our thirst we drank into the ocean. The wind helped the motor push us out again as it had when we left Balanye. It was clear there were too many of us for the boat's capacity. Were it not for the wind we might not even have gotten this far. I thought that in spite of our discomforts and misfortune, the wind's will re-

vealed God's own that this journey was meant to be. Yet I also felt
we were like rats in a dark, humid, airless, underground trap.

It quickly became hard to sit on the bare planks with nothing to
lean on. Before long we were all lying down, side by side, our backs
chilled by the water that had already filtered in and was swishing
around in accord with the boat's motion; chilled by our own sweat,
which could have been from the suffocating heat and airlessness
but actually was from increasing terror; chilled by the realization
we had been sold out by our very own, the people of Balanye —
Tony and all the men involved in the building of the boat. Some or
all of them would have known the boat had no gas, was too full, and
couldn't take us anywhere but to the bottom of the ocean. I shivered while I remembered Tony's words that the trip would take "no
time! No time at all!" So we took no food, no water, not even for the
children, who were by then in too much shock to even cry, including Anaïse's baby. There was silence among us, because we were beyond questioning, beyond arguing, beyond speech. We were without chains, yet unable to rise. Rising would have only exposed our
complete impotence.

I remembered what I had learned of Haitians' history. I wondered if there might really be some kind of biological memory.
What we were experiencing in Tony's *kanntè* was the same as when
we had left Ginen — Africa! This was the way our ancestors had
come to Haiti, to Balanye, although this time the choice was ours
and also the hope — to reach a promised land called Miami. And
there we are, so completely drenched we feel naked, so fearful we
are mute, bound anew to each other in ways that had become more
complex. We had always been burdened by an old, common Creole
experience. It seemed that for us then, history was copying an old
chapter. One that linked us to an African land by now so distant
that its very name — Ginen — had become only an evocative word,
a mythical realm for spirits and for the dead.

I held on to the belief that God certainly could not aimlessly allow such coincidence to take place. His presence and eye on me
throughout the journey was the blue rectangle that, during the day,
was the hold's opening cut out of the sky. I would not close my eyes.
I kept thinking, No, this is not just a meaningless trick of history —
we are on a mission, us black people. Shipped out, shipped off, we
are the people who can take any boat. Rip us out of anywhere, dis-

mantle us, and drop us anyplace, in the worst conditions for life, the best for dispersion and disintegration, and we regroup. We reshape ourselves from the void of hell. We are the people who can live how no people should, suffer what no people can spell out, the sacrificial lambs never comfortable on earth — home is not on earth. This is the meaning we bring. That is the mission.

By two o'clock in the afternoon we passed the Môle St. Nicolas. We had already run out of gas again and the motor had broken down. But wind was pushing us toward more wind — at dusk we fell into the accursed Wind Canal. We knew it because we felt it. The boat seemed made out of bone. It shook like a fleshless carcass. And also, at that moment, there was *Grann* Venante's song, a slow and soft lament: *"Nan Ginen m te ye, se nan Ginen m prale* — I came from Ginen, I am going back to Ginen — *nan Ginen m te ye, se nan Ginen m prale . . ."* And the baby started to cry.

Winds like the arms of a forest grab us as if to suck us out of the ocean's skin. But the ocean is hungry and wants us! Pull from above! Pull from below! The waves are a mad mother who grasps the boat like a child by the hair to slap him, and slap him, so that his eyes and face swell until he is blinded, his head gets spongy and rings, his teeth feel like abrasive grit shredding his lips. And yet she stills slaps and slaps and slaps, and in the hold of that ship we feel like the teeth in that child's mouth and we scream and scream.

Night falls onto our cries. We are tossed without end one against another with nothing firm to hold on to, bumping on heads, crashing on the hold's floor. Mothers grip tightly the light bodies of children to keep them from being hurled too high and too fast and yet they end up crushing them when they fall back on them with fuller weight after a blow. The winds have arms that don't let go, that howl at their extremities, and that will bleed all night for this catch if they have to. Chenèl of "doing fine after God" tries to tie himself to the mast like he wants to say "I was born-baptized on that boat, I will die on that boat." He yells at us that we should shut our eyes and pray.

But there are two feet of water now in the hold, and if someone falls and presses on anyone for too long he'd drown right here in the boat without having time to think "Jesus, Marie . . ." A man jumps up with a howl, climbs out of the hold mumbling repeatedly, "Get out of the way, I am going home, get out of the way, I am going home, get out of . . ." A kick in the chest from Chenèl on the deck throws him right back down. Two men wrap their arms around him to keep him from getting up and out again; someone from a corner of the hold yells, "Let him go! Throw him out in the ocean! Too many of us in here anyway!" Others echo him from everywhere in the hold: "Throw him out! Throw him out! Too many! Too many!"

The man now screams, *"Lage m! Lage m! Lage m, bagay dyab andedan —* Let go of me! The devil is in here!"

A beam of light suddenly shoots in the hold — it's Chenèl with a flashlight. He spotlights faces here and there. Then he aims the beam up the mast and sail. The light distracts us and stops the growing frenzy against the man. Chenèl's light is searching for something and finds it: a man on the deck stands briefly at the very edge of the black waters, arms wide open, his body an image of the cross, Bible in hand, face lifted to the sky, and, soundlessly, jumps. Suddenly, *"Grennen! Grennen! Grennen! —* Scatter! Scatter! Scatter!" we hear from all over the hold.

It was pitch black. Who was saying it? How many? To whom? What does it mean? What's happening? However brave anyone might have still felt, hearing this, one could only shiver. It has an urgency, a heartlessness, a madness about it — my body goes limp with fear. And again, repeatedly, *"Grennen! Grennen!"* Then, right after, "Shut your eyes! Shut your *eyes! Fèmen je w!"* Something terrible is here! Something odious is happening! I already could not see anything, but closing my eyes, I felt so completely vulnerable it was unbearable! At this very moment, *Grann* Venante squeezed my arms and ordered me as well, "Shut your eyes!" I did, and just then felt light going across my face — someone was flashing us. Voices were screaming, "Help! Help! Let go of me! Let go of me! — *Anmwe! Anmwe! Lage m!"*

√ "Mother! What's happening?" I asked with anguish and my eyes still shut. *"Bagay zonbi nan batiman an! Fèmen je w! —* Zombies at work on the boat! Shut your eyes!"

Her voice was calming. I felt calmed that she seemed able to think through all of this, even though I didn't know why she ordered me to shut my eyes nor what it meant that she kept hers open. People close to me overheard what she said and started screaming in a panic, repeating her words, "Zombies at work on the boat! Zombies at work on the boat!" Suddenly I felt a lot of vio-

lent motion around me. Then hands were pulling at me. But two
strong arms held me fast while I heard my mother lashing out: "My
child's not going! My child's not going!" Almost right after hearing
her, it seemed that every hand that had gripped and pulled at my
body relaxed and let go. I kept hearing, *"Grennen! Grennen!"* until
my heart could no longer take all the pounding in my chest and I
passed out.

When I came to, it still felt dark around me, but the boat was no
longer being slapped by waves and there was no sound of water
splashing in with every slap. My mother had told me to keep my
eyes closed, and I did until I sensed daybreak. When I opened
them I saw that she was not there. Where was she? Where could she
have gone? We were all in too much shock to make sense of the
night and of all that we had heard and suffered. I thought this must
have been a passage under water.

I used to hear stories about journeys under water made by the
dead but sometimes by the living. These come back transformed by
secret knowledge that can heal, give wisdom, attract wealth, challenge the world's sense of reality. The old folks said that the underwater world is a reverse reflection of the one above — that there
are trees, houses, everything as we know it on earth. How then do
we tell which one we are in and if we have crossed over? Was my
mother gone? Or was I? Which one is under? Which one is above?
The mast was broken and the sail was ripped. No matter what
amount of wind would lift, the boat could not be led forward. People started to worry that we were going to die if the boat could not
go forward anymore. But were we dead already? Was this broken
mast and torn sail an underworld metaphor for the full sails of the
living?

I sat on the deck with the others, amorphous, washed of feelings,
and with these thoughts in my mind until I saw it — the island! —
gleaming in the dawn, and with mist surrounding it that made it
seem to float in the sky. There was no more division between blue
water and blue sky. Morning mist smudged all boundaries and the
island seemed elevated and weightless. We were too worn out to
cheer, but some felt hope filling up their chests again as if a gentle
breeze had entered them. Claudine thought it was Miami. Chenèl
thought it was Cuba. Was it either one? Or was it maybe . . . Ginen?
Now, can you tell me? Is it? Is it Ginen? Is my mother here?

DEAN PASCHAL

Moriya

FROM ONTARIO REVIEW

HE'S VERY mechanically minded.

Oh?

Yes. It's scary at times.

How so?

There is a darkness to mechanical objects that he is a bit too quick to appreciate and understand.

(The elderly lady turned ahead of them down a long hall and the mother and the boy followed. The three of them turned again, passing a shelf covered with whiskey bottles and a mahogany cabinet which the boy noticed was full of wine and single-malt scotch.)

In that case (the elderly lady said) I have something — something mechanical — that he might like to see. The girl next door wanted to see it this morning, so it's already wound.

The boy to whom the two grown women are impolite enough to be indirectly referring is fourteen years old and is following them through a Victorian-looking house on his first day in New Orleans. He is to take six weeks of intensive French lessons in a special summer program for adolescents in a school on Jackson Avenue. The elderly woman is a moderately distant friend of his mother's who is going to put him up and who is leading both of them now into a parlor tinkling with prisms and light.

Indeed, the idea of "something mechanical" immediately had this boy's interest. Just as immediately, he saw it and was disappointed. Enough so, that it was difficult to fully conceal his disappointment. The mechanical thing was a clock. It was a glass clock in the center of a marble table. It was ticking steadily. The clock had an exposed mechanism, a pendulum weighted with dual glass tubes full of mercury, but otherwise was of a rather familiar style and unremarkable. There were some other antiquated objects in the room, some family pictures in ornate, somewhat brassy-looking shadow-box frames, a spinet-style piano, two medallion sofas facing one another beneath a third medallion on the ceiling. Indeed, there was something of a medallion "theme" to the entire center of the parlor. It is unlikely that the boy would have known or noticed this. He was, after all, mechanically, not architecturally, minded. On the left-hand sofa, however, there was something he *did* notice, couldn't help but, a doll, a virtually life-sized doll, not a "baby" doll either but a doll representing an adolescent girl, a girl in her mid-adolescence, perhaps. Had she been standing up she might have been over four feet high, perhaps well over. She was wearing a nineteenth-century, European, many-buttoned, fin-de-siècle dress, a maroon velvet jacket, and some high-topped black shoes. She had been positioned so that she was looking somewhat wistfully out of a long French window, one elbow on the arm of the sofa.

There was a black ribbon with a medallion on it around her neck.

(The boy went dutifully to the clock.)

We think a Swiss clockmaker made it, the woman continued. It's from 1892, over a hundred years old at this point.

The boy looked at the beveled glass, the spattering of color on the marble tabletop, the mercury-filled tubes, and stood there waiting for the woman to say something more about it. Actually, though, he knew the theory of the tubes himself. Heat causes metal to expand, and the pendulum, being metal, will lengthen, lowering the center of gravity and therefore slowing the clock — not much, of course, infinitesimally, as a matter of fact, but when one is counting seconds over months or years the differences become significant, then profound. The mercury in the tubes is confined so that it can only expand upward, *raising* the center of gravity so the effects cancel.

(Well, he thought, standing patiently, politely, at the table, at least he could show off his knowledge.)

Is this the original key? he said.

What?

It was only then that the boy realized that the woman was looking at neither him nor the clock.

Oh, that, she said. Not *that*. I know nothing about that. That's new, for *us* anyway. That was at an estate sale last year. Sit down.

Ma'am?

Sit down. Here. The woman patted the sofa beside her, rubbed the red velvet flirtatiously, made room between herself and the boy's mother.

This woman, with her well-applied makeup and at least one face-lift, was elegant in the slightly decadent manner of the best-pre-served of sixty-year-old females. She was the sort of woman who can successfully squeeze the last remnants of sensuality out of age, possessing still the power of crossed legs in cocktail dresses, know-ing well the uses of black chiffon, gold jewelry, French perfume, and alcohol. In fact, bringing a fourteen-year-old into a parlor tin-kling with such temptations might have given many a mother pause. But this particular woman had a husband she was still mod-erately crazy about, a handsome lawyer with an alcoholic nose who was a member of one of the old-line Mardi Gras krewes and a fixture at Galatoire's on Friday. (In fact, the husband was there now, this being a Friday.). So that particular story is possibly over before it starts.

Wait, the woman said, facing the other sofa now.

The doll continued looking out the window. The clock contin-ued ticking on its table.

The boy sat down, began waiting, leaned forward slightly.

It may take a while. Would you like a Coca-Cola?

The boy was equally puzzled by both sentences.

He was still facing the sofa. He had already noticed that the two sofas were not quite identical. The one the doll was on was slightly longer and had darker, somewhat different-looking woodwork. He was beginning to make other comparisons. But at that moment the doll began to turn. She began to turn toward him, slowly, as he watched, though not so slowly as to be unlifelike. It was as though she had been interrupted in the midst of a daydream. Her brilliant hazel eyes were not fixed, not what they call "doll-like"; they moved independently of her head and slightly in advance of it, giving an effect the realism of which was uncanny. Her hazel-colored eyes were crystalline, maybe literally. There was no movement of her mouth, which, like her face, was ceramic, or ivory, or alabaster, and *was* doll-like, though the lips were full and there was a feeling and even a glimpse of natural teeth. She moved her elbow and left hand from the armrest and crossed both hands (politely?) in her lap. She was wearing long white gloves which, had her jacket been removed, would have proved to extend past her elbows. She moved her right hand and tugged on the fabric of her left glove as though to straighten it or exorcise some ghost of disorder.

Then she looked at the boy again, directly at him, through him. There could have been no more steadfast stare. The most saucy and impudent thirteen-year-old that has ever taken the perilous step of trying the effects of lipstick on a stepfather could not have had such a gaze. The doll had a breathtaking face, not innocent, but breathtaking: high cheekbones, shadowy eyes, dark hair that seemed real. His own gaze flinched down somewhat to the black-and-white medallion around her neck. Her breasts were so well formed, her blouse so tucked in as to give a sense of suspended breathing.

The woman was talking to his mother now.

It's the only one like it we've ever seen. It's Swiss, we think. It stayed in the attic for decades in a cedar-lined box. It was in my husband Eric's family. Eric's grandfather would have had to know something about it, since this was his house and furniture. Eric himself says he had never seen it before. His grandfather never mentioned the thing, had forgotten about it, perhaps, or perhaps kept it a secret deliberately, since he had three daughters in addition to his son. Maybe he wanted to avoid a fight. We didn't find it till a few months ago. The year 1892 was stamped on — actually burned into — the wood of the box. It was in an alcove under an unbelievable number of blankets.

(The women, of course, are talking around the boy again.)

The crank is in that case, the woman said, pointing to a narrow leather box. There are a number of movements it goes through randomly, *sometimes* randomly, sometimes not. I'm not sure that we've seen them all as yet. It seems, at times, that where you touch it very much affects the internal program. You may touch it, if you like.

The boy came closer but could hear no sound of clockwork. The doll's eyes had not moved, her head had not moved, still she seemed to be following him. He grasped the tips of her gloved fingers, tremulously, as though shaking hands, as though saying hello.

After a moment, the doll turned slightly and looked up at him. Her eyes, once again, slightly leading the movement. It was impossible to believe it was coincidental.

It will run for days, the woman said. The spring must be enormous. It *feels* enormous when you wind it.

What's her name?

My God! You're the second person who has asked that today! Actually, we haven't named her. Or maybe we have. My husband and I have begun calling her "the doll." You can name her if you like.

(The boy was still waiting, still holding the doll's hand.)

Can you stop her? he said. Her motion, I mean. Is it possible to shut her off?

(Outside the house, he heard the shriek of a young girl's voice next door.)

Yes, there's a little wheel in the back of her neck, just under the ribbon.

The boy went behind her, behind the sofa, and rested both his hands on the doll's shoulders. Her eyelashes were almost assuredly real, her hair too, human, straight, long and luxurious. It seemed he could smell a trace of perfume. He looked down at the fabric of her dress, felt the little wheel beneath the ribbon.

Interesting, the woman said. See what I mean? (The woman was talking to the boy's mother now.) I've never seen her do that before.

The doll was turning around to look at the boy. She succeeded, too, to a surprising degree, finishing by staring up at him, her neck arched slightly.

During the first week, the boy attempted to make a complete catalog of the doll's movements. She seldom moved as much as she had the first day. Sometimes she would go a full hour or two without any motion of any kind. He would come into the parlor in the afternoon or evening and watch her and wait. Her activity was completely unpredictable: five minutes, thirty minutes, forty-seven and a half minutes between movements. Then she might do a lot, an entire series of things, as though bored by the long inactivity — straighten a glove, adjust her knees, slap at an invisible fly. The most elaborate thing she could do was the following: put both hands down, curl her knuckles slightly, and lift her entire body a fraction of an inch to the right. But before that motion was ever repeated, she would move to the left again, so that there was no overall change in position. Often she would fold her hands together, waiting; and from that position move her eyes, alone, so as to look slowly around the room. (Literally, she seemed very much to *look* at something for a while, then at something else.) Occasionally she would look down at the floor for quite a period of time, so that one would be very tempted to say, "This little doll once had a little dog."

Her eyes themselves, the boy noticed, seemed as though they should be able to close, the lids seemed to be hinged, or *potentially* hinged, but they never did, or he never saw them do it. They never blinked, even. He could hear her ticking only by holding his ear directly on her body, but anyplace on it would work — her back, for instance, or one of her shoulders. There was quite a *presence* in the sound, not a slow tick . . . tick . . . tick . . . tick . . . like a clock, but something faster, shorter, more breathless and passionate: a tic-tic-tic-tic-tic-tic-tic-tic-tic, full in its own way, of the quality of construction, of the click of micrometers, of the precise cut of lathes, of the tempering of steel for shafts and mainsprings.

The boy had other concerns, of course. Before leaving home, he had had daydreams that there might be some girl in New Orleans waiting just for him. But those dreams did not pan out. All the girls were older. He was literally the youngest individual in his class. Most of the girls had boyfriends with driver's licenses. They were friendly enough but definitely not interested in any fourteen-year-old "mechanically minded" boy. On several occasions he hunted for but did not find the girl next door, nor, for that matter, did he ever hear her again.

Under the circumstances, the question that became paramount for him was how long the doll would run. It dawned on him that it might be somewhat difficult to tell. The doll might continue to *tick* long after she had stopped moving because it should take less energy to do that. In fact, every day, after class, he would wonder, has she stopped already?

He began to leave things in her hands, little bits of paper, to see if she had moved in his absence. Infinitesimal, these pieces of paper were, some of them virtually the size of lint. He would find them later, on the sofa, on the armrest, on the floor beneath her feet. After a while he began writing tiny messages on them. To camouflage, as far as possible, what he was doing, he would write very small, so that what she ended up holding was an unreadable blob of ink. But in each case *he* knew what he had written and was pleased to think she did as well.

Hello.

Thinking of you.

Sleep well.

Or:

I think you're beautiful.

Will try to dream of Switzerland for your sake.

(He would find the messages on the cushion of the sofa, on the armrest, on the floor beneath her feet.)

The boy *did* try to dream of Switzerland for her; and, in order to get a focus for his dream, saturated himself with ideas and images of the area from two sets of encyclopedias in the house: pictures of the Alps, of cows, of cheese, of Zurich and Bern. He thought that perhaps she might come *alive* for him in a dream.

(And, as he began to learn more French, he tried speaking to her.)

Je t'aime.

On the sofa sometimes, unmoving for hours, he would stare at her, trying to saturate his brain with her beauty. Her hazel eyes were so realistic it was impossible to believe she was not seeing him too, watching him, waiting for something.

Nothing came of the dreams, though. That is, they did not happen.

In truth, the two of them didn't get much time absolutely alone together. Other things would intervene. The maid would come in. The husband would enter with his pipe, the wife with her cigarettes, or both, simultaneously. They seemed mainly to smoke in that room. The boy noticed one evening that the doll was looking directly at the husband as he fiddled with his pipe, and he suddenly realized he was feeling something very like jealousy.

One afternoon, while waiting for the doll to move, he began looking at the family pictures in the shadow-box frames. He noticed there was a resemblance, a definite resemblance, between this doll and certain of the women in the pictures. He thought they might be the wives. The maid came on Tuesdays and Thursdays and he began to ask her questions. She knew the answers to most of them, and the woman eventually provided him with the rest. He found that the daughters in the family had something of a resemblance, passed on, no doubt, genetically; but what he had guessed initially was the truth. The real resemblance was to the wives.

The boy opened the leather box, looked at the crank with its mahogany handle, lifted it up, set it back. There were some spare buttons for the blouse, a long Allen wrench with a T-shaped handle, some regular wrenches too, three screwdrivers, a button hook. (There was also an impression of these things crushed into the velvet lining of the top of the box.)

How long could the spring *last?* he wondered. It was already more than "days," as the woman had suggested. It was "weeks" now, past two, and well into a third. But then it quit. The boy came home one afternoon and found his last message (unread?) in her hand. The doll had run down. She was stopped, frozen, dead, caught in the middle of a motion. It was a most unnatural-looking position for her, her eyes on the floor, her neck in the process of a turn. Seeing it, he immediately understood the importance of a little-appreciated role and function of funeral directors, who have as their responsibility the final, strictly physical disposition of a human body: the adjusting of hands and feet, the closing of eyes, the stopping of life at a node.

The boy felt strongly that the doll shouldn't be left like this. Did they even notice, the man and woman? Why *didn't* they? Maybe they weren't really looking at her. He decided he would rewind her himself. He decided he would fix the problem.

It would be three days before he could do that, though. The man and woman were going to dinner at Commander's Palace on Saturday. Afterward they were going to a party in the French Quarter. He would have two full hours at least, maybe more, maybe considerably more.

(In the meantime, she sat there, gathering infinitesimal dust.)

Saturday evening he waited a full twenty minutes after they left. Then he waited another ten in case they had forgotten something. Finally he went into the parlor, locked the doors, closed the curtains, and opened the box of tools. He saw the mahogany handle, the black velvet lining, noted, in passing almost, that the top section of the box (where the images of the tools were crushed) was somewhat thicker than it had to be. He realized the velvet lining of the case might hold or conceal something, might, in fact, fold down *(did* fold down, he discovered with the aid of a bent paper clip). What he saw immediately inside was a certificate.

The certificate had a name, *Moriya,* printed in ornate black script at the top. There was some more writing too, near that, in a smaller, different script: Austral Kraftwerk, Prague. Then there was a paragraph of print and some handwritten specifications in an antique and purple-looking ink in a series of printed blanks. The writing might have been German, might have been Czech. He did not know. He had had two years of Latin and now, of course, a smattering of French. But he had no idea. Austral Kraftwerk, Prague. What he saw now was that the design on the medallion on the doll's neck was the trademark for the company. Not one word of the writing was meaningful to him. There was a serial number and part of a decorative scroll around the edge of the certificate. One of the bottom corners of the scroll had been torn off. He thought there might once have been an engraved picture of the doll in that corner. If so, it had been torn off. Why had it been torn off?

The boy thought that there might have been such a picture because there was something *else* engraved on the other corner, something totally unexpected: the sofa! But of course! The sofa was part of the doll! Not connected, obviously, but a platform for it, as it obviously had to be. Probably the doll had to be placed at the end of it, at the far left end, too. There might be things inside it, magnets, for instance, that allowed the doll to orient herself. Who, then, in this family had known to put her there? Someone was not telling the whole truth here.

Well, well, well, he thought. So, then, the doll's name was Moriya.

"Moriya," he said, coming around in front and looking at her, touching her fingertips.

But she continued to look dead to him, distorted; and, of course, there was no movement of her eyes.

Still, the boy realized, it was very possible that only *he* knew the rest of the story. This doll had not been made in Switzerland; she had been made in Prague. His hands were slightly tremulous now as he began to undress her. He was worried, at first, about how to handle her arms; but her maroon velvet jacket unhooked in the back, came off immediately, he discovered. He unlaced the back of the dress, which also came apart easily. The dress had innumerable pleats and revealed underneath what he would have called a black corset, but which the woman, outside of the house now, would have known was a bustier. The boy saw that he didn't have to remove that. There was a hole in the fabric itself in the low back. As a precaution, though, before he inserted the crank, he moved the wheel in her neck to the "off" position. He inserted the short, stubby, but rather massive crank and began to turn it. He was expecting a heavy sound like click . . . click . . . click. What he heard instead had more of a roaring quality and feel. He wound it on and on, tighter and tighter: ten, twelve, fifteen, twenty, thirty, a total of forty times before the spring began to feel really tight to him. At the end he relaxed the crank very carefully to be sure the ratchet would hold. Then he turned the wheel in her neck and watched as she completed the turn she had begun days ago. She came to rest in a position he had seen many times before, her eyes slightly averted. Was she being shy? Flirtatious?

Disheveled now, her jacket down, her young back showing, what he saw was the breathtaking, incredible modeling of her scapulas and vertebrae. Her skin was not ceramic, but what was it? Ivory? Alabaster? It was something that looked like ivory to him. It was slightly warm-feeling. He saw the dark bustier, the stunning shoulder blades, the pleated cloth hanging off her right shoulder, and all of a sudden the temptation became too great for him.

He began to undo the front of her dress.

The little fabric-covered buttons were somewhat difficult to manipulate. He saw it would be rather easy to break one. The doll's breasts were not overly large. Her nipples were of a deeper hue than her lips. Her pigments were getting darker, it seemed, in the more caudal direction (a word he would not have known but a principle he might have appreciated). What he noticed about the breasts was that they were not unfinished. The doll's breasts, like her back, were perfect; they were not just forms and armatures for fabric; they were meant to be seen. He began to see very clearly now; this doll was not designed around a dress. She was designed around a nude body.

The doll's nipples were of a rubbery material, darkly pink. Where the rubber came together centrally, it could be pulled and teased apart. It dawned on him that something might be hidden beneath the rubber. Screws, perhaps. This might be the way to take off the front of the doll.

The boy was well familiar with the deviousness of mechanical constructions. In disassembling such things as vacuum cleaners, radios, televisions, and lawn mowers, he had learned long ago (virtually in kindergarten, in fact) that the innocent-looking moldings and chrome strips frequently hid the mounting attachments for a motor or chassis. This was wildly different, of course; yet, all things considered, it was right up his alley. He turned the doll off, ran to the kitchen, and got a flashlight. With the light, he looked carefully as he pried gently into the rubber nipples with the tip of the button hook. No, there were no screw heads. The holes went deeper, though, so maybe something else would fit. The Allen wrench, perhaps. It was possible that he was on the right track. Another thought, though, was beginning to bother him. Would a dress of this era normally lace in the back and *button* in front? He had no idea.

It seemed this doll's clothes were made to be taken off quickly.

Behind him, on the marble table, the clock continued to tick. The boy was taking rather more time with all of this than he realized. And now, in his rush to get the flashlight, he had left the door to the parlor unlocked.

He took the T-shaped Allen wrench out of the case and tried to insert it directly through the rubber in the right nipple. He was not successful. He met resistance immediately. Still, to be thorough, he tried it in the left as well. It went in. Not a little. It went in the full length of the shaft.

With one hand on her back and one hand on the T-shaped handle, he now had a decision to make: whether or not to turn the wrench. The doll's eyes were still averted. This could possibly cause her body to spring open. He might not be able to get her back together again. There was no clue as to what was going to happen. He waited several seconds, thinking, deliberating, resting his full palm flat against her bare back. Then the doll's eyes began to move. They moved upward a matter of millimeters and began to drift steadily to the right toward him. It was a move he had never seen her make before. Finally her eyes met his, not exactly but almost. He leaned down to intersect her gaze. It was impossible to believe she was not seeing him, talking to him, begging him silently. He took a quick breath and turned the handle clockwise. Nothing happened. Absolutely nothing. He met complete resistance. (Actually, he was almost relieved to find it.) Then (being very thorough again) he turned the handle the other way.

Something clunked deep within the interior of the doll. Deep within the doll, he heard something rather heavy-sounding move into another position.

The boy listened quickly, almost desperately, holding his ear to her bare shoulder. There was no change whatsoever in the noise (tic-tic-tic-tic-tic-tic-tic-tic-tic). Then again, maybe there *was*. Maybe the ticking was faster now.

The boy held the Allen wrench in his hand, waiting, but nothing happened. He sat down beside her; still nothing. He looked at the clock on the table. Fifteen minutes, he thought.

He waited beside her, the doll with her breasts bared, her black bustier open. She seemed to be looking toward but not directly at the clock. A woman ignoring you might look in such a direction. Suddenly the boy remembered the unlocked door. He jumped up, ran to lock it, sat down again.

He should be safe anyway, he thought, should have plenty of time. They should still be at Commander's Palace now. He should have plenty . . . hours, maybe. On the other hand, what if they dropped by *here* on the way to the Quarter.

Fifteen minutes, he thought.

But it didn't take that long.

After six minutes of ticking, the doll blinked. Actually, what the doll did was a good deal more than a blink; it was slower, and more prolonged:

She fully closed and opened her eyes.

Then she began to move her right hand. The doll moved her right hand forward and set it down rather firmly near the boy's knee and began to pull along his leg and thigh. She did not stop. She pulled steadily and directly into his crotch and stayed there for a long time. What she was doing now was evidently not unintentional. She was steadily moving her hand. The boy did not know whether to look at her or not. He could barely see her dark and tender lashes. Then he felt her hand on his shoulder. The doll had changed positions somewhat; she had put her gloved hand on his left shoulder and leaned into him. This was an entirely different, beseeching, sort of movement. In a human being you would say that what was wanted now was a kiss; the girl — or lady — wants a kiss. In a doll, of course, you could not say that — not accurately, that is. But the boy said it anyway. He kissed her. He kissed her on her mouth. The doll's mouth was not unpleasant-feeling. Her mouth was electrifying. She looked up, seemed to lock onto his eyes. He felt more and more pressure in her kiss, more and more and more of the pressure. Then he realized what was happening.

The doll was climbing on top of him. The boy fell the full length of the sofa, and her sudden, unexpected heaviness was upon him. Her dark hair fell completely over both of them. By helping her slightly he got her legs on the sofa too, and centered in his groin area. She was as heavy as a small sack of fertilizer. Altogether the sensation was unexpected, weird, and magical; she *felt* real. Not that he had ever felt a girl in this situation. But then again there was no object that had ever felt like *this*. Her balance was perfect. He had already been phenomenally, wildly turned on by the kiss alone. With this extra activity, he was reaching unprecedented heights (or lengths). But he didn't feel any receptacle for what had now grown between them. Steadily, powerfully, the doll began to grind against him. Her searching eyes locked firmly onto his. He felt desperately, but her groin was perfectly smooth. He inserted his hand down beneath her clothes to make absolutely sure. There was nothing. She continued to pin him with her mouth and grind against him. What must such a doll have *cost?* was almost his last thought before he exploded into his own underwear. She ground into him for another full minute, then stopped, leaving him with her weight and the warm, soapy stickiness.

Je t'aime, the boy said. J'ai la tête de la mécanique.

The doll's eyes remained closed, as though sleeping. The boy put his hand on the back of her head. He stayed on the sofa an additional ten minutes, feeling her satisfying weight, the slight vibration of her body, all fear of being discovered gone, the glass clock on the table steadily ticking, all centers of gravity in the room perfectly balanced now. The boy waited another five minutes, even afterward, vaguely curious, vaguely thinking something else might happen. But nothing did.

At last the boy sat up, then sat *her* up and turned her off. Her dress was still more or less in place. But he wanted to take a closer look at her groin area. There was nothing there, nothing. The area was perfectly smooth, sexless in a way, an ivory groin. No, wait a minute. There was *something*, but it was not a part of her. There was something *written*, embroidered in the cloth of her underpants (they didn't really look like panties to him, but it was the last garment before her bare body). The writing was in script in dark letters, a phrase in Latin: *Talis umbras mundum regnant.*

The boy smiled and said it aloud, musingly. So the sole use, thus far, in his life of two full years of Latin was to understand the message written on a doll's underpants. He began to put the doll back together. He checked carefully for stains. All was fine, perfect; no stains, nothing. Finally, with the Allen wrench, he set her back to the clockwise position, waited a moment, looking.

The doll suddenly opened her eyes.

He kissed her and turned off the light.

Have you thought of a name for her?

No.

(This was three days later, in the parlor, where the boy was sitting after class, studying a list of verbs. The woman had come in to retrieve a pack of cigarettes from a carton.)

The boy was shocked at how quickly he had been able to lie, to think of all the unknowns and ramifications and know the name he now had for her, *her* name in fact, could never be said. It was one of those moments in life in which he knew for sure that he was developing the adult mind.

I think "the doll" is a perfectly fine name, he said, watching the woman.

The woman fished a pack of cigarettes from a carton. (Even *she* resembled the doll; could she possibly not *see* that?)

Who thought of putting her on the sofa? the boy said.

Oh? You think she looks good there?

Yes.

My husband.

Four times, and four times only, the boy and Moriya were able to intersect. During the last two, the boy was bare from the waist down and Moriya was almost perfectly nude. By diligently searching up and down Magazine Street, he had found a filling station with a condom machine in the restroom. He had bought several; they were a bit large, of course; still, they simplified certain worries — not so *much* of a problem, after all, for a fourteen-year-old, but enough for staining a sofa or a dress.

All through the days that followed, the boy had more energy than he had ever had in his life. He felt more *alive*. He would watch Moriya in the afternoon light, the saucy, impudent, perfectly beautiful face, the risqué and hungry mouth, cherish the memory and anticipation of her ivory groin grinding into his. In the actual sexual encounters, it helped to know, now, exactly what was going to happen, when her hand was going to move, when she was going to need assistance with her feet.

Since the boy now knew where Moriya was *really* from, he decided to try the trick of the dream again. It worked, too, this time, and magnificently. (But once, and once only.) He sneaked a heavy volume of the encyclopedia to bed with him and read the entire article about Prague, twice through, completely, just before turning out the light. Sure enough, during the night she came to him. Or, more correctly, *he* went to her. He went to Prague. He and Moriya were suddenly walking across the Charles Bridge together. She was tracing the veins in his hand with her gloved hand.

Then they were in a café, each with a glass of wine.

I have a *secret,* she said.

(There was a light heaviness to her voice; it was precisely articulate, as though English were her third or fourth language.)

What? he said.

She was bubbling over with excitement.

But she would not tell him.

I know a *secret!* she said again, later. She came around the little table and sat on his lap, dangling her feet above the ceramic tiles. She pressed the tips of her fingers into his cheeks, head to head, nose to nose, her eyes locked onto his, to fix and center his vision. There was an incredible glow of energy around her. She leaned forward as though to whisper something, but licked his ear instead.

Interestingly, the boy's dream was not set in 1892, not in the era of gaslights and horses, the era of her construction, but in a strange and intermediate time. It would have had to have been somewhere in the 1930s, just before the Second World War. There were only a few cars, very dark, dusty. But what cars! What magnificent machines! He saw a fair number of Mercedes, a couple of Rolls Royces (the great roadsters and dual-cowled phaetons), a Bugatti, an Invicta, a Hispano-Suiza. The cars were parked on the stone bridges, the stone streets, the horses clopping by them. The greatest cars of the twentieth century, covered with dust from the road.

It was a mechanically minded dream.

But four times, and four times only, the two of them had together. Not that that was absolutely all the possible chances. It was because on the last chance something disastrous happened.

The man and woman were going to another party (in Covington, this time, across Lake Pontchartrain and the causeway).

The boy knew he would have plenty of time.

Thirty minutes after they'd left, he had the doll perfectly nude. But with such a luxury of time, he began to look at her more carefully. On her flanks now, he saw several other places for the Allen wrench to insert, a total of six of them, between her arms and her waist. This had to be the way to get inside her. The boy's curiosity began to get the better of him. There was so much she could *do,* and he couldn't begin to imagine how. He simply had to *see* firsthand what was going on. He quickly removed six long machine screws with hexagonal insert heads and set them on the marble-topped table. He managed to get his fingernails into a seam in her back and then, with the smallest screwdriver, pry her alabaster skin up carefully, very carefully, so as not to crack it. He had to break a sort of suction. He could scarcely pull the skin off. This doll had probably not been opened in a hundred years. He saw some green felt, some brass gears, some shafting; then, suddenly, an incredible surprise: wires! Electrical wires! Yellow, cotton-covered wires! Bundles of them, everywhere, even attached to her back through a very odd-looking detachable connector. There was a flywheel between the doll's shoulder blades. It was not spinning, though, and would not spin even when he released the control in her neck. He suspected some chunks of unmachined metal that he saw near the flywheel might be magnets, and tested one of them with the blade of the screwdriver:

It was all he could do to pull it away again.

A magnet indeed, a very powerful magnet! What he was looking at was a dynamo. This doll generated her own electricity! There were several copper discs attached to the underside of her skin. He saw a number of others inside too, maybe an eighth of an inch thick, maybe thicker, and a couple of inches in diameter. For what? Capacitance effects? Probably not, at least not in this era. On the other hand, thermocouples were a definite possibility. Thermocouples were really old, he knew; he had seen a book from the 1880s that had them in it. Thermocouples would be sensitive to heat too, or to *changes* in heat. So she *could* know when and where she was being touched.

There was absolutely no dust, though. The doll's body might have been sealed yesterday. Only the dullness of the brass and some corrosion of the bearings revealed her true age. So moisture itself can enter, the boy thought (or perhaps it simply condensed inside her). He saw shafts with differential gearing and hard-rubber wheels pressing against discs to give integrals and derivatives of motion. Along her flanks and in the back side of her breasts there were areas where lead had been cast to give the proper weight distribution. All of this was so much more elaborate than he could have dreamed. There were banks of wire-wound resistors in what appeared to be a series of Wheatstone bridges, arranged, perhaps, in a sort of decision tree. (Wouldn't you need to *amplify* the current, though? Maybe not.) What must such a doll have *cost*? he thought. Her movements themselves were powered by the spring; but many of the decisions were evidently electromechanical. Not all of them, though, because he saw a cylindrical stack of metal discs with slots, like in a music box, tiny relays, strain gauges, electromagnetic clutches. The doll had to be pushing the absolute *limits* of the technology of the era. Still, the great majority of the time everything was evidently disengaged; she sat there ticking steadily, declutched and waiting.

(Tic-tic-tic-tic-tic-tic-tic-tic-tic.)

The boy sat the doll up and put her, very carefully now, in the counterclockwise position, since the motions were continuous there and he knew what they would be. The flywheel of the dynamo suddenly began to spin. He could slow it, stop it, though, by touching the escapement wheel. The escapement was finer-toothed than a clock's. Every time he put his finger down on the wheel, the doll's hand would stop. If he let it go, it would run. It would run, then stop, run, then stop. Tic-tic-tic-tic . . . tic-tic . . . He was watching the part of the movement where she would normally grab for his shoulder. But this time there was going to be no shoulder for her to grab. With his finger he had complete control of her: tic-tic-tic . . . tic-tic . . . tic-tic. She moved now an inch, now a quarter of an inch, now a matter of millimeters. Something seemed to have been filtered out of the movement, though. Something very real but difficult to describe. What? Well. *Something.* Passion, maybe. It seemed to be passion.

Was passion some function of time?

She would run, then stop, run, then stop: tic-tic-tic-tic . . . tic-tic. Her movements had become somewhat jerky at this speed. The boy was utterly fascinated. He found himself watching the tremor of her gloved hand. Had he inadvertently *aged* the doll? He touched her again and again, letting her move only incrementally. Tic . . . tic . . . tic . . . . tic. . . . . tic

At that moment the escapement wheel sheared off. It sheared completely off and dropped deep within the mechanism. What was left of the little shaft began to spin furiously. The gloved hand of the doll shot eight inches in less than a second. The boy's sense of panic could not have been greater had there been an artery spurting blood across the room. He quickly grabbed at the other control in her neck, stopped the motion, stopped the shaft, his heart pounding furiously.

Oh my God!

He couldn't get to the wheel. It had fallen deep inside. He could not reach it within the labyrinth of machinery. The boy tilted the doll, shook her a little, righted her. There was a tinkling springy noise as the wheel fell down and lodged somewhere near the bottom. It would take a major disassembly to get to it now and would do no good whatsoever since the shaft itself was broken.

There was absolutely no way to put the wheel back.

The boy stood there, terrified. In desperation, he tried inserting the wrench and turning her back to the clockwise position. He thought there possibly might be a second escapement for that position. (Just possibly.) At the same time, he knew in his heart that that would never be true. Absolutely knew, even before he turned the wrench. It was impossible. And yet there *was.* He heard it as soon as he released the control. There was indeed another escapement ticking more deeply inside her. He waited, sat her up, her back still open, waited, waited (tic-tic-tic). Suddenly she began to move. The normal position seemed to be OK. The boy held his ear close to her shoulder. (Tic-tic-tic-tic-tic-tic-tic.) The sound was exactly the same as always. The normal position was OK, or seemed to be. He began sealing her shut again.

After all, he thought, perhaps no one *knew* about the other position. Working furiously, he began to put Moriya back together. The precision of this doll's construction was absolutely unbelievable. He had to wait to let air escape before the two halves would seal together. He was virtually spinning the Allen wrench now, his hands moving as accurately as a surgeon's. Soon there was no trace whatsoever of his entering, no felt showing, no misalignment. It was all snug, tight, perfect.

The boy began to dress her, then to lace up her bustier. He had a sense that his time was limited, that something *else* was about to go wrong. He laced up the back of her dress, missed one position and had to start again. The normal position was OK, he thought, and perhaps no one knew about the other. Or if they did, they might assume they had broken her themselves. He straightened her dress, began to hook her velvet jacket. Get her dressed! Get her *dressed! Hurry!* he thought. The normal position is OK, he told himself (or *was* telling himself) until a question brought him up short in his thoughts:

Exactly which position was normal?

He finished hooking up her velvet jacket and quickly turned out the light.

There had been absolutely no need to rush. It was several hours before the man and woman returned. Still, afterward, for three full days, the boy worried himself sick about the doll. Why? Because of the escapement wheel. How could he be sure it was completely out of the way? For all possible movements, that is. It might still strip a gear or cause something to short-circuit. The boy studiously avoided entering the parlor. He didn't want to be physically in the same room if something within Moriya began to grind and malfunction. Each day before class, he looked in to see whether or not she had moved. When he was home, he went past the parlor doorway, nervously, almost hourly. Had she changed position? Yes. No. Maybe. Yes. (Yes, indeed.) The doll seemed to be running perfectly. Still, he could not study for worrying. All he thought of in class now was Moriya, alone, in that parlor, initiating each perilous new motion. Three days, four days, five days, six. She should have gone through most of her program now. The man and woman would go into the parlor, leave it, notice nothing, say nothing. Mostly, though, Moriya sat there all alone. The boy would watch her from the hall. He too noticed absolutely nothing. Indeed, it seemed absolutely nothing had changed.

But in those days of worry and despair, he began to see the doll in a new light, as something of an agent, ambassador, and spy. What kind of reasoning had gone into her? What was she all about? Her design was more than clever; it was *demonic* in its brilliance, compulsive in its perfection; perhaps the work of some famously dirty-minded old clockmaker from the Austral Kraftwerk in Prague who had sent her into the world in search of fourteen-year-old boys. From this point of view, the boy saw that he had been set up, framed, completely. There was nothing necessarily gentle or bright here. What dark imperatives was this doll fulfilling? The boy could imagine a shop with lathes and drill presses, wires and electromagnets, petticoats and steel filings — pipes too, and cheese, micrometers, and tankards of beer. What was *he* thinking of (the clockmaker) when he had designed her? Was he dreaming of the sex himself? And if so, with whom? Was it *his* hand that found its way up your leg? After all, the message on the underwear was not from her but from the clockmaker: *Talis umbras mundum regnant.* That was a message from the clockmaker, wasn't it?

The feeling did not last long. Another feeling soon replaced it in the boy's heart. The new feeling was loneliness, a bottomless loneliness, the most abject loneliness imaginable. He went through a daily agony. It was as though *he* were broken, not she. He would stand at the door, watch her adjust her position, straighten her glove, scratch an invisible fly off a sleeve. She was trapped now. *He* was trapped without her. His misery and guilt became unbearable. After dinner one evening, he realized he simply had to go in to see her again. Cautious, shy, nervous, he tucked his shirttail in, actually checked his appearance in a mirror before he went through the door. He sat down on the opposite sofa with his French book as though nothing had happened. He waited there nervously. *Why* was he nervous? What was this, silliness? Superstition? She was a *toy*, wasn't she? At last the doll began to turn and look directly at him. He held his breath as her eyes met his. Then he saw her, truly saw her, for the first time in a week. Her face. He had forgotten it. He had *not* forgotten it. He had . . . He went numb inside.

He went.

Then she continued her turn beyond him, seemed at last to be looking at something out the door. She adjusted her glove, became motionless once more.

She did not move again for two hours.

She was trapped now. *He* was trapped without her. The doll did not look at him again. She seemed to avert her eyes.

The boy's dream of Prague came back to him. What secret could she have had? What could it have possibly been? That she loved him? That she was pregnant? What could it have been?

It was an agony to remember it. It was simply too painful to think about.

There was nothing now, nothing. The doll would adjust her gloves, straighten them, fold her hands, look up, look down, and just about break his heart.

I have insulted her, he thought, with these thoughts of a clockmaker. He had met *her* in Prague, or at least had met something that very much *seemed* to be her. They had talked. She had talked *to* him. *She* was not bound by those wires. There was something, a shadow of something, within her that got beyond everything, beyond the gears, the shafts, the magnets — an umbra, so to speak; *umbras,* the plural would be. Was that her secret? Was that what she had wanted and not wanted to tell him? *Talis umbras mundum regnant.* ("Such shadows rule the world.") He could not have had that dream without her.

Did she say she *knew* a secret or *had* a secret?

His memory of the dream was already fading.

And then his French course was over.

And then there was the afternoon he came to visit her for the last time. He felt the briefest flush of hope when he entered the room. Everything was not perfectly gloomy. What can be broken can be fixed, he thought. What can be broken can be fixed. There was a dimension to all of this he had to ignore, a reality, if you will. But a balance wheel can be reattached, a shaft can be machined, from scratch if necessary. Still, it would be too late for him. The normal, or maybe *not* the normal, part of the doll still worked perfectly. The other could be fixed. But not for him, never for him, fixed or not, *that* was gone forever. He would never be in this parlor again, never have another chance, never be on the sofa with this girl, never feel her pressure against him, never see her close her eyes like a kitten to sleep.

The dangling prisms weighed heavily on his soul. The doll sat on her sofa, perfectly motionless. He stood there, watching her, breathing mainly out of his mouth. "Je t'aime," he said quietly.

It had been impossible, over the days, not to see longing, then reproach, then anger in those eyes.

He would leave tomorrow. He told her that. (Out loud, in fact.) He waited, waited a long time. She did not move.

Je t'aime. I love you, he said again, finally.

The doll still did not move. She continued staring out the window. She did not believe him anymore.

The boy picked up some papers that he had left in the parlor and walked toward the front of the house. He heard, outside, in another world, another block, the shriek of some children. On the spur of the moment, he decided to go out onto the front porch. He saw the streetlamps, the live oaks, stood there quietly, glum and melancholy. There was a solid hedge of boxwood in front of him and to his right.

The loveliness of the afternoon was almost but not completely lost on him.

Did she say I have or I *know?* he thought.

Strange, in six weeks, he had scarcely been on this porch. He stood there patiently in the late-afternoon light, looking out at the enormous hedge. Whatever life held for him, whatever *waited* for him, lay beyond it now. There was an immense stillness, a perfect quietness to the tiny leaves. He had learned some French in this town, some other things. Well, it would pass. Time itself would pass.

Passion was some function of time.

ZZ PACKER

Every Tongue Shall Confess

FROM PLOUGHSHARES

As PASTOR EVERETT made the announcements that began the
service, Clareese Mitchell stood with her choir members, knowing
that once again she had to Persevere, put on the Strong Armor of
God, the Breastplate of Righteousness, but she was having her
monthly womanly troubles, and all she wanted to do was curse the
Brothers' Church Council of Greater Christ Emanuel Church of
the Fire Baptized who'd decided that the Sisters had to wear *white*
every Missionary Sunday, which was, of course, the day of the
month when her womanly troubles were always at their absolute
worst! And to think that the Brothers' Church Council of Greater
Christ Emanuel Church of the Fire Baptized had been the first
place she'd looked for guidance and companionship nearly ten
years ago when her aunt Alma had fallen ill. And why not? They
were God-fearing, churchgoing men; men like Deacon Julian
Jeffers, now sitting in the first row of pews, closest to the altar, right
under the leafy top of the corn plant she'd brought in to make the
sanctuary more homey. Two months ago she'd been reading the
Book of Micah and posed the idea of a Book of Micah discussion
group to the Deacon Jeffers, and he'd said, "Oh, Sister Clareese!
We should make *you* a deacon!" Which of course they didn't. Deacons, like pastors, were men — not that she was complaining. But it
still rankled that Jeffers had said he'd get back to her about the Micah discussion group and he never had.

Clareese's cross-eyes roved to the back of the church, where Sister Drusella and Sister Maxwell sat, resplendent in their identical,
wide-brimmed, purple-flowered hats, their unsaved guests sitting

next to them. The guests wore frightened smiles, and Clareese
tried to shoot them reassuring looks. The gold-lettered banner behind them read, "We Are More Than Conquerors in Christ Our
Lord," and she tried to use this as a focal point, but her cross-eyes
couldn't help it, they settled at last on Deacon McCreedy, making
his way down the aisle for the second time. Oh, how she hated him!

She would never forget — never, never, never — the day he
came to the hospital where she worked; she was still wearing her
white nurse's uniform, and he'd said he was concerned about her
spiritual well-being — *Liar!* — then drove her to where she lived
with her aunt Alma, whose room resounded with perpetual snores
and hacking and wheezing — as if Clareese didn't have enough of
this at the hospital — and while Alma slept, Clareese poured Deacon McCreedy some fruit punch, which he drank between forkfuls
of chicken, plus half their pork roast. No sooner than he'd wiped
his hands on the napkin — didn't bother using a fork — he stood
and walked behind her, covering her cross-eyed eyes as though she
were a child, as though he were about to give her a gift — a Bible
with her very own name engraved on it, perhaps — but he didn't
give her anything, he just covered her wandering eyes and said,
"Sing 'On Christ the Solid Rock I Stand.' Make sure to do the
Waterfall." And she was happy to do it, happy to please Deacon
McCreedy, so she began singing in her best, cleanest voice until she
felt his hand slide up the scratchy white pantyhose of her nurse's
uniform and slide up toward the control top of her pantyhose. Before she could stop him, one finger wriggling around inside, and
by then it was too late to tell him she was having her monthly womanly troubles. He drew back in disgust — no, *hatred* — then rinsed
his hand in the kitchen sink and left without saying a word, not a
thanks for the chicken nor the pork roast nor her singing. Not a
single word of apology for anything. But she could have forgiven
him — if Sisters could even forgive Deacons — for she could have
understood that an unmarried man might have needs, *needs,* but
what really bothered her was how he ignored her. How a few weeks
later she and Aunt Alma had been waiting for the bus after
Wednesday night prayer meeting, and he *drove past.* That's right.
No offer of a ride, no slowing down, no nothing. Aunt Alma was
nearly blind and couldn't even see it was him, but Clareese recognized his car at once.

Yes, she wanted to curse the Brothers' Church Council of

Greater Christ Emanuel Church of the Fire Baptized, but Sisters and Brothers could not curse, could not even swear or take an oath, for *neither shalt thou swear by thy head, because thou canst not make one hair white or black.* So no oath, no swearing, and of course no betting — an extension of swearing — which was why she'd told the other nurses at University Hospital that she would not join their betting pool to predict who would get married first, Patty or Edwina. She told them about the black and white hairs, and all Nurse Holloway did was clomp her pumps — as if she was too good for the standard orthopedically correct shoes — down the green tiles of the hall and shout behind her back, "Somebody sure needs to get laid." Oh, how the other RNs tittered in their gossipy way.

Now everyone applauded when Pastor Everett announced that Sister Nina would be getting married to Harold, one of the Brothers from Broadway Tongues of Spirit Church. Then Pastor Everett said, "Sister Nina will be holding a Council so we can get husbands for the rest of you hardworking Sisters." Like Sister Clareese, is what he meant. The congregation laughed at the joke. Ha, ha. And perhaps the joke *was* on her. If she'd been married, Deacon McCreedy wouldn't have dared do what he did; if she'd been married, perhaps she'd also be working fewer shifts at the hospital, perhaps she would have never met that patient — the man who'd almost gotten her fired! And at exactly that moment, it hit her, right below the gut, a sharp pain, and she imagined her uterus, that Texas-shaped organ, the Rio Grande of her monthly womanly troubles flushing out to the Gulf.

Pastor Everett had finished the announcements. Now it was time for testimony service. She tried to distract herself by thinking of suitable testimonies. Usually she testified about work. Last week she'd testified about the poor man with a platelet count of seven, meaning he was as good as dead; Nurse Holloway had told him, "We're bringing you more platelets," and he'd said, "That's all right. God sent me more." No one at the Nurses' Station — to say nothing of those atheist doctors — believed him. But when Nurse Holloway checked, sure enough, Glory be to God, he had a count of sixteen. Clareese told the congregation how she knelt on the cold tiled floor of University Hospital's corridor, right then and there, arms outstretched to Glory. And what could the other nurses say to that? Nothing, that's what.

She remembered her testimony from a month ago, how she'd

been working the hotline and a mother had called to say that her son had eaten ants, and Sister Clareese had assured the woman that ants were God's creatures and wouldn't harm the boy. But the Lord told Clareese to stay on the line with the mother, not to rush the way other nurses often did, so Clareese stayed on the line. And Glory be to God that she did! Once the mother had calmed down she'd said, "Thank goodness. The insecticide I gave Kevin must have worked." Sister Clareese had stayed after her shift to make sure the woman brought her boy into Emergency. Afterwards she told the woman to hold hands with Kevin and give God the Praise he deserved.

But she had told these stories already. As she fidgeted in her choir mistress's chair, she tried to think of new ones. The congregation wouldn't care about how she had to stay on top of codes, or how she had to triple-check patients' charts. The only patients who stuck in her mind were Mrs. Geneva Bosma, whose toe was rotting off, and Mr. Toomey, who had prostate cancer. And, of course, Mr. Cleophus Sanders, the cause of all her current troubles. Cleophus was an amputee who liked to turn the volume of his television up so high that his channel-surfing sounded as if someone were being electrocuted, repeatedly. At the Nurses' Station she'd overheard that Cleophus Sanders was once a musician who in his heyday went by the nickname "Delta Sweetmeat." But he'd gone in and out of the music business, sometimes taking construction jobs. A crane had fallen on his leg, and he'd been amputated from below the knee. No, none of these cases were Edifying in God's sight. Her run-in with Cleophus had been downright un-Edifying.

When Mr. Sanders had been moved into Mr. Toomey's room last Monday, she'd told them both, "I hope everyone has a blessed day!" She'd made sure to say this only after she was safely inside with the door closed behind her. She had to make sure she didn't mention God until the door was closed *behind* her because Nurse Holloway was always clomping about, trying to say that this was a *university* hospital, as well as a *research* hospital, one at the very *forefront* of medicine, and didn't Registered Nurse Clareese Mitchell recognize and *respect* that not everyone shared her beliefs? That the hospital catered not only to Christians but to people of the Jewish faith? Muslims, Hindus, and agnostics? Atheists, even?

This Clareese knew only too well, which was why it was all the more important for her to Spread the Gospel. So she shut the door, and said to Mr. Toomey, louder this time, "I HOPE EVERYONE HAS A BLESSED DAY!"

Mr. Toomey grunted. Heavy and completely white, he reminded Sister Clareese of a walrus: everything about him drooped, his eyes like twin frowns, his nose, perhaps even his mouth, though it was hard to make out because of his frowning blond mustache. Well, Glory be to God, she expected something like a grunt from him, she couldn't say she was surprised: junkies who detox scream and writhe before turning clean; the man with a hangover does not like to wake to the sun. So it was with sinners exposed to the harsh, curing Light of the Lord.

"Hey, sanctified lady!" Cleophus Sanders called from across the room. "He got cancer! Let the man alone."

"I *know* what he *has*," Sister Clareese said. "I'm his *nurse*." This wasn't how she wanted the patient-RN relationship to begin, but Cleophus had gotten the better of her. Yes, that was the problem, wasn't it? *He'd* gotten the better of *her*. This was how Satan worked, throwing you off a little at a time. She would have to Persevere, put on the Strong Armor of God. She tried again.

"My name is Sister Clareese Mitchell, your assigned registered nurse. I can't exactly say that I'm pleased to meet you because that would be a lie and *lying lips are an abomination to the Lord*. I will say that I am pleased to do my duty and help you recover."

"*Me oh my!*" Cleophus Sanders said, and laughed big and long, the kind of laughter that could go on and on, rising and rising, re-starting itself if need be, like yeast. He slapped the knee of his amputated leg, the knee that would probably come off if his infection didn't stop eating away at it. But Cleophus Sanders didn't care. He just slapped that infected knee, hooting all the while in an ornery, backwoods kind of way that made Clareese want to hit him.

She busied herself by changing Mr. Toomey's catheter, then remaking his bed, rolling the walrus of him this way and that, with little help on his part. As soon as she was done with Mr. Toomey, he turned on the Knicks. The whole time she'd changed Toomey's catheter, however, Cleophus had watched her, laughing under his breath, then outright, a waxing and waning of hilarity as if her every gesture were laughably prim and proper.

"Look, Mr. *Cleophus*," she said, glad for the chance to bite on the ridiculous name, "I am a professional. You may laugh at what I do, but in doing so you laugh at the Almighty who has given me the breath to do it!"

She'd steeled herself for a vulgar reply. But no. Mr. Toomey did the talking.

"I tell *you* what!" Mr. Toomey said, pointing his remote at Sister Clareese. "I'm going to sue this hospital for lack of peace and quiet. All your 'Almighty this' and 'Oh Glory that' is keeping me from watching the game!"

While Sister Clareese murmured her apologies to Mr. Toomey, Cleophus Sanders put on an act of restraining his amusement, body and bed quaking in seizure-like fits.

Now sunlight filtered through the yellow-tinted windows of Greater Christ Emmanuel Church of the Fire Baptized, lighting Brother Hopkins, the organist, with a halo-like glow. The rest of the congregation had given their testimonies, and it was now time for the choir members to testify, starting with Clareese. Was there any way she could possibly turn her incident with Cleophus Sanders into an Edifying testimony experience? Just then, another hit, and she felt a cramping so hard she thought she might double over. It was her turn. Cleophus's laughter and her cramping womb seemed one and the same; he'd inhabited her body like a demon, preventing her from thinking up a proper testimony. As she rose, unsteadily, to her feet, all she managed to say was, "Pray for me."

All right. Get a hold of yourself. It was almost time for Pastor Everett to preach his sermon. To introduce it, Sister Clareese had the choir sing "Every Knee Shall Bow, Every Tongue Shall Confess." It was an old-fashioned hymn, unlike the hopped-up gospel songs churches were given to nowadays. And she liked the slow unfolding of its message: how without uttering a word, all the hearts of men and women would be made plain to the Lord; that He would know you not by what you said or did, but by what you'd hoped and intended. The teens, however, mumbled over the verses, and older choir members sang without vigor. The hymn ended up sounding like the national anthem at a school assembly: a stouthearted song rendered in monotone.

"Thank you, thank you, thank you, Sister Clareese," Pastor Everett said, looking back at her, "for that wonderful tune."

Tune? She knew that Pastor Everett thought she was not the kind of person a choir mistress should be; she was quiet, nervous, skinny in all the wrong places, and completely cross-eyed. She knew he thought of her as something worse than a spinster, because she wasn't yet old.

Pastor Everett hunched close to the microphone, as though about to begin a forlorn love song. From the corners of her vision she saw him smile — only for a second — but with every single tooth in his mouth. He was yam-colored, and given to wearing epaulets on the shoulders of his robes and gold braiding all down the front. Sister Clareese felt no attraction to him, but she seemed to be the only one who didn't; even the Sisters going on eighty were charmed by Pastor Everett, who, though not entirely handsome, had handsome moments.

"Sister Clareese," he said, turning to where she stood with the choir. "Sister Clareese, I know y'all just sang for us, but I need some *more* help. Satan got these Brothers and Sisters putting m' Lord on hold!"

Sister Clareese knew that everyone expected her and her choir to begin singing again, but she had been alerted to what he was up to; he had called her yesterday; he thought nothing of asking her to unplug her telephone — her *only* telephone, her *private* line — to bring to church so that he could use it in some sermon about call-waiting. Hadn't even asked her how she was doing, hadn't bothered to pray over her aunt Alma's sickness, nevertheless she'd said, "Why, certainly, Pastor Everett. Anything I can do to help."

Now Sister Clareese produced her Princess telephone from under her seat and handed it to the Pastor. Pastor Everett held the telephone aloft, shaking it as if to rid it of demons. "How many of y'all — Brothers and Sisters — got telephones?" the Pastor asked.

One by one, members of the congregation timidly raised their hands.

"All right," Pastor Everett said, as though this grieved him, "almost all of y'all." He flipped through his huge pulpit Bible. "How many of y'all — Brothers and Sisters — got call-waiting?" He turned pages quickly, then stopped, as though he didn't need to search for the scripture after all. "Let me tell ya," the Pastor said, nearly kissing the microphone, "there is Someone! Who won't *accept* your call-waiting! There is *Someone!* Who won't *wait,* when you put Him on hold!" Sister Nancy Popwell and Sister Drusella Davies now had their eyes closed in concentration, their hands waving slowly in the air in front of them as though they were trying to make their way through a dark room.

The last phone call Sister Clareese had made was on Wednesday, to Mr. Toomey. She knew both he and Cleophus were likely to reject the Lord, but she had a policy of sorts, which was to call patients who'd been in her care for at least a week. She considered it her Christian duty to call — even on her day off — to let them know that Jesus cared, and that she cared. The other RNs resorted to callous catch phrases that they bandied about the Nurses' Station: "Just because I care *for* them doesn't mean I have to care *about* them," or, "I'm a nurse, not a nursery . . ." Not Clareese. Perhaps she'd been curt with Cleophus Sanders, but she had been so in defense of God. Perhaps Toomey had been curt with her, but he was going into OR soon, and grouchiness was to be expected.

Nurse Patty had been switchboard operator that night, and Clareese had had to endure her sighs before the girl finally connected her to Toomey.

"Praise the Lord, Mr. Toomey!"

"Who's this?"

"This is your nurse, Sister Clareese, and I'm calling to say that Jesus will be with you through your surgery."

"Who?"

"Jesus," she said.

She thought she heard the phone disconnect, then a voice. Of course. Cleophus Sanders.

"Why ain't you called *me*?" Cleophus said.

Sister Clareese tried to explain her policy, the thing about the week.

"So you care more about some white dude than you care about good ol' Cleophus?"

"It's not that, Mr. Sanders. God cares for white and black alike. Acts 10:34 says, 'God is no respecter of persons.' Black or white. Red, purple, or green — He doesn't care, as long as you accept His salvation and live right." When he was silent on the other end, she said, "It's that I've only known you for two days. I'll see you tomorrow."

She tried to hang up, but he said, "Let me play something for you. Something interesting, since all you probably listen to is monks chanting and such."

Before she could respond, there was a noise on the other end that sounded like juke music. Then he came back on the phone and said, "Like that, don't you?"

"I had the phone away from my ear."

"I thought you said, 'Lying is the abomination.' Do you *like* or do you *don't?*" When she said nothing, he said, "Truth, now."

She answered yes.

She didn't want to answer yes. But she also didn't want to lie. And what was one to do in that circumstance? If God looked into your heart right then, what would He think? Or would He have to approve because He made your heart that way? Or were you suppose to train it against its wishes? She didn't know what to think, but on the other end Cleophus said, "What you just heard there was the blues. What you just heard there was me."

"Let me tell ya!" Pastor Everett shouted, his voice hitting its highest octave. "*Jeeeee-zus* — did not *tell* his *Daddy*, 'I'm sorry, Pops — but my girlfriend is on the other line.' *Jeeeee-zus* — never *told* the Omnipotent One, 'Can you wait a sec, I think I got a call from the electric company'! *Jeeeeeeee-zus* — never told Matthew, Mark, Luke, or John, 'I'm *sorry*, but I got to put you on hold; I'm sorry, Brother Luke, but I got some mac and cheese in the oven; I'm *sorry*, but I got to eat this fried chicken'" — and at this Pastor Everett paused, grinning in anticipation of his own punchline — "'cause it's finger-licking good'!"

Drops of sweat plunked onto his microphone.

Sister Clareese watched as the congregation cheered, the women flagging their Bibles in the air as though the Bibles were as light and yielding as handkerchiefs, their bosoms jouncing as though they were harboring sacks of potatoes in their blouses. They shook tambourines, scores of them all going at once, the sound of something sizzling and frying.

That was it? That was The Message? Of course, she'd only heard part of it, but still. Of course she believed that one's daily life shouldn't outstrip one's spiritual one, but there seemed no place for true belief at Greater Christ Emanuel Church. Everyone wanted flash and props, no one wanted the Word itself, naked in its fiery glory.

Most of the Brothers and Sisters were up on their feet. "Tell it!"

yelled some, while others called out, "Go 'head on!" The organist pounded out the chords to what could have been the theme song of a TV game show.

She looked to see what Sister Drusella and Sister Maxwell's unsaved guests were doing. Drusella's unsaved guest was her son, which made him easy to bring into the fold: he was living in her shed and had no car. He was busy turning over one of the cardboard fans donated by Hamblin and Sons Funeral Parlor, reading the words intently, then flipping it over again to stare at the picture of a gleaming casket and grieving family. Sister Donna Maxwell's guest was an ex-con she'd written to and tried to save while he was in prison. The ex-con seemed to watch the scene with approval, though one could never really know what was going on in the criminal mind. For all Sister Clareese knew, he could have been counting all the pockets he planned to pick.

And they called themselves missionaries. Family members and ex-cons were easy to convince of God's will. As soon as Drusella's son took note of the pretty young Sisters his age, he'd be back. And everyone knew you could convert an ex-con with a few well-timed pecan pies.

Wednesday was her only day off besides Sunday, and though a phone call or two was her policy on days off, she very seldom visited the hospital. And yet last Wednesday she had to. The more she considered Cleophus's situation — his loss of limb, his devil's music, his unsettling laughter — the more she grew convinced that he was her Missionary Challenge. That he was especially in need of Saving.

Minutes after she'd talked with him on the phone, she took the Number 42 bus and transferred to the crosstown H, then walked the rest of the way to the hospital.

Edwina had taken over for Patty as Nurse Station attendant, and she'd said, "We have an ETOH in — where's your uniform?"

"It's not my shift," she called behind her as she rushed past Edwina and into Room 204.

She opened the door to find Cleophus sitting on the bed, still plucking chords on his unplugged electric guitar that she'd heard him playing over the phone half an hour earlier. Mr. Toomey's bed was empty; one of the nurses must have already taken him to OR, so Cleophus had the room to himself. The right leg of Cleophus's hospital pants hung down limp and empty, and it was the first time she'd seen his guitar, curvy and shiny as a sports car. He did not acknowledge her as she entered, still picking away until he began to sing a song about a man whose woman had left him so high and dry, she'd taken the car, the dog, the furniture. Even the wallpaper. Only when he'd strummed the final chords did Cleophus look up, as if noticing her for the first time.

"Sister *Clare-reeeese!*" He'd said it as if he were introducing a showgirl.

"It's your soul," Clareese said. "God wants me to help save your soul." The urgency of God's message struck her so hard, she felt the wind knocked out of her. She sat on the bed next to him.

"Really?" he said, cocking his head a little.

"Really and truly," Clareese said. "I know I said I liked your music, but I said it because God gave you that gift for you to use. For Him."

"Uhnn-huh," Cleophus said. "How about this, little lady? How about if God lets me keep this knee, I'll come to church with you? We can go out and get some dinner afterwards. Like a proper couple."

She tried not to be flattered. "The Lord does *not make* deals, Mr. Sanders. But I'm sure the Lord would love to see you in church regardless of what happens to your knee."

"Well, since you seem to be His receptionist, how about you ask the Lord if He can give you the day off. I can take you out on the town. See, if I go to church, I *know* the Lord won't show. But I'm positive you will."

"Believe you me, Mr. Sanders, the Lord is at every service. *Where two or three are gathered together in my name, there am I in the midst of them.*" She sighed, trying to remember what she came to say. *"He is the Way, the Truth, and the Life. No man —"*

"— cometh to the Father," Cleophus said, *"but by me."*

She looked at him. "You know your Bible."

"Naw. You were speaking, and I just heard it." He absently strummed his guitar. "You were talking, saying that verse, and the rest of it came to me. Not even a voice," he said, "more like . . . kind of like music."

She stared. Her hands clapped his, preventing him from playing further. For a moment she was breathless. He looked at her, suddenly seeming to comprehend what he'd just said, that the Lord had actually spoken to him. For a minute they sat there, both over-joyed at what the Lord had done, but then he had to go ruin it. He burst out laughing his biggest, most sinful laugh yet.

"Awww!" he cried, doubled over, and then flopped backwards onto his hospital bed. Then he closed his eyes, laughing without sound.

She stood up, chest heaving, wondering why she even bothered with him.

"Clareese," he said, trying to clear his voice of any leftover laugh-ter, "don't go." He looked at her with pleading eyes, then patted the space beside him on the bed.

She looked around the room for some cue. Whenever she needed an answer, she relied on some sign from the Lord: a fresh beam of sunlight through the window, the hands of a clock folded in prayer, or the flush of a commode. These were signs that what-ever she was thinking of doing was right. If there was a storm cloud, or something in her path, then that was a bad sign. But nothing in the room gave her any indication whether she should stay and wit-ness to Mr. Sanders, or go.

"What, Mr. Sanders, do you want from me? It's my day off. I de-cided to come by and offer you an invitation to my church because God has given you a gift. A musical gift." She dug into her purse, then pulled out a pocket-sized Bible. "But I'll leave you with this. If you need to find us — our church — the name and number is printed inside."

He took the Bible with a little smile, turning it over, then flipping through it, as if some money might be tucked away inside. "Seri-ously, though," he said, "let me ask you a question that's gonna seem dumb. Childish. Now, I want you to think long and hard about it. Why the hell's there so much suffering in the world if God's doing his job? I mean, look at me. Take old Toomey, too. We done anything *that bad* to deserve all this put on us?"

She sighed. "Because of people, that's why. Not God. It's *people* who allow suffering, people who create it. Perpetrate it."

"Maybe that explains Hitler and all them others, but I'm talking about —" He gestured at the room, the hospital in general.

Clareese tried to see what he saw when he looked at the room. At one time the white and pale green walls of the hospital rooms had given her solace: the way everything was clean, clean, clean; the many patients that had been in each room, some nice, some dying, some willing to accept the Lord. But most, like Mr. Toomey, cast the Lord aside like wilted lettuce, and now the clean hospital room was just a reminder of the emptiness, the barrenness, of her patients' souls. Cleophus Sanders was just another one of those patients who disrespected the Lord.

"Why does He allow natural disasters to kill people?" Clareese said, knowing that her voice was raised beyond what she meant it to be. "Why are little children born to get some rare blood disease and die? Why," she yelled, waving her arms, "does a crane fall on your leg and smash it? I don't know, Mr. Sanders. And I don't like it. But I'll say this! No one has a *right* to live! The only right we have is to die. That's it! If you get plucked out of the universe and given a chance to become a life, that's more than not having become anything at all, and for that, Mr. Sanders, you should be grateful!"

She had not known where this last bit had come from, and, she could tell, neither had he, but she could hear the other nurses coming down the hall to see who was yelling, and though Cleophus Sanders looked to have more pity on his face than true belief, he had come after her when she turned to leave. She'd heard the clatter of him gathering his crutches, and even when she heard the meaty weight of him slam onto the floor, she did not turn back.

Then, there it was. Pastor Everett's silly motion of cupping his hand to his ear, like he was eavesdropping on the choir, his signal that he was waiting for Sister Clareese to sing her solo, waiting to hear the voice that would send the congregation shouting, "Thank you, Jesus, Blessed Savior!"

How could she do it? She thought of Cleophus on the floor and felt ashamed. She hadn't seen him since; her yelling had been brought to the attention of the hospital administrators, and although understaffed, the administration had suggested that she not return until next week. They handed her the card of the staff psychiatrist. She had not told anyone at church what had happened. Not even her aunt Alma.

She didn't want to sing. Didn't feel like it, but she thought, *I will freely sacrifice myself unto thee; I will praise thy name, O Lord, for it is good.* Usually thinking of a scripture would give her strength, but this time it just made her realize how much strength she was always needing.

She didn't want to, but she'd do it. She'd sing a stupid solo part

— the Waterfall, they called it — not even something she'd *invented* or *planned* to do who knows how many years ago when she'd had to sneeze her brains out — but oh no, she'd tried holding it in, and when she had to do her solo, those years ago, her near-sneeze made the words come out tumbling in a series of staccato notes that were almost fluid, and ever since then she'd had to sing *all* solos that way, it was expected of her, everyone loved it, it was her trademark. She sang: *"All-hall other-her her grooouund — is sinking sand!"*

The congregation applauded.

"Saints," the Pastor said, winding down, "you know this world will soon be over! Jesus will come back to this tired, sorry Earth in *a moment and a twinkling of an eye!* So you can't use call-waiting on the Lord! *Jeeee-zus,* my friends, does not accept conference calls! You are Children of God! You need to PRAY! Put down your phone! Say goodbye to AT&T! You cannot go in God's *direction,* without a little — *genuflection!"*

The congregation went wild, clapping and banging tambourines, whirling in the aisles. But the choir remained standing in case Pastor Everett wanted another song. For the first time, Clareese found her monthly troubles had settled down. And now that she had the wherewithal to concentrate, she couldn't. Her cross-eyes wouldn't keep steady, she felt them roaming like the wheels of a defective shopping cart, and from one roving eye she saw her aunt Alma, waving her arms as though listening to leftover strains of Clareese's solo.

What would she do? She didn't know if she'd still have her job when she went back on Monday; didn't know what the staff psychiatrist would try to pry out of her. More importantly, she didn't know what her aunt Alma would do without the special referrals Clareese could get her. What was a Sister to do?

Clareese's gaze must have found him just a moment after everyone else had. A stranger at the far end of the aisle, standing directly opposite Pastor Everett as though about to engage him in a duel. There was Cleophus Sanders with his crutches, the right leg of his pinstriped pants hollow, wagging after him. Over his shoulder was a strap, attached to which was his guitar. Even Deacon McCreedy was looking.

What in Heaven's name was Cleophus doing here? To bring his soul to salvation? To ridicule her? For another argument? Perhaps the doctors had told him he did not need the operation after all, and Cleophus was keeping his end of the deal with God. But he didn't seem like the type to keep promises. Not unless they threatened to break him. She saw his eyes search the congregation, and when he saw her, they locked eyes as if he had come to claim her. He did not come to get Saved, didn't care about his soul in that way, all he cared about was —

Now she knew why he'd come. He'd come for her. He'd come *despite* what she'd told him, despite his disbelief. Anyhow, she disapproved. It was God he needed, not her. Nevertheless, she remained standing for a few moments, even after the rest of the choir had already seated themselves, waving their cardboard fans to cool their sweaty faces.

NICOLE KRAUSS

Future Emergencies

FROM ESQUIRE

FOR A LONG TIME they said we didn't need one, but then something changed and they said that we did. I was standing barefoot in the kitchen listening to the radio turned up loudly, as I like to do in the morning. It gives the news a greater impact and increases the drama of beginning another day in a world I've grown used to but know can change at any moment. When the announcement was made, my first instinct was to hold my breath in case whatever it was had already been released into the air. "What?" Victor asked, coming in and turning down the volume. I exhaled. "Gas masks," I said.

But outside the window, the morning was pale and clear. There appeared to be nothing in the atmosphere beyond the invisible blessing of oxygen. Other things too, equally invisible: a trace of benzene, a low-level reading of mercury or dioxin, maybe. But nothing we hadn't learned to live with. Sometimes at dusk I watch runners on the track around the reservoir, their lungs pumping to take in the maximum cubic feet of air, and the thought occurs to me that maybe they belong to a more evolved subspecies, one actually benefiting from — actually able to break down and harness for energy — elements still toxic to the rest of us. Victor calls it the flagellation parade. He says that they're wearing away their joints, grinding down cartilage. He says they'll leave the world limping or crawling on all fours. But to me they seem the image of health: lithe, agile, unharmed by pollution. It makes the sunsets more beautiful, all of those particles in the air. The sky turns colors that seem to reflect the peculiar ache of being alive at that hour.

"The threat may not come from common pollutants or shifting

winds," the radio said. "It may not come from airborne pesticides or a factory fire or underground tests." The coffeemaker purred, and Victor took two mugs off the shelf. "Where will the threat come from?" I asked aloud. I felt an intimate connection to the voice, at liberty to ask it questions. "The threat may come from an unknown source," the radio replied. Even when the news is bad, I am glad to have been answered.

For the time being, the air was still safe to breathe, the radio said. It was all right to go outside, so long as you remembered to stop and get a mask at one of the distribution centers being set up in each neighborhood. Victor had been planning on staying in to grade papers, so I offered to pick up masks for both of us on my way back from work.

"If there's a choice, I'd like the kind with the eyeholes and the snout. The anteater one," Victor joked, going to the door for the newspaper.

"I don't think this is a time to be picky."

It was November, and outside the air was crisp and seemed to carry the promise of snow. What I miss about living in the country is the morbid beauty of the autumns. In the city the leaves just turn brown and scatter. Once I took Victor back to the farm where I grew up and it rained the whole time. We tramped around in the mud and I tried to show him how to milk a cow, but he couldn't stand the smell of the hot milk. When we finally left, he said that one had to have a sense of humor to grow up in a place like that. I didn't explain to him how the dogs used to come into the house smelling of the fields.

I met Victor in my last year of college. He was the professor of my medieval history class. Victor is French and so he didn't have any hangups about going out with a student. After graduation I moved in with him and got a job giving tours at the museum. Though the life we live together now feels like the only one I know, there are moments when I still imagine another life, with different things in it. A life with someone who is not Victor and who is nothing like him.

On the steps down to the subway I passed a man coming up wearing a gas mask. It wasn't the kind Victor was talking about. This one was fancier, like a motorcycle helmet, with circles over the nose and mouth and on each cheek, the one on the left twice the size of the others. The man was wearing a red silk tie and a suit that looked like it had just been unwrapped from the dry cleaner. The sight of him was unnerving, and people stopped to stare. Some probably hadn't heard the news that morning, and the ones who had were wondering if there had been an update. There had been warnings before about the possible need for the masks, but this was the first time they were actually being distributed, and obviously it set everyone on edge. When I went down to the subway platform, there were a few people who'd already gone to the distribution centers and were carrying their masks in corrugated plastic boxes. I thought about going to pick ours up, but I was late for work and the first tour of the day is always my favorite. The light comes in softly through the eastern windows, lighting up the madonnas and the saints.

There were only five people in my morning tour: a couple from Texas, a mother and daughter from Munich, and a man named Paul. He had beautiful hands. I noticed them when he touched his forehead. Everyone was feeling a little nervous, and we spent the first few minutes talking about the news in the hushed tones used in museums. When the group is small, I usually ask the visitors what they're interested in and try to tailor the tour to their tastes. The man from Texas, who had a gold ring on his pinkie, said he was a big fan of Renoir. He pronounced it *Rin-waa,* and his wife smiled in agreement.

The man named Paul was interested in the museum's photography collection, so I started off in the room with the Walker Evans portraits. I've always been struck by his photographs, their sparse and formal beauty. Here were these people caught in grim and hopeless lives, and he photographed them with the same precise detachment as he would an old signboard. There's something breathtaking about it, the lack of compassion in favor of cold clarity. There were a couple of photographs by Diane Arbus at the other end of the room, and I decided to show them to the group to give them a sense of the other end of the spectrum, someone who seemed to identify with her subjects on a terrifying level. Not only does Arbus seem to feel their unhappiness, I explained, but what's more, they — the twins and the triplets, the misfit children, the odd couples, the tramps, the queens, the freaks — seem to regard her as if they recognize something darker and more haunting than their own lot. I'd never exactly realized this before. Sometimes on a good day that happens: you're giving a tour, and as you talk you find things you didn't know you had to say.

I let the group look for a while in silence at the child clutching the toy grenade and the old woman in a wheelchair holding a witch's mask over her face. I was a little worried about how the man from Texas would react, but I should have given him the benefit of the doubt, because he ended up taking a big interest, going right up close and screwing up his face in concentration. Paul had drifted back over to the Walker Evans photographs. I watched his hands, the fingers long and elegant. I imagined him as a musician — a pianist, or maybe a cellist.

Before Victor I had always dated men my own age. It's hard to remember what they were like now, the smoothness of their skin, and how when I took my clothes off they seemed almost grateful. It's even hard to remember what it felt like to be the person they loved, for whom the world was still opening. A person who is not, in some form, a refraction of Victor. When I first met him I was practically a kid. He struck me as strong and utterly remarkable, a man against whose finished form I could lean to feel the pleasure of a permanent shape.

While I was eating lunch, one of the other guides, a thin woman named Ellen with a long neck, came into the staff room. She'd gone to pick up her mask already and put it on as a joke. She got right up in my face like the Texan in front of the Arbus and peered down at me through the eyeholes. I let out a playful scream, but the truth was that the way she looked, like a giant praying mantis, gave me the creeps. Ellen has an odd sense of humor, and she started to bark with laughter, the sound trapped and muffled by the rubber mouthpiece. After she'd calmed down, she pushed the mask back onto her head and finished the rest of her tunafish sandwich with the eyeholes staring blindly up at the ceiling. Sometimes Ellen and I talk about our relationships. Her boyfriend practices rock climbing in an atrium, calls her Lou, and once got arrested for scalping tickets. She says I'm lucky to have a man with such refined taste, who's dedicated his life to the pursuit of ideas.

Victor's sense of humor is also unusual. He's a medievalist, which already suggests something about his tastes, but add to that the fact that he wrote his dissertation on the penal system in thirteenth-century Burgundy and you begin to have a real sense of what a person like Victor might find funny. When we first started dating, I found the blackness of his humor charming. It drew attention to the difference in our ages, leaving me free to take on the role of the naive, uncorrupted youth. Soon Victor will be forty-five. When he doesn't shave, some of the hairs in his beard come in silver, and sometimes, lying with my cheek against his, a sense of gratitude still comes over me and I love him more than ever. I have the feeling then that Victor is standing between me and some distant harm, and that his presence is what shields me from it.

My last tour at the museum ended at quarter to five, and I got my coat and headed outside. A week earlier the clocks had been turned back, and I still hadn't gotten used to the dark coming in so early. I always feel a little pang of hurt that first day when darkness falls without warning. It's the slight, sickening feeling of being reminded of the reckless authority of time, of losing your bearings in a world whose dimensions you thought you'd learned to live with. I took my time getting back. I imagined Paul practicing somewhere in an empty auditorium. The park was mostly deserted, but the runners were still out, sprinting under the bare trees around the reservoir, the light from the lamps shining off the reflector guards on their sneakers and clothing.

The distribution center for our neighborhood was an elementary school on a quiet street of townhouses. There were paper cutouts of turkeys and Pilgrims in the window. When I got there, people were bustling in and out, gathering in little clots on the steps to share whatever they knew. Judging from what I overheard on the way in, it wasn't much. At work I'd heard various speculations — the man from Texas thought that there had been some sort of meltdown at a nuclear plant, and Ellen insisted that a crop duster from Colombia had disappeared — but none of them were particularly credible. It seemed strange that no one was explaining the sudden need for gas masks, and also how the city had been prepared with enough masks on hand for everyone. But I assumed there were reasons. Victor says that I don't question things enough. He said I accept the way things are without challenge. The first words he ever directed at me were written on the top of an essay I'd handed in. *Your argument is unclear,* he wrote. *See me.*

The distribution was set up in one of the classrooms. There was some sort of master list with all of the residents' names, and when I got to the front of the line for *M* through *R,* I had to explain that I was also picking one up for Victor Assoulen, and could I please have his without having to stand in the line for *A* through *F*? There was a small bureaucratic scuffle among the volunteers working on the other side of the blockade of children's desks, but after I showed them an ID with an address that matched up to Victor's it got straightened out and a woman in a velour sweatsuit handed me two boxes. On my way out I stopped to smile at a little girl hopping around in ballet slippers, and when I looked up again I noticed a note left on the blackboard. It read, in elegant teacher's cursive, *Due Monday: your predictions for the future.* I started to laugh but caught myself when I turned back and met the cool gaze of the small prophet in scuffed ballet slippers.

Ask Victor and he'll tell you that the Middle Ages were more passionate times than these. Extreme contrasts and violent conflicts existed side by side, lending a thrilling vigor to life that order can't provide. He'll sit with you over a bottle of wine and explain to you in a breathlessly articulate manner how now all anyone wants is conflict resolution. They want to shake hands and settle matters; they want tolerance for all points of view, so long as those points of view are expressed through the proper channels and procedures. It's not that Victor would have us all back in the thirteenth century, cheering in spasmodic effusion at public executions. His sense of morality is finely tuned. But he refuses to accept a system designed to reject conflict and force us all, like a fat lady through a keyhole, in the direction of a stable average. That's the phrase he uses, a fat lady through a keyhole.

When I got home, Victor was standing in the kitchen knee-deep in shopping bags. He'd bought more food than we normally eat in a month and was trying to find room for it all in our tiny kitchen. When he saw me standing in the door he put down a jar of peanut butter he was trying to wedge between some soup cans, waded across the sea of plastic bags, and hugged me hard. Normally when I come home Victor peeks out from behind some book about minstrels and barely raises an eyebrow. It's not that he isn't glad to see me; he just likes to greet me in his own time. It's as if there are two Victors, and between the intellectual Victor engaged in an ongoing critique of the suppression of conflict and the Victor who rubs my toes when I'm cold there is a powerful force field, and each day, like a superhero morphing back into his normal life, Victor must cross back through it to get to me.

"Hi," I said into the flannel of his shirt.

"I was worried," said Victor. "I tried to call you at the museum to come home early."

"Was there more news?"

"No. They're giving instructions on how to seal the windows with duct tape, but they're not saying why. I went to the supermarket."

We both looked around the kitchen at the bags of apricots and pears, the cheese wrapped in butcher paper, the loaves of bread, the chocolate bars and pints of ice cream, the cold cuts and condiments, the plastic tubs of dips and spreads.

"The store was being emptied. I grabbed what I could," Victor said. "I'm going to make you dinner," he said, nipping my ear between his lips.

Victor is a talented cook, and in the ten minutes it took me to change into my sweatpants and curl up on the sofa in front of the TV, the apartment was already filled with the smell of something good simmering on the stove. I watched as the news channel flashed images of ransacked shelves at the supermarkets and lines snaking out onto the streets outside the distribution centers, and then the picture cut to a little girl with blond curls and a nose crusted with snot trying to work a gas mask down over her face. When I looked up from the TV screen I caught a reflection of myself in the window, tucked under a blanket like a child before a hurricane, and I realized that I was full of happy anticipation. Outside, the world was cold and dark, but inside the rooms were lit with the yellow glow of lamps, and waiting for Victor to call me for dinner I felt the rush of pleasure that I used to seek in made-up games of my childhood, in which all things were eclipsed by the singular goal of survival.

Victor must have felt it too, because despite the grim uncertainty of the news and the future threat of scarcity, the meal he'd prepared was a feast. We ate Japanese-style, sitting on cushions around the coffee table, the television turned down low behind us. There was duck cooked with apricots and raspberries, and salad with pomegranate seeds. He turned off the lights, lit candles, and opened a bottle of wine from the region where his family comes from in Languedoc. I told him about the scene at the distribution center. He stopped eating and stared at me the way he used to when I was a student and would sit in his office scratching my bare knees. In the middle of a sentence he leaned across the corner of the table and kissed me. His tongue was in my mouth, and he slipped his hand under my bra. When I pushed my hand against his jeans, he groaned and rolled on top of me. He unbuckled his belt and then I inhaled sharply. We clawed at each other's clothes, and I felt my spine crack and my ribs pressing into the floorboards.

We ate dessert flushed and damp with sweat. It had been a long time since we'd done something like that. Despite Victor's interest in the passion of the Middle Ages, his campaign in favor of friction and conflict, even he would have had to admit that our own relationship was closer to the stable average of which he was so critical. We'd been living together for five years, and our days and nights had taken on a certain familiar order dictated by my hours at the museum, Victor's at the university, and the great, silent country of hours that Victor spent at work in his study.

The candles were burning deep, their centers already liquid. Victor shared out what was left of the wine into our glasses, and even though I was already feeling a little tipsy, I swallowed mine down in a couple of gulps. We turned up the news again and listened, but there wasn't any new information, just the same images, over and over, of people trying on gas masks and walking around with them as if they were testing the feel of new shoes. Neither of us was tired, or maybe we didn't want the evening to end, didn't want to go to sleep and wake up to whatever the world would bring us tomorrow, so we decided to play a game of Scrabble. Victor is obsessed with the game and must know every three-letter word in the language. It helps that his English is impeccable. My ear is so used to his accent that there are times when I almost forget that most of Victor's life took place in another idiom, with different expressions for pleasure and pain, in sentences to me foreign and incomprehensible. Sometimes I come across Victor exclaiming aloud to himself in French, and I am reminded of this other life, for a moment thrown off guard, and forced to add a third, secret Victor to the Victors I already know.

While Victor went to get the Scrabble board I cleared our plates, piling them in the sink with the dirty pots and pans in which the remains of our dinner were already congealing. The sight of them gave me a vague nauseated feeling. On the way back to the living room I passed the boxes with our gas masks where I'd left them sitting by the door. I picked them up and carried them over to the sofa, one under each arm, and while Victor was setting up the board I opened one and pulled the mask out of the wrapping.

"Look," I said, holding it up.

"Let me see," Victor said. He turned it over in his hands and examined it. He pulled the bands back and slipped it over his face, then turned and regarded me calmly through the clear plastic lenses. He looked ugly and menacing, a strange creature I'd never seen before who was Victor nonetheless, and I felt a flash of anger rise to my cheeks. Without thinking, I leaned forward and blasted each eyehole with a shot of breath. For a moment neither of us moved. Victor continued to sit in silence, and I watched as the clouds of breath slowly evaporated, revealing the distant, dull stars of his eyes.

"Take it off," I demanded. Victor was motionless, as if the mask had made him demented. "I said, take it *off.*" My heart was beating fast. I was about to wrestle it off him, but before I could do anything he slipped it from his face and laid it on the floor.

"It stinks of rubber," he said. Then he happily went about choosing his seven letters. I watched his face in silence, surprised at myself.

Victor put down *lemur* for the first word, to which I added *nut,* and then Victor did *geek* and I did *guns.* Everything was fine for a while, the little crux of wooden letters expanding like some kind of self-multiplying message, garbled at first, but, if you looked carefully enough using the right decoder, possessing its own intelligence, its subtle eloquence, *neck* sprouting from *geek,* and *tongue* from *neck,* like some kind of confused desire trapped in the language with nothing to do but try desperately to spell its want. Maybe it was just the wine, but as we played I started to think that if we tried hard enough, we could figure out what it was that we were trying to say to each other after all these years, and then he put down *positron* and all of a sudden I realized that I wanted to tell Victor that I was thinking of leaving him.

Victor won, as he often does, and as he was dumping the letters back into the drawstringed pouch I began to cry. At first he didn't notice, but at last he glanced up, and a look of surprise crossed his face.

"It's only a game," he said.

I tried to smile and shook my head. I wanted to tell him about what I'd realized about the Arbus photographs, about the old woman in a wheelchair who lifted a witch's mask to her face when the shutter clicked, maybe to protect herself from the photographer's acute gaze, or to send back to Arbus an image of herself, or to throw a wrench into the eternal chain of reflections between two people who gaze upon each other and see, in the stranger looking back, a startling image of themselves. But I said nothing. Victor kneeled in front of me and wiped a tear from my cheek.

"It's okay."

"I'm scared," I whispered.

"It happens," Victor said, taking me in his arms. "A necessary scourge, natural or manmade, that comes through periodically to control the population."

I looked up at him. I knew he thought that I was frightened of whatever it was that we were waiting to hear news of, the thing that might threaten the very air we breathed and the life we'd grown used to. And maybe I was. Or maybe I was just tired and drunk, fed up with the argument in my head — for or against a life with Victor — that all this time later was still unclear. It was already midnight. The glasses smeared with fingerprints were still on the table, holding the last few drops of wine from the place Victor might have come from had his father not moved to Paris to become a doctor, beginning the chain of events that would lead to Victor's childhood spent in the shadow of L'Hôpital Saint-Vincent-de-Paul, his youthful interest in plagues and infectious diseases, his passion for the Middle Ages, his teaching job in America, and, finally, me. One of the candles sputtered and went out, and Victor leaned away from me and blew out the other. He lay on the rug and pulled me down next to him, and we held each other in the blue glow of the television.

And then we fell asleep, sprawled there among the Scrabble letters and the empty wineglasses, and when I woke up again the sky outside was already starting to lighten. My right hand had fallen asleep, and when I touched it with the fingers of the left the sensation was chilling. I untangled myself from Victor and shook it until

the feeling came back. I had a headache and my mouth was dry, so
I got up to get some water from the kitchen. When I came back the
television was mutely flickering, and in its light I saw the gas mask
lying on its side by Victor's face. I picked it up and turned it over,
and then I slipped it over my face. It was snug inside, safe like a
catcher's mask, and I lay down on my back, blinking up through
the eyeholes. I wondered how long it would be until we would
know what it was we were going to need to learn to protect ourselves from, or if it was too late, if the only ones who would survive
were those who had been training all the while, with reflective
clothing and superior lungs. Maybe whatever it was had already
seeped through the cracks of the windows and under the door. But
I was drowsy and too tired to object. Without turning to look, I
moved my hand until my fingertips touched Victor's cheek. Then I
closed my eyes to wait, grateful for what was left of the dark.

The next morning was Saturday, and we woke up to the news that
the whole thing had been some sort of test. Victor perched on the
edge of the couch, his hair sticking up at a strange angle as if he
had fought through a windstorm to make it through to daybreak.
He held the coffee mug between his hands and took little sips, his
gaze fixed on the television. After I got out of the shower I sat down
next to him. The mayor was giving a press conference, explaining
how they'd wanted to make certain that the city was prepared. We
were instructed to keep the masks in a safe and dry place where we
would be able to find them easily. He apologized for any inconvenience or unnecessary fright the test had caused anyone, thanked all
of the volunteers, and congratulated the city for the admirable way
it had performed in test conditions. When the reporters began to
bark out questions, I went to the kitchen to pour myself some coffee, and when I switched on the radio the mayor's answers echoed
through the apartment in an eerie duet.

It had snowed during the night, and Victor and I decided to take
a walk together. It had been a long time since we'd done that, almost as long as since we'd last interrupted dinner to screw each
other on the living room floor. It was cold, so we bundled up in hats
and scarves, and Victor wore the red wool mittens I'd knitted for
him when that was something I did. I wore a pair of gloves that were
frayed at the thumb, and when we stopped to wait for the light to
change, Victor lifted my thumb to his mouth like a horn and blew

hot air through the hole. On the way to the park, we passed some-one — it was impossible to tell if it was a man or a woman — with a gas mask on. Maybe it was a joke, or maybe the person didn't trust the mayor, or maybe he or she had simply gotten used to wearing it, had grown to like it, in fact, and was reluctant to part with it now and go back to walking around with a naked face, exposed to everything.

In the park, the snow crunched under our feet. The sun had come out and reflected brightly off everything. Victor made a snowball and threw it at a tree, and when it hit, it exploded in a blast of white. I kept slipping because my shoes didn't have any treads, but Victor held my arm so that I wouldn't fall. There were some kids running around with a dog in the snow, and Victor laughed out loud as he watched.

I thought about that day some weeks later when I did one of those home tests and found out that I was pregnant. I did it twice because the first time the pink line showed up in the box I couldn't believe it, even though I'm never late. For a few days I didn't tell Victor. I went to work and did the tours with the knowledge that in me something tiny was growing — a human insistence — steadily growing until the day it would finally make its way out into the world to tell us what all this time we had been without. A small be-ing with a clear argument. Perhaps there was a time during those days while I carried around that secret, a small window of opportu-nity. But it never occurred to me not to keep the baby. During the long months of my pregnancy, before I became too big to walk as far as the park, I often stood outside the fence and watched the runners on the track. I possessed the unreasonable hope that if I watched them enough, the child might be born into their race, not mine.

ADAM HASLETT

Devotion

FROM THE YALE REVIEW

THROUGH THE OPEN French doors, Owen surveyed the garden. The day was hot for June, a pale sun burning in a cloudless sky, wilting the last of the irises, the rhododendron blossoms drooping. A breeze moved through the laburnum trees, carrying a sheet of the Sunday paper into the rose border. Mrs. Giles's collie yapped on the other side of the hedge. With his handkerchief, Owen wiped sweat from the back of his neck.

His sister, Hillary, stood at the counter sorting strawberries. She'd nearly finished the dinner preparations, though Ben wouldn't arrive for hours yet. She wore a beige linen dress he'd never seen on her before. Her black-and-gray hair, usually kept up in a bun, hung down to her shoulders. For a woman in her midfifties, she had a slender, graceful figure.

"You're awfully dressed up," he said.

"The wine," she said. "Why don't you open a bottle of the red? And we'll need the tray from the dining room."

"We're using the silver, are we?"

"Yes, I thought we would."

"We didn't use the silver at Christmas."

He watched Hillary dig for something in the fridge.

"It should be on the right under the carving dish," she said.

Raising himself from the chair, Owen walked through into the dining room. From the sideboard he removed the familiar gravy boats and serving dishes until he found the tarnished platter. The china and silver had come from their parents' when their father died, along with the side tables and sitting chairs and the pictures on the walls.

"It'd take an hour to clean this," he called into the kitchen.

"There's polish in the cabinet."

"We've *five* perfectly good trays in the cupboard."

"It's behind the drink, on the left."

He gritted his teeth. She could be so bloody imperious.

"This is some production," he muttered, seated again at the kitchen table. He daubed a cloth in polish and drew it over the smooth metal. They weren't in the habit of having people in to dinner. Aunt Philippa from Shropshire, their mother's sister, usually came at Christmas and stayed three or four nights. Now and again Hillary had Miriam Franks, one of her fellow teachers from the comprehensive, in on a Sunday. They'd have coffee in the living room afterward and talk about the students. Occasionally they'd go out if a new restaurant opened on the High Street, but they'd never been gourmets. Most of Owen's partners at the firm had professed to discover wine at a certain age and now took their holidays in Italy. He and Hillary rented a cottage in the Lake District the last two weeks of August. They had been going for years and were perfectly happy with it. A nice little stone house that caught all the afternoon light and had a view of Lake Windermere.

He pressed the cloth harder onto the tray, rubbing at the tarnished corners. Years ago he'd gone to dinners, up in Knightsbridge and Mayfair. Richard Stallybrass, an art dealer, gave private gentlemen's parties, as he called them, at his flat on Belgrave Place. All very civilized. Solicitors, journalists, the odd duke or MP, there with the implicit and, in the 1970s, safe assumption that nothing would be said. Half of them had wives and children. Saul Thompson, an old friend from school, had introduced Owen to this little world, and for several years Owen had been quite taken with it. He'd looked at flats in central London, encouraged by Saul to leave the suburbs and enjoy the pleasures of the city.

But there had always been Hillary and this house. She and Owen had lost their mother when they were young, and it had driven them closer than many siblings were. He couldn't see himself leaving her here in Wimbledon. The idea of his sister's loneliness haunted him. One year to the next he'd put off his plans to move.

Then Saul was dead, one of the first to be claimed by the epidemic. A year later Richard Stallybrass died. Owen's connection to the gay life had always been tenuous. AIDS severed it. His work for the firm went on, work he enjoyed. And despite what an observer might assume, he hadn't been miserable. Not every fate was alike. Not everyone ended up paired off in love.

"The wine, Owen? Aren't you going to open it?"

But then he'd met Ben, and things had changed.

"Sorry?" he said.

"The wine. It's on the sideboard."

Hillary held a glass to the light, checking for smudges.

"We're certainly pulling out all the stops," he said. When she made no reply, he continued. "Believe it or not, I commented on your dress earlier, but you didn't hear me. I haven't seen that one before. Have you been shopping?"

"You didn't comment on my dress, Owen. You said I was awfully dressed up."

She looked out the window over the kitchen sink. They both watched another sheet of the *Sunday Times* tumble gently into the flowerbeds.

"I thought we'd have our salad outside," she said. "Ben might like to see the garden."

Standing in stocking feet before the open door of his wardrobe, Owen pushed aside the row of gray pinstripe suits, looking for a green summer blazer he remembered wearing the year before to a garden party the firm had given out in Surrey. Brushing the dust off the shoulders, he put it on over his white shirt.

On the shelf above the suits was a boater hat — he couldn't imagine what he'd worn that to — and just behind it, barely visible, the shoebox. He paused a moment, staring at the corner of it. Ben would be here in a few hours. His first visit since he'd gone back to the States, fifteen years ago. Why now? Owen had asked himself all weekend.

"I'll be over for a conference," he'd said when Owen took the call Thursday. And yet he could so easily have come and gone from London with no word to them.

As he had each of the last three nights, Owen reached behind the boater hat and took down the shoebox. Fourteen years it had sat there untouched. Now the dust on the lid showed his fingerprints again. He listened for the sound of Hillary downstairs, then crossed the room and closed the door. Perching on the edge of the side chair, he removed the lid of the box and unfolded the last of the four letters.

November 4, 1985
Boston

Dear Hillary,

It's awkward writing when I haven't heard back from my other letters. I suppose I'll get the message soon enough. Right now I'm still bewildered. My only thought is you've decided my leaving was my own choice and not the *Globe*'s, that I have no intention of trying to get back there. I'm not sure what more I can say to convince you. I've told my editor I'll give him six months to get me reassigned to London or I'm quitting. I've been talking to people there, trying to see what might be available. It would be a lot easier if I thought this all had some purpose.

I know things got started late, that we didn't have much time before I had to leave. Owen kept you a secret for too long. But for me those were great months. I feel like a romantic clown to say I live on the memory of them, but it's not altogether untrue. I can't settle here again. I feel like I'm on a leash, everything so depressingly familiar. I'm tempted to write out all my recollections of our weekends, our evenings together, just so I can linger on them a bit more, but that would be maudlin, and you wouldn't like that — which is, of course, why I love you.

If this is over, for heaven's sake just let me know.

Yours,
Ben

Owen slid the paper back into its envelope and replaced it in the box on his lap. Dust floated in the light by the window. The rectangle of sun on the floor crept over the red pile carpet.

For most of his life he'd hated Sundays. Their gnawing stillness, the faint memories of religion. A day loneliness won. But in these last years that quiet little dread had faded. He and Hillary made a point of cooking a big breakfast and taking a walk on the common afterward. In winter they read the paper together by the fire in the front room and often walked into the town for a film in the evening. In spring and summer they spent hours in the garden. They weren't unhappy people.

From the pack on his bedside table he took a cigarette. He rolled it idly between thumb and forefinger. Would it be taken away, this life of theirs? Was Ben coming here for an answer?

He smoked the cigarette down to the filter, then returned the shoebox to its shelf and closed the door of his wardrobe. Ben was married now, had two children. That's what he'd said on the phone; they'd spoken only a minute or two. Did he still wonder why he'd never heard?

Through the window Owen could see his sister clearing their tea mugs from the garden table. There had been other men she'd gone out to dinner with over the years. A Mr. Kreske, the divorced father of a sixth-form student, who'd driven down from Putney. The maths teacher, Mr. Hamilton, had taken her to several plays in the city before returning to Scotland. Owen had tried to say encouraging things about these evenings of hers, but then the tone of her voice had always made it clear that that's all they were, evenings.

In the kitchen, Hillary stood by the sink, arranging roses in a vase.

"I see you made up the guest room," he said.

She looked directly at him, failing to register the comment. He could tell she was trying to remember something. They did that: rested their eyes on each other in moments of distraction, as you might stare at a ring on your finger.

"The guest bed. You made it up."

"Oh, yes. I did," she said, drawn back into the room. "I thought if dinner goes late and he doesn't feel like taking a train . . ."

"Of course."

Sitting again at the table, Owen picked up the tray. In it he could see his reflection, his graying hair. What would Ben look like now? he wondered.

"Chives," she said. "I forgot the chives."

They'd met through the firm, of all places. The *Globe* had Ben working on a story about differences between British and American lawyers. They went to lunch and somehow the conversation wandered. "You ask all sorts of questions," Owen could remember saying to him. And it was true. Ben had no hesitation about inquiring into Owen's private life, where he lived, how he spent his time. All in the most guileless manner, as though such questions were part of his beat.

"I hope he hasn't become allergic to anything," Hillary said, setting the chives down on the cutting board.

Though Ben had been in London nearly a year, he hadn't seen much of the place. Owen offered himself as a guide. On weekends they traveled up to Hampstead or Camden Town, or out to the East End, taking long walks, getting lunch along the way. They talked about all sorts of things. It turned out Ben too had lost a parent at a young age. When Owen heard that, he understood why he'd been drawn to Ben: he seemed to comprehend a certain register of sadness intuitively. Other than Hillary, Owen had never spoken to anyone about the death of his mother.

"I come up with lots of analogies for it," he could remember Ben saying. "Like I was burned and can't feel anything again until the flame gets that hot. Or like people's lives are over and I'm just wandering through an abandoned house. None of them really work. But you have to think the problem somehow."

Not the sort of conversation Owen had with colleagues at the office.

He picked up the cloth and wiped it again over the reflective center of the tray. Owen and his sister were so alike. Everyone said that. From the clipped tone of their voices, their gestures, right down into the byways of thought, the way they considered before speaking, said only what was needed. That she too had been attracted to Ben made perfect sense.

Hillary crossed the room and stood with her hands on Owen's shoulders. He could feel the warmth of her palms through his cotton blazer. Unusual, this: the two of them touching.

"It'll be curious, won't it?" she said. "To see him so briefly after all this time."

"Yes."

Twenty-five years ago he and Hillary had moved into this house together. They'd thought of it as a temporary arrangement. Hillary was doing her student teaching; he'd just started with the firm and had yet to settle on a place. It seemed like the beginning of something.

"I suppose his wife couldn't come because of the children." Her thumbs rested against his collar.

She was the only person who knew of his preference for men, now that Saul and the others were gone. She'd never judged him, never raised an eyebrow.

"Interesting he should get in touch after such a gap," Owen said.

She removed her hands from his shoulders. "It strikes you as odd, does it?"

"A bit."

"I think it's thoughtful of him," she said.

"Indeed."

In the front hall, the doorbell rang.

"Goodness," Hillary said, "he's awfully early."

He listened to her footsteps as she left the room, listened as they stopped in front of the hall mirror.

"I've been with a man once myself," Ben had said on the night Owen finally spoke to him of his feelings. Like a prayer answered, those words were. Was it such a crime he'd fallen in love?

A few more steps and then the turning of the latch.

"Oh," he heard his sister say. "Mrs. Giles. Hello."

Owen closed his eyes, relieved for the moment. Her son lived in Australia; she'd been widowed the year before. After that she'd begun stopping by on the weekends, first with the excuse of borrowing a cup of something but later just for the company.

"You're doing all right in the heat, are you?" she asked.

"Yes, we're managing," Hillary said.

Owen joined them in the hall. He could tell from the look on his sister's face she was trying to steel her courage to say they had company on the way.

"Hello there, Owen," Mrs. Giles said. "Saw your firm in the paper today."

"Did you?"

"Yes, something about the law courts. There's always news of the courts. So much of it on the telly now. Old Rumpole."

"Right," he said.

"Well . . . I was just on my way by . . . but you're occupied, I'm sure."

"No, no," Hillary said, glancing at Owen. "Someone's coming later . . . but I was just putting a kettle on."

"Really, you don't have to," Mrs. Giles said.

"Not at all."

They sat in the front room, Hillary glancing now and again at her watch. A production of *Les Misérables* had reached Perth, and Peter Giles had a leading role.

"Amazing story, don't you think?" Mrs. Giles said, sipping her tea.

The air in the room was close, and Owen could feel sweat soaking the back of his shirt.

"Peter plays opposite an Australian girl. Can't quite imagine it done in that accent, but there we are. I sense he's fond of her, though he doesn't admit it in his letters."

By the portrait of their parents over the mantel, a fly buzzed. Owen sat motionless on the couch, staring over Mrs. Giles's shoulder.

His sister had always been an early riser. Up at five-thirty or six for breakfast and to prepare for class. At seven-thirty she'd leave the house in time for morning assembly. As a partner, he never had to be at the firm until well after nine. He read the *Financial Times* with his coffee and looked over whatever had come in the post. There had been no elaborate operation, no fretting over things. A circumstance had presented itself. The letters from Ben arrived. He took them up to his room. That's all there was to it.

"More tea?"

"No, thank you," Owen said.

The local council had decided on a one-way system for the town center, and Mrs. Giles believed it would only make things worse. "They've done it down in Winchester. My sister says it's a terrible mess."

"Right," Owen said.

They had kissed only once, in the small hours of an August night, on the sofa in Ben's flat, light from the streetlamps coming through the high windows. Earlier, strolling back over the bridge from Battersea, Owen had told him the story of him and Hillary being sent to look for their mother: walking out across the fields to a wood where she sometimes went in the mornings; the rain starting up and soaking them before they arrived under the canopy of oaks, and looked up to see their mother's slender frame wrapped in her beige overcoat, her face lifeless, her body turning in the wind. And he'd told Ben how his sister — twelve years old — had taken him in her arms right then and there, sheltering his eyes from the awful sight, and whispered in his ear, "We will survive this, we will survive this." A story he'd never told anyone before. And when he and Ben had finished another bottle of wine, reclining there on the sofa, they'd hugged, and then they'd kissed, their hands running through each other's hair.

"I can't do this," Ben had whispered as Owen rested his head against Ben's chest.

"Smells wonderful, whatever it is you're cooking," Mrs. Giles said. Hillary nodded.

For that moment before Ben had spoken, as he lay in his arms, Owen had believed in the fantasy of love as the creator, your life clay in its hands.

"I should check the food. Owen, why don't you show Mrs. Giles a bit of the garden. She hasn't seen the delphiniums, I'm sure."

"Of course," he said, looking into his sister's taut smile.

"I suspect I've mistreated my garden," Mrs. Giles said as the two of them reached the bottom of the lawn. "John it was who had the green thumb. I'm just a bungler really."

The skin of her hands was mottled and soft-looking. The gold ring she still wore hung rather loosely on her finger.

"I think Ben and I might have a weekend away," Hillary had said one evening in the front room as they watched the evening news. The two of them had only met a few weeks before. An accident really, Hillary in the city on an errand, coming to drop something by for Owen, deciding at the last minute to join them for dinner. When the office phoned the restaurant in the middle of the meal, Owen had to leave the two of them alone.

A weekend at the cottage on Lake Windermere is what they had.

Owen had always thought of himself as a rational person, capable of perspective. As a schoolboy, he'd read *Othello*. *O, beware, my lord, of jealousy! It is the green-eyed monster, which doth mock the meat it feeds on.* What paltry aid literature turned out to be when the feelings were yours and not others'.

"Funny, I miss him in the most peculiar ways," Mrs. Giles said. "We'd always kept the chutney over the stove, and as we only ever had it in the evenings, he'd be there to fetch it. Ridiculous to use a stepladder for the chutney, if you think about it. Does just as well on the counter."

"Yes," Owen said.

They stared together into the blue flowers.

"I expect it won't be long before I join him," she said.

"No, you're in fine shape, surely."

"Doesn't upset me — the idea. It used to, but not anymore. I've been very lucky. He was a good person."

Owen could hear the telephone ringing in the house.

"Could you get that?" Hillary called from the kitchen.

"I apologize, I —"

"No, please, carry on," Mrs. Giles said.

He left her there and, passing through the dining room, crossed the hall to the phone.

"Owen, it's Ben Hansen."

"Ben."

"Look, I feel terrible about this, but I'm not going to be able to make it out there tonight."

"Oh."

"Yeah, the meetings are running late here and I'm supposed to give this talk, it's all been pushed back. Horrible timing, I'm afraid."

Owen could hear his sister closing the oven door, the water coming on in the sink.

"I'm sorry about that. It's a great pity. I know Hillary was looking forward to seeing you. We both were."

"I was looking forward to it myself, I really was," he said. "Have you been well?"

Owen laughed. "Me? Yes. I've been fine. Everything's very much the same on this end . . . It does seem awfully long ago you were here."

For a moment, neither of them spoke.

Standing there in the hall, Owen felt a sudden longing. He imagined Ben as he often saw him in his mind's eye, tall and thin, half a step ahead on the Battersea Bridge, hands scrunched into his pockets. And he pictured the men he sometimes saw holding hands in Soho or Piccadilly. In June, perhaps on this very Sunday, thousands marched. He wanted to tell Ben what it felt like to pass two men on the street like that, how he had always in a sense been afraid.

"You're still with the firm?"

"Yes," Owen said. "That's right." And he wanted to say how frightened he'd been watching his friend Saul's ravaged body die, how the specter of disease had made him timid. How he, Ben, had seemed a refuge.

"And with you, things have been well?"

He listened as Ben described his life — columnist now for the paper, the children beginning school; he heard the easy, slightly weary tone in his voice — a parent's fatigue. And he wondered how Ben remembered them. Were Hillary and Owen Simpson just two people he'd met on a year abroad ages ago? Had he been coming here for answers, or did he just have a free evening and a curiosity about what had become of them?

What did it matter now? There would be no revelation tonight. He was safe again.

"Might you be back over at some point?" he asked. He sensed their conversation about to end and felt on the edge of panic.

"Definitely. It's one of the things I wanted to ask you about. Judy and I were thinking of bringing the kids — maybe next summer — and I remembered you rented that place up north. Is there a person to call about getting one of those?"

"The cottages? . . . Yes, of course."

"Yeah, that would be great. I'll try to give you a call when we're ready to firm up some plans."

"And Judy? She's well?"

"Sure, she's heard all about you, wants to meet you both sometime."

"That would be terrific," Owen said, the longing there again.

"Ben?"

"Yes?"

"Who is it?" Hillary asked, stepping into the hall, drying her hands with a dishcloth. A red amulet their mother had worn hung round her neck, resting against the front of her linen dress.

"Ben," he mouthed.

Her face stiffened slightly.

"Hillary's just here," he said into the phone. "Why don't you have a word?" He held the receiver out to her.

"He can't make it."

"Is that right?" she said, staring straight through him. She took the phone. Owen walked back into the dining room; by the sideboard, he paused.

"No, no, don't be silly," he heard his sister say. "It's quite all right."

"A beautiful evening, isn't it?" Mrs. Giles said as he stepped back onto the terrace. The air was mild now, the sun beginning to shade into the trees. Clouds like distant mountains had appeared on the horizon.

"Yes," he said, imagining the evening view of the lake from the garden of their cottage, the way they checked the progress of the days by which dip in the hills the sun disappeared behind.

Mrs. Giles stood from the bench. "I should be getting along."

He walked her down the side of the house and out the gate.

Though the sky was still bright, the streetlamps had begun to flicker on. Farther up the street a neighbor watered her lawn.

"Thank you for the tea."

"Not at all," he said.

"It wasn't bad news just now, I hope."

"No, no," he said. "Just a friend calling."

"That's good, then." She hesitated by the low brick wall that separated their front gardens. "Owen, there was just one thing I wanted to mention. In my sitting room, the desk over in the corner, in the top drawer there. I've put a letter in. You understand. I wanted to make sure someone would know where to look. Nothing to worry about, of course, nothing dramatic . . . but in the event . . . you see?"

He nodded, and she smiled back at him, her eyes beginning to water. Owen watched her small figure as she turned and passed through her gate, up the steps, and into her house.

He stayed awhile on the sidewalk, gazing onto the common: the expanse of lawn, white goalposts on the football pitch set against the trees. A long shadow, cast by their house and the others along this bit of street, fell over the playing field. He watched it stretching slowly to the chestnut trees, the darkness slowly climbing their trunks, beginning to shade the leaves of the lower branches.

In the house, he found Hillary at the kitchen table, hands folded in her lap. She sat perfectly still, staring into the garden. For a few minutes they remained like that, Owen at the counter, neither of them saying a word. Then his sister got up and, passing him as though he weren't there, opened the oven door.

"Right," she said. "It's done."

They ate in the dining room, in the fading light, with the silver and the crystal. Roses, pink and white, stood in a vase at the center of the table. As the plates were already out, Hillary served her chicken marsala on their mother's china. The candles remained unlit in the silver candlesticks.

"He'll be over again," Owen said. Hillary nodded. They finished their dinner in silence. Afterward, neither had the appetite for the strawberries set out on the polished tray.

"I'll do these," he said when they'd stacked the dishes on the counter. He squeezed the green liquid detergent into the baking dish and watched it fill with water. "I could pour you a brandy if you like," he said over his shoulder. But when he turned, he saw his sister had left the room.

He rinsed the bowls and plates and arranged them neatly in the rows of the dishwasher. Under the warm running water, he sponged the wineglasses clean and set them to dry on the rack. When he'd finished, he turned the taps off, and then the kitchen was quiet.

He poured himself a scotch and took a seat at the table. The door to the garden had been left open, and in the shadows he could make out the azalea bush and the cluster of rhododendron. Up the lane from where they'd lived as children, there was a manor with elaborate gardens and a moat around the house. An old woman they called Mrs. Montague lived there, and she let them play on the rolling lawns and in the labyrinth of the topiary hedge. They would play for hours in the summer, chasing each other along the embankments, pretending to fish in the moat with a stick and string. He won their games of hide-and-go-seek because he never closed his eyes completely, and could see which way she ran. He could still remember the peculiar anger and frustration he used to feel after he followed her to her hiding place and tapped her on the head. He imagined that garden now, the blossoms of its flowers drinking in the cooler night air, the branches of its trees rejuvenating in the darkness.

From the front room, he heard a small sound — a moan let out in little breaths — and realized it was the sound of his sister crying.

He had ruined her life. He knew that now in a way he'd always tried not to know it — with certainty. For years he'd allowed himself to imagine she had forgotten Ben, or at least stopped remembering. He stood up from the table and crossed the room but stopped at the entrance to the hall. What consolation could he give her now?

Standing there, listening to her tears, he remembered the last time he'd heard them, so long ago it seemed like the memory of a former life: a summer morning when she'd returned from university, and they'd walked together over the fields in a brilliant sunshine and come to the oak trees, their green leaves shining, their branches heavy with acorns. She'd wept then for the first time in all the years since their mother had taken herself away. And Owen had been there to comfort her — his turn at last, after all she had done to protect him.

At the sound of his footsteps entering the hall, Hillary went quiet. He stopped again by the door to the front room. Sitting at the breakfast table, reading those letters from America, it wasn't only Ben's affection he'd envied. Being replaced. That was the fear. The one he'd been too weak to master.

Holding on to the banister, he slowly climbed the stairs, his feet pressing against the worn patches of the carpet. They might live in this silence the rest of their lives, he thought.

In his room, he walked to the window and looked again over the common.

When they were little they'd gone to the village on Sundays to hear the minister talk. Of charity and sacrifice. A Norman church with hollows worked into the stones of the floor by centuries of parishioners. He could still hear the congregation singing, *Bring me my bow of burning gold! Bring me my arrows of desire!* Their mother had sung with them. Plaintive voices rising. *And did those feet in ancient time walk upon England's mountains green?* Owen could remember wanting to believe something about it all, if not the words of the Book, perhaps the sorrow he heard in the music, the longing of people's song. He hadn't been in a church since his mother's funeral. Over the years, views from the train or the sight of this common in evening had become his religion, absorbing the impulse to imagine larger things.

Looking over it now, he wondered at the neutrality of the grass and the trees and the houses beyond, how in their stillness they neither judged nor forgave. He stared across the playing field a moment longer. And then, calmly, he crossed to the wardrobe and took down the box.

Sitting in the front room, Hillary heard her brother's footsteps overhead and then the sound of his door closing. Her tears had dried and she felt a stony kind of calm, gazing into the wing chair opposite — an old piece of their parents' furniture. Threads showed at the armrests, and along the front edge the ticking had come loose. At first they'd meant to get rid of so many things, the faded rugs, the heavy felt curtains, but their parents' possessions had settled in the house, and then there seemed no point.

In the supermarket checkout line, she sometimes glanced at the cover of a decor magazine, a sunny room with blond wood floors, bright solid colors, a white sheet on a white bed. The longing for it usually lasted only a moment. She knew she'd be a foreigner in such a room.

She sipped the last of her wine and put the glass down on the coffee table. Darkness had fallen now, and in the window she saw the reflection of the lamp and the mantel and the bookcase.

"Funny, isn't it? How it happens." That's all her friend Miriam Franks would ever say if the conversation turned onto the topic of why neither of them had married. Hillary would nod and recall one of the evenings she'd spent with Ben up at the cottage, sitting in the garden, talking of Owen, thinking to herself she could only ever be with someone who understood her brother as well as Ben did.

She switched off the light in the front room and walked to the kitchen. Owen had wiped down the counters, set everything back in its place. For a moment, she thought she might cry again. Her brother had led such a cramped life, losing his friends, scared of what people might know. She'd loved him so fiercely all these years, the fears and hindrances had felt like her own. What good, then, had her love been? she wondered as she pulled the French doors shut.

Upstairs, Owen's light was still on, but she didn't knock or say goodnight as she usually did. Across the hall in her own room, she closed the door behind her. The little stack of letters lay on her bed. Years ago she had read them, after rummaging for a box at Christmastime. Ben was married by then, as she'd found out when she called. Her anger had lasted a season or two, but she had held her tongue, remembering the chances Owen had to leave her and how he never had.

Standing over the bed now, looking down at the pale blue envelopes, she was glad her brother had let go of them at last. Tomorrow they would have supper in the kitchen. He would offer to leave this house, and she would tell him that was the last thing she wanted.

Putting the letters aside, she undressed. When she'd climbed into bed, she reached up and turned the switch of her bedside lamp. For an instant, lying in the sudden darkness, she felt herself there again in the woods, covering her brother's eyes as she gazed up into the giant oak.

RYAN HARTY

Why the Sky Turns Red
When the Sun Goes Down

FROM TIN HOUSE

I GET THE CALL as my wife is setting the table for dinner. It's our neighbor Ben Hildeman, who tells me in a breathless voice that my son has had a problem.

"This is bad, Mike," Ben says, and in the background I hear his boys, Tanner and Phillip, talking in excited tones. "He fell and hurt his leg, is I guess what happened, but then he just sort of lost control. By the time I got there he was in the Kohlers' yard, banging his head against their air-conditioning unit."

"God, you're kidding," I say.

"I'm afraid it's pretty bad, Mike. Some of the kids are upset now. I wish you'd come down."

"I'll be right there," I say, and hang up the phone.

Dana comes into the doorway with a bunch of utensils in her hand. "It's not about Cole?" she says, but she can see in my face that it is. "You should go, Mike. Hurry."

Running down Keehouatupa, past the subterranean houses, I'm hoping that whatever happened to Cole will have nothing to do with the trouble we had in Portland. I know Dana is thinking the same thing back at the house. We came to Arizona at the height of the D3 crisis, with high hopes that the desert air would be good for Cole. Amazingly, in the seven months we've been here he's had not a single problem — no shutdown or twitching hands, no problems with speech or movement. We've only just begun to believe that things might be all right again.

Ben's house comes into view, a newly built subterranean with smoke-tinted skylights, a couple of date palms shimmering in the day's waning heat. Ben stands atop the grassy dome, a stocky man in jeans. Behind him are the red peaks of the Superstition Mountains. A half-dozen boys in shorts and tank tops stand at his side. Cole, I see, is not among them.

Ben jogs down and puts a hand on my shoulder. "I didn't want to touch him, Mike," he says. "He's around the back now. I think he might be unconscious."

"That's good, actually. It means he's in shutdown."

We climb the hill. From the top I see Cole lying belly down on the back slope, his legs splayed out behind him. He *is* in shutdown — there's that stillness about him — and I'm relieved to see it, though it's clear he's in horrible shape. His neck has twisted around so far that his chin seems to rest in the shallow valley between his shoulder blades. His right arm has come off completely and lies, bent at the elbow, a few yards away, multicolored wires curling out of the torn end. I get a lightheaded feeling and have to crouch for a moment and catch my breath.

"You all right?" Ben asks.

"I'll be okay."

"He just — " Ben gives me a squint-eyed look. "It's hard to describe it, Mike. It was crazy."

"So all this happened when he fell? The arm and everything?"

"That's what I was saying." He jerks a thumb at a metal box at the edge of the Kohlers' yard. "When I came out he was just banging against that thing like he wanted to knock it down or something. He made an electrical noise in his throat, sort of, a whirring sound."

I glance at the boys, who are all studying me carefully — six boys in a line on the hill.

"Everybody all right?"

They nod.

"I asked them to go home, but they wouldn't go," Ben says. "They're worried about their friend."

"Sure," I say. "Well, listen, guys, Cole's gonna be all right, you hear me?"

They nod again and glance at one another. These are good kids, all of them — Ben's son Tanner and our next-door neighbor Sean

Ho, and a Devin something whose parents I've met a few times. One of them, a red-haired boy I haven't seen before, looks as though he might be D3 himself; his skin seems to reflect the sun a little more directly than the other boys'. He holds his shoulders unusually straight. Most people can't see the difference, but D3 parents can more often than not. This kid looks as stunned as the rest of them.

I walk down the grassy slope and kneel beside Cole. His eyes are wide open and staring at nothing, and that's something I hate to see. I lay a hand on each of his cheeks, turn his head to the side, and feel a pop — things seem looser inside him than they should be. I brush his bangs from his forehead, roll him to his back, and slip a hand under his T-shirt, feeling for the power button. I give it a push.

Cole's head jerks just slightly. His eyes change, almost imperceptibly, as if the dimmest light has gone on behind them. It's enough, though: he looks like my son again.

"Hey, buddy," I say.

He blinks at me. "Hey, Dad. What are you doing here?"

"I came to take you home."

He glances around, and I see the disappointment in his eyes, the look of understanding. "I had an accident," he says.

"I'm afraid so, kid. Do you remember what happened?"

"We were playing kick the can," he says, and draws his lips in, concentrating. "I was running, I think. I had a bad headache. I don't remember anything else."

I'm relieved he's come out of it alert and lucid, much better than at times in the past. During the bad period in Portland there were always problems upon switchback — inability to focus, slowed-down speech and movement.

"So listen, there are a few things I need to tell you," I say. "Things you may not want to hear." I help him to a sitting position, a hand at the small of his back. "For one thing, your arm's come off."

He touches his shoulder where the arm should be. A look of panic overtakes him.

"It's all right," I say. "It's just down the hill. We'll get it fixed up as soon as we can. I just want you to know what's going on, okay? The other thing is that I think there might be a little problem with your neck, but that'll be fine too, I promise."

He swallows hard and looks at me. "What about my arm?" he says. "Aren't you going to put it on again?"

"I can't, pal. I wish I could. We'll have to take it along to the hospital tomorrow."

He glances up at his friends on the hill. I know he's embarrassed about what's happened.

"Maybe you ought to say something to them," I tell him. "Let them know you're all right."

"I don't know what to say," he says.

"Just whatever you want. It'll make it easier when you see them the next time."

He seems to think for a moment, his tongue poking out between his lips. Then he glances up the hill and says, "Hey, guys, I'm all right and everything. I gotta go home, but I can probably come back tomorrow."

"Hey, that's terrific," Ben says, and glances around at the boys. "Isn't that great, guys?"

"Yeah," Tanner Hildeman says quietly. "That's great, Cole."

"We just hope you're okay and everything," Sean Ho says, then glances at Cole's arm where it lies on the grass. He turns to the other kids, and as if given a signal they all start down the hill. A couple of them raise their hands to Cole, and Cole waves back.

"That wasn't so bad, was it?"

"I guess not," he says.

"You ready to go home to Mom now?"

"All right," he says, but there's a hint of hesitation in his eyes.

"What's the matter, kid?"

He shakes his head, then says, "Does Mom know what happened?"

"She knows you got hurt," I say. "She'll be glad to see you."

He glances up at the date palms in front of the house.

"What's the matter, pal?"

"Nothing," he says, but I can see there is. For the first time it occurs to me that he might know more about Dana and me than I've imagined.

Dana is outside when we get home, standing at the edge of the lawn with an uneasy look on her face. I try to give her a reassuring nod, but there's little use in that with Cole's arm tucked under my own like a rolled-up newspaper.

"Oh boy," she says, glancing from Cole to me and back. "You all right, kid?"

"I guess," he says, and looks at me.

"He's disappointed," I say.

"Of course," she says. "Who wouldn't be?" She brushes her hands down her sides, glances at the house. Dana is an attorney at an intellectual property firm in Phoenix and makes a good living appearing composed when everything is going to hell around her. But I can see she's flustered now, and it makes me feel suddenly tender toward her. Together we go into the house, where the air is cool and smells of pork chops and mashed potatoes.

While Cole goes upstairs to get cleaned up, I walk into the kitchen. Dana is washing her hands and staring out the window. It's six o'clock and the sky has taken on the pinks and silvers of an abalone shell.

"Don't you think we ought to shut him down?" she says, and turns to me. "I can't stand to see him with his arm like that."

"I think it's better to keep him running if we can," I say. "We don't want him to get any more disoriented than he has to."

"I guess not," she says.

"He seems pretty good in most ways. This is probably nothing too serious."

"He's torn his own arm off, Mike," she says. "Of course it's serious."

"All right. I just mean it might be a mechanical problem. It's not necessarily anything chronic."

Her face is doubtful, weary. "Well, let's hope so," she says.

At the top of the stairs I hear the faucet running in the bathroom. Cole bumps a knee against the cabinet under the sink and says "Ouch," then the faucet shuts off with a knock. I walk into the master bathroom, where the face I see in the mirror is so pale it shocks me. I have to sit on the toilet for a while with my head between my knees. It's that echoey feeling I had in the Hildemans' yard, a feeling I had a lot as a kid — at swim meets and at summer camps, and later during final exams in college. A doctor put me on Zoladex for a while when I was in my twenties, but I didn't like the way it made me feel — sedate and strangely detached from my life. I sit blotting my forehead with toilet paper, breathing deeply until my heartbeat slows.

I had these symptoms back in Portland too, when Cole was at his worst and Dana and I disagreed about how to handle it. Dana wanted to get a new center chip for Cole then, one of the D4 units that seemed to work well for people at the time. To me that would have been like getting a new child altogether, since his personality wouldn't be the same. In D-children, experience affects development the way it affects a human child: D-children become who they are because of the lives they've lived. While it's possible to transfer memory, you cannot transfer a personality that's been formed over the years. We'd been told that the engineers could *approximate* Cole's personality type, which to me was worthless, though a lot of people disagreed with me. My wife happened to be one of them.

Dana's brother Davis had a D3 child of his own, a boy named Brice, who suffered for years from the same kinds of problems as Cole — intermittent breakdown, loss of motor control. A year before we moved to Arizona, on the Tuesday before Thanksgiving, Brice disappeared after a martial arts class, and it was almost a week before they found him in a wooded field two miles north of Davis's house, where he'd apparently collapsed taking a shortcut home. A week later, Davis had a new center chip installed. The results were so positive he couldn't help calling us about it during our worst stretch with Cole. He knew how I felt about center chips; we'd discussed it many times. Davis had always been protective of Dana, and I'd never got the feeling he approved of me. I began to see his calls as a way of stirring up trouble between Dana and me.

And it worked, too. Brice was a high school junior then, a scholar-athlete and a truly fine kid, a boy Dana and I had always liked. But it was less his personality and accomplishments that impressed Dana, I think, than the sheer absence of D3-related problems. I remember Davis being worried about drugs at one point (he'd found a marijuana cigarette in Brice's underwear drawer), and even that became a selling point, because it was a *normal* problem. You couldn't miss the pride in Davis's voice when he told us about it — about the awkward talk he'd had with Brice, the two of them hashing it out for nearly an hour before finally hugging and crying. The point seemed to be that Brice was living a life of uninterrupted normalcy, and the insinuated question was, Why settle for a child who breaks down all the time when you can have a new one who won't?

I was dead set against it. It mattered absolutely to me that Cole be *my* child, the boy I'd come to know over the years. Dana and I fought about it more than we'd ever fought about anything, and in the end I think it changed the way we saw each other. She came to seem harder to me, less nurturing; I must have come to seem weak and sentimental. We'd met during our final year at the University of Oregon, and for the longest time had been amazed by how much we had in common — a penchant for old books and antiques, a respect for nature, a desire to have kids while we were still young enough to do everything with them. But as problems with Cole became worse, Dana receded, took on longer hours at work, grew distant when she was home. We argued about small, unrelated things, like the antiques we'd collected over the years. She said she felt hemmed in by them, even suggested we sell the old gas-powered Bonneville we'd loved to drive in college. For a few months that fall, I became convinced she was having an affair with a man named Stuart Solomon, a high-tech consultant at her firm. I never had solid evidence. Stuart's name turned up a few times on the caller ID, though he and Dana worked on different accounts. Twice, when Dana was supposed to be working late, I drove to her office and found that her car was not in the parking lot. I tried to confront her about it a few times, but always lost my nerve. There's no describing the relief I felt when the reports came in about D3 kids going problem-free in the Southwest. Suddenly there seemed reason to hope our lives could return to normal if we moved.

I stand and walk to the window. Outside, the rows of subterranean houses lie spread out like the fairways of a golf course. Mine is one of the few two-story houses left in the neighborhood now, and it costs so much to cool I'm sure I won't be able to keep it long — though I hate to think of giving it up, since it's a link to my past, to the two-story colonial my family still owns in Eugene. From where I stand, I can see the other two-story on the street, a big stucco home with a pool in the back. A light goes on in an upstairs window, and a man passes through a room. I've never spoken to this man before, but now I find myself thinking about him, wondering if he's anything like me, wondering if he feels himself being ushered into the future, away from the things that brought him comfort in the past.

Downstairs, Cole is carrying a basket of rolls to the table with his one good hand, singing "My Bonnie Lies Over the Ocean." It's a song he learned at summer camp, but he seems to have gotten some of the words wrong. Instead of singing "Bonnie," he sings "body." "My body lies over the ocean / My body lies over the sea." He sets the rolls on the table and goes back for more.

"Sit, honey," Dana says from the kitchen. "I'll get the rest."

"I don't mind," he says.

He takes a pitcher of water from the counter and starts into the dining room. Dana touches the back of his neck. I give her a look meant to say, "Doesn't he seem fine?" and she gives me a more doubtful look, which says, I suppose, "We'll see." But she comes over and puts her arms around me — an offering of peace.

"All right, break it up," Cole says, hurrying back in. "Can't you see I'm starving here?"

We bring the rest of the food to the table. As we begin to pass dishes and talk I feel a little better. It seems as if we've gotten past the day's bad luck and tension.

"Good dinner, Mom," Cole says, forking up a bite of pork chop.

"Flattery will get you everywhere," she says, and gives him a small smile.

"Listen," I say, passing the rolls, "how'd you guys like to take the Bonneville out tomorrow? After we get everything taken care of at the hospital, we could head out to Papago Lake and have a picnic. Maybe drive around Tortilla Flats."

"All right," Dana says. "Sounds like a good idea."

"Cool with me," says Cole, and glances up from his plate.

Something is wrong with his eyes, I see. One of them points directly at me while the other seems to shoot off at a crazy angle toward the kitchen. I glance at Dana, who's noticed it too.

"What?" Cole says, looking from me to Dana. "What's wrong?"

"Nothing," Dana says, carefully. "It's just — can you see all right?"

"Yeah," he says, "why?"

I set the bowl of broccoli down and say, "Listen, kid, try this." I put a hand in front of his face, then slowly move it until my fingers enter the line of his wayward eye. "Can you see my fingers now?"

"No," he says, and a flash of panic comes over him. "What's happening, Dad?"

"Well, I don't think it's anything to worry about. It looks like you've lost vision in one of your eyes, is all. But we're going to the hospital tomorrow anyway, right? They can fix this in a snap."

For a minute I think Cole might start to cry. "Gaw!" he says, and throws his balled-up napkin on the table. "I can't believe this!"

"Hey, come on," Dana says, her tone gentle but firm. She goes to Cole and kisses the crown of his head, and says, "Don't let it get you down." Then she gives me a look and walks into the kitchen. Cole and I keep on with our dinners. When Dana's been gone for a minute, I get up and go after her. She's at the sink, staring out the window at the fading sunset.

"We've got to shut him down, Mike. This is just scary. It's scaring *him.*"

"I know," I say, because it's scaring me too. I can't think of anything else to do about it.

"Hey, Dad," Cole calls from the dining room.

"What's up, pal?" I wait for an answer, but it doesn't come. "Be out in a second, all right?"

"Hey, Dad, what makes the sky red when the sun goes down?"

Dana breathes out a small laugh. Her face softens. For a moment she looks like the young woman I met in Oregon. I give her a kiss on the cheek and go into the dining room.

"That's just dust," I say. "Dust and pollution, actually."

But Cole isn't looking at me. He's pushing food across the table with his fingers, staring at the mess he's made. An electric drone comes from his throat.

"Cole?"

"I gotta go to the bathroom," he says, staring at the table. "I don't feel so hot." The drone in his throat gets louder.

"What's the matter, kid?"

He glances up, his expression suddenly sly. "I'll bet you a dollar," he says.

"What are you talking about, pal?"

Dana comes into the doorway. "What's going on, Mike?"

"Jesus H. Christ," Cole says, and suddenly laughs. "Holy frickin' shit!"

"Cole! Look up here," I say. "Look at me."

He raises his head, but his eyes veer in different directions. His jaw makes a clicking noise. Then he suddenly raises his head high and brings it down with a violent crack against the table.

"Cole!" I say.

He lifts his head again, his face covered with pork chop grease and broccoli. I try to get around the table to hold him down, but before I can get there his head hits the table with another crack, rattling the silverware. Dana shrieks. This time, when Cole's head comes up, it swings way back over one shoulder, loose and wild.

"My God, his neck!" Dana says.

"I see it! Help me hold him down."

I get a hand on his shoulder and try to reach under his shirt for the power button, but it's hard to get to with his head lolling around like a jack-in-the-box.

"Whoa!" he says. "Help me, Dad."

The smell of burning wires comes off him. He breathes out an electric wheeze, his head lolling, and then his face seems to fill with wonder and he goes perfectly still my arms. He turns to me, eyes clear and perfectly aligned.

"This is the best Christmas ever," he says.

I shut him down. His head thumps against the table. The electric drone cuts out. I wipe his face with a napkin and go into the kitchen, where I get a bottle of beer from the fridge. When I come back Dana is at the table, arms folded across her chest. She glances out the window.

"That's it, Mike," she says. "I mean it. This has got to stop."

The next morning I pull the Bonneville out of the driveway and carry Cole downstairs. Even with the seat belt over his shoulder, it's hard to prop him up in a way that looks natural. His head tips forward, making his mouth fall open. Dana and I have not talked about taking the Bonneville out since last night, and a picnic no longer seems like the best idea, but I'm in the mood to feel the thrum of the big gasoline engine, the vibration of the catalytic converter under my legs.

After a few minutes, Dana comes down and we take Highway 1073 past the mall and the hydroponics yards. The D-pediatric is twelve miles away, a sprawling complex on the outskirts of Olberg. As we drive, Dana stares out the window, her eyes steady and serious, her mouth drawn into a line.

Last night, after I shut Cole down and we cleaned up the mess in the dining room, Dana went into the den and called her brother Davis, and through the door I heard her talking softly. I couldn't make out what she said, though I'm certain it was something she couldn't say to me, since we went through the evening without another word about Cole. Sometime late in the night I woke to the sound of her crying and put a hand on her shoulder, and she moved into my arms for a while. It was like holding an injured animal; I couldn't help feeling she just needed a little time to heal, then she'd be out of my arms for good.

Afterward I lay awake, looking at the tiny red light of a smoke detector, listening as the wind pulled an ocotillo branch across the window. Dana was asleep, and Cole, I knew, was much farther away than that, gone in a sense, so that he was not even dreaming and would not wake up and call my name. I waited until the sky whitened in the window, then got up and walked down the hall and into his room. Cole lay dressed on top of the covers, his eyes closed, an inappropriate smile on his face. I had an urge to put his pajamas on him and tuck him into bed, but I knew it wouldn't make me feel better. Eventually I went down and started coffee and made bacon and eggs as the sky whitened through the windows.

We pass Mesa now, and the ground opens up to uncultivated fields and cacti. Just past Alvarado, I catch a glimpse of a coyote between the clumps of sage, golden brown and moving quickly, nose to the ground. It makes me think of driving out to Salmon Creek with Dana when we first got the Bonneville, years ago, laying a blanket across the back seat and making love right in the car with the windows open, the sound of the wind coming through the firs.

In the rearview mirror I see Cole propped against the door, his eyes closed, his mouth open. Dana is staring out the window. For some reason I imagine she's thinking of Davis, and it makes me angry.

"So suppose things get bad again," I say, and glance at her. "What do you think would happen then?"

"What do you mean, Mike?"

"Suppose this is the beginning of more bad times with Cole. We'd have to make some decisions then, right?" I know my voice is sharp, but it seems beyond my power to control it.

"Of course," she says.

"But you already know what you'd want to do," I say. "Isn't that right too?"

"Come on, Mike, don't do this," she says. "I'm not in the mood for an argument right now."

"But suppose I need to know. Suppose it's important for me to know where we stand on this."

She sighs and glances out at the fields of brush. "Why do you have to push things all the time? What if I *can't* say what I'd do in every single situation? Can you?"

"I think I can. Yes."

"Can you really, Mike? You can say what you'd do no matter what happens to him or to us?"

"What do you mean, 'to us'?"

"Oh, God, I don't know," she says, and shakes her head wearily. "I just get tired of waking from the dream, don't you? Don't you get tired of being reminded he's not real?"

"He's as real to me as you are," I say, but when I glance at Cole in the rearview mirror he looks like what he is — a mechanical boy, a sophisticated doll for adults.

The desert floor runs out to a line of purple mountains. A ranch house slips past, then an electric plant, huge and complicated. For a moment I feel as if I don't know what's important to me, what matters the most. Dana has closed her eyes and is leaning back against the headrest.

"There was a coyote back there in a field," I say in a small voice. "I should have pointed him out to you."

We wait for hours in the air-conditioned lobby, sitting on a vinyl couch, trying to read magazines while other parents come and go with their children. Through a tinted window, I see a slice of blue sky. A peregrine falcon dips into view now and then. Finally Dr. Otsuji comes down the hall in a crisp white coat and yellow tie. He gives us his doctor's smile and sits on the chrome magazine table across from us.

"He's fine," he says. "We've fixed the arm and the neck, and right now he's just going through some tests to make sure everything's in good shape. He seems terrific."

Dana nods the way she does in court when conceding a point made by the opposition. "Do you have any idea what happened?" she asks.

The doctor turns up his eyes in concentration. "I'd call it an anomaly," he says, "though it could be more than that. It's like if you have an arrhythmia — unless we can check your heart when it's happening, we have a hard time knowing what causes it."

"But in your opinion, is it likely we'll have more problems?" she asks. "Now that this has happened?"

Dr. Otsuji looks from one of us to the other, as if he's just noticed the tension between us. "He's not showing any symptoms that would point to that, no," he says, "but to be honest, I don't see it as a good sign. For someone with Cole's history, you want as few problems as possible. Problems can lead to problems, is one way of looking at it."

Dana nods.

"Can we see him?" I ask.

"In a few minutes. He's a little upset, as you might expect. He's had a rough day. What I'd like to do is to put him out for a few minutes and run some numbers, then let him wake up naturally. I'll have the receptionist tell you when you can see him." He smiles in his professional way, then stands and shakes our hands and walks down the hall.

"Well, there it is," I say.

"I should call Davis," Dana says, and takes her bag up from the floor. "He'll want to know what happened."

She opens her cell phone, but before dialing she looks at me with an expression I've never seen before — her face hard, her eyes narrowed with what seems like pity. It's as if she's far away and needs to squint just to see me. "Listen, if you still want to go for a drive, that's fine. We can do that."

"Forget it. I don't really feel like it anymore."

"Well. Whatever. We'll go if you want to."

"I said I don't want to." The tone of my voice makes us both fall silent. She stands and walks down the hall.

Outside, clouds move across the sky, changing the light. A young family rushes into the lobby, the man carrying a blond, catatonic-looking girl in his arms. The child stares straight ahead with vacant eyes. I pick up a magazine, but there's no use trying to read or even think about anything before I'm able to see Cole. Finally the receptionist calls my name and I get Cole's room number and go down the hall.

Cole's in a bed in a pale yellow hospital gown, asleep with his arms at his sides. His cheeks are flushed, his hair a little tousled. I stand above him and watch his chest rise and fall. He opens his eyes and glances around, then nods in a resigned way. "The hospital," he says.

"I'm afraid so, pal. They've fixed your arm, though. Check it out."

He raises the arm and rolls his shoulder. I can see he's trying to appear calm for my sake.

"Does it feel all right?"

"Pretty good," he says.

"We'll test it out with a game of catch. How's that sound?"

"All right."

"Maybe we'll drop your mom off at home and head out to Papago Park. I've got the Bonneville. We can just grab some mitts and go."

"Where *is* Mom?" he says, and gives me a worried look.

"Down the hall. Talking to your uncle Davis."

"Is she mad at me?"

"Of course not. Why would you say that?"

"I don't know," he says. "I know she doesn't like it when I break down all the time."

"You don't break down all the time," I say. "And anyway, none of this is your fault."

He seems distracted, as if he's trying to listen to Dana's voice down the hall. I can just hear her, a low, familiar sound coming over the tiles.

"Let's get you dressed and get your hair combed," I say. "We don't want people to think you were raised by wolves now, do we?"

He lifts the covers away and lowers his legs to the floor. I help him with the ties at the back of his gown. His clothes are on a chair by the window, and as he puts them on I see the seam where his arm has been reattached, a thin band where the skin is a little lighter, nothing you'd notice unless you were a parent or a doctor. I comb his hair, crouching in front of him, watching his eyes, which are alive with private thoughts and worries.

"Now you look like a gentleman," I say. "You ready to go?"

"I guess so," he says, and together we walk into the hall.

On the ride home, we play a game called Blackout. The object is to find the letters of each other's names in the license plates of passing cars, then call them out before the other person does. If you call them all, the person is out of the game. There's very little traffic until we hit the highway, and then we're suddenly in a sea of

Why the Sky Turns Red When the Sun Goes Down

sedans and sport utility vehicles. Cole picks up a *D* for Dana and an *M* for Mike. I get an *A* for Dana, who seems not to be paying attention to the game.

"You better hurry up, Mom," Cole says, leaning over the front seat. "You've got two letters already."

She gazes straight out the windshield, a distant look on her face. Ever since our exchange in the hospital, she's been stiff and far away. I've seen the effect on Cole — the way he keeps his eyes on her, the way he won't stop trying to draw her attention.

"There's an *I*, Dad," he says, and glances at Dana.

We get off the highway and drive down Auwatukee, past the golf course and the hydroponic yards. At a red light, I call an *O* and an *N*, and then Cole and I both see a Honda in front of us, the license plate ALA-36940. We meet each other's gaze in the mirror, but neither of us calls the *A*.

At home I park on the street and kill the engine. Dana steps out of the car. She pretends not to hear Cole when he asks if she's coming to the park with us. He watches her walk up to the house with a stricken look on his face.

"She's having a rough time," I say. "It's not your fault, pal. I'll go get the mitts."

He nods, his face tight and willfully composed.

When I go inside, Dana is at the dining table, staring out the window. The sky has burst into color and filled the room with yellow light.

"So what's the plan?" I say. "Treat him badly? Make him feel like he doesn't have a mother?"

She turns, and I see that she's been crying. Her cheeks shine where the light strikes them from the side. "Are you really going to do this?" she asks. "Would you really take him and leave me?"

"I guess I don't know what my legal options are," I say.

"No one said anything about legal options," she says, "though I guess I shouldn't be surprised if you're thinking in that direction." She gives her head a small shake and glances up at me in a surprisingly open way, her eyes soft and even. "If I try hard enough, I can almost imagine how I look to you right now."

"Can you really?"

"Yes, I can," she says. "And it's not pretty."

"I don't think either of us looks very good to the other right now," I say, and try a smile.

"I guess not," she says.

"Of course, we don't know what will happen. He might be fine. He might just get better and surprise both of us."

"Do you think it would even matter?" she asks, smiling sadly.

"Why wouldn't it?"

"I just think you reach a point where you can't go on. Don't you? I feel as if we've gotten close to that point."

"Have we really?"

"I was very in love with you," she says, and puts a hand on top of my own. "You know that, right? I still love you very much."

"I love you too," I say, and let out a laugh, because it all seems so crazy. "It's not as if we've lost everything, is it? It's not as if everything's gone."

"I don't know," she says. "That's what I worry about sometimes."

Cole and I drive out Clementine Road, past orange groves and fields of yuccas. Cole takes his mitt up from the floorboard and socks the ball into the pocket. He's been quiet and somber since I returned to the car, but now he seems to be cheering up under the influence of the drive. We pass an old stable building, the wood planks faded to silver-gray. He asks if I remember a drive we took a couple of winters ago, when it hailed so hard I had to pull to the side of the road and wait for it to stop.

"We were on our way to see the rodeo," I say, remembering.

"I thought the hail would dent the car," he says, and gives a small laugh. "There was a little dog out in the street, remember? You went out and brought him back to the car."

"I remember he smelled like rotten garbage."

Cole laughs. "He did not." He's excited, and seems to be coming to the point of his story, which I'm guessing will be that we should allow him to have a dog. It's an argument he's been making the last few months. Before he can get to that, though, the fingers of his right hand begin to twitch and he slips the hand into his mitt. As we drive past the arboretum, I see the tendons of his forearm jumping. I don't say anything. It's not like him to hide anything from me.

I'm thinking of Dana, of course, thinking she seems like a different person now, though I suppose we'll both have to change if we

intend to go our separate ways. Our conversation has made it necessary to imagine raising Cole by myself. I imagine taking him to
the grocery store, having him break down in the produce aisle, carrying his inert body back to some empty apartment. It's hard to be
optimistic when you know you'll be alone, when you know it will be
only you in the D-pediatric waiting room, waiting to hear whether
your son will seem like a child again.

At the park we walk across a field of fresh-mowed grass, the sun cutting over a long line of oleanders. A Mexican family barbecues
flank steak under a picnic stand, and the smell of charred beef is in
the air. Cole's hand seems to have improved enough for him to
play catch, so we take our usual positions on a strip of grass near
the snack bar.

"So, Dad," he says, winding up like a big-league pitcher, "you
think I'll be able to play Little League next year?" He looks an
imaginary runner back to first.

"You'll be eligible. You can try it if you want to."

His sidearm pitch skids on the ground. "Sorry about that," he
says.

"Your arm all right?"

"Little sore," he says, and takes his mitt off and massages the
shoulder. Even from twenty feet I can see the hand twitching,
though he's playing it cool. "I'm trying to decide if it would be too
much to do baseball *and* soccer," he says, and puts the mitt back on.

"What are Tanner and Sean going to do?"

"Tanner's gonna do both. Sean hasn't decided yet."

"Maybe you should just play baseball and see how it goes." I
throw him a grounder, and he fields it and makes a pretend throw
to first.

"Soccer's my main sport, though," he says with intensity. "I want
to play soccer for sure." He throws a pitch that hits the grass a few
feet in front of him, then hustles up like a catcher going after a
bunt. But his throwing arm is shaking so badly he can hardly hold
the ball, let alone make the throw. He falls abruptly to a sitting position on the grass, pressing his bad hand into the mitt.

"Let's take a break," he says.

I walk over and sit down beside him.

He's gazing off at the covered picnic tables, watching a young

Mexican girl in a white lace dress swing at a piñata with a broom-
stick. He hunches over his mitt, rocking back and forth. What
seems remarkable is not that he's having problems, but that he's
been able to throw a ball at all, ever — that we've stood here and
played catch and it's seemed normal.

"Maybe we ought to go home," I say. "It's been a long day for everyone."

"I'll be all right in a second," he says.

I lean into him, touch his face. When he's looking at me, I say,
"It's really all right if you're having problems. You don't have to
hide anything from your dad."

"I'm not hiding," he says, but his eyes suddenly fill with tears and
he has to glance off at the picnic tables, where the girl has opened
up the piñata now and kids are clamoring underneath. He watches,
his jaw set tight. His voice, when he speaks again, is as thin and
frightened as I've heard it before. "What's going to happen, Dad?"
he asks. "What'll become of me?"

"You'll be fine," I say, because sometimes it's a father's job to lie.
"Don't worry, kid. You'll be great."

LOUISE ERDRICH

Shamengwa

FROM THE NEW YORKER

I

AT THE EDGE of our reservation settlement there lived an old
man whose arm was twisted up winglike along his side, and who was
for that reason named for a butterfly — Shamengwa. Other than
his arm, he was an extremely well-made person. Anyone could see
that he had been handsome, and he still cut a graceful figure, slim
and of medium height. His head was covered with a startling thick
mane of white hair, which he was proud of. Every few weeks, he had
it carefully trimmed and styled by his daughter, Geraldine, who
traveled in from the bush just to do it.

Shamengwa was a man of refinement, who prepared himself
carefully to meet life every day. In the Ojibwa language that is spoken on our reservation, *owehzhee* is the way men get themselves up
— pluck stray hairs, brush each tooth, make a precise part in their
hair, and, these days, press a sharp crease down the front of their
blue jeans — in order to show that, although the government has
tried in every way possible to destroy their manhood, they are
undefeatable. *Owehzhee.* We still look good and we know it. The old
man was never seen in disarray, and yet there was more to it.

He played the fiddle. How he played the fiddle! Although his
arm was so twisted and disfigured that his shirts had to be carefully
altered and pinned to accommodate the gnarled shape, he had
agility in that arm, even strength. Ever since he was very young,
Shamengwa had, with the aid of a white silk scarf, tied his elbow
into a position that allowed the elegant hand and fingers at the end

of the damaged arm full play across the fiddle's strings. With his other hand, he drew the bow. When I try to explain the sound he made, I come to some trouble with words. Inside became outside when Shamengwa played music. Yet inside to outside does not half sum it up. The music was more than music — at least, more than what we are used to hearing. The sound connected instantly with something deep and joyous. Those powerful moments of true knowledge which we paper over with daily life. The music tapped our terrors, too. Things we'd lived through and wanted never to repeat. Shredded imaginings, unadmitted longings, fear, and also surprising pleasures. We can't live at that pitch. But every so often, something shatters like ice, and we fall into the river of our own existence. We are aware. This realization was in the music somehow, or in the way Shamengwa played it.

Thus Shamengwa wasn't wanted at every party. The wild joy his jigs and reels brought forth might just as easily send people crashing onto the rocks of their roughest memories and they'd end up stunned and addled or crying in their beer. So it is. People's emotions often turn on them. Geraldine, a dedicated, headstrong woman who six years back had borne a baby, dumped its father, and earned a degree in education, sometimes drove Shamengwa to fiddling contests, where he could perform in more of a concert setting. He even won awards, prizes of the cheap sort given at local musical contests — engraved plaques and small tin cups set on plastic pedestals. These he placed on a triangular scrap of shelf high in one corner of his house. The awards were never dusted, and sometimes, when his grandchild asked him to take them down for her to play with, they came apart. Shamengwa didn't care. He was, however, fanatical about his violin.

He treated this instrument with the reverence we accord our drums, which are considered living beings and require from us food, water, shelter, and love. He fussed over it, stroked it clean with a soft cotton handkerchief, laid it carefully away in the cupboard every night in a leather case that he kept as well polished as his shoes. The case was lined with velvet that had been faded by time from a heavy blood red to a pallid and streaked violet. I don't know violins, but his was thought to be exceptionally beautiful; it was generally understood to be old and quite valuable, too. So when Geraldine came to trim her father's hair one morning and found him on the floor, his good hand bound behind his back, his ankles tied, she was not surprised to see the lock of the cupboard smashed and the violin gone.

I am a tribal judge, and things come to me through the grapevine of the court system or the tribal police. Gossip, rumors, scuttlebutt, BS, or just flawed information. I always tune in, and I even take notes on what I hear around. It's sometimes wrong, or exaggerated, but just as often it contains a germ of useful truth. In this case, for instance, the name Corwin Peace was on people's lips, although there was no direct evidence that he had committed the crime.

Corwin was one of those I see again and again. A bad thing waiting for a worse thing to happen. A mistake, but one that we kept trying to salvage, because he was so young. Some thought he had no redeeming value whatsoever. A sociopath. A clever manipulator, who drugged himself dangerous each weekend. Others pitied him and blamed his behavior on his mother's drinking. FAE. FAS. ADD. He wore those initials after his name the way educated people append their degrees. Still others thought they saw something in him that could be saved — perhaps the most dangerous idea of all. He was a petty dealer with a string of girlfriends. He was, unfortunately, good-looking, with the features of an Edward Curtis subject, though the crack and vodka were beginning to make him puffy.

Drugs now travel the old fur-trade routes, and where once Corwin would have sat high on a bale of buffalo robes and sung traveling songs to the screeching of an oxcart, now he drove a 1991 Impala with hubcaps missing and its back end dragging. He drove it hard and he drove it all cranked up, but he was rarely caught, because he traveled such erratic hours. He drove without a license — it had long ago been taken from him. DUI. And he was always looking for money — scamming, betting, shooting pool, even now and then working a job that, horrifyingly, put him on the other side of a counter frying Chinese chicken strips. He was one of those whom I kept track of because I imagined I'd be seeing the full down-arcing shape of his life's trajectory. I wanted to make certain that if I had to put him away I could do it and sleep well that same night. So far, he had confirmed this.

As the days passed, Corwin lay low and picked up his job at the deep fryer. He made one of those rallying attempts that gave heart to so many of his would-be saviors. He straightened out, stayed sober, used his best manners, and when questioned was convincingly hopeful about his prospects and affable about his failures. "I'm a jackass," he admitted, "but I never sank so low as to rip off the old man's fiddle."

Yet he had, of course. And while we waited for him to make his move, there was the old man, who quickly began to fail. I had not realized how much I loved to hear him play — sometimes out on his scrubby back lawn after dusk, sometimes at those little concerts, and other times just for groups of people who would gather round. After weeks had passed, a dull spot opened and I ached with surprising poignance for Shamengwa's loss, which I honestly shared, so that I had to seek him out and sit with him as if it would help to mourn the absence of his music together. I wanted to know, too, whether, if the violin did not turn up, we could get together and buy him a new, perhaps even better instrument. So I sat in Shamengwa's little front room one afternoon and tried to find an opening.

"Of course," I said, "we think we know who took your fiddle. We've got our eye on him."

Shamengwa swept his hair back with the one graceful hand and said, as he had many times, "I was struck from behind."

Where he'd hit the ground, his cheekbone had split and the white of his eye was an angry red. He moved with a stiff, pained slowness, the rigidity of a very old person. He lowered himself piece by piece into a padded brown rocking chair and gazed at me, or past me, really. I soon understood that although he spoke quietly and answered questions, he was not fully engaged in the conversation. In fact, he was only half present, and somewhat disheveled, irritable as well, neither of which I'd ever seen in him before. His shirt was buttoned wrong, the plaid askew, and he hadn't shaved that morning. His breath was sour, and he didn't seem at all glad that I had come.

We sat together in a challenging silence until Geraldine brought two mugs of hot, strong, sugared tea and got another for herself. Shamengwa's hand shook as he lifted the cup, but he drank. His face cleared a bit as the tea went down, and I decided that there would be no better time to put forth my idea.

"Uncle," I said, "we would like to buy a new fiddle for you."

Shamengwa said nothing, but put down the cup and folded his hands in his lap. He looked past me and frowned in a thoughtful way.

"Wouldn't he like a new violin?" I appealed to Geraldine. She shook her head as if she were both annoyed with me and exasperated with her father. We sat in silence. I didn't know where to go from there. Shamengwa had leaned back in his chair and closed his eyes. I thought he might be trying to get rid of me. But I was stubborn and did not want to go. I wanted to hear Shamengwa's music again.

"Oh, tell him about it, Daddy," Geraldine said at last.

Shamengwa leaned forward and bent his head over his hands as though he were praying.

I relaxed now and understood that I was going to hear something. It was that breathless gathering moment I've known just before composure cracks, the witness breaks, the truth comes out. I am familiar with it, and although this was not exactly a confession, it was, as it turned out, something not generally known on the reservation.

II

My mother lost a baby boy to diphtheria when I was but four years old, Shamengwa said, and it was that loss that turned my mother to the Church. Before that, I remember my father playing chansons, reels, and jigs on his fiddle, but after the baby's death he put the fiddle down and took the Holy Communion. My mother out of grief became strict with my father, my older sister, and me. Where before we'd had a lively house that people liked to visit, now there was quiet. No wine and no music. We kept our voices down because our noise hurt, my mother said, and there was no laughing or teasing by my father, who had once been a dancing and hilarious man.

I don't believe my mother meant things to change so, but the sorrow she bore was beyond her strength. As though her heart, too, were buried underneath that small white headstone in the Catholic cemetery, she turned cold, turned away from the rest of us. Now that I am old and know the ways of grief, I understand she felt too much, loved too hard, and was afraid to lose us as she had lost my brother. But to a little boy these things are hidden. It only seemed to me that, along with that baby, I had lost her love. Her strong arms, her kisses, the clean soap smell of her face, her voice calming me — all of this was gone. She was like a statue in a church. Every so often we would find her in the kitchen, standing still, staring through the wall. At first we touched her clothes, petted her hands. My father kissed her, spoke gently into her ear, combed her hair into a shawl around her shoulders. Later, after we had given up, we just walked around her as you would a stump. My sister took up the cooking, and gradually we accepted that the lively, loving mother we had known wasn't going to return. We didn't try to coax her out. She spent most of her time at the church, her ivory-and-silver rosary draped over her right fist, her left hand wearing the beads smoother, smaller, until I thought one day for sure they would disappear between her fingers.

We lived right here then, but in those days trees and bush still surrounded us. There were no houses to the west. We pastured our horses where the Dairy Queen now stands. One day, while my family was in town and I was home with a cold, I became restless. I began to poke around, and soon enough I came across the fiddle that my mother had forced my father to stop playing. There it was. I was alone with it. I was only five or six years old, but I could balance a fiddle and I remembered how my father had used the bow. I got sound out of it all right, though nothing pleasing. The noise made my bones shiver. I put the fiddle back carefully, well before my parents came home, and climbed underneath my blankets when they walked into the yard. I pretended to sleep, not because I wanted to keep up the appearance of being sick but because I could not bear to return to the way things had been. Something had changed. Something had disrupted the nature of all that I knew. This deep thing had to do with the fiddle.

After that, I contrived, as often as I could, to stay alone in the house. As soon as everyone was gone I took the fiddle from its hiding place, and I tuned it to my own liking. I learned how to play it one string at a time, and I started to fit these sounds together. The sequence of notes made my brain itch. It became a torment for me to have to put away the fiddle when my family came home. Sometimes, if the wind was right, I sneaked the fiddle from the house and played out in the woods. I was always careful that the wind should carry my music away to the west, where there was no one to hear it. But one day the wind may have shifted. Or perhaps my mother's ears were more sensitive than my sister's and my father's. Because when I came back into the house I found her staring out the window, to the west. She was excited, breathing fast. Did you hear it? she cried out. Did you hear it? Terrified to be discovered, I said no. She was very agitated, and my father had a hard time calming her. After he finally got her to sleep, he sat at the table with his head in his hands. I tiptoed around the house, did the chores. I felt terrible not telling him that my music was what she'd heard. But now, as I look back, I consider my silence the first decision I made as a true musician. An artist. My playing was more important to me than my father's pain. It was that clear. I said nothing, but after that I was all the more sly and twice as secretive.

It was a question of survival, after all. If I had not found the music, I would have died of the silence. There are ways of being abandoned even when your parents are right there.

We had two cows, and I did the milking in the morning and evening. Lucky, because if my parents forgot to cook at least I had the milk. I can't say I really ever suffered from a stomach kind of hunger, but another kind of human hunger bit me. I was lonely. It was about that time that I received a terrible kick from the cow, an accident, as she was usually mild. A wasp sting, perhaps, caused her to lash out in surprise. She caught my arm and, although I had no way of knowing it, shattered the bone. Painful? Oh, for certain it was, but my parents did not think to take me to a doctor. They did not notice, I suppose. I did tell my father about it, but he only nodded, pretending that he had heard, and went back to whatever he was doing.

The pain in my arm kept me awake, and at night, when I couldn't distract myself, I moaned in my blankets by the stove. But worse was the uselessness of the arm in playing the fiddle. I tried to prop it up, but it fell like a rag doll's arm. I finally hit upon a solution. I started tying up my broken arm, just as I do now. I had, of course, no idea that it would heal that way and that as a result I would be considered a permanent cripple. I only knew that with the arm tied up I could play, and that playing saved my life. So I was, like most artists, deformed by my art. I was shaped.

School is where I got the name I carry now. Shamengwa, the black-and-orange butterfly. It was a joke on my "wing arm." Although a nun told me that a picture of a butterfly in a painting of Our Lady was meant to represent the Holy Spirit, I didn't like the name at first. My bashfulness about the shape of my arm caused me to avoid people even once I was older, and I made no friends. Human friends. My true friend was my fiddle, anyway, the only friend I really needed. And then I lost that friend.

My parents had gone to church, but there was on that winter's day some problem with the stove. Smoke had filled the nave at the start of Mass and everyone was sent straight home. When my mother and father arrived, I was deep into my playing. They listened, standing at the door rooted by the surprise of what they heard, for how long I do not know. I had not heard the door open and, with my eyes shut, had not seen the light thereby admitted. Finally I noticed the cold breeze that swirled around me, turned, and we stared at one another with a shocked gravity that my father broke at last by asking, "How long?"

I did not answer, although I wanted to. *Seven years. Seven years!*

He led my mother in. They shut the door behind them. Then he said, in a voice of troubled softness, "Keep on."

So I played, and when I stopped he said nothing.

Discovered, I thought the worst was over. But the next morning, waking to a silence where I usually heard my father's noises, hearing a vacancy before I even knew it for sure, I understood that the worst was yet to come. My playing had woken something in him. That was the reason he left. But I don't know why he had to take the violin. When I saw that it was missing, all breath left me, all thought, all feeling. For a while after that I was the same as my mother. In our loss, we were cut off from the true, bright, normal routines of living. I might have stayed that way, joined my mother in the darkness from which she could not return. I might have lived on in that diminished form, if I had not had a dream.

The dream was simple. A voice. *Go to the lake and sit by the southern rock. Wait there. I will come to you.*

I decided to follow these instructions. I took my bedroll, a scrap of jerky, and a loaf of bannock, and sat myself down on the crackling lichen of the southern rock. That plate of stone jutted out into the water, which dropped off from its edges into a green-black depth. From that rock, I could see all that happened on the water. I put tobacco down for the spirits. All day I sat there waiting. Flies bit me. The wind boomed in my ears. Nothing happened. I curled up when the light left and I slept. Stayed on the next morning. The next day, too. It was the first time that I had ever slept out on the shores, and I began to understand why people said of the lake that there was no end to it, even though it was bounded by rocks. There were rivers flowing in and flowing out, secret currents, six kinds of weather working on its surface and a hidden terrain beneath. Each wave washed in from somewhere unseen and washed out again to somewhere unknown. I saw birds, strange-feathered and unfamiliar, passing through on their way to somewhere else. Listening to the water, I was for the first time comforted by sounds other than my fiddle-playing. I let go. I thought I might just stay there forever, staring at the blue thread of the horizon. Nothing mattered. When a small bit of the horizon's thread detached, darkened, proceeded forward slowly, I observed it with only mild interest. The speck seemed to both advance and retreat. It wavered back and forth. I lost sight of it for long stretches, then it popped closer, over a wave.

It was a canoe. But either the paddler was asleep in the bottom or the canoe was drifting. As it came nearer, I decided for sure that it must be adrift, it rode so lightly in the waves, nosing this way, then the other. But always, no matter how hesitantly, it ended up advancing straight toward the southern rock, straight toward me. I watched until I could clearly see there was nobody in it. Then the words of my dream returned. *I will come to you.* I dove in eagerly, swam for the canoe — I had learned, as boys do, to compensate for my arm, and although my stroke was peculiar, I was strong. I thought perhaps the canoe had been badly tied and slipped its mooring, but no rope trailed. Perhaps high waves had coaxed it off a beach where its owner had dragged it up, thinking it safe. I pushed the canoe in to shore, then pulled it up behind me, wedged it in a cleft between two rocks. Only then did I look inside. There, lashed to a crosspiece in the bow, was a black case of womanly shape that fastened on the side with two brass locks.

That is how my fiddle came to me, Shamengwa said, raising his head to look steadily at me. He smiled, shook his fine head, and spoke softly. And that is why no other fiddle will I play.

III

Corwin shut the door to his room. It wasn't really his room, but some people were letting him stay in their basement in return for several favors. Standing on a board propped on sawhorses, he pushed his outspread fingers against the panel of the false ceiling. He placed the panel to one side and groped up behind it among wires and underneath a pad of yellow fiberglass insulation, until he located the handle of the case. He bore it down to the piece of foam rubber that served as his mattress and through which, every night, he felt the hard cold of the concrete floor seep into his legs. He had taken the old man's fiddle because he needed money, but he hadn't thought much about where he would sell it or who would buy it. Then he had an inspiration. One of the women in the house went to Spirit Lake every weekend to stay with her boyfriend's family. He'd put the fiddle in the trunk and hitch along. They'd let him out at Miracle Village Mall, and he'd take the violin there and sell it to a music lover.

Corwin got out of the car and carried the violin into the mall. There are two kinds of people, he thought, the givers and the takers. I'm a taker. Render unto Corwin what is due him. His favorite movie of recent times was about a cop with such a twisted way of looking at the world that you couldn't tell if he was evil or good — you only knew that he could seize your mind with language. Corwin had a thing for language. He inhaled it from movies, rap and rock music, television. It rubbed around inside him, word against word. He thought he was writing poems sometimes in his thoughts, but the poems would not come out. The words stuck in odd configurations and made patterns that raced across the screen of his shut eyes and off the edge, down his temples and into the darkness of his neck. So when he walked through the airlock doors into the warm cathedral-like space of the central food court, his brain was a mumble.

Taking a seat, peering at the distracted-looking shoppers, he quickly understood that none of them was likely to buy the fiddle. He walked into a music store and tried to show the instrument to the manager, who said only, "Nah, we don't take used." Corwin walked out again. He tried a few people. They shied away or turned him down flat.

"Gotta regroup," Corwin told himself, and went back to sit on the length of bench he had decided to call his own. That was where he got the idea that became a gold mine. He remembered a scene from a TV show, a clip of a musician in a city street. He was playing a saxophone or something of that sort, and at his feet there was an open instrument case. A woman stopped and smiled and threw a dollar in the case. Corwin took the violin out and laid the open case invitingly at his feet. He took the fiddle in one hand and drew the bow across the strings with the other. It made a terrible, strange sound. The screech echoed in the food court and several people raised their lips from the waxed-paper food wrappers to look at Corwin. He looked back at them, poised and frozen. It was a moment of drama — he had them. An audience. He had to act instantly or lose them. Instinctively he gave a flowery, low bow, as though he were accepting an ovation. There were a few murmurs of amusement. Someone even applauded. These sounds acted on Corwin Peace at once, more powerfully than any drug he had tried. A surge of unfamiliar zeal filled him, and he took up the instrument again, threw back his hair, and began to play a swift, silent passage of music.

His mimicry was impeccable. Where had he learned it? He didn't know. He didn't touch the bow to the strings, but he played music all the same. Music ricocheted around between his ears. He could hardly keep up with what he heard. His body spilled over with drama. When the music in his head stopped, he dipped low and did the splits, which he'd learned from Prince videos. He held the violin and the bow overhead. Applause broke over him. A skein of dazzling sound.

They picked up Corwin Peace pretending to play the fiddle in a Fargo mall, and brought him to me. I have a great deal of latitude in sentencing. In spite of myself, I was intrigued by Corwin's unusual treatment of the instrument, and I decided to set a precedent. First I cleared my decision with Shamengwa. Then I sentenced Corwin to apprentice himself with the old master. Six days a week, two hours each morning. Three hours of practice after work. He would either learn to play the violin or he would do time. In truth, I didn't know who was being punished, the boy or the old man. But at least now, from Shamengwa's house, we began to hear the violin again.

It was the middle of September on the reservation, the mornings chill, the afternoons warm, the leaves still green and thick in their final sweetness. All the hay was mowed. The wild rice was beaten flat. The radiators in the tribal offices went on at night, but by noon we had to open the windows to cool off. The woodsmoke of parching fires and the spent breeze of diesel entered then, and sometimes the squall of Corwin's music from down the hill. The first weeks were not promising. Then the days turned uniformly cold, we kept the windows shut, and until spring the only news of Corwin's progress came through his probation officer. I didn't expect much. It was not until the first hot afternoon in early May that I opened my window and actually heard Corwin playing.

"Not half bad," I said that night when I visited Shamengwa. "I listened to your student."

"He's clumsy as hell, but he's got the fire," Shamengwa said, touching his chest. I could tell that he was proud of Corwin, and I allowed myself to consider the possibility that something as idealistic as putting an old man and a hardcore juvenile delinquent together had worked, or hadn't, anyway, ended up a disaster.

The lessons and the relationship outlasted, in fact, the sentence. Fall came, and we closed the windows again. In spring, we opened them, and once or twice heard Corwin playing. Then Shamengwa died.

His was a peaceful death, the sort of death we used to pray to Saint Joseph to give us all. He was asleep, his violin next to the bed, covers pulled to his chin. Found in the morning by Geraldine.

There was a large funeral with the usual viewing, at which people filed up to his body and tucked flowers and pipe tobacco and small tokens into Shamengwa's coffin to accompany him into the earth. Geraldine placed a monarch butterfly upon his shoulder. She said that she had found it that morning on the grille of her car. Halfway through the service, she stood up and took the violin from the coffin, where it had been tucked up close to her father.

"A few months ago, Dad told me that when he died I was to give this violin to Corwin Peace," she told everyone. "And so I'm offering it to him now. And I've already asked him to play us one of Dad's favorites today."

Corwin had been sitting in the back and now he walked up to the front, his shoulders hunched, hands shoved in his pockets. The sorrow in his face surprised me. It made me uneasy to see such a direct show of emotion in one who had been so volatile. But Corwin's feelings seemed directed once he took up the fiddle and

began to play. He played a chanson everyone knew, a song typical
of our people because it began tender and slow, then broke into a
wild strangeness that pricked our pulses and strained our breath.
Corwin played with passion, if not precision, and there was enough
of the old man's energy in his music that by the time he'd finished
everybody was in tears.

Then came the shock. Amid the dabbing of eyes and discreet
nose-blowing, Corwin stood gazing into the coffin at his teacher,
the violin dangling from one hand. Beside the coffin there was
an ornate communion rail. Corwin raised the violin high and
smashed it on the rail, once, twice, three times, to do the job right.
I was in the front pew, and I jumped from my seat as though I'd
been prepared for something like this. I grasped Corwin's arm as
he laid the violin carefully back beside Shamengwa, but then I let
him go, for I recognized that his gesture was spent. My focus moved
from Corwin to the violin itself, because I saw, sticking from its
smashed wood, a roll of paper. I drew the paper out. It was old and
covered with a stiff, antique flow of writing. The priest, somewhat
shaken, began the service again. I put the roll of paper into my
jacket pocket and returned to my seat. I didn't exactly forget to
read it. There was just so much happening after the funeral, what
with the windy burial and then the six-kinds-of-fry-bread supper in
the Knights of Columbus Hall, that I didn't get the chance to sit
still and concentrate. It was evening and I was at home, comfortable in my chair with a bright lamp turned on behind me, so the ra-
diance fell over my shoulder, before I finally read what had been
hidden in the violin for so many years.

IV

I, Baptiste Parentheau, also known as Billy Peace, leave to my
brother Edwin this message, being a history of the violin which on
this day of Our Lord August 20, 1897, I send out onto the waters to
find him.

A recapitulation to begin with: Having read of LaFountaine's
mission to the Iroquois, during which that priest avoided having
his liver plucked out before his eyes by nimbly playing the flute,
our own Father Jasprine thought it wise to learn to play a musical
instrument before he ventured forth into the wastelands past the

Lake of the Woods. Therefore, he set off with music as his protection. He studied and brought along his violin, a noble instrument, which he played less than adequately. If the truth were told, he'd have done better not to impose his slight talents on the Ojibwa. Yet, as he died young and left the violin to his altar boy, my father, I should say nothing against good Jasprine. I should, instead, be grateful for the joys his violin afforded my family. I should be happy in the hours that my father spent tuning and then playing the thing, and in the devotion that my brother and I eagerly gave to it. Yet, as things ended so hard between my brother and myself because of the instrument, I find myself imagining that we never knew the violin, that I'd never played its music or understood its voice. For when my father died he left the fiddle to both my brother Edwin and myself, with the stipulation that were we unable to decide who should have it, then we were to race for it as true sons of the great waters, by paddling our canoes.

When my brother and I heard this declaration read, we said nothing. There was nothing to say, for as much as it was true that we loved each other, we both wanted that violin. Each of us had given it years of practice, each of us had whispered into its hollow our sorrows and taken hold of its joys. That violin had soothed our wild hours, courted our wives. But now we were done with the passing of it back and forth. And if it had to belong to one of us two brothers, I determined that it would be me.

Two nights before we took our canoes out, I conceived of a sure plan. When the moon slipped behind clouds and the world was dark, I went out to the shore with a pannikin of heated pitch. I had decided to interfere with Edwin's balance. Our canoes were so carefully constructed that each side matched ounce for ounce. By thickening the seams on one side with a heavy application of pitch, I'd throw off Edwin's paddle stroke enough, I was sure, to give me a telling advantage.

Ours is a wide lake and full of islands. It is haunted by birds who utter sarcastic or sad cries. One loses sight of others easily, and sound travels skewed, bouncing off the rock cliffs. There are flying skeletons, floating bogs, caves containing the spirits of little children, and black moods of weather. We love it well, and we know its secrets — in some part, at least. Not all. And not the secret that I put in motion.

We were to set off on the far northern end of the lake and arrive at the south, where our uncles had lit fires and brought the violin, wrapped in red cloth, in its fancy case. We started out together, joking. Edwin, you remember how we paddled through the first two narrows, laughing as we exaggerated our efforts, and how I said, as what I'd done with the soft pitch weighed on me, "Maybe we should share the damn thing after all."

You laughed and said that our uncles would be disappointed, waiting there, and that when you won the contest things would be as they were before, except all would know that Edwin was the faster paddler. I promised you the same. Then you swerved behind a skim of rock and took your secret shortcut. As I paddled, I had to stop occasionally and bail. At first I thought that I had sprung a slow leak, but in time I understood. While I was painting on extra pitch, you were piercing the bottom of my canoe. I was not, in fact, in any danger, and when the wind shifted all of a sudden and it began to storm — no thunder or lightning, just a buffet of cold rain — I laughed and thanked you. For the water I took on actually helped to steady me. I rode lower, and stayed on course. But you foundered. It was worse to be set off balance. You must have overturned.

The bonfires die to coals on the south shore. I curl in blankets but I do not sleep. I am keeping watch. At first when you are waiting for someone, every shadow is an arrival. Then the shadows become the very substance of dread. We hunt for you, call your name until our voices are worn to whispers. No answer. In one old man's dream everything goes around the other way, the not-sun-way, counterclockwise, which means that the dream is of the spirit world. And then he sees you there in his dream, going the wrong way too.

The uncles have returned to their houses, pastures, children, wives. I am alone on the shore. As the night goes black, I sing for you. As the sun comes up, I call across the water. White gulls answer. As the time goes on, I begin to accept what I have done. I begin to know the truth of things.

They have left the violin here with me. Each night I play for you, brother, and when I can play no more I'll lash our fiddle into the canoe and send it out to you, to find you wherever you are. I won't have to pierce the bottom so it will travel the bed of the lake. Your holes will do the trick, brother, as my trick did for you.

V

Of course, the canoe did not sink to the bottom of the lake. Nor did it stray. The canoe and its violin eventually found a different Peace, through the person of Shamengwa. The fiddle had searched long, I had no doubt of that. For what stuck in my mind, what woke me in the middle of the night, was the date on the letter: 1897. The violin had spoken to Shamengwa and called him out onto the lake more than twenty years later.

"How about that?" I said to Geraldine. "Can you explain such a thing?"

She looked at me steadily.

"We know nothing" is what she said. I was to marry her. We took in Corwin. The violin lies buried in the arms of the man it saved, while the boy it also saved plays for money now and prospers here on the surface of the earth. I do my work. I do my best to make the small decisions well, and I try not to hunger for the greater things, for the deeper explanations. For I am sentenced to keep watch over this little patch of earth, to judge its miseries and tell its stories. That's who I am. *Mii'sago iw.*

ANTHONY DOERR

The Shell Collector

FROM THE CHICAGO REVIEW

THE SHELL COLLECTOR was scrubbing limpets at his sink when he heard the water-taxi come scraping over the reef. He cringed to hear it — its hull grinding the calices of finger corals and the tiny tubes of pipe organ corals, tearing the flower and fern shapes of soft corals, and damaging shells too: punching holes in olives and murexes and spiny whelks, sending *Hydatina physis* and *Turis babylonia* spinning. It was not the first time people had hired a motorboat taxi to seek him out.

He heard their feet splash ashore and the taxi motor off, back to Lamu, and the light singsong pattern of their knock. Tumaini, his German shepherd, let out a low whine from where she was crouched under his sleeping cot. He dropped a limpet into the sink, wiped his hands, and went, reluctantly, to greet them.

They were both named Jim, overweight reporters from a New York tabloid. Their handshakes were slick and hot. He poured them chai. They occupied a surprising amount of space in the kitchen. They said they were there to write about him: they would stay only two nights, pay him well. How did $10,000 American sound? He pulled a shell from his shirt pocket — a cerith — and rolled it in his fingers. They asked about his childhood: did he really shoot caribou as a boy? Didn't he need good vision for that?

He gave them truthful answers. It all held the air of whim, of unreality. These two big Jims could not actually be at his table, asking him these questions, complaining of the stench of dead shellfish. Finally they asked him about cone shells and the strength of cone venom, about how many visitors had come. They asked nothing about his son.

All night it was hot. Lightning marbled the sky beyond the reef. From his cot he heard siafu feasting on the big men and heard them claw themselves in their sleeping bags. Before dawn he told them to shake out their shoes for scorpions, and when they did one tumbled out. He heard its tiny scrapings as it skittered under the refrigerator.

He took his collecting bucket and clipped Tumaini into her harness, and she led them down the path to the reef. The air smelled like lightning. The Jims huffed to keep up. They told him they were impressed he moved so quickly.

"Why?"

"Well," they murmured, "you're blind. This path ain't easy. All these thorns."

Far off, he heard the high, amplified voice of the muezzin in Lamu calling prayer. "It's Ramadan," he told the Jims. "The people don't eat when the sun is above the horizon. They drink only chai until sundown. They will be eating now. Tonight we can go out if you like. They grill meat in the streets."

By noon they had waded a kilometer out, onto the great curved spine of the reef, the lagoon slopping quietly behind them, a low sea breaking in front. The tide was coming up. Unharnessed now, Tumaini stood panting, half out of the water on a mushroom-shaped dais of rock. The shell collector was stooped, his fingers middling, quivering, whisking for shells in a sandy trench. He snatched up a spindle shell, ran a fingernail over its prickled spiral. *Fusinius colus,* "he said.

Automatically, as the next wave came, the shell collector raised his collecting bucket so it would not be swamped. As soon as the wave passed he plunged his arms back into sand, his fingers probing an alcove between anemones, pausing to identify a clump of brain coral, running after a snail as it burrowed away.

One of the Jims had a snorkeling mask and was using it to look underwater. "Lookit these blue fish," he gasped. "Lookit that *blue.*"

The shell collector was thinking, just then, of the persistence of nematocysts. Even after death the tiny cells will discharge their poison — a single dried tentacle on the shore, severed eight days, stung a village boy last year and swelled his legs. A weeverfish bite bloated a man's entire right side, blacked his eyes, turned him dark purple. A stone fish sting corroded the skin off the sole of the shell collector's own heel, years ago, left the skin smooth and printless. How many urchin spikes, broken but still spurting venom, had he squeezed from Tumaini's paw? What would happen to these Jims if a banded sea snake came slipping up between their fat legs?

"Here is what you came to see," he announced, and pulled the snail — a cone — from its collapsing tunnel. He spun it and balanced its flat end on two fingers. Even now its poisoned proboscis was nosing forward, searching out his fingers. The Jims waded noisily over.

"This is a Geography Cone," he said. "It eats fish."

"*That* eats fish?" one of the Jims asked. "But my pinkie's bigger."

"This animal," said the shell collector, dropping it into his bucket, "has twelve kinds of venom in its teeth. It could paralyze you and drown you right here."

This all started when a malarial Seattle-born Buddhist named Nancy was stung by a cone shell in the shell collector's kitchen. It crawled in from the ocean, slogging a hundred meters under coconut palms, through acacia scrub, bit her, and made for the door.

Or maybe it started before Nancy, maybe it grew outward from the shell collector himself, the way a shell grows, spiraling upward from the inside, whorling around its inhabitant, all the while being worn down by the weathers of the sea.

The Jims were right: the shell collector did hunt caribou. Nine years old in Whitehorse, Canada, and his father would send the boy leaning out the bubble canopy of his helicopter in cutting sleet to cull sick caribou with a scoped carbine. But then there was choroideremia and degeneration of the retina; in a year his eyesight was tunneled, spattered with rainbow-colored halos. By twelve, when his father took him four thousand miles south, to Florida, to see a specialist, his vision had dwindled into darkness.

The ophthalmologist knew the boy was blind as soon as he walked through the door, one hand clinging to his father's belt, the other arm held straight, palm out, to stiff-arm obstacles. Rather than examine him — what was left to examine? — the doctor ushered him into his office, pulled off the boy's shoes, and walked him out the back door down a sandy lane onto a spit of beach. The boy had never seen the sea and he struggled to absorb it: the blurs that were waves, the smears that were weeds strung over the tideline.

The doctor showed him a kelp bulb, let him break it in his hands and scrape its interior with his thumb. There were many such discoveries: a small horseshoe crab mounting a larger one in the wavebreak, a fistful of mussels clinging to the damp underside of rock. And then, as he waded ankle-deep, his toes came upon a small round shell no longer than a segment of his thumb. His fingers dug up the shell, he felt the sleek egg of its body, the toothy gap of its aperture. It was the most elegant thing he'd ever held. "That's a mouse cowry," the doctor said. "A lovely find. It has brown spots, and darker stripes at its base, like tiger stripes. You can't see it, can you?"

But he could. His fingers caressed the shell, flipped and rotated it. He had never felt anything so smooth — had never imagined something could possess such deep polish. He asked, nearly whispering, "Who *made* this?" The shell was still in his hand a week later, when his father pried it out, complaining of the stink.

Overnight his world became shells, conchology, the phylum Mollusca. In Whitehorse, during the sunless winter, he learned Braille, mail-ordered shell books, turned up logs after thaws to root for wood snails. At sixteen, burning for the reefs he had discovered in books like *The Wonders of Great Barrier,* he left Whitehorse for good and crewed sailboats through the tropics: Sanibel Island, St. Lucia, the Batan Islands, Colombo, Bora Bora, Cairns, Mombassa, Moorea. All this blind. His skin went brown, his hair white. His fingers, his senses, his mind — all of him — obsessed over the geometry of exoskeletons, the sculpture of calcium, the evolutionary rationale for ramps, spines, beads, whorls, folds. He learned to identify a shell by flipping it up in his hand; the shell spun, his fingers assessed its form, classified it: *Ancilla, Ficus, Terebra.* He returned to Florida, earned a bachelor's in biology, a Ph.D. in malacology. He circled the equator; got terribly lost in the streets of Fiji; got robbed in Guam and again in the Seychelles; discovered new species of bivalves, a new family of tusk shells, a new *Nassarius,* a new *Fragum.*

Four books, three Seeing Eye shepherds, and a son named Josh later, he retired early from his professorship and moved to a thatch-roofed kibanda just north of Lamu, Kenya, one hundred kilometers south of the equator in a small marine park in the remotest elbow of the Lamu Archipelago. He was fifty-eight years old. He had realized, finally, that he would only understand so much, that malacology only led him downward, to more questions. He had never comprehended the endless variations of design: Why this lattice ornament? Why these fluted scales, these lumpy nodes? Ignorance was, in the end, and in so many ways, a privilege: to find a shell, to feel it, to understand only on some unspeakable level why it bothered to be so lovely. What joy he found in that, what utter mystery.

Every six hours the tides plowed shelves of beauty onto the beaches of the world, and here he was, able to walk out into it, thrust his hands into it, spin a piece of it between his fingers. To gather up seashells — each one an amazement — to know their names, to drop them into a bucket: this was what filled his life, what overfilled it.

Some mornings, moving through the lagoon, Tumaini splashing comfortably ahead, he felt a nearly irresistible urge to bow down.

But then, two years ago, there was this twist in his life, this spiral which was at once inevitable and unpredictable, like the aperture in a horn shell. (Imagine running a thumb down one, tracing its helix, fingering its flat spiral ribs, encountering its sudden, twisting opening.) He was sixty-three, moving out across the shadeless beach behind his kibanda, poking a beached sea cucumber with his toe, when Tumaini, who was not yet so confused by visitors that she crouched under a cot daylong, yelped and skittered and dashed away, galloping down-shore, her collar jangling. When the shell collector caught up, he caught up with Nancy, sunstroked and incoherent, wandering the beach in a khaki travel suit as if she had dropped from the clouds, fallen from a 747. He took her inside and laid her on his cot and poured warm chai down her throat. She shivered awfully; he radioed Dr. Kabiru, who boated in from Lamu.

"A fever has her," Dr. Kabiru pronounced, and poured seawater over her chest, swamping her blouse and the shell collector's floor. Eventually her fever fell, the doctor left, and she slept and did not wake for two days. To the shell collector's surprise, no one came looking for her — no one called; no taxi-boats came speeding into the lagoon ferrying frantic American search parties.

As soon as she recovered enough to talk she talked tirelessly, a torrent of divulged privacies. She'd been coherent for a half-hour when she explained she'd left a husband and kids. She'd been naked in her pool, floating on her back, when she realized that her life — two children, a three-story Tudor, an Audi wagon — was not what she wanted. She'd left that day. At some point, traveling through Cairo, she ran across a neo-Buddhist who turned her on to words like inner peace and equilibrium. She was on her way to live with him in Tanzania when she contracted malaria. "But look!" she exclaimed, tossing up her hands. "I wound up here!" As if it were all settled.

The shell collector nursed and listened and made her toast. Every three days she faded into shivering delirium. He knelt by her and trickled seawater over her chest, as Dr. Kabiru had prescribed.

Most days she seemed fine, babbling her secrets. He fell for her, in his own unspoken way. In the lagoon she would call to him and he would swim to her, show her the even stroke he could muster with his sixty-three-year-old arms. In the kitchen he tried making her Mickey Mouse pancakes and she assured him, giggling, that they were delicious.

And then one midnight she climbed onto him. Before he was fully awake, they had made love. Afterward he heard her crying. Was sex something to cry about? "You miss your kids," he said.

"No." Her face was in the pillow and her words were muffled. "I don't need them anymore. I just need balance. Equilibrium."

"Maybe you miss your family. It's only natural."

She turned to him. "Natural? You don't seem to miss *your* kid. I've seen those letters he sends. I don't see you sending any back."

"Well, he's thirty . . ." he said. "And I didn't run off."

"Didn't run off? You're three trillion miles from home! Some retirement. No fresh water, no friends. Bugs crawling in the bathtub."

He didn't know what to say: what did she want, anyhow? He went out collecting.

Tumaini seemed grateful for it, to be in the sea, under the moon, perhaps just to be away from her master's garrulous guest. He unclipped her harness; she nuzzled his calves as he waded. It was a lovely night, a cooling breeze flowing around their bodies, the warmer tidal current running against it, threading between their legs. Tumaini paddled to a rock perch, and he began to roam, stooped, his fingers probing the sand. A marlinspike, a crowned nassa, a branched murex, a lined bullia, small voyagers navigating the current-packed ridges of sand. He admired their sleekness and put them back where he found them. Just before dawn he found two cone shells he couldn't identify, three inches long and audacious, attempting to devour a damselfish they had paralyzed.

When he returned, hours later, the sun was warm on his head and shoulders and he came smiling into the kibanda to find Nancy catatonic on his cot. Her forehead was cold and damp. He rapped his knuckles on her sternum and she did not reflex. Her pulse measured at twenty, then eighteen. He phoned Dr. Kabiru, who motored his launch over the reef and knelt beside her and spoke in her ear. "Bizarre reaction to malaria," the doctor mumbled. "Her heart hardly beats."

The shell collector paced his kibanda, blundered into chairs and tables that had been unmoved for ten years. Finally he knelt on the kitchen floor, not praying so much as buckling. Tumaini, who was agitated and confused, mistook despair for playfulness, and rushed to him, knocking him over. Lying there on the tile, Tumaini slobbering on his cheek, he felt the cone shell, the snail inching its way, blindly, purposefully, toward the door.

Under a microscope, the shell collector had been told, the teeth of cones look long and sharp, like tiny translucent bayonets. The proboscis slips out the siphonal canal, unrolling, the barbed teeth spring forward. In victims the bite causes a spreading insentience, a rising tide of paralysis. First your palm goes horribly cold, then your forearm, then your shoulder. The chill spreads to your chest. You can't swallow, you can't see. You burn. You freeze to death.

"There is nothing," Dr. Kabiru said, eyeing the snail, "I can do for this. No antivenom, no fix. I can do nothing." He wrapped Nancy in a blanket and sat by her in a canvas chair and ate a mango with his penknife. The shell collector boiled the cone shell in the chai pot and forked the snail out with a steel needle. He held the shell, fingered its warm pavilion, felt its mineral convolutions.

Ten hours of this vigil, a sunset and bats feeding and the bats gone full-bellied into their caves at dawn, and then Nancy came to, suddenly, miraculously, bright-eyed.

"That," she announced, sitting up in front of the dumbfounded doctor, "was the most incredible thing ever." As if she had just fin-

ished viewing some hypnotic twelve-hour cartoon. She claimed the sea had gone slushy and snow blew down around her and all of it — the sea, the snowflakes, the white frozen sky — pulsed. *"Pulsed!"* she shouted. "Sssshhh!" she yelled at the doctor, at the stunned shell collector. "It's still pulsing! *Whump! Whump!"*

She was, she exclaimed, cured of malaria, cured of delirium; she was *balanced*. "Surely," the shell collector said, "you're not entirely recovered," but even as he said this he wasn't so sure. She smelled different, like meltwater, like slush, glaciers softening in spring. She spent the morning swimming in the lagoon, squealing and splashing. She ate a tin of peanut butter, practiced high leg-kicks on the beach, sang Neil Diamond songs in a high, scratchy voice.

That night there was another surprise: she begged to be bitten with a cone again. She promised she'd fly directly home to be with her kids, she'd phone her husband in the morning and plead forgiveness, but first he had to sting her with one of those incredible shells one more time. She was on her knees. She pawed up his shorts. "Please," she begged. She smelled so different.

He refused. Exhausted, dazed, he sent her away on a water-taxi to Lamu.

The surprises weren't over. The course of his life was diving into its reverse spiral by now, into that dark, whorling aperture. A week after Nancy's recovery, Dr. Kabiru's motor-launch again came sputtering over the reef. And behind him were others; the shell collector heard the hulls of four or five dhows come over the coral, heard the splashes as people hopped out to drag the boats ashore. Soon his kibanda was crowded. They stepped on whelks drying on the front step, trod over a pile of chitons by the bathroom. Tumaini retreated under the shell collector's cot, put her muzzle on her paws.

Dr. Kabiru announced that a mwadhini, the mwadhini of Lamu's oldest and largest mosque, was here to visit the shell collector, and with him were the mwadhini's brothers, and his brothers-in-law. The shell collector shook the men's hands as they greeted him, dhow-builders' hands, fishermen's hands.

The doctor explained that the mwadhini's daughter was terribly ill; she was only eight years old, and her already malignant malaria had become something altogether more malignant, something the doctor did not recognize. Her skin had gone mustard-seed yellow, she threw up several times a day, her hair fell out. Worse yet: she had degenerated rapidly. For the past three days she had been delirious, wasted. She tore at her own skin. Her wrists had to be bound to the headboard. These men, the doctor said, wanted the shell collector to give her the same treatment he had given the American woman. He would be paid.

The shell collector felt them crowded into the room, these ocean Muslims in their rustling kanzus and squeaking flip-flops, each stinking of his work — gutted perch, fertilizer, hull tar — each leaning in to hear his reply.

"This is ridiculous," he said. "She will die. What happened to Nancy was some kind of fluke. It was not a treatment."

"We have tried everything," the doctor said.

"What you ask is impossible," the shell collector repeated. "Worse than impossible. Insane."

There was silence. Finally a voice directly before him spoke, a strident, resonant voice, a voice he heard five times a day as it swung out from loudspeakers over the rooftops of Lamu and summoned people to prayer. "The child's mother," the mwadhini began, "and I, and my brothers, and my brothers' wives, and the whole island of Lamu, we have prayed for this child. We have prayed for many months. It seems sometimes that we have always prayed for her. And then today the doctor tells us of this American who was cured of the same disease by a snail. Such a simple cure. Elegant, would you not say? A snail which accomplishes what laboratory capsules cannot. Allah, we reason, must be involved in something so elegant. So you see. These are signs all around us. We must not ignore them."

The shell collector refused again. "She must be small, if she is only eight. Her body will not withstand the venom of a cone. Nancy could have died — she *should* have died. Your daughter will be killed."

The mwadhini stepped closer, took the shell collector's face in his hands. "Are these," he intoned, "not strange and amazing coincidences? That this American was cured of her afflictions and that my child has similar afflictions? That you are here and I am here, that animals right now crawling in the sand outside your door harbor the cure?"

The shell collector paused. Finally he said, "Imagine a snake, a terribly venomous sea snake. The kind of venom that swells a body to bruising. It stops the heart. It causes screaming pain. You're asking this snake to bite your daughter."

"We're sorry to hear this," said a voice behind the mwadhini. "We're very sorry to hear this." The shell collector's face was still in the mwadhini's hands. After long moments of silence, he was pushed aside. He heard men, uncles probably, out at the washing sink, splashing around.

"You won't find a cone out there," he yelled. Tears rose to the corners of his dead sockets. How strange it felt to have his home overrun by unseen men.

The mwadhini's voice continued: "My daughter is my only child. Without her my family will go empty. It will no longer be a family."

His voice bore an astonishing faith, in the slow and beautiful way it trilled sentences, in the way it enunciated each syllable. The mwadhini was convinced, the shell collector realized, that a snail bite would heal his daughter.

The voice raveled on: "You hear my brothers in your back yard, clattering among your shells. They are desperate men. Their niece is dying. If they must, they will wade out onto the coral, as they have seen you do, and they will heave boulders and tear up corals and stab the sand with shovels until they find what they are looking for. Of course they too, when they find it, may be bitten. They may swell up and die. They will — how did you say it? — have screaming pain. They do not know how to capture such animals, how to hold them."

His voice, the way he held the shell collector's face. All this was a kind of persuasion.

"You want this to happen?" the mwadhini continued. His voice hummed, sang, became a murmurous soprano. "You want my brothers to be bitten also?"

"No. I want only to be left alone."

"Yes," the mwadhini said, "left alone. A stay-at-home, a hermit, a mtawa. Whatever you want. But first, you will find one of these cone shells for my daughter, and you will sting her with it. Then you will be left alone."

At low tide, accompanied by an entourage of the mwadhini's brothers, the shell collector waded with Tumaini out onto the reef and began to upturn rocks and probe into the sand beneath, to try to extract a cone. Each time his fingers flurried into loose sand, or into a crab-guarded socket in the coral, a volt of fear would speed down his arm and jangle his fingers. *Conus tessulatus, Conus obscurus, Conus geographus,* who knew what he would find. The waiting proboscis, the poisoned barbs. You spend your life avoiding these things; you end up seeking them out.

He whispered to Tumaini, "We need a small one, the smallest we can," and she seemed to understand, wading with her ribs against his knee, or paddling when it became too deep, but these men leaned in all around him, splashing in their wet kanzus, watching with their dark, redolent attention.

It was exhausting, but he'd handled cones a thousand times before and knew how to spin the shell and hold it by its apex, how to do this so rapidly the animal had no time to spear his fingertip. By noon he had one, a tiny tessellated cone he hoped couldn't paralyze a housecat, and he dropped it in a mug with some seawater.

They ferried him to Lamu, to the mwadhini's home, a surfside jumba with marble floors. They led him to the back, up a vermicular staircase, past a tinkling fountain, to the girl's room. He found her hand, her wrist still lashed to the bedpost, and held it. It was small and damp and he could feel the thin fan of her bones through her skin. He poured the mug out into her palm and folded her fingers, one by one, around the snail. It seemed to pulse there, in the delicate vaulting of her hand, like the small dark heart at the center of a songbird. He was able to imagine, in acute detail, the snail's translucent proboscis as it slipped free, the quills of its teeth probing her skin, the venom spilling into her.

"What," he asked into the silence, "is her name?"

Further amazement: the girl, whose name was Seema, recovered. Completely. For ten hours she was cold, catatonic. The shell collector spent the night standing in a window, listening to Lamu: donkeys clopping up the street, nightbirds squelching from somewhere in the acacia to his right, hammer strokes on metal, far off, and the surf, washing into the pylons of the docks. He heard the morning prayer sung in the mosques. He began to wonder if he'd been forgotten, if hours ago the girl had passed gently into death and no one had thought to tell him. Perhaps a mob was silently gathering to drag him off and stone him, and wouldn't he have deserved every stone?

But then the cooks began whistling and clucking, and the mwadhini, who had squatted by his daughter nightlong, palms up in supplication, hurried past. "Chapatis," he gushed. "She wants chapatis." The mwadhini brought her them himself, cold chapatis slathered with mango jam.

By the following day everyone knew a miracle had occurred in the mwadhini's house. Word spread, like a drifting cloud of coral eggs, spawning, frenzied; it left the island and lived for a while in the daily gossip of coastal Kenyans. The *Daily Nation* ran a back-page story, and KBC ran a minute-long radio spot featuring soundbites from Dr. Kabiru: "I did not know one hundred percent that it would work, no. But, having extensively researched, I was confident . . ."

Within days the shell collector's kibanda became a kind of pilgrim's destination. At almost any hour he heard the buzz of motorized dhows, or the oar-knocking of rowboats, as visitors came over the reef into the lagoon. Everyone, it seemed, had a sickness that required remedy. Lepers came, and children with ear infections, and it was not unusual for the shell collector to blunder into someone as he made his way from the kitchen to the bathroom. His conches were carted off, and his neat mound of scrubbed limpets. His entire collection of Flinders' vase shells disappeared.

Tumaini, thirteen years old and long settled into her routine with her master, did not fare well. Never aggressive, now she became terrified of nearly everything: termites, fire ants, stone crabs. She barked her voice out at the moon's rising. She spent nearly all her hours under the shell collector's cot, wincing at the smells of strangers' sicknesses, and didn't perk up even when she heard her food dish come down upon the kitchen tile.

There were worse problems. People were following the shell collector out into the lagoon, stumbling onto the rocks or the low benches of living coral. A choleric woman brushed up against fire coral and fainted from the pain. Others, thinking she had swooned in rapture, threw themselves on the coral and came away badly welted, weeping. Even at night, when he tried stealing down the path with Tumaini, pilgrims rose from the sand and followed him — unseen feet splashing nearby, unseen hands sifting quietly through his collecting bucket.

It was only a matter of time, the shell collector knew, before something terrible would happen. He had nightmares about finding a corpse bobbing in the wavebreak, bloated with venom. Sometimes it seemed to him that the whole sea had become a tub of poison harboring throngs of villains. Sand eels, stinging corals, sea snakes, crabs, men-of-war, barracuda, mantas, sharks, urchins — who knew what septic tooth would next find skin?

He stopped shelling. He was supposed to send shells back to the university — he had permits to send a boxful every two weeks — but he filled the boxes with old specimens, ceriths or cephalopods he had lying in cupboards or wrapped in newspaper.

And there were always visitors. He made them pots of chai, tried politely to explain that he had no cone shells, that they would be seriously injured or killed if they were bitten. A BBC reporter came, and a wonderful-smelling woman from the *International Tribune;* he begged them to write about the dangers of cones. But they were more interested in miracles than snails; they asked if he had tried pressing cone shells to his eyes and sounded disappointed to hear he had not.

After some months without miracles the number of visits fell off, and Tumaini slunk out from under the cot, but people continued to taxi in, curious tourists or choleric elders without the shillings for a doctor. Still the shell collector did not shell for fear he would be followed. Then, in the mail that came in by boat twice a month, a letter from Josh arrived.

Josh was the shell collector's son, a camp coordinator in Kalamazoo. Like his mother (who had kept the shell collector's freezer stocked with frozen meals for thirty years, despite being divorced from him for twenty-six), Josh was a goody-goody. At age ten he grew zucchini on his mother's back lawn, then distributed them, squash by squash, to soup kitchens in St. Petersburg. He picked up litter wherever he walked, took his own bags to the supermarket, and airmailed a letter to Lamu every month, letters that filled half a page of exclamation-laden Braille without employing a single substantial sentence: *Hi Pop! Things are just fabulous in*

Michigan! I bet it's sunny in Kenya! Have a wonderful Labor Day! Love
you tons!

This month's letter, however, was different.

"Dear Pop!" it read.

I've joined the Peace Corps! I'll be working in Uganda for three years! And guess
what else? I'm coming to stay with you first! I've read about the miracles you've
been working — it's news even here. You got blurbed in The Humanitarian!
I'm so proud! See you soon!

Six mornings later Josh splashed in on a taxi-boat. Immediately
he wanted to know why more wasn't being done for the sick people
clumped in the shade behind the kibanda. "Sweet Jesus!" he exclaimed, slathering suntan lotion over his arms. "These people are
suffering! These poor orphans!" He crouched over three Kikuyu
boys. "Their faces are covered with tiny flies!"

How strange it was to have his son under his roof, to hear him
unzip his huge duffel bags, to come across his Schick razor on the
sink. Hearing him chide ("You feed your dog prawns?"), chug pa-
paya juice, scrub pans, wipe down counters — who was this person
in his home? Where had he come from?

The shell collector had always suspected that he did not know
his son one whit. Josh had been raised by his mother; as a boy
he preferred the baseball diamond to the beach, cooking to conchology. And now he was thirty. He seemed so energetic, so good
. . . so stupid. He was like a golden retriever, fetching things, sloppy-
tongued, panting, falling over himself to please. He used two days
of fresh water giving the Kikuyu boys showers. He spent seventy
shillings on a sisal basket that should have cost him seven. He
insisted on sending visitors off with care packages: plantains or
House of Mangi tea biscuits, wrapped in paper and tied off with
yarn.

"You're doing fine, Pop," he announced one evening at the table. He had been there two weeks. Every night he invited strangers,
diseased people, to the dinner table. Tonight it was a paraplegic
girl and her mother. Josh spooned chunks of curried potato onto
their plates. "You can afford it." The shell collector said nothing.
What could he say? Josh shared his blood; this thirty-year-old do-
gooder had somehow grown out of him, out of the spirals of his
own DNA.

Because he could only take so much of Josh, and because he could not shell for fear of being followed, he began to slip away with Tumaini to walk the shady groves, the sandy plains, the hot, leafless thickets of the island. It was strange moving away from the shore rather than toward it, climbing thin trails, moving inside the ceaseless cicada hum. His shirt was torn by thorns, his skin chewed by insects; his cane struck unidentifiable objects: was that a fence-post? A tree? Soon these walks became shorter; he would hear rustles in the thickets, snakes or wild dogs, perhaps — who knew what awful things bustled in the thickets of that island? — and he'd wave his cane in the air and Tumaini would yelp and they would hurry home.

One day he came across a cone shell in his path, toiling through dust half a kilometer from the sea. *Conus eburneus,* a common enough danger on the reef, but to find it so far from water was impossible. How would a cone come all the way up here? And why? He picked the shell from the path and pitched it into the high grass. On subsequent walks he began coming across cones more frequently: his outstretched hand would come across the trunk of an acacia and on it would be a wandering cone; he'd pick up a hermit crab wandering in the mango grove and find a freeloading cone on its back. Sometimes a stone worked itself into his sandal and he jumped, terrified, thinking it would sting him. He mistook a pinecone for *Conus gloriamaris,* a tree snail for *Conus spectrum.* He began to doubt his previous identifications: maybe the cone he had found in the path was not a cone at all, but a miter shell, or a rounded stone. Maybe it was an empty shell dropped by a villager. Maybe there was no strangely blooming population of cone shells; maybe he had imagined it all. It was terrible not to know.

Everything was changing: the reef, his home, poor frightened Tumaini. Outside, the entire island had become sinister, viperous, paralyzing. Inside, his son was giving away everything — the rice, the toilet paper, the Vitamin B capsules. Perhaps it would be safest just to sit, hands folded, in a chair, and move as little as possible.

Josh had been there three weeks before he brought it up.

"Before I left the States I did some reading," he said, "about cone shells." It was dawn. The shell collector was at the table, waiting for Josh to make him toast. He said nothing.

"They think the venom may have real medical benefits."

"Who is they?"

"Scientists. They say they're trying to isolate some of the toxins and give them to stroke victims. To combat paralysis."

The shell collector felt like saying that injecting cone venom into someone already half paralyzed sounded miraculously stupid.

"Wouldn't that be something, Pop? If what you've done winds up helping thousands of people?"

The shell collector fidgeted, tried to smile.

"I never feel so alive," Josh continued, "as when I'm helping people."

"I can smell the toast burning, Josh."

"There are so many people in the world, Pop, who we can *help*. Do you know how lucky we are? How amazing it is just to be healthy? To be able to reach out?"

"The toast, son."

"Screw the toast! Jesus! Look at you! People are dying on your doorstep and you care about toast!"

He slammed the door on his way out. The shell collector sat and smelled the toast as it burned.

Josh started reading shell books. He'd learned Braille as a Little Leaguer, sitting in his uniform in his father's lab, waiting for his mother to drive him to a game. Now he took books and magazines from the kibanda's one shelf and hauled them out under the palms where the three Kikuyu orphan boys had made their camp. He read aloud to them, stumbling through articles in journals like *Indo-Pacific Mollusca* and *American Conchologist*. "The Blotchy Ancilla," he'd read, "is a slender shell with a deep suture. Its columella is mostly straight." The boys stared at him as he read, hummed senseless, joyful songs.

The shell collector heard Josh, one afternoon, reading to them about cones. "The Admirable Cone is thick and relatively heavy, with a pointed spire." As he read, the boys stared at him and hummed senseless, joyful songs.

Gradually, amazingly, after a week of afternoon readings, the boys grew interested. The shell collector would hear them sifting through the banks of shell fragments left by the spring tide. "Bubble shell!" one would shout. "Kafuna found a bubble shell!" They plunged their hands into the rocks and squealed and shouted and dragged shirtfuls of clams up to the kibanda, identifying them with made-up names: "Blue Pretty! Mbaba Chicken Shell!"

One evening the three boys were eating with them at the table, and he listened to them as they shifted and bobbed in their chairs and clacked their silverware against the table edge like drummers. "You boys have been shelling," the shell collector said.

"Kafuna swallowed a butterfly shell!" one of the boys yelled.

The shell collector continued: "Do you know that some of the shells are dangerous, that dangerous things — bad things — live in the water?"

"Bad shells!" one squealed.

"Bad sheelllls!" the others chimed.

Then they were eating, quietly. The shell collector sat, and wondered.

He tried again the next morning. Josh was hacking coconuts on the front step. "What if those boys get bored with the beach and go out to the reef? What if they get into some fire coral? What if they step on an urchin?"

"Are you saying I'm not keeping an eye on them?" Josh said.

"I'm saying that they might be looking to get bitten. Those boys came here because they thought I could find some magic shell that will cure people. They're here to get stung by a cone shell."

"You don't have the slightest idea," Josh said, "why those boys are here."

"But you do? You think you've read enough about shells to teach them how to look for cones. You *want* them to find one. You hope they'll find a big cone, get stung, and be cured. Cured of whatever ailment they have. I don't even see anything wrong with them."

"Pop," Josh groaned, "those boys are mentally handicapped. I do *not* think some sea snail is going to cure them."

So, feeling very old, and very blind, the shell collector decided to take the boys shelling. He took them out into the lagoon, where the water was flat and warm, wading almost to their chests, and worked alongside them, and did his best to show them which animals were dangerous. "Bad sheelllls!" the boys would scream, and cheered as the shell collector tossed a testy blue crab out, over the reef, into deeper water. Tumaini barked too, and seemed her old self, out there with the boys, in the ocean she loved so dearly.

Finally it was not one of the boys or some other visitor who was bitten, but Josh. He came dashing along the beach, calling for his father, his face bloodless.

"Josh? Josh, is that you?" the shell collector hollered. "I was just showing the boys here this Girdled Triton. A graceful shell, isn't it, boys?"

In his fist, his fingers already going stiff, the back of his hand reddening, the skin distended, Josh held the cone that had bitten him, a snail he'd plucked from the wet sand, thinking it was pretty.

The shell collector hauled Josh across the beach and into some shade under the palms. He wrapped him in a blanket and sent the boys for the phone. Josh's pulse was already weak and rapid and his breath was short. Within an hour his breathing stopped, then his heart, and then he was dead.

The shell collector knelt, dumbfounded, in the sand, and Tumaini lay on her paws in the shade watching him with the boys crouched behind her, their hands on their knees, terrified.

The doctor boated in twenty minutes too late, wheezing, and behind him were police, in small canoes with huge motors. The police took the shell collector into his kitchen and quizzed him about his divorce, about Josh, and about the boys.

Through the window he heard more boats coming and going. A damp breeze came over the sill. It was going to rain, he wanted to tell these men, these half-aggressive, half-lazy voices in his kitchen. It will rain in five minutes, he wanted to say, but they were asking him to clarify Josh's relationship with the boys. Again (was it the third time? the fifth?) they asked why his wife had divorced him. He could not find the words. He felt as if thick clouds were being shoved between him and the world; his fingers, his senses, the ocean — all this was slipping away. My dog, he wanted to say, my dog doesn't understand this. I need my dog.

"I am blind," he told the police finally, turning up his hands. "I have nothing."

Then the storm came, a monsoon assaulting the thatched roof. Frogs, singing somewhere under the floorboards, hurried their tremolo, screamed into the storm.

When the rain let up he heard the water dripping from the roof, and a cricket under the refrigerator started singing. There was a new voice in the kitchen, a familiar voice, the mwadhini's. He said, "You will be left alone now. As I promised."

"My son —" the shell collector began.

"This blindness," the mwadhini said, taking an auger shell from the kitchen table and rolling it over the wood, "it is not unlike a shell, is it? The way a shell protects the animal inside? The way an animal can retreat inside it, tucked safely away? Of course the sick came, of course they came to seek out a cure. Well, you will have your peace now. No one will come to seek miracles now."

"The boys —"

"They will be taken away. They require care. Perhaps an orphanage in Nairobi. Malindi, maybe."

A month later and these Jims were in his kibanda, pouring bourbon into their evening chai. He had answered their questions, told them about Nancy and Seema and Josh. Nancy, they said, had given them exclusive rights to her story. The shell collector could see how they would write it — midnight sex, a blue lagoon, a dangerous African shell-drug, a blind medicine guru with his wolf-dog. There for all New York to peer at: his shell-cluttered kibanda, his pitiful tragedies.

At dusk he rode with them into Lamu. The taxi let them off on a pier and they climbed a hill to town. He heard birds call from the scrub by the road, and from the mango trees that leaned over the path. The air smelled sweet, like cabbage and pineapple. The Jims labored as they walked.

In Lamu the streets were crowded and the street vendors were out, grilling plantains or curried goat over driftwood coals. Pineapples were being sold on sticks, and children moved about yoked with boxes from which they hawked maadazi or chapatis spread with ginger. The Jims and the shell collector bought kebabs and sat in an alley, their backs against a carved wooden door. Before long a passing teenager offered hashish from a water pipe, and the Jims accepted. The shell collector smelled its smoke, sweet and sticky, and heard the water bubble in the pipe.

"Good?" the teenager asked.

"You bet," the Jims coughed. Their speech was slurred.

The shell collector could hear men praying in the mosques, their chants vibrating down the narrow streets. He felt a bit strange, listening to them, as if his head were no longer connected to his body.

"It is Taraweeh," the teenager said. "Tonight Allah determines the course of the world for next year." *Allah is a black stone !*

"Have some," one of the Jims said, and passed the pipe in front of the shell collector's face. "More," the other Jim said, and giggled.

The shell collector took the pipe, inhaled.

It was well after midnight. A crab fisherman in a motorized mtepe was taking them up the archipelago, past banks of mangroves, toward home. The shell collector sat in the bow on a crab trap made from chicken wire and felt the breeze in his face. The boat slowed. "Tokeni," the fisherman said, and the shell collector did, the Jims with him, splashing down from the boat into chest-deep water.

The crab boat motored away and the Jims began murmuring about the phosphorescence, admiring the glowing trails blooming behind each other's bodies as they moved through the water. The shell collector took off his sandals and waded barefoot, down off the sharp spines of coral rock into the deeper lagoon, feeling the hard furrows of intertidal sand and the occasional mats of algal turf, fibrous and ropy. The feeling of disconnectedness had continued, been amplified by the hashish, and it was easy for him to pretend that his legs were unconnected to his body. He was, it seemed suddenly, floating, rising above the sea, feeling down through the water with impossibly long arms into the turquoise shallows and coral-lined alleys. This small reef: the crabs in their expeditions, the anemones tossing their heads, the blizzards of tiny fish wheeling past, pausing, bursting off . . . he felt it all unfold simply below him. A cow fish, a trigger fish, the harlequin Picasso fish, a drifting sponge — all these lives were being lived out, every day, as they always had been. His senses became supernatural: beyond the breaking combers, the dappled lagoon, he heard terns, and the thrum of insects in the acacias, and the heavy shifting of leaves in avocado trees, the sounding of bats, the dry rasping of bark at the collars of coconut palms, spiky burrs dropping from bushes into hot sand, the smooth seashore roar inside an empty trumpet shell, the rotting smell of conch eggs beached in their black pouches, and far down the island, near the horizon — he could walk it down — he knew he would find the finless trunk of a dolphin, rolling in the swash, its flesh already being carted off, piece by piece, by stone crabs.

"What," the Jims asked, their voices far off and blended, "does it feel like to be bitten by a cone shell?"

What strange visions the shell collector had been having, just now. A dead dolphin? Supernatural hearing? What was that? Were they even wading toward his kibanda? Were they anywhere near it?

"I could show you," he said, surprising himself. "I could find some small cones, tiny ones. You would hardly know you'd been bitten. You could write about it."

He began to search for cone shells. He waded, turned in a circle, became quickly disoriented. He moved out to the reef, stepping carefully between the rocks; he was a shorebird, a hunting crane, his beak poised to stab down at any moment, to impale a snail, a wayward fish.

The reef wasn't where he thought it was; it was behind him, and soon he felt the foam of the waves, long breakers clapping across his back, churning the shell fragments beneath his feet, and he sensed the algal ridge just ahead of him, the steep shelf, the rearing, twisting swells. A whelk, a murex, an olive; shell debris washed past his feet. Here, this felt like a cone. So easy to find. He spun it, balanced its flat end on his palm. An arrhythmic wave sucker-punched him, broke over his chin. He spit saltwater. Another wave drove his shin into the rocks.

He thought: God writes next year's plan for the world on this night. He tried to picture God bent over parchment, dreaming, puzzling through the possibilities. "Jim," he shouted, and imagined he heard the big men splashing toward him. But they were not. "Jim!" he called. No answer. They must be in the kibanda, hunkered at the table, folding up their sleeves. They must be waiting for him to bring this cone he has found. He will press it into the crooks of their arms, let the venom spring into their blood. Then they'd know. Then they'd have their story.

He half swam, half clambered back toward the reef and climbed

onto a coral rock, and fell, and went under. His sunglasses came
loose from his face, pendulumed down. He felt for them with his
heels, finally gave up. He'd find them later.

Surely the kibanda was around here somewhere. He moved into
the lagoon, his shirt and hair soaked through. Where were his sandals? They had been in his hand. No matter.

The water became more shallow. Nancy had said there was a
pulse, slow and loud. She said she could still hear it, even after she
woke. The shell collector imagined it as a titanic pulse, the three-
thousand-pound heart of an ice whale. Gallons of blood at a beat.
Perhaps that was what he heard now, the drumming that had begun in his ears.

He was moving toward the kibanda now, he was certain. He felt
the packed ridges of lagoon sand under his soles. He heard the
waves behind him collapsing onto the reef, the coconut palms
ahead rustling, husk on husk. He was bringing an animal from the
reef to paralyze some writers from New York, perhaps kill them.
They had done nothing to him, but here he was, planning their
deaths. Was this what he wanted? Was this what God's plan for his
sixty-some years of life led up to?

His chest was throbbing. Where was Tumaini? He imagined the
Jims clearly, their damp bodies prone in their sleeping bags, exhal-
ing booze and hashish, tiny siafu biting their faces. These were men
who were only doing their jobs.

He took the cone shell and flung it, as far as he could, back into
the lagoon. He would not poison them. It felt wonderful to make a
decision like this. He wished he had more shells to hurl back into
the sea, more poisons to rid himself of. His shoulder seemed terribly stiff.

Then, with a clarity that stunned him, a clarity that washed over
him like a wave, he knew he'd been bitten. He was lost in every way:
in this lagoon, in the shell of his private darkness, in the depths and
convolutions of the venom already crippling his nervous system.
Gulls were landing nearby, calling to each other, and he had been
poisoned by a cone shell.

The stars rolled up over him in their myriad shiverings. His life
had made its final spiral, delving down into its darkest whorl, where
shell tapered into shadow. What did he remember, as he faded, poisoned finally, into the tide? His wife, his father, Josh? Did his child-

hood scroll by first, like a film reel, a boy under the northern lights, clambering into his father's Bell 47 helicopter? What was there, what was the hot, hard kernel of human experience at his center — a dreamy death in water, poison, disappearing, dissolution, the cold sight of his arctic origins or fifty years of blindness, the thunder of a caribou hunt, lashing bullets into the herd from the landing strut of a helicopter? Did he find faith, regret, a great sad balloon of emptiness in his gut, his unseen, barely known son, just one of Josh's beautiful, unanswered letters?

No. There was no time. The venom had spread to his chest. He remembered this: blue. He remembered how that morning one of the Jims had praised the blue body of a reef fish. "That *blue*," he'd said. The shell collector remembered seeing blue in ice fields, in Whitehorse, as a boy. Even now, fifty-five years later, after all his visual memories had waned, even in dreams — the look of the world and his own face long since faded — he remembered how blue looked at the bottom pinch of a crevasse, cobalt and miraculous. He remembered kicking snow over the lip, tiny slivers disappearing into that icy cleft. How strange that his mind hung on to this, that neurons dredged up this one memory from its forgotten bin.

Then his body abandoned him. He felt himself dissolve into that most extravagantly vivid of places, into the clouds rising darkly at the horizon, the stars blazing in their lightless tracts, the trees sprouting up from the sand, the ebbing, pulsing waters. What he must have felt, what awful, frigid loneliness.

The girl, Seema, the mwadhini's daughter, found him in the morning. She was the one who had come, every week since her recovery, to stock his shelves with rice and dried beef, to bring him toilet paper and bread and what mail he had and Uhu milk in paper cartons. Rowing there from Lamu with her nine-year-old arms, out of sight of the island, of other boats, only the mangroves to see, sometimes she would unpin her black wraparound and let the sun down on her shoulders, her neck, her hair.

She found him awash, face up, on a stretch of white sand. He was a kilometer from his home. Tumaini was with him, curled around his chest, her fur sopped, whining softly.

He was barefoot; his left hand was badly swollen, the fingernails black. She dragged his body, which smelled so much like the sea, of the thousands of boiled gastropods he had tweezered from shells, into the surf and heaved him into her little boat, amazed that she could lift him. She fitted the oarlocks and rowed him to his kibanda. Tumaini raced alongside, bounding along the shore, pausing to let the boat catch up, yelping, galloping off again.

When they heard the girl and the dog come clattering up to the door, the Jims burst from their sleeping bags, their hair matted, eyes red, and helped in the best ways they knew. They carried the shell collector in and with the girl's help dialed Dr. Kabiru. They wiped the shell collector's face with a washcloth and listened to his heart beating shallowly and slowly. Twice he stopped breathing, and twice one of those big writers put his mouth on the shell collector's and blew life into his lungs.

He was numb forever. What clockless hours passed, what weeks and months? He didn't know. He dreamed of glass, of miniature glass-blowers making cone teeth like tiny snow-needles, like the thinnest bones of fish, veins on the arms of a snowflake. He dreamed of the ocean glassed over with a thick sheet, and he skated out on it, peering down at the reef, its changing, perilous sculpture, its vast, miniature kingdoms. All of it — the limp tentacles of a coral polyp, the chewed and floating body of a clownfish — was gray and lonesome, torn down. A freezing wind rushed down his collar. The clouds, stringy and ragged, poured past in a terrible frozen hurry. He was the only living thing on the whole surface of the earth, and there was nothing to meet, nothing to see, no ground to stand on.

Sometimes he woke to chai pouring into his mouth. He felt his body freeze it, ice chunks rattle through his guts.

It was Seema who warmed him, finally. She visited every day, rowing from her father's jumba to the shell collector's kibanda, under the white sun, over the turquoise waters. She nursed him out of bed, shooed the siafu from his face, fed him toast. She began walking him outside and sitting with him in the sun. He shivered endlessly. She asked him about his life, about shells he had found, and about the cone shell that saved her life. Eventually she began to hold his wrists and walk him out into the lagoon, and he shivered whenever air touched his wet skin.

*

The shell collector was wading, feeling for shells with his toes. It had been a year since he'd been bitten.

Tumaini perched on a rock and sniffed at the horizon, where a line of gulls threaded along beneath stacks of giant cumulus. Seema was on the reef with them, as she had been nearly every day, her shoulders free of her wraparound. Her hair, usually bound back, hung across her neck and reflected the sun. What comfort it was to be with a person who could not see, who did not care anyway.

Seema watched as a school of fish, tiny and spear-shaped, flashed just below the surface of the water. They stared up at her with ten thousand round eyes, then turned lazily. Their shadows glided over the rutted sand, over a fern-shaped colony of coral. Those are needlefish, she thought, and that is Xenia soft coral. I know their names, how they rely on each other.

The shell collector moved a few meters, stopped, and bent. He had come across what he thought was a bullia — a blind snail with a grooved, high-spired shell — and he kept his hand on it, two fingers resting lightly on the apex. After a long moment, waiting, tentative, the snail brought its foot from the aperture and resumed hauling itself over the sand. The shell collector, using his fingers, followed it for a while, then stood. "Beautiful," he murmured. Beneath his feet the snail kept on, feeling its way forward, dragging the house of its shell, fitting its body to the sand, to the private, unlit horizons that whorled all around it.

E. L. DOCTOROW

Baby Wilson

FROM THE NEW YORKER

I HAD TAKEN UP WITH HER, knowing she was this crazy lovesick girl. It was against my better judgment. I was too accustomed to having my life made easy. I was stopped in my tracks by the smitten sweet smile and the pale eyes. With straight brown hair she never fussed with but to wash it. And she wore long cotton dresses and no shoes in the business district. Karen. A whole year ago. And now she had gone and done this thing.

She held it out to me all rolled up in a blanket.

Where'd you get that?

Lester, this is our baby. He is named Jesu because he is a Spanish-looking child. He will be a dark saturnine young man with slim hips like yours.

The face was still red with its effort to be born, and its hair was slick with something like pomade, and it had small dark eyes struggling to see. Around his wrist was a plastic band.

I don't want to hold him, I said. Take him back.

Oh, silly man, she said, smiling, cradling it in her arms. It's not hard to hold a dear child.

No, Karen, I mean take him back to the hospital where you stole him.

I couldn't do that, Lester. I couldn't do that, this is my newborn child, this is my tiny little thing his momma loves so that I am giving him to you to be your son.

And she smiled at me, that dreamland smile of hers.

She moved her shoulders from side to side and sang to it, but the little arms sort of jerked and waved a bit and she didn't seem to notice. There was a dried blob of blood on the front of its wrappings.

I looked at the clock. It was just noon. Was this a reasonable day, Karen should have been at Nature's Basket doing up her flowers.

I went into the bedroom and put on my jeans and a fresh shirt. I wet my hair and combed it and got a beer from the kitchen.

There were two hospitals in Crenshaw, the private one, in the historic district, and the county one, out by the interstate. What did it matter where she took it from, either one would be just as good. Or I could drive it direct to the police station, not the smartest move in the world. Or I could just take the Durango and leave.

Instead of doing any of these things by which I would finally reform into a person who makes executive decisions, I thought to myself, I would not want to shock such a woman in her dangerous blissful state of mind, and so went back and tried again as if you could argue sense into someone who was never too steady to begin with and was now totally bereft of her remaining faculties.

This is wrong, Karen. It is wrong to go around stealing babies.

But this is my baby, she said, staring into its face. I mean our baby, Lester. Yours and mine. I bore it as you conceived it.

I went over to the couch where she had sat down, and I looked again at the wristband. It said "Baby Wilson."

My name is not Wilson and your name is not Wilson, I said.

That is a simple clerical error. Jesu is our love child, Lester. He is the indissoluble bond God has placed upon our union. God commanded this. We can never part now, we are a family.

And she looked at me with her pale eyes all a-dazzle.

Jesu, if it was him, was crying in little yelps, and its head was turning this way and that with its mouth open and its little hands were all a-tremor.

I had known she would finally put me at risk. I tried to pay no attention when she stole things and presented them to me, because they were little things and of no use. A Mexican embroidered nightshirt — whereas I like to sleep in the altogether — or a silver money clip in the shape of an *L* for Lester, like I was some downtown lawyer, or an antique music box, for Christ's sake, that plays "Columbia, the Gem of the Ocean," as if anyone would want to hear it more than once. Totally the wrong things for me, if it was me she was stealing for, whereas I was hard pressed to get a decent meal in this household.

Karen opened her blouse and put the baby to her breast. It

hadn't changed any that I could see — of course, there was no milk there.

I sat down next to her and pointed the remote at the TV: cartoon, a rerun, puppets, a rerun, nature, a preacher, and then I found the local news station.

Just like them, they hadn't heard the news yet.

Karen, I said, I'll be right back, and I drove into town to the Bluebird. It was lunchtime, busy as hell, and Brenda wasn't too pleased, but seeing the look in my eyes she took a cigarette break out the back door. I told her what was what.

She stood listening, Brenda, and shook her head.

Lester, she said, your brains are in your balls. That is the way you are and the way you'll always be.

God damn it, Brenda, it's not something I've done, you understand. Is this what I need to hear from you right now?

She was squinting at me from the smoke drifting up into her eyes.

I said, And you sometimes haven't minded if that's where my brain is, as I recall.

Brenda is as unlike Karen as two women can be. Sturdier in mind, and shaped as if for the Bluebird clientele in her powder-blue uniform with the *Brenda* stitched on the bosom pocket.

Are you aware, she said, that kidnapping is a federal offense? Are you aware that if something happens to that infant the both of you — I'm saying the both of you, don't shake your head no — let's see, how do they do it in this state, I forget, electricity or the needle? I mean all Alice in Wonderland will end up is in the loony bin, but you as aiding and abetting — goodbye, Charlie.

I was beginning to feel sick to my stomach standing there out in the sun with the Bluebird garbage bins in full reek.

She ground out her cigarette and took me by the arm and walked me around to the parking lot.

Now, Lester, the first thing is to go to the Kmart and buy you some infant formula — I believe it comes in their own plastic bottles these days. You follow the instructions and feed that baby so it doesn't die, as it surely will if you don't step in here. And while you're at it buy you an armload of diapers, they come with Velcro now, and a nightie or three and a cap for its head — she looked up at the sky — it's supposed to get cooler later on. And whatever else

you see there in Infants and Toddlers that might come in useful.
You understand me?

I nodded.

And then, when it turns out you haven't killed that child you get
it back to its rightful parents as soon as you possibly can, any way
you can, and see to it that your darling poetess up there on cloud
nine takes the rap that is justly hers to take. Do you hear me?

I nodded.

Brenda opened the door for me and saw me up behind the
wheel.

And Lester? If I don't hear on the TV tonight that you've settled
this to a happy conclusion, I personally will call the cops. You understand me?

Thanks, Brenda.

She slammed the door. And don't ever try to see me anymore,
Lester, you asshole, she said.

I had done everything Brenda advised by way of food and sanita-
tion, and now there was peace in the house. I didn't want to alarm
Karen in any way, so I treated her with nothing but cooperation. By
the time I'd gotten back from the store, she had just begun to realize that a baby needed taking care of. She was so grateful she
hugged me, and I helped her fuss over that child as if it was truly
ours. Isn't he the sweetest thing? Karen said. How he seems to
know us — oh, that is so dear! Look at that sweet face, he is surely
the most beautiful baby I ever have seen!

Now, with everything calmed down and both Karen and Baby
Wilson asleep on our bed, it was time to do some thinking. I put on
the five o'clock news to get the lay of the land.

Oh my. The Crenshaw commissioner of police saying the entire
CPD had been put on alert and deployed throughout the city to
find the infant and apprehend the kidnapper or kidnappers. He'd
also notified the FBI.

Hey, I said, it is just my slightly crazy girl Karen, you don't have to
worry, we're not kidnappers, man.

The female they wanted for questioning was probably in her
twenties, white, about five-six, slight of build, with straight brown
hair. She had brought a bouquet of flowers and, when approached
by a nurse, claimed to be a friend of Mrs. Wilson's.

She was that cool, my Karen? Behind the commissioner was a

worried-looking hospital official and, I supposed, the nurse in question, tearful now for having turned her back for a moment to look for a vase.

Then a doctor stepped to the microphone and said whoever had the baby should remember that there was an open wound at the site of the umbilical cord. It should be kept clean and dressed with an antibacterial agent and a fresh bandage at least once a day.

Well, I knew that. I had seen it for myself. In the medicine chest I'd found the Polysporin I had once bought for a cut on my forehead and applied it only after I washed my hands. I am not stupid. The doctor said the baby should have only sponge baths until the wound healed. I would have figured that out, too.

A reporter asked if a ransom note had been received. That really got me riled. Of course not, you moron, I said. What do you think we are?

No ransom note as yet, the commissioner said, emphasizing the "as yet," which offended me even more.

Then we were back in the studio with the handsome news anchor: he said Mrs. Wilson, the mother, was under sedation. He quoted Mr. Wilson, the father, as saying he didn't understand — that they were not rich people, he was a CPA who worked for his living like everyone else.

I had seen enough. I woke up Karen and hustled her and the baby and all the Kmart paraphernalia into the Durango. Why, whatever is the matter, Lester? Karen said. She was still half asleep. Are we going somewhere? She looked frightened for a moment until I put Baby Wilson in her arms. I ran back to the house and grabbed some clothes and things for each of us. Then I ran back again and turned off the lights and locked the door.

I could imagine them any minute coming up the road and through the woods around us at the same time. We were in a cul-de-sac at the end of a dirt road here. I drove down to the two-lane. It was a mile from there to the freeway ramp. I pointed east for Nevada, though not planning to go there, necessarily, but just to be out on the highway away from town, feeling safer on the move, even if expecting any moment to see a cop car in the rearview.

I wasn't worried about Brenda, she would think twice before getting involved. But I reasoned that if the police were smart they would talk to every florist in the city. Of course, their being Crenshaw's finest, it was only even odds they would make the connection to an employee of Nature's Basket who had not shown up for work, one Karen Robileaux, age twenty-six. But even odds was not good enough as far as I was concerned, besides which the FBI were getting on the case, so say the odds were now sixty-forty, and if they made an ID of Karen it would be too late for an anonymous return of the baby. And if they came knocking on the door before we had the chance to deliver him back of our own accord, as appeared likely, there would be no alleviating circumstances for a judge to consider, that I could see.

And so we were out of there.

I had picked up her shoulder bag when running out of the house. Of course, it was of Indian design, knitted, with all sorts of jagged lines, sectioned like a map in different colors of sand and rust and aqua. Inside she kept not what women usually keep in their bags, no lipstick or powder compacts, or portable tampon containers, or any such normal things as that. She had some crumbs of dried flowers, and a packet of Kleenex, and her house keys, and a paperback book about the Intergalactic Council, a kind of UN of advanced civilizations around the universe, and how it was trying to send messages of peace to Earth. It was a nonfiction book, she had told me all about it. She had been thinking of becoming an Earth Representative of the Council. And two crumpled dollar bills and a handful of change.

Karen, don't you have any money? Didn't you get paid this week?

Oh, I forgot, yes, Lester, let's see, she said and rooted about in the pocket of her dress. And she handed me her pay envelope.

She had her hundred and twenty in there. I was carrying thirty-five in my wallet. Not great. I could cover gas, food, and a motel room for a night.

After a couple of hours on the road, I was calming down. It occurred to me that, despite everything, I was not mad at Karen. Given her state of mind, she couldn't be held responsible. If anyone, I was the one to blame for not springing into action the minute she walked in the door with the kid. And she was so trusting, sitting up there beside me with Baby Wilson in her arms and her eyes on the road ahead. She didn't ask where we were going, not that I could have told her. And the moving car seemed to soothe him, too. He was quiet in her arms. A weird feeling, something like a pride of ownership, came over me, which I would compare now to falling asleep at the wheel. My God, I woke up quickly enough.

By now it had gotten dark, it was all desert now, the road flat and straight. Karen opened her window and leaned out to see the stars. I had to slow down so Baby Wilson would not have a cold wind blowing into his face. I stuck my hand over the back of the seat and rummaged around till I found the package of diapers. I pulled one out and told her to put it around his little head.

Babies don't get sick the first three months of their life, Karen said. No viruses or anything. They are automatically insured by God for three months exactly. Did you know that, Lester?

But she did as I asked. By midnight, I had us tucked away in a Days Inn outside of Dopple City, Nevada. So, without consciously thinking about it till we were practically there, this was where I had meant to come.

I brought in a hamburger dinner, French fries, chicken wings, a milkshake, and for Karen a garden salad. She never drank anything but water. I left her sitting on one of the double beds and feeding the child. I went outside for a smoke and then got back in the SUV.

I knew Dopple. It was a city in its dreams only — what, a railroad yard, a string of car dealerships? It wasn't much of anything. Anyone could find the strip by seeing where the night sky was lit up.

I decided on Fortunato's. The lady dealers, with their little black bow ties and white shirts and black vests and ass-tight slacks, were the one bit of class. Bells ringing, someone singing with a karaoke, the usual din of losers. A cheap mob place trying to be Vegas, with an understocked bar and slots from yesteryear. It smelled, too, like there was a stable or a cow barn out back.

In the men's room, where the floor was all wet and some drunk had lost it, I carefully combed my hair. Then I went out and sat down at a five-dollar table that looked about right and bought fifty dollars in chips. Little blond lady dealer, a pitman just behind her. Four decks in the shoe, but my system is not counting cards. My system is betting modestly while sitting next to a high roller with a big stack in front of him. Kind who talks too much and swivels around with each winning hand to see if he's gathered the audience he deserves.

I didn't look at the dealer but smiled as if to myself every now and then. I was very quiet. When I doubled, if the pitman had moved on, I put down a chip for her. She didn't look at me but nodded slightly and smiled as if to herself. Tiny mouth but well shaped. There arose a sympathy between us. It's not as if any cheating goes on — it's more like a flirtation through the cards. Things happen. At the end of a half-hour, it was as if she'd taken the edge of her plump little hand and cut one of the high roller's stacks and slid it over to me. I got up at that point — it was supposed to be a fun thing, nothing to take too far. That would lack class, ruin the whole game between us. I left twenty for her and cashed in for a hundred and twenty-five dollars net.

It was a short drive to the Mexican part of town. Dark there, quiet, not many lights. I parked into the curb, rolled down the window, and sat there and had a smoke, and pretty soon a kid came along. He couldn't have been more than thirteen, fourteen. Peered in at me for a good look. When I told him what I was buying, he went to the front of my car and looked at the California plate. Then he went around a corner, and a few minutes later someone who could have been his mother was standing at my window. She was a heavyset woman with a handsome broad face and a black dress too tight for her, but she acted tired, or fed up. She wanted one-fifty for a six-pack, which was cheap enough, but I told her as honestly as I could I had only one and a quarter to spend. She said something in Spanish indicating her disgust, but then she nodded, and I drove away with two Visas, two MasterCards, and two Amexes, one of them Gold.

What was I up to if not executive decisions? I felt almost proud of myself by the time I got back to the motel. Karen was asleep with her arm around the infant. Her shift had ridden up. She was weird and maybe even a witch of some sort, but those were the smoothest young legs and artfully draped crescents of backside a man could ever hope to gaze upon. But I was tired too, and decided to wait till morning. I conformed one of my driver's licenses, practiced my signature, and then went to sleep in the other bed, thinking what a great country this was.

Of course, the infernal problem remained, whatever the stupid mood I happened to be in. How was I going to get little Junior away from Karen without making her crazier than she was? And if I managed that, how to avoid the law while finding a way to deliver him to his proper parents? And thirdly, how to keep Karen out of a U.S. district court, as well as the newspapers, as an object of public odium, to say nothing of myself?

And then in the morning, wouldn't you know it, she was so busy with the baby that she didn't have time for me. Or inclination. Everything was Jesu this and Jesu that, all her love flowing out of her and none of it coming in my direction. She sent me off for more supplies, so careless of my feelings she didn't even find it necessary to explain that the baby was taking all her weakened strength, as if she was a real mother recovering from the act of giving birth. She just expected me to understand that from the way she moved about, holding her hand in the small of her back for a moment of thought, or blowing back from the corner of her mouth a strand of hair that had fallen over her eye because both her hands were busy diapering the kid, and so on.

It is strange how different the same woman can be at different times, even a lovesick crazy one like this, who was so moony about me from the first moment I caught her attention when I walked into Nature's Basket to wire flowers to Illinois for my mother's birthday. There was this lovely girl in a long dress and barefooted who seemed to have risen out of the smell of earth and the heavy humidity you get in a florist's. Karen looked at me as if struck dumb. She tucked her hair behind her ears and said it was nice that I had a mother I thought so well of. I didn't tell her otherwise. I went along with her illusion, whereas the twenty-five dollars I laid down for the mixed bouquet was an investment against a return of ten times or twenty times that which I hoped to wheedle out of the old bat after a decent interval.

So after I get back with doughnuts and coffee, and a yogurt for Karen, and this and that from the drugstore, it starts to rain in Dopple City. Lightning and thunder, an unlikely spring torrent, and what does she do but take Baby Wilson outside behind the Days Inn, where she steps over the scraggly attempt at landscaping and walks out into the desert dirt, laughing and hugging the poor child and holding her head up to drink rainwater while not listening to what I am saying, and shaking me off when I try to hustle her back inside. And as suddenly as it came the rain passes, and Karen is standing there with her hair wet, as if she'd just had a shower, and she says, Look, my sweet baby, you see what God is doing? And to me she says, You too, Lester, wait for the runoff, where the rivulets leave their traces. Keep your eyes focused — it is the pure magic of the desert you are about to see.

And all she meant was those desert wildflowers that hurry to blossom from the least encouragement of rain, which they did — little settlements of blue and yellow and white spikes and petals and tiny cups in the declivities, clustered close to the land as if not wanting to take the chance of growing up too far away from it, flowers that you don't actually see opening but just have the feeling that they were there all along, only you didn't happen to notice them before.

And that was pretty, if you go for that sort of thing, but the child still couldn't see, although he seemed to be peering out from under her hand, which she held over his head like an umbrella, and for a moment I had the ridiculous feeling of real communication between them, this mad girl and a stolen infant just two or three days old, who were now poking about together under the sun out there in the flowering desert behind the Days Inn.

I left them there and got the keys to the Durango and took it down the highway to a used-car place. I wanted to get out of Dopple City as soon as possible. My theory was to keep moving if nothing else. Besides which, I did not want to have to pay another day's rent on the motel room, the checkout time for which was twelve noon.

The Durango was registered in both our names, although in truth it was Karen's savings that had bought it, but under my influence, I might add, since I had always held Durangos in high esteem.

It was already used when we bought it, though in reasonable condition, with just fifty thousand miles on the odometer, which I had since added twenty to, but the front tires were almost new, which is what I explained to the guy at the car lot, uselessly, since he would only give me seven-fifty for it, six if I wanted cash. I took the six hundred. He was a short, fat, underhanded thief in a white shirt and string tie but then again did not ask too many questions as he unscrewed my plates and handed them to me.

His man gave me a ride a mile down the road to the Southwest Car Rental, and I used my Amex Gold to secure a new Windstar van whose greatest if not only attribute was a Nevada license plate.

It was in this sad, shining new van that I wouldn't ordinarily be

caught dead in that I packed up my imitation wife and child and
headed west, back to California. I had no idea what to do. But we
were well disguised in our domestic vehicle with a little baby boy
adorably asleep in the new car chair I had got him. Karen stroked
the upholstery. She marveled at the drink containers at each seat.
She accepted the Windstar without question, as she did any mysterious moves on my part. My feeling about things began to change: I
had cash in my pocket and now some pride in my heart because Karen loved the new car. She turned the radio on, and there we were,
heading west with the sun behind us and the great Patsy Cline singing "Sweet Dreams of You," Karen giving me a sly amused and
weirdly sane glance that caused me nearly to swerve into the opposite lane as we sang along with Patsy, *I know I should hate you the whole
night through, instead of having sweet dreams of you.*

Now I do admit that there came over me an idea I not only hadn't
considered but that wouldn't have come even glancingly to my
mind before this moment, which was to let it all hang out — to embrace my mad girl's madness as, before all this happened, I had
customarily embraced her. Why not? Baby Wilson already had a
certain character that I found agreeable. He cried only when he
had to, and seemed thoughtful most of the time, if that was possible, full of serious attention to the new world in which he found
himself, as if, seeing it only as a blur, he was by way of compensation
listening very carefully. And though Karen told me that what I
thought was a smile as he looked at me was in reality a bit of indi-
gestion, it was hard for me not to smile back. She was an instant
mother, who seemed to have the wise love that mothers have as
soon as they become mothers, as if the maternal hormones or
whatever chemicals are involved had begun to operate within her
from the moment she calmly walked out of that hospital with some
other woman's newborn in her arms.

I didn't know anything about the Wilsons except that Mr. Wilson
was an accountant, which didn't foretell a particularly exciting life
for this kid, who had already seen, and not yet a week old, two
states and a rare rain in the desert that not many people not living
in the desert would ever see. And his beautiful though self-ap-
pointed and by law criminally insane mother had picked one tiny
blue flower and put its stem in his little hand, and his fingers had
curled around it, automatically, of course, but he still clutched it,

though fast asleep in his car chair as we crossed the state line into California.

And from all of this and the sun lighting our way ahead like a golden road I had this revelation of a new life for myself, a life I had never thought of aspiring to, where I would be someone's husband and someone else's father, dependable, holding a full-time job and building a respectable place in the world for himself and his family. So that when he died they would mourn grievously and bless his departing spirit for the love and meaningful life he had given them.

A special news bulletin on the radio was like cold water on my face: Baby Wilson's parents had received a ransom note.

We were about a hundred miles east of Crenshaw. I pulled over to the side of the road.

The details of the note had not been divulged, but it was believed the Wilsons intended to meet the kidnapper's demands.

God damn!

What, Lester?

Can you believe this?

I pounded the steering wheel. The baby woke and began to cry. Karen reached back and unbuckled him and lifted him over the seat and held him in her arms as if to protect him from me.

Lester, you're frightening us!

Can you believe the evil in this world? That some slime would con those poor people to cash in on their suffering?

She was silent for a moment. She said, I do believe there is evil in this world, yes, but I believe people can be redeemed? Her voice clouded up, she could barely finish the sentence. She began rocking the kid in her arms and soon the tears were coming, and now I had the two of them bawling away.

I got out of the van and lit a cigarette and paced up and down the grass shoulder. A car sped by, and its wind made the van shudder. Then another. I wanted to be in one of those cars. There was some sort of green crop growing in bunches low to the ground behind the fence and it seemed to go on for miles. I wanted to be the farmer out here in the middle of nowhere quietly growing his cash crop of whatever it was, spinach or cauliflower or some other damn inedible vegetable. I wanted to be anyone but who I was and anywhere but where I was. What was I supposed to do now?

I motioned for her to roll down her window: Has it occurred to you, Karen, that you have provided him or them the opportunity?

Gone were all my diplomatic strategies, all the anger that I had pent up cascaded over this sad pathetic girl sitting rocking the baby in her arms and her pale eyes reddened and enlarged with the tears rolling down her cheeks.

Yes, you have stirred up something really grand, you know that? You have inspired others to do evil, Karen Robileaux. And not only this slime or slimes. Supposing he really had possession of the baby? Is it in the baby's interest of safety to have the news broadcast all around the country that there is a ransom note? Of course not. How could this slimeball trust them now, these poor parents, thinking they had told everyone about his private communication. What would you do under the circumstances if you couldn't trust the parents to deal without calling in the cops, the FBI, and the media — I mean, this is a goddamn radio station in Los Angeles. Los Angeles! They don't give a shit if the baby turns up dead. They just want people to listen so they can sell their advertising. They are happy to violate such delicate confidences. They are proud to be good reporters! So the evil is going out in all directions, Karen, like radio waves from an antenna.

He can't do anything bad to this baby, she sobbed. None of them can. He doesn't have this baby. I have this baby, she said, kissing the child fervently on the cheeks, on his head, every part of him that was not swaddled.

Well, maybe not, I said, quieter now. But how do the Wilsons know that? He has already done something to them when they find out he is a fraud and a hoax and they are who knows how many thousands of dollars poorer. And not only that, I said more to myself than to her, everyone thinks now you have an accomplice, a male accomplice, because no woman alone who stole a child would do it for purposes of ransom.

Karen opened the door and stepped out of the van and handed me Baby Wilson, and then went off a ways on the shoulder behind a tree and lifted her dress and squatted down to pee.

I had not held him before to any extent. He was a warm little fellow, I could feel his heart beat, and he squirmed around a bit trying to look at me who was holding him. And he had stopped crying.

When Karen came back, she took Baby Wilson and got back in

the van and sat there frowning and staring straight ahead, and she wasn't crying anymore either. It was like she was waiting for the car to move, as if it really didn't need a driver to get up there beside her and put the key in the ignition.

A few miles on, at the edge of a town, I pulled into a gas station with a convenience store. I bought us bottled waters and presented one to Karen by way of a peace offering. Without looking at me, she took it. I bought the newspapers they carried, the local and the L.A. and San Diego papers. They all had the story, they were blissed out with excitement. And every story came with a composite police drawing of someone who looked like Karen, though with her ears grown bigger and her mouth thinner and her eyes transplanted from someone else. It was both not a good likeness and too close for comfort.

I tossed the papers away. I didn't feel the need to show her any-thing more by way of persuasion. She had no voice in the matter, as far as I was concerned. We drove on, and this turned out to be a well-groomed little town with big trees shading the streets and the retail stores uniformly in good taste so as not to offend the eye. And there was nobody in sight, as if the townsfolk were having their afternoon nap, even the police. It hit me then, my idea: if the story was in every paper, if it was all over the damn state, did it matter where we dropped off Baby Wilson? And I thought, Why not here? And if not now, when?

I peered right and left as I rolled to a stop at each corner until I saw something along the lines of what I wanted — a neat white stucco church with a red barrel-tile roof. It was a Catholic church, as uniformly tasteful as everything else in this town. It had a Christ on the Cross in relief on the stucco steeple. I can't now remember the saintly name of it, even the town's name escapes me, this was a moment of such stressful fatedness that the surroundings remain in my mind only as bodily impressions. I remember the sun on my neck as I carried the car seat by its handles as a portable carryall for the baby after Karen had been in there a few minutes, I remember my instructions to her beforehand as we sat in the van with the mo-tor running in the neatly ruled empty parking lot around the side, and, though the air conditioning was on, I felt the sweat dripping down the small of my back.

It was very peculiar that she seemed as ready as I was, as if some-

where at some moment — I couldn't have told you when — we had
made magnetic contact. As if it had never been otherwise than that
we were both sane and synchronized in our thoughts. So I experienced something also like a feeling of estrangement as I realized,
looking at her, that I loved Karen Robileaux. I loved her. I mean it
just came over me — an incredible welcoming rush of gladness
that welled up in my throat and threatened to spill out of my eyes. I
loved her. Her frail being was strong. Her kookiness was mystical.
And it was even eerier to hear in my mind, at last, what she had
been telling me time and time again before this all happened —
how she adored me, how she actually did love me in all the ways
that people understand as love. It was a bonding that was true, if it
was this scary. Of course, I said nothing and did not declare myself.
I really didn't have to. She knew. Our intimacy was in the fact of our
conspiring together as she concentrated on what I was saying with
her pale wolf eyes staring into mine, so much so that once she got
out of the car and walked up the steps into the church, I wondered
if this hadn't really been her plan, and that she had brought me to
this moment as I believed I had brought her. Because I remember
her only problem was technical, whereas you might have expected
much more in the way of resistance.

Lester, she said, I don't know the right words for confessing.

It's O.K., I said, just go in there and sit down in that box they
have. It is somewhere off to the side. You don't have to be Catholic
for them to listen to you. When he hears you, the priest will sit
down on the other side, and you just tell him you want to confess
something. And he will listen and never betray your trust that it is
just between the two of you. And you don't have to cross yourself or
anything, he will tell you what to do if you put it in the form of asking for his advice. And you will thank him, and you will mean it,
and maybe thank God, too, that there are people who are sworn to
do this for a living.

And what will he say?

Well, I have to believe priests read the papers and watch the TV
like everyone else, so he will know what baby you are talking about.
He will say, And where is the Wilson baby now? And you will tell
him, Father, the baby is here. You will find him in his carryall just
inside the front door. And a paper sack with his formula and his diapers and a tube of Polysporin for his belly button.

And when he gets up and runs down the aisle, you slip out the side door to right here where we are parked.

Karen is a brave woman. She has always been brave and never more than at this moment. She walked in there with her skirt swaying from her lovely hips, and her hair, which she had tied up in a ponytail, given the solemnity of the occasion, also swinging from side to side, and for the same reason her usually bare feet were in a pair of sandals.

But before she took her deep breath and stepped down from the Windstar, she held the baby in her arms and caressed his round little head and brushed his dark hairs with the tips of her fingers as he stared up at her in his impassive manner and then looked away. And then Karen slipped him gently into my arms like a friend of the mother's who has been given the privilege for just that moment of holding another woman's child.

That whole day, as we drove, she slept in the back seat, curled up with her hands under her chin. I had decided to head north, staying off the freeways for the most part. When it was evening, I pulled into a motel, and she went right from the car to the bed, where she got under the covers and went immediately back to sleep. I didn't want to take any chance that she would wake up and watch the TV, so I pulled the plug and bent it out of shape before I went to the restaurant they had there and watched as on the bar TV Mr. and Mrs. Wilson were shown hugging their baby and laughing through their tears. They were not the youngest of couples. They were both on the portly side, and in fact Mr. Wilson had quite a paunch on him, to make me think I would never let myself go that way. And it turned out they had six other children of various sizes standing around the couch looking at the camera with what I recognized as the same unsmiling quietness of expression as Baby Wilson himself.

Meanwhile, an announcer was telling the story of the return, and quoting Mr. Wilson saying he and his wife were so happy that they forgave whoever had kidnapped their child, but before I could breathe a sigh of relief, the camera cut to the FBI official now in charge of the investigation, and he said that the FBI would continue the search — that regardless of the outcome, a federal crime had been committed and it was never up to the Wilsons to decide whether or not to prosecute. And then another shot of the bad drawing of Karen.

In the gift shop there I bought a pair of sunglasses and an Angels baseball cap, and we got up at dawn and drove away. Karen wore the glasses and that cap with her hair tucked up inside all the way through California. I used the credit cards sparingly, each one never more than once until the last one, which I hazarded a couple of times and then threw away, not wanting to press my luck, and now we were down to our diminishing cash funds.

In San Francisco, I parked Karen in a movie theater and went around to Noe Street to see if Fran still lived there. She did. When she opened her door, she said, Well, will you look what the cat dragged in! Fran was never the sort to bear a grudge. She was a song stylist who made her living singing in clubs. She had a housemate now, a kind of blowsy older woman who nevertheless had the tact to excuse herself on some errand or other, probably to her chosen bar. I visited with Fran almost the whole two hours of a feature movie, and then she walked with me to the ATM at the local grocery. As I left, I swore I would return her generosity in full. I knew she didn't believe me, because she gave a goodhearted laugh and said time would tell and she was smiling and shaking her head as I waved and turned the corner.

Just before the Oregon state line, I removed the Nevada plates from the Windstar and replaced them with the Durango's old California plates.

In Seattle, we took the ferry to Canada, standing at the rail in the gray and green mist of that day, with the foghorns coming over the water and the smell of the sea and gulls appearing and disappearing in the bad visibility. Karen loved this part of the trip. There was a new peace between us, and she held my arm with both her hands with a kind of fervent wifeliness.

At the hotel in Vancouver, we resumed our lovemaking as in our first days together and it was action-packed, she had really come awake to life as I realized now, reflecting on the last months between us, when she was more withdrawn than I wanted to admit.

Vancouver is a squeaky clean town, like all of Canada that I have ever seen — the glass office buildings reflecting the sky color, the waterside filled with flag-flying yachts and motorboats that are so well kept they look like they've never been used except for advertis-

ing, and the downtown without litter of any kind, and everyone going about their business so as not to disturb anyone else. Not a
town you want to stay in very long. But you find things if you look,
and I found a man in the import-export business who would take
the Windstar off my hands, and if he gave me three thousand
American for it I knew he would clear at least ten at the other end.

Then I bought Karen an opal engagement ring and a gold wedding band for one thousand Canadian, though we didn't actually get legally married till we were settled in this town in Alaska
where she is known not as Karen Robileaux but as Mrs. Lester
Romanowski, although she doesn't get around enough to be
known very well in her condition but stays in this hillside cabin we
rent and tends her garden and cooks good things, not only for
me but for herself, since she is eating for two, while I am working
down below, at sea level, between the mountains and the waterside,
which is where the town is crammed.

I have different jobs, one scrubbing pots and pans in this phony
frontier restaurant, where the monster hamburger menu is up on
blackboards, and the bartender has a red beard and wears a lum-
berjack shirt with the sleeves rolled, and there is sawdust on the
floor. I also drive a school bus in the early morning and midafter-
noon, and another job, when I have to, is the slime line, which is
how they handle the fish off the boats — a heavy-hauling, slippery
job requiring rubber apron and gloves and hip boots and a shower
and a good deodorant at the end of the shift.

Just now I have a new opportunity, on the weekend, and it is easy
enough. I put on a funny bear costume and meet the cruise-ship
passengers as they come down the gangway. I do it because, A, nobody knows it's me in that stupid outfit, and B, it gives me a chance
to get close to those ships without drawing attention to myself. I
dance the ladies around a bit and make them laugh and pose with
them for a photo to record their historic visit to Alaska.

On my day off, Karen and I have found a place to watch the bears
fishing in the shallows for their salmon dinner. Lots of birds busy in
the forest, and animals I don't get up out of bed to identify rustle
around the cabin at night. Up through the tops of the trees every
morning we see the black bald eagle that lives up on the side of the
mountain and likes to soar about in the thermals.

Most people living here like us don't quite fit into the greater

U.S. for one reason or another, so nobody asks too many questions. Everyone I've met mostly has an attitude of big plans for themselves, which I certainly can appreciate. I'm beginning to think my big plan must have something to do with those cruise ships. They sail up every day to rest their block-long hulls against the dockside. When the tourists pour down the gangways, well, this, plus the fish, is what keeps the Panhandle in the money. But more of the money stays aboard at the gaming tables. So I'm thinking I find a way to get a passenger ID, take an overnight cruise to the next landing, come back flush the next day — I don't know — the modus is there, and it is only a matter of time till it makes itself known to me.

Karen hugs me when I come home and always has a good dinner waiting, and sits across the table with her chin in her hand and stares at me as I eat. Of course, she praises the reformed man I have become, and as a person who has not been without bold ideas of her own she can appreciate that I am alert and ready for inspiration. But basically she has no mind for anything but the baby growing inside her. She has a wise, contented smile these days, my young wife. No one meeting her for the first time would think she was anything but sane. She said last night that she hopes I don't mind not being consulted but she got used to the name Jesu, and so that is what he will be called.

EDWIDGE DANTICAT

Night Talkers

FROM CALLALOO

HE THOUGHT that the mountain would kill him, that he would never see the other side. He had been walking for two hours when suddenly he felt a sharp pain in his side. He tried some breathing exercises he remembered from medical shows on television, but it was hard to concentrate. All he could think of, besides the pain, was his roommate Michel, who'd had an emergency appendectomy a few weeks before in New York. What if he was suddenly stricken with appendicitis, here on top of a mountain, deep in the Haitian countryside, where the closest village seemed like a grain of sand in the valley below?

Hugging his midsection, he took cover from the scorching midday sun under a tall, arched, wind-deformed tree. He slid down onto his back, over the grainy pebbled soil, and closed his eyes, shutting out, along with the indigo sky, the sloping hills and craggy mountains that made up the rest of his journey.

He was on his way to visit his aunt Estina, his father's older sister, whom he'd not seen since he'd moved to New York six years before. He had lost his parents to the dictatorship when he was a boy, and his aunt Estina had raised him in the capital. After he'd moved to New York, she had returned to her home in the mountains, where she had always taken him during school holidays. This was the first time he was going to her village, as he had come to think of it, without her. If she were with him, she would have made him start his journey earlier in the day. They would have boarded a camion at the bus depot in Port-au-Prince before dawn and started climbing the mountain at sunrise to avoid sunstroke at high noon. If she

knew he was coming, she would have hired him a mule and sent a
child to accompany him, a child who would have known all the
shortcuts to her village. She also would have advised him to wear a
sun hat and bring more than the two bottles of water he'd consumed hours ago.

But no, he wanted to surprise her. However, the only person he
was surprising was himself, by getting lost and nearly passing out
and possibly lying there long enough to draw a few mountain vul-
tures to come pick his skeleton clean.

When he finally opened his eyes, the sun was beating down on
his face in pretty, symmetrical designs. Filtered through the long
upturned branches of what he recognized as a giant saguaro cactus, the sunrays had patterned themselves into hearts, starfishes,
and circles looped around one another.

He reached over and touched the cactus's thick trunk, which felt
like a needle-filled pincushion or a field of dry grass. The roots
were close to the soil, which his aunt Estina had once told him were
designed to collect as much rainwater as possible. Further up along
the spine, on the stem, was a tiny cobalt flower. He wanted to pluck
it and carry it with him the rest of the way, but his aunt would scold
him if she knew what he had done. Cactus flowers bloomed only
for a few short days, then withered and died. He should let the cactus enjoy its flower for this brief time, his aunt would say.

The pain in his midsection had subsided, so he decided to get up
and continue his walk until he reached his destination. There were
many paths to his aunt's house, and seeing the lone saguaro had
convinced him that he was on one of them.

He soon found himself in a village where a girl was pounding a
pestle into a mortar, forming a small crater in the ground beneath
the mortar as a group of younger children watched.

The girl stopped her pounding as soon as she saw him, causing
the other children to turn their almost identical brown faces toward him.

"Bonjou, cousins," he said, remembering the childhood greeting
his aunt had taught him. When he was a boy, in spite of the loss of
his parents, he had thought himself part of a massive family, every
child his cousin and every adult his aunt or uncle.

"Bonjou," the children replied.

"Ki jan ou ye?" How are you? the oldest girl added, distinguish-
ing herself.

"Could I have some water, please?" he said to the oldest girl, determining that she was indeed the one in charge.

The girl turned her pestle over to the next oldest child and ran into the limestone house as he dropped his backpack on the ground and collapsed on the front gallery. The ground felt chilly against his bare legs, as though he had stumbled into a cold stream.

As one of the younger boys ran off behind the house, the other children settled down on the ground next to him, some of them reaching over and stroking his backpack.

The oldest girl came back with a glass in one hand and an earthen jar in the other. He watched as she poured the water, wondering if it, like her, was a mirage fabricated by his intense thirst. When she handed him the water, he drank it faster than it took her to pour him another glass, then another and another, until the earthen jar was clearly empty.

She asked if he wanted more.

"No," he replied. "Mèsi anpil." Thank you.

The girl went back into the house to put the earthen jar and glass away. The children were staring up at him, too coy to question him and too curious not to stare. When the girl returned, she went back to her spot behind the mortar and pestle and just stood there as though she no longer knew what to do.

An old man carrying a machete and a sisal knapsack walked up to the bamboo gate that separated the road from the house. The boy who had run off earlier was at his side.

"How are you, konpè?" the old man asked.

"Uncle," he said, "I was dying of thirst until your granddaughter here gave me some water to drink."

"My granddaughter?" the old man laughed. "She's my daughter. Do you think I look that old?"

He looked old, with a grizzly salt-and-pepper beard and a face full of folds and creases that seemed to map out every road he had traveled in his life.

The old man reached over and grabbed one of three wooden poles that held up the front of the house. He stood there for a while, saying nothing, catching his breath. After the children had brought him a calabash filled with water — the glass was obviously reserved for strangers — and two chairs for him and the stranger, he lit his pipe and exhaled a fragrant cloud of fresh tobacco and asked, "Where are you going, my son?"

"I am going to see my aunt, Estina Estème," he replied. "She lives in Beau Jour."

The old man removed the pipe from his mouth and reached up to scratch his beard.

"Estina Estème? The same Estina Estème from Beau Jour?"

"The same," he said, growing hopeful that he was not too far from his aunt's house.

"You say she is your aunt?"

"She is," he replied. "You know her?"

"Know her?" the old man retorted. "There are no strangers in these mountains. My grandfather Nozial and her grandfather Osnac were cousins. Who was your father?"

"My father was Maxo Jean Osnac," he said.

"The one who was killed in that explosion?" the old man asked. "He only had one boy. The mother died too, didn't she? Estina nearly died in that explosion too. Only the boy came out whole."

"I am the boy," he said, an egg-sized lump growing in his throat.

He didn't expect to be talking about these things so soon. He had prepared himself for only one conversation about his parents' death, the one he would inevitably have with his aunt.

The children moved a few inches closer to him, their eyes beaming as though they were being treated to a frightening folktale in the middle of the day.

"Even after all these years," the old man said, "I am sad for you. So you are that young man who used to come here with Estina, the one who left for New York some years back?"

The old man looked him up and down, as if searching for burn marks on his body, then ordered the children to retreat.

"Shoo," he commanded. "This is no talk for young ears."

The children quickly vanished, the oldest girl resuming her work with the mortar and pestle.

Rising from his chair, the old man said, "Come, I will take you to Estina Estème."

Estina Estème lived in a valley between two lime-green mountains and a giant waterfall, which was constantly spraying a fine mist over the banana grove that surrounded her one-room house and the teal mausoleum that harbored the bones of her forebears. Her nephew recognized the house as soon as he saw it. It had not changed much, the sloped tin roof and the wooden frame intact. His aunt's banana grove seemed to have flourished, however. It was greener and denser than he remembered; her garden was packed with orange and avocado trees, a miracle given the barren mountain range he had just traveled through.

When he entered his aunt's yard, he was greeted by a flock of hens and roosters, which scattered quickly, seeking shelter on top of the family mausoleum.

He rushed to the front porch, where an old faded skirt and blouse were drying on the wooden railing. The door was open, so he ran into the house, leaving behind the old man and a small group of neighbors whom the old man had enticed into following them by announcing as he passed their houses that he had with him Estina Estème's only nephew.

In the small room was his aunt's cot, covered with a pale blue sheet. Nearby was a calabash filled with water, within easy reach so she could drink from it at night without leaving her bed. Under the cot was her porcelain chamber pot and baskets filled with her better dresses and a few Sunday hats and shoes.

The old man peeked in to ask, "She's not here?"

"No," he replied. "She is not."

He was growing annoyed with the old man, even though he was now certain that he would have never found his aunt's house so quickly without his help.

When he walked out of the house, he found himself facing a dozen or so more people gathered in his aunt's yard. He scanned the faces and recognized some, but could not recall their names. Many in the group were nudging each other, whispering while pointing at him. Others called out, "Dany, don't you know me anymore?"

He walked over and kissed the women, shook hands with the men, and patted the children's heads.

"Please, where is my aunt?" he asked of the entire crowd.

"She will soon be here," a woman replied. "We sent for her."

Once he knew his aunt was on her way, he did his best to appear interested in catching up. Many in the crowd complained that once he got to New York, he forgot about them, never sending the watch or necklace or radio he had promised. Surprised that they had taken his youthful pledges so seriously, he made feeble excuses:

"It's not so easy to earn money in New York . . . I thought you had moved to the capital . . . I didn't know your address."

"Where would we have gone?" one of the men rebutted. "We were not so lucky as you."

He was glad when he heard his aunt's voice, calling his name from the back of the crowd. The crowd parted and she appeared, pudgy yet graceful in a drop-waist dress. Her face was round and full, her few wrinkles more like tribal marks than signs of old age. Two people were guiding her by the elbows. As they were leading her to him, she pulled herself away and raised her hands in front of her, searching for him in the breeze. He had to remind himself once more that she was blind, had been since the day of the fire that had taken his parents' life.

The crowd moved back a few feet as he ran into her arms. She held him tightly, angling her head to kiss the side of his face.

"Dany, is it you?" She patted his back and shoulders to make sure.

"I brought him here for you," the old man said.

"Old Zo, why is it that you're always mixed up in everything?" she asked, joking.

"True to my name," the old man replied, "I am a bone that fits every stew."

The crowd laughed.

"Let's go in the house, Da," his aunt said. "It's hot out here."

As they started for her front door, he took her hand and tried to guide her, but found himself an obstacle in her path and let go. Once they were inside, she felt her way to her cot and sat down on the edge.

"Sit with me, Da," she said. "You have made your old aunt a young woman again."

"How are you?" He sat down next to her. "Truly?"

"*Truly* fine," she said. "Did Popo tell you different?"

For many years now, he had been paying a boyhood friend in Port-au-Prince, Popo, to come and check on her once a month. He would send Popo money to buy her whatever she needed, and Popo would in turn call him in New York to brief him on how she was doing.

"No," he said, "Popo didn't tell me anything."

"Then why did you come?" she asked. "I am not unhappy to see you, but you just dropped out of the sky, there must be a reason."

She felt for his face, found it, and kissed it for what seemed like a hundredth time since he'd seen her. "Were you sent back?" she asked. "We have a few boys here in the village who have been sent back. Many don't even speak Creole anymore. They come here because this is the only place they have any family. There's one boy not far from here. I'll take you to visit him. You can speak to him, one American to another."

"You still go on your visits?" he asked.

"When they came to fetch me, I was with a girl in labor," she said.

"Still a midwife?"

"Helping the midwife," she replied. "You know I know every corner of these mountains. If a new tree grows, I learn where it is. Same with children. A baby's still born the same way it was when I had sight."

"I meant to come sooner," he said, watching her join and separate her fingers randomly, effortlessly, like tree branches brushing against each other in a gentle breeze.

"I know," she said. "But why didn't you send word that you were on your way?"

"You're right," he said. "I didn't just drop out of the sky. I came because I wanted to tell you something."

"What is it, Da?" she asked, weaving and unweaving her fingers. "Are you finally getting married?"

"No," he said. "That's not it. I found him. I found him in New York, the man who killed Papa and Manman and took your sight."

Why the old man chose that exact moment to come through the door he will never know. Perhaps it was chance, serendipity, or maybe simply because the old man was a nosy pain in the ass. But just then Old Zo appeared in the doorway, pushing the mortar-and-pestle girl ahead of him with a covered plate of food in her hand.

"We brought you something to refresh you," he told Dany.

His aunt seemed neither distressed nor irritated by the interruption. She could have sent Old Zo and the girl away, but she didn't. Instead she told them to put their offering down on an old table in the corner. The girl quietly put the plate down and backed out of the room, avoiding Dany's eyes.

"I hope you're both hungry," the old man said, not moving from his spot. "Everyone is going to bring you something."

Clusters of food-bearing people streamed in and out of the house all afternoon. He and his aunt would sample each plate, then share the rest with the next visitor, until everyone in the valley had tasted at least one of their neighbor's dishes.

By the time all the visitors had left and he and his aunt were alone together, it was dark and his aunt showed no interest in hearing what he had to say. Instead she offered him her cot, and he talked her into letting him have the sisal mat that she had laid out on the floor for herself.

She fell asleep much more quickly than he did. Mid-dream, she laughed, paid compliments, made promises, or gave warnings. "Listen, don't go too far. Come back soon. What a strong baby! I'll make you a dress. I'll make you coffee." Then she sat up in her cot to scold herself — "Estina, you are waking the boy" — before drifting once again into the movie in her head.

In the dark, listening to his aunt conduct entire conversations in her sleep, he realized that aside from blood, she and he shared nocturnal habits. They were both night talkers. He too spoke his dreams aloud in the night, in his sleep, to the point of sometimes jolting himself awake with the sound of his own voice. Usually he could only remember the very last words he spoke, but a lingering sensation remained that he had been talking, laughing, and at times crying all night long.

His aunt was already awake by the time he got up the next morning. With help from Old Zo's daughter, who seemed to have been rented out to his aunt for the duration of his visit, she had already set up breakfast on the small table brought out to the front gallery from inside the house. His aunt seemed fidgety, almost anxious, as if she had been waiting for him to rise for hours.

"Go wash yourself, Da," she said, handing him a towel. "I'll be waiting for you here."

Low shrubs covered in dew brushed against his ankles as he made his way down a trail toward the stream at the bottom of the fall. The water was freezing cold when he slipped in, but he welcomed the sensation of having almost every muscle in his body contract, as if to salute the dawn.

Had his father ever bathed in this stream? Had his parents bathed here together when they'd come to stay with his aunt? Had they enjoyed it, or had they wished for warmer waters and more privacy?

A group of women were coming down the path with calabashes and plastic jugs balanced on top of their heads. They would bathe, then fill their containers farther up, closer to the fall. He remembered spending hours as a boy watching the women bathe topless, their breasts flapping against their chests as they soaped and scrubbed themselves with mint and parsley sprigs, as if to eradicate every speck of night dust from their skin.

When he got back to his aunt's house, he had a visitor. It was a boy named Claude, a deportee. Claude was sitting next to his aunt, on the top step in front of the house; he was dipping his bread in the coffee that Old Zo's daughter had just made.

"I sent for Claude," his aunt announced. "Claude understands Creole and is learning to speak bit by bit, but he has no one to speak English to. I would like you to talk with him."

It was awkward at first, especially with the giant, overly muscular Claude looking so absolutely thrilled to see him, yet trying to hide it with a restrained smile and an overly firm handshake. Both of Claude's brawny arms were covered with tattoos from his shoulders down to his wrists, his skin a collaged canvas of Chinese characters plus kings and queens from a card deck: One-Eyed Jack, Hector, Lancelot, Judith, Rachel, Argine and Palas, they were all there, carved into his coal-black skin in blue ink. His hands were large too, his fingers long, thick, callused, perhaps the hands of a killer.

"What's up?" Claude stood up only to sit down again. "How you doing?"

Claude was probably in his late teens — too young, it seemed, to have been expatriated twice, from both his native country and his adopted land. Dany sat down on the step next to Claude as Old Zo's daughter handed him a cup of coffee and a piece of bread.

"How long you been here?" he asked Claude.

"Too long, man," Claude replied, "but I guess it could be worse. I could be down in the city, in Port, eating crap and sleeping on the street. Everyone here's been really cool to me, especially your aunt. She's kind of taken me under her wing. When I first got here, I thought I would get stoned. I mean I thought people would throw rocks at me, man, not the other kind of stoned. I mean, coming out of New York, then being in prison in Port for like three months because no one knew what to do with me, then finally my moms, who didn't speak to me for like the whole time I was locked up, came to Port and hooked me up with some family up here."

His aunt was leaning forward with both hands holding up her face, her white hair braided like a crown of gardenias around her head. She was listening to them speak, like someone trying to capture the indefinable essence of a great piece of music. Watching her face, the pleasure she was taking in the unfamiliar words, made him want to talk even more, find something drawn-out to say, tell a story of some kind, even recite some poetry, if only he knew any.

"So you're getting by all right?" he asked Claude.

"It took a lot of getting used to, but I'm settling in," Claude replied. "I got a roof over my head and it's quiet as hell here. No trouble worth a damn to get into. It's cool that you've come back to see your aunt, man. Some of the folks around here told me she had someone back in New York. I had a feeling when she'd ask me to speak English for her, it was because she really wanted to hear somebody else's voice, maybe yours. It's real cool that you didn't forget her, that you didn't forget your folks. I really wish I had stayed in touch more with my people, you know, then it wouldn't be so weird showing up here like I did. These people don't even know me, man. They've never seen my face before, not even in pictures. They still took me in, after everything I did, because my moms told them I was their blood. I look at them and I see nothing of me, man, blank, nada, but they look at me and they say he has so-and-so's nose and his grandmother's forehead, or some shit like that. It's like a puzzle, man, a weird-ass kind of puzzle. I am the puzzle and these people are putting me back together, telling me things about myself and my family that I never knew or gave a fuck about. Man, if I had run into these people back in Brooklyn, I would have laughed my ass off at them. I would have called them backward-ass peasants. But here I am, man, one of those backward-ass peasants myself."

His aunt was engrossed, enthralled by Claude's speech, smiling at times while the morning sunrays danced across her eyes, never penetrating her pupils. He was starting to think of his aunt's eyes as a strange kind of prism, one that consumed light rather than reflected it.

"I can't honestly say I love it here, man" — Claude seemed to be wrapping up — "but it's worked out all right for me. It saved my life. I am at peace here and my family seems to have made peace with me. I came around, man. I can honestly say I was reformed in prison. I would have been a better citizen than most if they hadn't deported me."

"You still have a chance," Dany said, not believing it himself. "You can do something with your life. Maybe you're back here for a reason, to make things better."

He was growing tired of Claude, tired of what he considered his lame excuses and an apparent lack of remorse for whatever it was he had done.

"How long will you be staying?" Claude asked.

"A while," Dany said.

"Is there anything you want to do?" Claude asked. "I know the area pretty well now. I take lots of walks to clear my head. I could show you around."

"I know where things are," Dany said. "And if I don't remember, my aunt can —"

"It's just with her not being able to see —"

"She can see, in her own way —"

"All right, cool, my man. I was just trying to be helpful."

Even with the brusque way their conversation ended, Claude seemed happy as he left. He had gotten his chance to speak English and tell his entire life story in the process.

After Claude's departure, Old Zo's daughter came up and took the empty coffee cup from Dany's hand. She lingered in front of him for a minute, her palm accidentally brushing against his fingertips. At times she seemed older than she looked. Maybe she was twenty, twenty-five, but she looked twelve. He wondered what her story was. Were those children he had seen in Old Zo's yard hers? Did she have a husband? Was he in the city? Dead?

She hesitated before stepping away, as though she gave too much thought to every move she made. When she finally walked away, Dany's aunt asked him, "Do you know why Claude was in prison?"

"He didn't say."

"Do you know what his people say?"

"What do his people say?"

"They say he killed his father."

That night, Dany dreamed that he was having the conversation he'd come to have with his aunt. They were sitting on the step where he and Claude had spoken. He began the conversation by recalling with his aunt the day his parents died.

He was six years old and his father was working as a driver for a family in Port-au-Prince. The morning of the fire, his father had rushed home to tell his mother and aunt, who was visiting from Beau Jour, that his father's employer's family home had been burned down, but not before the family had escaped and gone into hiding. His father thought they should leave for Beau Jour, for the people who were looking for his employer might think his workers were hiding him. His parents and Estina were throwing a few things in a knapsack when his father told him to go out in the yard and watch out for any strangers. He was watching the street carefully, for even then he felt that he had never been given such an important job. That's when a very large man came up and threw two grenades in quick succession at his house. Before he could even turn his head, the house was on fire, pieces of wood and cement chunks flying everywhere. The man got back in his car, a black German DKW — he remembered it very well because it was the same type of car many of the military men drove and his father had pointed out to him that he should avoid those cars as much as possible — and drove away, but not before Dany got a good look at the man's large round face, a widow's peak dipping into the middle of his forehead.

A few moments later, his aunt came crawling out of the house, unable to see. His parents never came out.

He dreamed his aunt saying, "Yes this is how it happened," then urging him to elaborate on what he had begun to tell her before Old Zo had walked into the room. "You said you saw that same man in New York? Are you sure it was him?"

"Yes," he replied. "He is a barber now."

The man who had killed his parents was calling himself Albert Bienaimé these days. He had a wife and a grown daughter, both of whom seemed unaware of his past. Some men he had met at work told him that Albert Bienaimé was renting a room in the basement of his house, where they also lived. When he went to Albert Bienaimé's barbershop to ask about the room, he recognized Albert Bienaimé as the same man who had thrown the grenades at his parents' house. When he asked Albert Bienaimé where he was from, Albert Bienaimé said that he was from the mountains somewhere above Jacmel and had never lived in a city before moving to New York.

"You see," the dream aunt said, "he may not be the one."

He took the empty room in Albert Bienaimé's basement. He couldn't sleep for months, spending his weekends in nightclubs to pass the time. He visited Albert Bienaimé's barbershop regularly for haircuts, in order to observe him and reassure himself that he was indeed the same man who had thrown the explosives at his house. Finally, two nights ago, when Albert Bienaimé's wife was away at a religious retreat — he looked for such opportunities all the time and hadn't found one until then — he climbed the splintered steps to the first floor, then made his way with a flashlight to Albert Bienaimé's bedroom.

"What did you do?" the dream aunt asked.

He stood there and listened to Albert Bienaimé breathing. Albert Bienaimé was snoring, each round of snores beginning in a low groan and ending in a high-pitched shrill. He lowered his face toward Albert Bienaimé's widow's peak, hoping Albert Bienaimé would wake up and be startled to death. Even when he was a boy, he had heard about how some of the military people, like Albert Bienaimé, would choke their prisoners in their sleep, watching their faces swell and their eyes bulge out of their heads. He was certain when he'd come up the stairs that he was going to kill Albert Bienaimé. He thought of pressing a pillow down on Albert Bienaimé's face, but something stopped him. It wasn't fear, because he was feeling bold, fearless. It wasn't pity; he was too angry to feel pity. It was something else, something less measurable. Perhaps it was the dread of being wrong, of harming the wrong man, of making the wrong woman a widow and the wrong child an orphan. At that moment, all he wanted to do was run as far away from Albert Bienaimé as possible, leave and never come back. He left Albert Bienaimé's room and went down to the basement, booking himself on the next available flight to Port-au-Prince and knowing he would never be coming back. Even though he knew he wouldn't be able to return on his expired visa, he wanted to see Beau Jour again. He needed to see his aunt. He needed to see a place where perhaps his parents had been happy.

Dany woke himself with the sound of his own voice reciting his story. His aunt was awake too, sitting up on her cot.

"Da, were you dreaming your parents?" she asked. "You were calling their names."

"Was I?" He would have thought he was calling Albert Bienaimé's name.

"You were calling your parents," she said, "just this instant."

He was still back there, in the yard, waiting for his parents to come out of that burning house, in the room with Albert Bienaimé, wishing he could watch Albert Bienaimé die. His aunt's voice was just an echo of things he could no longer hear, his mother's voice praying, his father's voice laughing.

"I am sorry I woke you," he said, wiping the sweat off his forehead with the backs of his hands.

"I should have let you continue telling me what you came here to say. It's like walking up these mountains and losing something precious halfway. For you it would be no problem walking back, because you are still young and strong, but for me it would take a lot more time and effort."

He heard the cot squeak as she lay back down.

"I understand," he said.

She went back to sleep, whispering something under her breath, then growing completely silent. When he woke up the next morning, she was dead.

It was Old Zo's daughter who let out the first cry, announcing the death to the entire valley. Sitting near the body, on the edge of his aunt's cot, Dany was doubled over with an intense bellyache. Old Zo's daughter took over immediately, brewing him some tea while waiting for their neighbors to arrive.

The tea did nothing for him. He was not expecting it to. Part of him was grateful for the pain, for the physically agonizing diversion it was providing him.

Soon after Old Zo's daughter's cry, a few of the village women began to arrive. It was only then that he learned Old Zo's daughter's name, at least her nickname, Ti Fanm (Little Woman), which the others kept shouting as they badgered her with questions.

"What happened, Ti Fanm?"

"Ti Fanm, did she die in her sleep?"

"Did she fall, Ti Fanm?"

"Ti Fanm, did she suffer?"

"Ti Fanm, she wasn't even sick."

"She was old," Ti Fanm said in a firm and mature voice. "It can happen like that."

They did not bother asking him anything. He wouldn't have known how to answer anyway. After he and his aunt had spoken in the middle of the night, he thought she had fallen asleep. When he woke up in the morning, even later than he had the day before, she was still lying there, her eyes shut, her hands resting on her belly, her fingers intertwined. He tried to find her pulse, but she had none. He lowered his face to her nose and felt no breath. Then he walked out of the house and found Ti Fanm, sitting on the steps, waiting to cook his breakfast. The pain was already starting in his stomach. Ti Fanm came in and performed her own investigation, then let out that cry, a cry as loud as any siren he had heard on the streets of New York or the foghorns that blew occasionally from the harbor near the house where he had lived with his parents as a boy.

His aunt's house was filled with people now, each of them taking turns examining his aunt's body for signs of life, and when finding none immediately assigning themselves, and each other, tasks related to her burial. One group ran off to get purple curtains, to hang shroudlike over the front door to show that this was a household in mourning. Another group went off to fetch an unused washbasin to bathe the corpse. Others were searching through the baskets beneath his aunt's cot for an appropriate dress to change her into after her bath. Another went looking for a carpenter to build her coffin.

The men assigned themselves to him and his pain.

"He is in shock," they said.

"Can't you see he's not able to speak?"

"He's not even looking at her. He's looking at the floor."

"He has a stomachache," Ti Fanm intercepted.

She brought him some warm salted coffee, which he drank in one gulp.

"He should lie down," one of the men said.

"But where?" Another rebutted. "Not next to her."

"He must have known she was going to die." He heard Old Zo's voice rising above the others. "He came just in time. Blood calls blood. She made him come so he could see her before she died. It would have been sad if she had died behind his back, especially since he never buried his parents."

They were speaking about him as though he couldn't understand, as if he were solely an English-speaker, like Claude. Perhaps this was the only way they could think of to console him right then, to offer him solace.

He wished that his stomach would stop hurting, that he could rise from the edge of the cot and take control of the situation, or at least participate in the preparations, but all he wanted to do was lie down next to his aunt, rest his head on her chest, and wrap his arms around her, the way he had done when he was a little boy. He wanted to close his eyes until he could wake up from this unusual dream where everyone was able to speak except the two of them.

By midday he felt well enough to join Old Zo and some of the men, who were opening up a slot in the family mausoleum. He was in less pain now, but was still uncomfortable and moved slower than the others.

The women were inside the house, bathing his aunt's body and changing her into a blue dress he had sent her through Popo. He had seen it in a store window in Brooklyn and had chosen it for her, remembering that blue was her favorite color. The wrapping was still intact; she had never worn it.

Once the slot was opened, Old Zo announced that a Protestant minister would be coming by the next morning to say a prayer during the burial. Old Zo had wanted to transport the body to a church in the next village for a full service, but he didn't want his aunt to travel so far, only to return to her own yard to be buried.

"The coffin is almost ready," Old Zo said. "She will be able to rest in it during the wake."

He had always been perplexed by the mixture of jubilation and sorrow that was part of Beau Jour's wakes, by the fact that some of the participants played cards and dominoes while others served tea and wept. But what he had always enjoyed was the time carved out for the mourners to tell stories about the deceased, singular tales of first or last encounters, which could either make him holler with laughter or have his stomach spasms return as his grief grew.

The people of his aunt's village were telling such stories about her now. They told of how she once tried to make coffee and filtered dirt through her coffee pouch even though she was able to deliver twins without any trouble. They told of how as a young

woman she had embroidered a trousseau that she carried everywhere with her, thinking it would attract a husband. They spoke of
her ambition, of her wanting to be a baby seamstress, so she could
make clothes for the very same children she was ushering into the
world. If he could have managed it, he would have spoken of her
sacrifices, of the fact that she had spent most of her life trying to
keep him safe. He would have told of how he hadn't wanted to
leave her, to go to New York, but she had insisted that he go so he
would be as far away as possible from the people who had murdered his parents.

Claude arrived at the wake just as it was winding down, at a time
when everyone was too tired to do anything but sit, stare, and
moan, when through sleepy eyes the reason for the all-night gathering had become all too clear, when the purple shroud blowing
from the doorway into the night breeze could no longer be ignored.

"I am so sorry, man," Claude said. "I was in Port today and when I
came back my people told me. I am truly sorry, man. Your aunt was
such good people. One of a kind, really. I am so sorry."

Claude moved forward, as if to hug him, Claude's broad shoulders towering over his head. Dany stepped back, moving away,
cringing. Perhaps it was what his aunt had told him, about Claude's
having killed his father, but he did not want Claude to touch him.

Claude got the message and walked away, drifting toward a group
of men who were nodding off at a table near the porch railing.

When he walked back inside the house, he found a small group
of women sitting near the open coffin, keeping watch over his
aunt. He was still unable to look at her in the coffin for too long.
He envied these women the six years they had spent with her while
he was gone. He dragged his sisal mat, the one he had been sleeping on these last two nights, to a corner as far away from the coffin
as he could get, coiled himself into a ball, and tried to fall asleep.

It could happen like that, Ti Fanm had said. A person his aunt's age
could fall asleep talking and wake up dead. He wouldn't have believed it if he hadn't seen it for himself. Death was supposed to be
either quick and furious or drawn-out and dull, after a long illness.
His aunt had chosen a middle ground. Perhaps Old Zo was right.

Blood calls blood. Perhaps she had summoned him here so he could at last witness a peaceful death and see how it was meant to be mourned. Perhaps Albert Bienaimé was not his parents' murderer after all, but just a phantom who'd shown up to escort him back here. He didn't know what to believe anymore.

He could not fall asleep, not with the women keeping watch over his aunt's body being so close by. Not with Ti Fanm coming over every hour with a cup of tea, which was supposed to cure his bellyaches forever.

He didn't like her nickname, was uncomfortable using it. It was too generic, as though she was one of many from a single mold, with no distinctive traits of her own.

"What is your name?" he asked when she brought him her latest brew.

She seemed baffled, as though she were thinking he might need a stronger infusion, something to calm his nerves and a memory aid, too.

"Ti Fanm," she replied.

"Non," he said, "your true name, your full name."

"Alice Denise Auguste," she said.

The women who were keeping watch over his aunt were listening to their conversation, cocking their heads ever so slightly in their direction.

"How old are you?" he asked.

"Thirty," she said.

"Thank you," he said.

"You're deserving," she said, using an old-fashioned way of acknowledging his gratitude.

She was no longer avoiding his eyes, as though his grief and stomach ailment and the fact that he had asked her real name had rendered them equals.

He got up and walked outside, where many of his aunt's neighbors were sleeping on mats on the porch. There was a full moon overhead and a calm in the air that he was not expecting. In the distance he could hear the waterfall, a sound that, once you got used to it, you never paid much attention to. He walked over to the mausoleum, removed his shirt, and began to wipe the mausoleum with it, starting at the base and working his way up toward the headstone. It was clean already. The men had done a good job removing the leaves, pebbles, and dust that had accumulated on it while they were opening his aunt's slot, but he wanted to make sure it was spotless, that every piece of debris that had fallen on it since was gone.

"Need help?" Claude asked from a few feet away.

He must have been sleeping somewhere on the porch with the others before he saw Dany.

Dany threw his dusty shirt on the ground, climbed up on one of the mausoleum ledges, and sat down. He had wanted to do something, anything, to keep himself occupied until dawn.

"I'm sorry," Dany said, "for earlier."

"I understand," Claude said. "I'd be a real asshole if I got pissed off at you for anything you did or said to me at a time like this. You're in pain, man. I get that."

"I don't know if I'd call it pain," Dany said. "There's no word yet for it. No one has thought of a word yet."

"I know, man," Claude said. "It's a real bitch."

In spite of his huge muscles and oversized tattoos, Claude seemed oddly defenseless, like a refugee lost at sea, or a child looking for his parents in a supermarket aisle. Or maybe that's just how Dany wanted to see him, to make him seem more normal, less frightening.

"I hear you killed your father," Dany said.

The words sounded less severe coming out of his mouth than they did rolling around in his head.

"Can I sit?" Claude asked, pointing to a platform on the other side of the headstone.

Dany nodded.

"Yes, I killed my old man," Claude said. "Everyone here knows that shit by now. I wish I could say it was an accident. I wish I could say he was a bastard who beat the crap out of me and forced me to defend myself. I wish I could tell you I hated him, never loved him, didn't give a fuck about him at all. I was fourteen and strung out on shit. He came into my room and took the shit. It wasn't just my shit. It was shit I was hustling for someone else. I was really fucked up and wanted the shit back. I had a gun I was using to protect myself out on the street. I threatened him with it. He wouldn't give my shit back, so I shot him."

There was even less sorrow in Claude's voice than Dany had

been able to muster over these past twenty-four hours. Dany was still numb, even as tears rolled down Claude's face; he had never known how to grieve or help others grieve. It was as though his parents' death had paralyzed that instinct in him.

"I am sorry," he said, feeling that someone should also think of a better word for this type of commiseration.

"Sorry?" Claude wiped the tears from his face with a quick swipe of his hand. "I am the luckiest fucker alive. I have done something really bad that now makes me want to live my life like a fucking angel. If I hadn't been a minor, I would have been locked up for the rest of my life. And if the prisons in Port had had more room, or if the police down there was worth a damn, I'd be in a small cell with a thousand people right now, not sitting here talking to you. Even with everything I've done, with everything that's happened to me, I am the luckiest fucker on this goddamned planet. Someone, somewhere, must be looking out for my ass."

It would be an hour or so before dawn. The moon was already fading, slipping away, on its way someplace else.

The only thing he could think to do for his aunt now was to get Claude to speak and speak and speak, which wouldn't be so hard, since Claude was already one of them, a member of their tribe. Claude was a night talker, one of those who spoke their nightmares out loud, to themselves, except Claude was also able to speak his nightmares to others, in the daytime, even when the moon had completely vanished and the sun had come out.

Johnny Hamburger

FROM ESQUIRE

IT'S HOT.

Day after day of record-breaking, neck-searing, mid-July heat —
heat that sweats you all day long and then, toward five when it
should be easing off, cooks you all over again. Johnny Hamburger
works two jobs, weekend nights at the Sea Shanty flipping burgers
and weekdays on the water with a dock-building crew, driving piles
on Don Lopatka's rusty iron barge: two griddle jobs, he jokes, one
where he's the cook, and one where he's the meat.

Johnny Frickin' Hamburger, says Denny the Mountain Man. *No wonder they call you that!*

Today they're doing a ninety-foot dock at a condo just past the
beach, Johnny Hamburger and Brian tacking down planking as
Denny sharpens points on the piles they'll drive tomorrow and
the Don sits in the crane cab, smoking. They've been at it since
early morning, and Johnny's wondering whether the Don will let
him leave at four and, if so, whether to stop by and have sex with his
girlfriend, Brenda, before his Friday-night shift at the Sea Shanty.
Lately it's been almost too hot for sex. Last time, he was underneath, and afterward there was a sweat stain on the sheet in the exact shape of his body, like the shroud of whatchamacallit in the
news, the Jesus thing.

"Hey, Mountain Man," he says as Denny's chain saw whines to a
stop. "You read about that hail in the paper today?"

"What hail?"

"Out in North Dakota. Five-inch hail." He skips the headline stories in the paper every morning — Bush versus Dukakis, or that

Iranian airliner the navy shot down — and looks for weather news.
Weather is beating the shit out of America. Yesterday it was a tornado in Michigan that hit a kennel and blew a poodle into a tree a
mile away. And today it's five-inch hail. Hail big as softballs, he tells
them, big as grapefruit.

"What paper you been reading, Johnny?" says the Don. "The *Wiz-
ard of Oz Times?*"

"No, it's true." He looks at Denny, who's laughing. "I'm telling
you, there's some weird weather going on."

Johnny tries to imagine what it would be like to hold one in your
hand, a hailstone the size of a grapefruit. Meanwhile, he and Brian
work in tandem, spacing the planks and hammering them in.

"Hey, Don," he calls over. "You need me after this?"

"Why? You got a big date tonight?"

He pictures Brenda. Her ass, plush and soft and shaped like a
heart; those two muscles in the small of her back.

"He's got a date, all right," says Brian. "A date with Mrs. Haffen-
reffer. A date with Mrs. Piel's."

Tell me about it, Johnny's supposed to say. But he doesn't. A mis-
hit nail goes skipping across the board and plops into the water. He
watches it sink. Nobody notices; it's just another bit of trash that
will find the bottom and stay there.

On the beach, four girls in bikinis lie stretched out on towels,
all boobs and butts, lined up in a row. A fishing boat chugs past
the breakwater. What strikes Johnny, what he feels without putting
words to the idea, is the sameness of it all — the same work, same
heat, same jokes, same idiot songs on the radio, day after day, *Together forever and never to part, together forever with you-oo-oo!* He's
floating in the deep pool of summer, with nothing to mark one day
from the next and nothing to tell him that this particular day, Friday, July 15, 1988, is the one that will change everything.

After work, in his piece-of-shit Escort, he pulls a Miller from the
cooler and knocks it back in thick gulps; then, a second can
snugged down in the crotch of his blue jeans where a cop can't see,
he drives off. The rearview mirror is angled down for night driving,
and he bats it back up. He hates seeing himself — his freckles, his
mouth that turns up at the corners, smiling even when he's not.
His smile is a girl's smile: his mother has it, his sister Nell, who's

twenty-five and a teacher, she has it, and now here he is, six feet tall, with a girl's freckles and smile. *I look like a faggot,* he says to Brenda, standing naked in front of the mirror. *You're getting it on with a guy who looks like a girl.*

Girls like girls, Haggerty, she says to him. *Don't you get that yet?*

His old man hates his smile. *What's this Johnny Hamburger crap, anyway?* he'll say. *You're twenty-two years old, you wanna go around sounding like a cartoon?* It's like a song between them, back and forth. Johnny will make some remark, and then his father says, *At your age I was back from Korea and building my first house.* Or, *You really don't have the foggiest goddamn idea, do you?*

He drives past the Yankee Village mall and under I-95. It's true, Johnny believes, he doesn't have an idea, not even a foggy one. As far as he can tell, all he has is feelings. Good feelings, like daydreaming about Brenda naked, and bad ones, like sitting at the armed forces office downtown while a recruiter tells him how the marines will whip his butt into shape. Some nights he'll be working at the Sea Shanty and someone in a passing car will yell out, *Yo, Johnny Hamburger!* and it's ridiculous, but he feels like the mayor. Then the next day he'll wake up into his same old clueless life. He smokes too much. He drinks too much. His apartment reeks — spilled bong water and old socks and green fung growing in Dunkin' Donuts coffee cups, and two plants his mother gave him that he thinks are dead, and T-shirts slimy with grill grease. A year ago Johnny was living at home, with a job at the sub shipyard he'd gotten through a connection of his father's. The money was good, and after three months he was set to snag his union card, when suddenly it felt like getting married and he backed out. *What do you mean, you don't feel like it?* his father demanded. *What if I don't feel like paying your rent?*

He's not lazy: he likes pulling a monster day on the barge, then taking a six-pack with Denny to Denny's truck and drinking the fuckers down. Doing the six-pack after the ten-hour, it's one feeling his father might understand, Johnny thinks, if only he could get it across. But he'd have to be drunk to try, drunk with his old man: working a day together, kicking back and shooting the shit, the whole routine. That's the thing about a feeling, you can't just tell it, you have to actually be having it, or it vanishes. His father has it ass-backward about ideas being foggy, he decides. It's feelings that are like fog. What he needs is some idea that would be there no matter how he felt. A lighthouse idea to cut through the fog.

But for now he's just cruising, Led Zeppelin blasting and his driver's seat cranked back like a La-Z-Boy as he winds along River Road. He steers Don Lopatka–style, one hand on the center bar, takes in the scenery — white houses and stone walls, ducks on the marsh, the road coming at him in little curves and bigger ones, finally the huge bend by the woods at Mallard Point. Johnny knows it blind, but heading in he's going too fast, and halfway through the curve he starts to fishtail. He can feel the car trying to break free — until, at the last instant, it torques back with a little wiggly snap and slings him out onto the straightaway. His heart thumps.

That piece of shit you sold me? he'll tell Brenda. *It almost got me killed today.*

He's been ragging her about the Escort ever since the day he answered her ad for it ten months ago. The engine overheats, the clutch pops out of reverse, one headlight shines at an angle. The floor between the seats is matted with golden hair. *That's dog hair,* she said after he'd bought the car and things were starting to happen between them. *The guy before me had a golden retriever. I slept with him — the guy, not the dog.*

And they laughed. Life with Brenda means laughing at things that used to make him jealous. Either she's turning him into a better person, Johnny thinks, or a fool. Maybe a fool for sex. They do a lot of it, trying out the best times of day (she likes dawn), or the best weather (rain), or the most outrageous place (under a blanket behind the top row at a Patriots game in Foxborough). Brenda can spend a whole day having sex: bored sex, buzzed sex, sleepy sex, even sex on a full stomach — belly banging, she calls it. It's all new for Johnny. How Brenda cries when she comes, or laughs, and sometimes both: like being everything all at once, she tells him. As for their future, they fucked their way through winter and spring and now into summer, and for all the fun of it, Johnny doesn't know whether it's getting them anywhere or whether they're just fucking in place.

He parks in the driveway behind the house where she rents a third-floor apartment. He has a key, but downstairs isn't locked, upstairs either, and he walks right in. She's got her radio on; he hears Tracy Chapman's "Fast Car," currently number one on Johnny's make-me-puke list. Brenda's in her room, wearing bikini underwear and a hand-me-down shirt from her brother and swaying to the music, eyes closed. Reaching down to the tuner on the table, he turns it off.

She opens her eyes. "And hello to you too, Haggerty," she says.

"So." He looks around. "Where's the toot?"

"What do you mean, where's the toot?"

"I mean you only dance when you're coked up."

"That's so false."

"That's so true." He looks over, sees the little mirror lying on her bureau, the rolled-up dollar bill. "See? You're lying to me."

"I'm not lying. I just said it's not true I only dance when I'm coked up. Music, please."

He turns it back on and goes to the kitchen for a beer. Brenda's fridge is crammed full: he has to fight his way past the jars of jam and health-food peanut butter, the containers of olives and pickled peppers and tofu and other stuff he can't even name. Brenda likes strange combinations. The last time she made dinner, she gave him a cherry-tomato salad with nuts and mint. It tasted good, but he wondered, Who puts mint in salad? Johnny thinks of her fridge and everything in it as a part of her personality that's on hold, waiting for someone to come along and appreciate it more than he does.

Back in her room with a bottle of Heineken, he leans an elbow on the bureau and stands there, watching her dance. Granules of powder dot the little mirror. He wets his finger and tastes.

"You do too much of this shit," he says.

"*Oooo*, listen to Mr. Just Say No." She dances by, giving him a nympho look. Kisses him on his neck and down his T-shirt, kneels and unzips his Levi's.

"Hey," he says.

"What? You don't want me to suck your cock, Mr. Just Say No?" She laughs; her fingers go tiptoeing in his boxers. They've had some epic sex in this situation, the hour between jobs, but today for some reason he doesn't feel like it.

He steps back, zips up, shakes his head. "You know, sometimes I wonder who I'm having sex with, Brenda," he says. "You or the blow."

Her smile collapses. Glaring, she backs off, then jabs the power button on the receiver. "You're a bastard, Haggerty, you know that?"

She goes for a Marlboro on the nightstand, but the pack's empty and she crumples it up and falls onto the bed. Her long braid lies down her back like a rope. When she's on top of him and undoes the braid, hair hangs down all around, enclosing them in a dark world. The magic tent, Johnny calls it.

"Brenda? You want one of my cigs?"

"Fuck you."

He sits on the bed, careful not to touch her; he wonders how he can spend all day thinking about her, then mess things up this badly. "Look," he says. "I'm an asshole. You don't have to tell me."

"Yeah? Maybe I want to."

"Go ahead."

"You're an asshole."

She doesn't turn around. Johnny looks out the window, past telephone lines to a clump of thunderheads. Day after day storm clouds gather, but the heat just gets worse.

"This frickin' weather," he says. "I don't know, something's gotta happen." He thinks about the hail out in Dakota and the photo he saw in the paper, some family's patio furniture all dented and bashed. "Can you imagine hail big as a grapefruit?" he says to Brenda. "I mean, you're just walking along and *whonk* — right on your head."

She looks at him, suspicious. But Johnny isn't trying to change the subject. He really does want to talk about the hail. For instance, how heavy would it be? A pound? Two? And how could an ice ball that big be floating around up there in the first place, how could it take shape out of nothing at all, way up in the sky?

He considers asking Brenda her opinion, but it's too bizarre. "Look, I gotta go," he says. "You want me to stop by later?"

She turns back to the window. "Are you still going to be an asshole?"

It annoys him. "Just fuck it, okay?" he says. "I'll see you when I see you." And walks out.

Back in the Escort, heading for work, he realizes he forgot to tell her how her piece-of-shit car almost got him killed — how if he hadn't happened to rotate his bald front tires with the halfway-decent back ones just last week, he'd probably be wrapped around a tree on River Road. He ponders the implications. If all that's separating him from being someone who drives off a road is, say, one thirty-sixth of an inch of tire tread, then he basically is that kind of person already, isn't he? Then again, he thinks, maybe you're not the kind of guy who drives off the road until you actually do drive off. And he didn't.

The way to the Shanty goes by his old neighborhood. Heat simmers off the pavement; the sign at the drive-in bank reads 99 degrees. It hasn't been this hot in years, not since he was a little kid. Back then, his father would take him over to the park and hit fly balls to him until they were both tired and sweaty. Then they'd get in the car — keeping the windows rolled up — and drive ten minutes to the beach, torturing themselves, sweltering the whole way. He remembers the noise his father would make when they hit the water. *Jesus, that's good,* he'd say, gasping.

At his parents' house, his father's car is nowhere to be seen, and Johnny pulls over and parks. Coming round the yard, he sees his mother through the kitchen window, working away, a fan on the counter blowing air into her face.

"Hey, good-looking," she says as he opens the screen door. "What brings you here?"

"Just heading over to the Shanty. Where's Dad?"

"He'll be back. Have a seat. Iced tea's in the fridge." He pours himself a glass and sits at the table as his mother scoops pickle relish out of a big bowl into jars. "I just talked to Nell," she says. "It's a hundred and six in St. Louis. She and the baby are down in the basement because it's cooler."

He nods, flipping through a gardening magazine. When he lived here, he was always doing something and talking to her on the side; it's harder when talk's the only reason he's here. His mother asks about his apartment, the plants she gave him. It's all fine, Johnny tells her; everything's fine.

"And you're still seeing the same girl? What's her name — Belinda?"

"Brenda. Who calls their kid Belinda?"

"Maybe if you brought her round, I'd get her name right. Is it her you're embarrassed about, or us?"

"I'm not embarrassed, Ma," he says. "I'm just working a lot, that's all."

She nods. "By the way, it's five-thirty. Won't George be mad?"

He waves a hand. George Santos owns the Shanty — a man eve-

ryone hates, running a business everyone loves. "Let him go ahead
and fire me. I'm not working at a burger stand the rest of my life
anyway."

His mother looks at him, and a little silence creeps by. He thinks
about Brenda and whether the two of them could ever have a future together, maybe even get married, like his sister Nell. He and
his sister are from different planets — Nell, the straight-A girl, the
brownnoser who wrote letters to her teachers for years afterward.
Back then he held it against her. But those teachers were her role
models, Johnny understands, her lighthouse idea; they got her out.

"I've been thinking," he says to his mother. "Maybe I should join
up after all. You know, the marines. What do you think?"

"I think it's a bad idea," she says.

"Why? Dad did it. It was good enough for him."

His mother dries her hands, then sits. "First of all, just because
he did it doesn't mean it was good enough for him. And second,
you're not your father. You don't need the marines, John."

"No?"

"No." She's looking at him again, carefully. "You like people,"
she says. "And people like you back. That's your life raft."

"I don't get it."

She pushes her chair back. "I know," she says. "That's why I
told you."

They walk together to the back door. "One other thing, Ma," he
says to her. "I lied about those plants. They kinda died."

His mother smiles. "I'm going to give you some genius advice
about keeping plants. Something my mother told me once.
Ready?"

He nods, and she leans up and whispers in his ear: "Water them."

It's a busy night at the Shanty, but aside from the heat it's no different from dozens of others he's worked before. Crowds come in
waves, a rhythm of rush and lull he settles into like music. It's a fantasy of his, that his grill gig is like playing in a rock band. Another
rush hits, and he's juggling ten things at once, burgers and dogs,
order slips clipped up like tiny shirts on a clothesline, and the fry-o-
lator bubbling away, and the chili and sauerkraut in their nasty little tubs. He's cruising, razzing the counter girls and Mrs. S, cracking jokes and twirling his spatula like a gunslinger and singing as

he tosses sliced cheddar onto a burger, *Together forever and never to part, together forever with cheeeeeese!* He swigs from his personal half-gallon of lemonade. Droplets of sweat fall off his face and sizzle on the grill. *You're eating Johnny Hamburger's sweat, motherfuckers,* he thinks; *you're licking Johnny Hamburger's salt!*

The only flaw is Santos. The Shanty has made Santos rich, but he's too much the penny-pinching slave driver to kick back on his boat and let them milk his cash cow for him in peace. The place would be perfect if only there were no Santos, and even his own mother knows it — Mrs. S, who's seventy and tiny and speaks Portugenglish. "Get out of my *cozinha!*" she yells at Santos, only half joking. For his part, Johnny takes every chance to piss the man off. At least once a weekend, it's clear that the only thing keeping Santos from canning his ass is knowing how much Johnny's worth to him, and it's fun to watch him twist.

But tonight Johnny doesn't feel up to it. The big rush goes by, and afterward he'd rather just talk to Mrs. S. "Let me ask you something," he says to her. "What would you do if hail five inches big fell on your head?"

"If hell fall on my head?"

"No, hail. You know, ice. Right out of the sky. I read about it in the paper. A ball of ice this big." He holds up an onion.

"That's big," she says. *"Milagrosamente."*

"Don't believe everything you read," says Santos.

"I tell you something," Mrs. S says to Johnny, ignoring her son. "I need that big ball of ice. Is too hot for quarter of ten. Please God, if you listen, please give me one miracle ball of ice." She takes up a pile of slips and starts counting in Portuguese. "You want you take a break, Johnny? Go ahead."

He grabs his Kools and ducks outside. Usually there's a splash of breeze off the river, but tonight the air hangs still and smothering. He leans back against the garbage pen, looking out over the marinas below, the lamps and lanterns tracing rectangular patterns on the water. Some of those docks are Don Lopatka jobs, ones Johnny worked on himself, from the very first pile to the copper sheeting capped onto the last, Denny finishing it off with his usual *If they don't like it, fuck 'em,* the Don silently smoking a Camel. That's the Don, man of few words, busting his butt three hundred sixty days a year, even in the dead of January, out there driving piles like a maniac. The bottom line with the Don, Johnny understands, is that you do a good job, and you do it even when no one's looking. It's the exact opposite of Santos, who pays dirt wages and looks over every shoulder. Even now he's yelling Johnny's name — a built-in employee-break clock, set to exactly three quarters of a cigarette. Johnny decides to finish his smoke. Sure enough, here comes Santos, sticking his head around the corner

"Hey, space case," he says, and walks over. "Ground control to Johnny H." He taps him on the side of the head.

Johnny jerks his head back, and Santos's hand freezes in midair. "Whoa, now, hold on," he says. "We got a problem here?"

"Nope. All I'm saying is, I don't like people going for my face, that's all."

Santos stares. "Fine. And all I'm saying is, don't make me come out here two times looking for you. Okay?"

He goes back in, and a moment later Johnny follows. "Good night, boys," says Mrs. S, taking her handbag and leaving for her apartment building next door. It's the winding-down time of the night; Santos sits at his tiny desk, going through order sheets, while Johnny starts scraping burnt crud off the grill. He imagines launching a simple *Fuck you*, right in the man's sunburned fat face. He wonders what's keeping him from doing it.

A couple comes to the counter. Johnny takes their order — a hot fudge sundae — and piles it high, an outrageous mountain of soft-serve and whipped cream with cherries and nuts everywhere. "Hey, thanks!" the guy says as Johnny hands it over. He rings them up, shuts the cash register. Then walks over to Santos, who's still poring over paperwork at his desk.

"George."

Santos raises a finger, and Johnny stands there, balancing on top of the moment. It's like wrapping your car around a tree, he thinks: either it's about to happen or some little bit of tread is going to hold him on the road.

"George," he says again. "I'm outta here."

Santos frowns at his watch.

"No, I mean, I'm through." He unties his apron. "I'm done."

Pulling his cheapo CVS glasses down his nose, Santos stares up at him. "Whaddya mean, you're done?"

"I mean, it's played out here, you know? I'm just . . . done."

Santos stands. "Tell you what," he says, a hand on Johnny's shoulder. "It's hot tonight, we're both a little tired. Why don't you go on home. We'll forget the whole thing."

Johnny shakes his head. "I don't think so."

"So what're you telling me? You're quitting? Listen, I need you. Tomorrow, the next day. This is midsummer business we're talking about."

"Sorry," Johnny says.

"Don't give me sorry. Sorry is bullshit." Santos glances away, then comes back again in his face. "Now, come on, Johnny. You walk in here forty-five minutes late on the hottest night of the summer, and do I bust your ass about it? I'm being fair here. Let's not burn any bridges." His look says, This is your last chance. Johnny says nothing, feels nothing.

"Fine," Santos says, and turns away. "But don't count on me being so nice when you come back."

Sitting in his car across the street, he fishes a Miller from the melted ice in his cooler and watches Santos scrub down, alone in the Shanty under the sign, FAMOUS SINCE 1976. He remembers there was actually a time when he, Johnny, fantasized about being cut in on the business one day. After all, when people thought Sea Shanty, didn't they think Johnny Hamburger, and vice versa?

The sign flicks off, and before Santos can come out and see him, he starts the Escort and pulls away. In his rearview mirror he watches the place disappear; he's leaving it behind, and Johnny Hamburger too. He was good at being Johnny Hamburger. But what's the use of being good at something worthless? It's like digging your own grave.

"So long," he says, and raises his beer.

It's only eleven, and he doesn't feel like waiting for Brenda at her place, so he drives. He heads away from town, past the high school and fairgrounds and out again onto River Road. Air pours up his arm, thick as warm milk. He turns on the radio — and out comes Brenda's song, this same deep-voiced black chick who's been yodeling away all summer about driving too fast in her boyfriend's car. It isn't even a real driving song, Johnny thinks, just a folky tune with a rinky-dink little guitar curlicue stuck onto it. But he leaves it on as a kind of apology to Brenda. He likes that she dances by herself in her room, coke or no coke. He shouldn't have gotten in her face like that.

At Mallard Point he drives toward the big curve. The river is on his left this time, the woods on his right, rising behind a culvert and a mossy bank. Frogs and ducks and crickets are whooping it up in the darkness, a regular nighttime jubilee. But something's wrong. His crooked headlight, the one that stabs out at an angle, catches taillight reflectors where no taillights should be. Slowing, Johnny sees a car, an aqua-green Honda Civic, up on the mossy bank, its front end rammed against a tree. And fire: little licks of flame, curling out from underneath.

His first crazy thought, even as he pulls over and jumps out, is that someone has made a campfire and parked on top of it. Then he sees the second car, a Volvo station wagon stopped on the other side of the road. There's a hippie-looking woman in a long skirt standing there, staring, eyes huge.

"What happened?" Johnny asks her. "Where's the other driver?"

"She just — my God, she just went right off and —" The woman points at the Honda. "She's in there."

"In there?"

"My husband went to get help. He didn't want to move her — David!"

The husband runs up, panting hard. He's bearded, with shorts and sandals and John Lennon glasses. "They're on their way," he says, taking in Johnny at a glance. Then he sees the Honda and the licks of flame. "Oh, shit."

The two of them rush over the culvert and up to the car. There's a hissing sound, and the acid smells of antifreeze and burning engine parts. And gasoline. Johnny can see the driver inside, a dark-haired girl slumped across the seat, miniskirt and tank top and one dangly earring and no seat belt. He tries the door but it's locked, windows closed — the fucking AC, he thinks.

"She's out cold!" he says. "We gotta break the window!"

He looks around for a rock, but just then a jet of flame shoots out from beneath the car, and he and the husband stagger backward. "David!" the woman at the Volvo yells. "David, get away, please!" The husband backs off farther.

"Where are the goddamn cops?" he says.

Behind them the wife screeches, hysterical. Johnny looks both ways along the empty road. Then he plunges forward, running up the bank, arms in front of his face to shield himself. There's no time to think, and reaching the car, he rears back a karate kick, Bruce Lee–style, right into the heart of the heat, toward the driver's window. His boot thwacks the glass and the window caves inward, exploding in little bits. He doesn't bother opening the door, just leans in and grabs the girl with both hands and hauls her right out through the window, weightless, a sack. Carrying her, he stumbles down past the culvert and across River Road and lays her on the pavement in front of the Volvo. There's a cut on her head, but he thinks she's alive. Head cuts bleed. He puts his ear to her mouth. She's breathing.

"Come on," he says to her.

Across the road, the Honda burns. It isn't like in the movies; there's no fireball, no explosion, just flames feeding upward and outward until it's all fire and no car. They stare, watching it burn. At forty feet they can feel the harsh heat and hear things fizzing and popping and being consumed.

"Jesus fucking Christ," says the husband.

Behind them, sirens.

By the time the paramedics clear out, along with the firemen and cops and county sheriff and somebody from the newspaper who wants to know his whole life story, it's almost 2:00 A.M. The girl's name is Antonia Nieves, she's nineteen, and she's okay, they radio back from the hospital; cuts and bruises and shock, but nothing serious.

Johnny says goodbye to the Volvo couple. "You were amazing," the woman tells him. He can see that the husband, David, is already feeling a little scratchy about how things played out. "You were great," says the woman.

"Nah," Johnny says. "I work at a grill. I'm kind of fireproof." He shakes their hands, then crosses River Road to his car.

At Brenda's apartment the lights are out and he creeps in. He washes up in the bathroom — shocked at what looks back at him from the mirror: his face smeared, one eyebrow singed away entirely. He turns off the light and stands there, his legs suddenly weak. In the dark he washes his face and hands and arms, then goes back out into the bedroom, peels off his clothes, and gets onto the bed next to her.

Brenda doesn't like sleeping with the AC on, and it's hot in the room — or maybe he's hot, still smoldering like an ember. His body feels as though it has worked three Don Lopatka shifts in a row, but he lies awake, seeing the girl's face as he leaned over her and her eyes fluttered open. *It's okay,* he told her. *You drove off the road.* She nodded. Her forehead bloody and glistening in the glow of the burning car.

You're a hero, the cop said to him after taking his statement — *enjoy it.* But all Johnny can think about as he floats toward sleep is how many little things could have gone differently. Maybe the Don keeps him another hour at work, in which case he doesn't drive along River Road in the first place and probably doesn't go back later on. Or maybe he doesn't stop off at his mother's, in which case he isn't late to the Shanty, and Santos isn't pissed off enough to piss him off enough to quit, and so when Antonia Nieves drives off the road, he's still breaking down the grill. Every little change leads to his not being there and the girl being dead.

And yet he was there; she isn't dead. He saved her. And not only her, but everything she's going to do from now on. Jobs, boyfriends, the kids she's going to have someday — he saved them too. He's their father, he thinks, or cofather, just like whoever it was in a village in Ireland a hundred years ago who loaned money for a boat ticket to some dirt-farming Haggerty is his cofather, or the golden retriever guy who sold the piece-of-shit Escort is the cofather of whatever he and Brenda might someday manage to become. He pictures Antonia Nieves's future kids, three or four of them, and how they'll come over on a summer afternoon to visit, everyone sitting around together, cooking out on the patio and playing games in the yard, listening to music and hitting fly balls and drinking iced tea.

He doesn't even know he is asleep until a tumbling crash of noise wakes him. The clock says 3:34. Outside, trees thrash, tossing shadows and light around the room. Wind whips through the screen. Lightning. Thunder.

"Hey," he says, and touches Brenda's shoulder.

"Mmmm," she murmurs, "you smell all toasty." But she's not awake. He can have a whole conversation with her like this, and she won't remember it tomorrow. He lies there, listening to the storm close in, rumbling and clanking as it comes. And suddenly he knows: it's up there somewhere. Rotating, revolving slowly, taking shape. Glinting like a big round cool gem.

"Hey," he says again to Brenda. "Wake up."

He joggles her shoulder, and at the same moment lightning blitzes with a huge tearing rip of the heavens, and she's awake — he sees her in the blue-gray flicker, looking at him.

"It's happening," he says to her. "It's up there."

"You smell —"

"Toasty. I know. I burned my eyebrows off."

"You what?" She touches his face.

"*Shhhhh.*" He puts a finger to her lips. Reaches down with his other hand, takes hold of her T-shirt, and hikes it up. Presses his body against her. "You can read about it in the paper tomorrow," he whispers.

He closes his eyes, kissing her, and move by slow move they begin to touch. It's like magic, he thinks, cold spun out of heat itself, the perfect ball of ice; and he reaches one hand out in the dark, palm up, to catch it.

DAN CHAON

The Bees

FROM MCSWEENEY'S

GENE'S SON Frankie wakes up screaming. It has become fre-
quent, two or three times a week, at random times: midnight —
three A.M. — five in the morning. Here is a high, empty wail that
severs Gene from his unconsciousness like sharp teeth. It is the
worst sound that Gene can imagine, the sound of a young child dying violently — falling from a building, or caught in some machinery that is tearing an arm off, or being mauled by a predatory animal. No matter how many times he hears it he jolts up with such
images playing in his mind, and he always runs, thumping into the
child's bedroom to find Frankie sitting up in bed, his eyes closed,
his mouth open in an oval like a Christmas caroler. Frankie appears
to be in a kind of peaceful trance, and if someone took a picture of
him he would look like he was waiting to receive a spoonful of ice
cream rather than emitting that horrific sound.

"Frankie!" Gene will shout, and claps his hands hard in the child's
face. The clapping works well. At this, the scream always stops
abruptly, and Frankie opens his eyes, blinking at Gene with vague
awareness before settling back down into his pillow, nuzzling a little
before growing still. He is sound asleep, he is always sound asleep,
though even after months Gene can't help leaning down and pressing his ear to the child's chest, to make sure he's still breathing, his
heart is still going. It always is.

There is no explanation that they can find. In the morning the
child doesn't remember anything, and on the few occasions that
they have managed to wake him in the midst of one of his screaming attacks, he is merely sleepy and irritable. Once, Gene's wife

Karen shook him and shook him, until finally he opened his eyes, groggily. "Honey?" she said. "Honey? Did you have a bad dream?" But Frankie only moaned a little. "No," he said, puzzled and unhappy at being awakened, but nothing more.

They can find no pattern to it. It can happen any day of the week, any time of the night. It doesn't seem to be associated with diet, or with his activities during the day, and it doesn't stem, as far as they can tell, from any sort of psychological unease. During the day he seems perfectly normal and happy.

They have taken him several times to the pediatrician, but the doctor seems to have little of use to say. There is nothing wrong with the child physically, Dr. Banerjee says. She advises that such things are not uncommon for children of Frankie's age group — he is five — and that more often than not, the disturbance simply passes away.

"He hasn't experienced any kind of emotional trauma, has he?" the doctor says. "Nothing out of the ordinary at home?"

"No, no," they both murmur, together. They shake their heads, and Dr. Banerjee shrugs.

"Parents," she says. "It's probably nothing to worry about." She gives them a brief smile. "As difficult as it is, I'd say that you may just have to weather this out."

But the doctor has never heard those screams. In the mornings after the "nightmares," as Karen calls them, Gene feels unnerved, edgy. He works as a driver for the United Parcel Service, and as he moves through the day after a screaming attack, there is a barely perceptible hum at the edge of his hearing, an intent, deliberate static sliding along behind him as he wanders through streets and streets in his van. He stops along the side of the road and listens. The shadows of summer leaves tremble murmurously against the windshield, and cars are accelerating on a nearby road. In the treetops, a cicada makes its trembly, pressure-cooker hiss.

Something bad has been looking for him for a long time, he thinks, and now, at last, it is growing near.

When he comes home at night everything is normal. They live in an old house in the suburbs of Cleveland, and sometimes after dinner they work together in the small patch of garden out in back of the house — tomatoes, zucchini, string beans, cucumbers — while Frankie plays with Legos in the dirt. Or they take walks around the neighborhood, Frankie riding his bike in front of them, his training wheels recently removed. They gather on the couch and watch cartoons together, or play board games, or draw pictures with crayons. After Frankie is asleep, Karen will sit at the kitchen table and study — she is in nursing school — and Gene will sit outside on the porch, flipping through a newsmagazine or a novel, smoking the cigarettes that he has promised Karen he will give up when he turns thirty-five. He is thirty-four now, and Karen is twenty-seven, and he is aware, more and more frequently, that this is not the life he deserves. He has been incredibly lucky, he thinks. Blessed, as Gene's favorite cashier at the supermarket always says. "Have a blessed day," she says when Gene pays the money and she hands him his receipt, and he feels as if she has sprinkled him with her ordinary, gentle beatitude. It reminds him of long ago, when an old nurse held his hand in the hospital and said that she was praying for him.

Sitting out in his lawn chair, drawing smoke out of his cigarette, he thinks about that nurse, even though he doesn't want to. He thinks of the way she leaned over him and brushed his hair as he stared at her, imprisoned in a full body cast, sweating his way through withdrawal and DTs.

He had been a different person, back then. A drunk, a monster. At nineteen, he'd married the girl he'd gotten pregnant, and then had set about slowly, steadily, ruining all their lives. When he'd abandoned them, his wife and son, back in Nebraska, he had been twenty-four, a danger to himself and others. He'd done them a favor by leaving, he thought, though he still felt guilty when he remembered it. Years later, when he was sober, he'd even tried to contact them. He wanted to own up to his behavior, to pay the back child support, to apologize. But they were nowhere to be found. Mandy was no longer living in the small Nebraska town where they'd met and married, and there was no forwarding address. Her parents were dead. No one seemed to know where she'd gone.

Karen didn't know the full story. She had been, to his relief, uncurious about his previous life, though she knew he had some drinking days, some bad times. She knew that he'd been married before, too, though she didn't know the extent of it, didn't know that he had another son, for example, didn't know that he had left them one night, without even packing a bag, just driving off in the car, a flask tucked between his legs, driving east as far as he could go. She didn't know about the car crash, the wreck he should have died in. She didn't know what a bad person he'd been.

She was a nice lady, Karen. Maybe a little sheltered. And truth to tell, he was ashamed — and even scared — to imagine how she would react to the truth about his past. He didn't know if she would have ever really trusted him if she'd known the full story, and the longer they knew one another, the less inclined he was to reveal it. He'd escaped his old self, he thought, and when Karen got pregnant, shortly before they were married, he told himself that now he had a chance to do things over, to do it better. They had purchased the house together, he and Karen, and now Frankie will be in kindergarten in the fall. He has come full circle, has come exactly to the point when his former life with Mandy and his son DJ had completely fallen apart. He looks up as Karen comes to the back door and speaks to him through the screen. "I think it's time for bed, sweetheart," she says softly, and he shudders off these thoughts, these memories. He smiles.

He's been in a strange frame of mind lately. The months of regular awakenings have been getting to him, and he has a hard time getting back to sleep after an episode with Frankie. When Karen wakes him in the morning, he often feels muffled, sluggish — as if he's hung over. He doesn't hear the alarm clock. When he stumbles out of bed, he finds he has a hard time keeping his moodiness in check. He can feel his temper coiling up inside him.

He isn't that type of person anymore, and hasn't been for a long while. Still, he can't help but worry. They say that there is a second stretch of craving, which sets in after several years of smooth sailing; five or seven years will pass, and then it will come back without warning. He has been thinking of going to AA meetings again, though he hasn't in some time — not since he met Karen.

It's not as if he gets trembly every time he passes a liquor store, or even as if he has a problem when he goes out with buddies and spends the evening drinking soda and nonalchoholic beer. No. The trouble comes at night, when he's asleep.

He has begun to dream of his first son. DJ. Perhaps it is related to his worries about Frankie, but for several nights in a row the image of DJ — aged about five — has appeared to him. In the dream, Gene is drunk, and playing hide-and-seek with DJ in the yard behind the Cleveland house where he is now living. There is the thick weeping willow out there, and Gene watches the child appear from behind it and run across the grass, happily, unafraid, the way Frankie would. DJ turns to look over his shoulder and laughs, and Gene stumbles after him, at least a six-pack's worth of good mood, a goofy, drunken dad. It's so real that when he wakes, he still feels intoxicated. It takes him a few minutes to shake it.

One morning after a particularly vivid version of this dream, Frankie wakes and complains of a funny feeling — "right here," he says, and points to his forehead. It isn't a headache, he says. "It's like bees!" he says. "Buzzing bees!" He rubs his hand against his brow. "Inside my head." He considers for a moment. "You know how the bees bump against the window when they get in the house and want to get out?" This description pleases him, and he taps his forehead lightly with his fingers, humming, zzzzzzz, to demonstrate.

"Does it hurt?" Karen says.

"No," Frankie says. "It tickles."

Karen gives Gene a concerned look. She makes Frankie lie down on the couch and tells him to close his eyes for a while. After a few minutes he rises up, smiling, and says that the feeling has gone.

"Honey, are you sure?" Karen says. She pushes her hair back and slides her palm across his forehead. "He's not hot," she says, and Frankie sits up impatiently, suddenly more interested in finding a matchbox car he dropped under a chair.

Karen gets out one of her nursing books, and Gene watches her face tighten with concern as she flips slowly through the pages. She is looking at Chapter Three: Neurological System, and Gene observes as she pauses here and there, skimming down a list of symptoms. "We should probably take him back to Dr. Banerjee again," she says. Gene nods, recalling what the doctor said about "emotional trauma."

"Are you scared of bees?" he asks Frankie. "Is that something that's bothering you?"

"No," Frankie says. "Not really."

When Frankie was three, a bee stung him above his left eyebrow.

They had been out hiking together, and they hadn't yet learned that Frankie was "moderately allergic" to bee stings. Within minutes of the sting, Frankie's face had begun to distort, to puff up, his eye swelling shut. He looked deformed. Gene didn't know if he'd ever been more frightened in his entire life, running down the trail with Frankie's head pressed against his heart, trying to get to the car and drive him to the doctor, terrified that the child was dying. Frankie himself was calm.

Gene clears his throat. He knows the feeling that Frankie is talking about — he has felt it himself, that odd, feathery vibration inside his head. And in fact he feels it again, now. He presses the pads of his fingertips against his brow. Emotional trauma, his mind murmurs, but he is thinking of DJ, not Frankie.

"What are you scared of?" Gene asks Frankie after a moment. "Anything?"

"You know what the scariest thing is?" Frankie says, and widens his eyes, miming a frightened look. "There's a lady with no head, and she went walking through the woods, looking for it. "Give . . . me . . . back . . . my . . . head . . ."

"Where on earth did you hear a story like that!" Karen says.

"Daddy told me," Frankie says. "When we were camping."

Gene blushes, even before Karen gives him a sharp look. "Oh, great," she says. "Wonderful."

He doesn't meet her eyes. "We were just telling ghost stones," he says softly. "I thought he would think the story was funny."

"My God, Gene," she says. "With him having nightmares like this? What were you thinking?"

It's a bad flashback, the kind of thing he's usually able to avoid. He thinks abruptly of Mandy, his former wife. He sees in Karen's face that look Mandy would give him when he screwed up. "What are you, some kind of idiot?" Mandy used to say. "Are you crazy?" Back then, Gene couldn't do anything right, it seemed, and when Mandy yelled at him it made his stomach clench with shame and inarticulate rage. I was trying, he would think, I was trying, damn it, and it was as if no matter what he did, it wouldn't turn out right. That feeling would sit heavily in his chest, and eventually, when things got worse, he hit her once. "Why do you want me to feel like shit," he had said through clenched teeth. "I'm not an asshole," he said, and when she rolled her eyes at him, he slapped her hard enough to knock her out of her chair.

That was the time he'd taken DJ to the carnival. It was a Saturday, and he'd been drinking a little so Mandy didn't like it, but after all — he thought — DJ was his son too, he had a right to spend some time with his own son. Mandy wasn't his boss even if she might think she was. She liked to make him hate himself.

What she was mad about was that he'd taken DJ on the Velocerator. It was a mistake, he'd realized afterward. But DJ himself had begged to go on. He was just recently four years old, and Gene had just turned twenty-three, which made him feel inexplicably old. He wanted to have a little fun.

Besides, nobody told him he couldn't take DJ on the thing. When he led DJ through the gate, the ticket-taker even smiled, as if to say, "Here is a young guy showing his kid a good time." Gene winked at DJ and grinned, taking a nip from a flask of peppermint schnapps. He felt like a good dad. He wished his own father had taken him on rides at the carnival!

The door to the Velocerator opened like a hatch in a big silver flying saucer. Disco music was blaring from the entrance and became louder as they went inside. It was a circular room with soft padded walls, and one of the workers had Gene and DJ stand with their backs to the wall, strapping them in side by side. Gene felt warm and expansive from the schnapps. He took DJ's hand, and he almost felt as if he were glowing with love. "Get ready, kiddo," Gene whispered. "This is going to be wild."

The hatch door of the Velocerator sealed closed with a pressurized sigh. And then, slowly, the walls they were strapped to began to turn. Gene tightened on DJ's hand as they began to rotate, gathering speed. After a moment the wall pads they were strapped to slid up, and the force of velocity pushed them back, held to the surface of the spinning wall like iron to a magnet. Gene's cheeks and lips seemed to pull back, and the sensation of helplessness made him laugh.

At that moment, DJ began to scream. "No! No! Stop! Make it stop!" They were terrible shrieks, and Gene grabbed the child's hand tightly. "It's all right," he yelled jovially over the thump of the music. "It's okay! I'm right here!" But the child's wailing only got louder in response. The scream seemed to whip past Gene in a circle, tumbling around and around the circumference of the ride like a spirit, trailing echoes as it flew. When the machine finally stopped, DJ was heaving with sobs, and the man at the control panel glared. Gene could feel the other passengers staring grimly and judgmentally at him.

Gene felt horrible. He had been so happy — thinking that they were finally having themselves a memorable father-and-son moment — and he could feel his heart plunging into darkness. DJ kept on weeping, even as they left the ride and walked along the midway, even as Gene tried to distract him with promises of cotton candy and stuffed animals. "I want to go home," DJ cried, and "I want my mom! I want my mom!" And it had wounded Gene to hear that. He gritted his teeth.

"Fine!" he hissed. "Let's go home to your mommy, you little crybaby. I swear to God, I'm never taking you with me anywhere again." And he gave DJ a little shake. "Jesus, what's wrong with you? Lookit, people are laughing at you. See? They're saying, 'Look at that big boy, bawling like a girl.'"

This memory comes to him out of the blue. He had forgotten all about it, but now it comes to him over and over. Those screams were not unlike the sounds Frankie makes in the middle of the night, and they pass repeatedly through the membrane of his thoughts, without warning. The next day he finds himself recalling it again, the memory of the scream impressing his mind with such force that he actually has to pull his UPS truck off to the side of the road and put his face in his hands: awful! awful! He must have seemed like a monster to the child.

Sitting there in his van, he wishes he could find a way to contact them — Mandy and DJ. He wishes that he could tell them how sorry he is, and send them money. He puts his fingertips against his forehead, as cars drive past on the street, as an old man parts the curtains and peers out of the house Gene is parked in front of, hopeful that Gene might have a package for him.

Where are they? Gene wonders. He tries to picture a town, a house, but there is only a blank. Surely, Mandy being Mandy, she would have hunted him down by now to demand child support. She would have relished treating him like a deadbeat dad, she would have hired some company who would garnish his wages.

Now, sitting at the roadside, it occurs to him suddenly that they are dead. He recalls the car wreck that he was in, just outside Des Moines, and if he had been killed they would never have known. He recalls waking up in the hospital, and the elderly nurse who said, "You're very lucky, young man. You should be dead."

Maybe they are dead, he thinks. Mandy and DJ. The idea strikes him a glancing blow, because of course it would make sense. The reason they'd never contacted him. Of course.

He doesn't know what to do with such premonitions. They are ridiculous, they are self-pitying, they are paranoid, but especially now, with their concerns about Frankie, he is at the mercy of his anxieties. He comes home from work and Karen stares at him heavily.

"What's the matter?" she says, and he shrugs. "You look terrible," she says.

"It's nothing," he says, but she continues to look at him skeptically. She shakes her head.

"I took Frankie to the doctor again today," she says after a moment, and Gene sits down at the table with her, where she is spread out with her textbooks and notepaper.

"I suppose you'll think I'm being a neurotic mom," she says. "I think I'm too immersed in disease, that's the problem."

Gene shakes his head. "No, no," he says. His throat feels dry. "You're right. Better safe than sorry."

"Mmm," she says thoughtfully. "I think Dr. Banerjee is starting to hate me."

"Naw," Gene says. "No one could hate you." With effort, he smiles gently. A good husband, he kisses her palm, her wrist. "Try not to worry," he says, though his own nerves are fluttering. He can hear Frankie in the back yard, shouting orders to someone.

"Who's he talking to?" Gene says, and Karen doesn't look up.

"Oh," she says. "It's probably just Bubba." Bubba is Frankie's imaginary playmate.

Gene nods. He goes to the window and looks out. Frankie is pretending to shoot at something, his thumb and forefinger cocked into a gun. "Get him! Get him!" Frankie shouts, and Gene stares out as Frankie dodges behind a tree. Frankie looks nothing like DJ, but when he pokes his head from behind the hanging foliage of the willow, Gene feels a little shudder — a flicker — something. He clenches his jaw.

"This class is really driving me crazy," Karen says. "Every time I read about a worst-case scenario, I start to worry. It's strange. The more you know, the less sure you are of anything."

"What did the doctor say this time?" Gene says. He shifts uncomfortably, still staring out at Frankie, and it seems as if dark specks circle and bob at the corner of the yard. "He seems okay?"

Karen shrugs. "As far as they can tell." She looks down at her textbook, shaking her head. "He seems healthy." He puts his hand gently on the back of her neck, and she lolls her head back and forth against his fingers. "I've never believed that anything really terrible could happen to me," she had once told him, early in their marriage, and it had scared him. "Don't say that," he'd whispered, and she'd laughed.

"You're superstitious," she said. "That's cute."

He can't sleep. The strange presentiment that Mandy and DJ are dead has lodged heavily in his mind, and he rubs his feet together underneath the covers, trying to find a comfortable posture. He can hear the soft ticks of the old electric typewriter as Karen finishes her paper for school, words rattling out in bursts that remind him of some sort of insect language. He closes his eyes, pretending to be asleep when Karen finally comes to bed, but his mind is ticking with small, scuttling images: his former wife and son, flashes of the photographs he didn't own, hadn't kept. They're dead, a firm voice in his mind says, very distinctly. They were in a fire. And they burned up. It is not quite his own voice that speaks to him, and abruptly he can picture the burning house. It's a trailer, somewhere on the outskirts of a small town, and the black smoke is pouring out of the open door. The plastic window frames have warped and begun to melt, and the smoke billows from the trailer into the sky in a way that reminds him of an old locomotive. He can't see inside, except for crackling bursts of deep orange flames, but he's aware that they're inside. For a second he can see DJ's face, flickering, peering steadily from the window of the burning trailer, his mouth open in an unnatural circle, as if he's singing.

He opens his eyes. Karen's breathing has steadied, she's sound asleep, and he carefully gets out of bed, padding restlessly through the house in his pajamas. They're not dead, he tries to tell himself, and stands in front of the refrigerator, pouring milk from the carton into his mouth. It's an old comfort, from back in the days when he was drying out, when the thick taste of milk would slightly calm his craving for a drink. But it doesn't help him now. The dream, the vision, has frightened him badly, and he sits on the couch with an afghan over his shoulders, staring at some science program on television. On the program, a lady scientist is examining a mummy. A child. The thing is bald — almost a skull but not quite. A membrane of ancient skin is pulled taut over the eye sockets. The lips are stretched back, and there are small, chipped, rodentlike teeth. Looking at the thing, he can't help but think of DJ again, and he looks over his shoulder, quickly, the way he used to.

The last year that he was together with Mandy, there were times when DJ would actually give him the creeps — spook him. DJ had been an unusually skinny child, with a head like a baby bird and long, bony feet with toes that seemed strangely extended, as if they were meant for gripping. He can remember the way the child would slip barefoot through rooms, slinking, sneaking, watching, Gene had thought, always watching him.

It is a memory that he has almost, for years, succeeded in forgetting, a memory he hates and mistrusts. He was drinking heavily at the time, and he knows now that alcohol grotesquely distorted his perceptions. But now that it has been dislodged, that old feeling moves through him like a breath of smoke. Back then, it had seemed to him that Mandy had turned DJ against him, that DJ had in some strange way almost physically transformed into something that wasn't Gene's real son. Gene can remember how sometimes he would be sitting on the couch, watching TV, and he'd get a funny feeling. He'd turn his head and DJ would be at the edge of the room, with his bony spine hunched and his long neck craned, staring with those strangely oversized eyes. Other times, Gene and Mandy would be arguing and DJ would suddenly slide into the room, creeping up to Mandy and resting his head on her chest, right in the middle of some important talk. "I'm thirsty," he would say, in imitation baby-talk. Though he was five years old, he would play-act this little toddler voice. "Mama," he would say. "I is firsty." And DJ's eyes would rest on Gene for a moment, cold and full of calculating hatred.

Of course, Gene knows now that this was not the reality of it. He knows: he was a drunk, and DJ was just a sad, scared little kid, trying to deal with a rotten situation. Later, when he was in detox, these memories of his son made him actually shudder with shame, and it was not something he could bring himself to talk about even when he was deep into his twelve steps. How could he say how repulsed he'd been by the child, how actually frightened he was? Jesus Christ, DJ was a poor wretched five-year-old kid! But in Gene's memory there was something malevolent about him, resting his head pettishly on his mother's chest, talking in that sing-song, lisping voice, staring hard and unblinking at Gene with a little smile. Gene remembers catching DJ by the back of the neck. "If you're going to talk, talk normal," Gene had whispered through his teeth, tightening his fingers on the child's neck. "You're not a baby. You're not fooling anybody." And DJ had actually bared his teeth, making a thin, hissing whine.

He wakes and he can't breathe. There is a swimming, suffocating sensation of being stared at, being watched by something that hates him, and he gasps, choking for air. A lady is bending over him, and for a moment he expects her to say, "You're very lucky, young man. You should be dead."

But it's Karen. "What are you doing?" she says. It's morning, and he struggles to orient himself — he's on the living room floor, and the television is still going.

"Jesus," he says, and coughs. "Oh, Jesus." He is sweating, his face feels hot, but he tries to calm himself in the face of Karen's horrified stare. "A bad dream," he says, trying to control his panting breaths. "Jesus," he says, and shakes his head, trying to smile reassuringly for her. "I got up last night and I couldn't sleep. I must have passed out while I was watching TV."

But Karen just gazes at him, her expression frightened and uncertain, as if something about him is transforming. "Gene," she says. "Are you all right?"

"Sure," he says hoarsely, and a shudder passes over him involuntarily. "Of course." And then he realizes that he is naked. He sits up, covering his crotch self-consciously with his hands, and glances around. He doesn't see his underwear or his pajama bottoms anywhere nearby. He doesn't even see the afghan, which he had draped over him on the couch while he was watching the mummies on TV. He starts to stand up, awkwardly, and he notices that

Frankie is standing there in the archway between the kitchen and the living room, watching him, his arms at his sides like a cowboy who is ready to draw his holstered guns.

"Mom?" Frankie says. "I'm thirsty."

✓ He drives through his deliveries in a daze. The bees, he thinks. He remembers what Frankie had said a few mornings before, about bees inside his head, buzzing and bumping against the inside of his forehead like a windowpane they were tapping against. That's the feeling he has now. All the things that he doesn't quite remember are circling and alighting, vibrating their cellophane wings insistently. He sees himself striking Mandy across the face with the flat of his hand, knocking her off her chair; he sees his grip tightening around the back of DJ's thin, five-year-old neck, shaking him as he grimaced and wept; and he is aware that there are other things, perhaps even worse, if he thought about it hard enough. All the things that he'd prayed that Karen would never know about him.

He was very drunk on the day that he left them, so drunk that he can barely remember. It was hard to believe that he'd made it all the way to Des Moines on the interstate before he went off the road, tumbling end over end into darkness. He was laughing, he thought, as the car crumpled around him, and he has to pull his van over to the side of the road, out of fear, as the tickling in his head intensifies. There is an image of Mandy sitting on the couch as he stormed out, with DJ cradled in her arms, one of DJ's eyes swollen shut and puffy. There is an image of him in the kitchen, throwing glasses and beer bottles onto the floor, listening to them shatter.

And whether they are dead or not, he knows that they don't wish him well. They would not want him to be happy — in love with his wife and child. His normal, undeserved life.

When he gets home that night, he feels exhausted. He doesn't want to think anymore, and for a moment it seems that he will be allowed a small reprieve. Frankie is in the yard, playing contentedly. Karen is in the kitchen, making hamburgers and corn on the cob, and everything seems okay. But when he sits down to take off his boots, she gives him an angry look.

"Don't do that in the kitchen," she says icily. "Please. I've asked you before."

He looks down at his feet: one shoe unlaced, half off. "Oh," he says. "Sorry."

But when he retreats to the living room, to his recliner, she follows him. She leans against the doorframe, her arms folded, watching as he releases his tired feet from the boots and rubs his hand over the bottom of his socks. She frowns heavily.

"What?" he says, and tries on an uncertain smile.

She sighs. "We need to talk about last night," she says. "I need to know what's going on."

"Nothing," he says, but the stern way she examines him activates his anxieties all over again. "I couldn't sleep, so I went out to the living room to watch TV. That's all."

She stares at him. "Gene," she says after a moment. "People don't usually wake up naked on their living room floor and not know how they got there. That's just weird, don't you think?"

Oh, please, he thinks. He lifts his hands, shrugging — a posture of innocence and exasperation, though his insides are trembling. "I know," he says. "It was weird to me too. I was having nightmares. I really don't know what happened."

She gazes at him for a long time, her eyes heavy. "I see," she says, and he can feel the emanation of her disappointment like waves of heat. "Gene," she says. "All I'm asking is for you to be honest with me. If you're having problems, if you're drinking again, or thinking about it. I want to help. We can work it out. But you have to be honest with me."

"I'm not drinking," Gene says firmly. He holds her eyes earnestly. "I'm not thinking about it. I told you when we met, I'm through with it. Really." But he is aware again of an observant, unfriendly presence, hidden, moving along the edge of the room. "I don't understand," he says. "What is it? Why would you think I'd lie to you?"

She shifts, still trying to read something in his face, still, he can tell, doubting him. "Listen," she says at last, and he can tell she is trying not to cry. "Some guy called you today. A drunk guy. And he said to tell you that he had a good time hanging out with you last night, and that he was looking forward to seeing you again soon." She frowns hard, staring at him as if this last bit of damning information will show him for the liar he is. A tear slips out of the corner of her eye and along the bridge of her nose. Gene feels his chest tighten.

"That's crazy," he says. He tries to sound outraged, but he is in fact suddenly very frightened. "Who was it?"

She shakes her head sorrowfully. "I don't know," she says. "Something with a *B*. He was slurring so badly I could hardly understand him. BB or BJ or . . ."

Gene can feel the small hairs on his back prickling. "Was it DJ?" he says softly.

And Karen shrugs, lifting a now teary face to him. "I don't know!" she says hoarsely. "I don't know. Maybe." And Gene puts his palms across his face. He is aware of that strange, buzzing, tickling feeling behind his forehead.

"Who is DJ?" Karen says. "Gene, you have to tell me what's going on."

But he can't. He can't tell her, even now. Especially now, he thinks, when to admit that he'd been lying to her ever since they met would confirm all the fears and suspicions she'd been nursing for — what? Days? Weeks?

"He's someone I used to know a long time ago," Gene tells her. "Not a good person. He's the kind of guy who might . . . call up, and get a kick out of upsetting you."

They sit at the kitchen table, silently watching as Frankie eats his hamburger and corn on the cob. Gene can't quite get his mind around it. DJ, he thinks as he presses his finger against his hamburger bun but doesn't pick it up. DJ. He would be fifteen by now. Could he, perhaps, have found them? Maybe stalking them? Watching the house? Gene tries to fathom how DJ might have been causing Frankie's screaming episodes. How he might have caused what happened last night — snuck up on Gene while he was sitting there watching TV and drugged him or something. It seems farfetched.

"Maybe it was just some random drunk," he says at last, to Karen. "Accidentally calling the house. He didn't ask for me by name, did he?"

"I don't remember," Karen says softly. "Gene . . ."

And he can't stand the doubtfulness, the lack of trust in her expression. He strikes his fist hard against the table, and his plate clatters in a circling echo. "I did not go out with anybody last night!" he says. "I did not get drunk! You can either believe me, or you can . . ."

They are both staring at him. Frankie's eyes are wide, and he puts down the corncob he was about to bite into, as if he doesn't like it anymore. Karen's mouth is pinched.

"Or I can what?" she says.

"Nothing," Gene breathes.

There isn't a fight, but a chill spreads through the house, a silence. She knows that he isn't telling her the truth. She knows that there's more to it. But what can he say? He stands at the sink, gently washing the dishes as Karen bathes Frankie and puts him to bed. He waits, listening to the small sounds of the house at night. Outside, in the yard, there is the swing set, and the willow tree — silver-gray and stark in the security light that hangs above the garage. He waits for a while longer, watching, half expecting to see DJ emerge from behind the tree as he'd done in Gene's dream, creeping along, his bony hunched back, the skin pulled tight against the skull of his oversized head. There is that smothering, airless feeling of being watched, and Gene's hands are trembling as he rinses a plate under the tap.

When he goes upstairs at last, Karen is already in her nightgown, in bed, reading a book.

"Karen," he says, and she flips a page, deliberately.

"I don't want to talk to you until you're ready to tell me the truth," she says. She doesn't look at him. "You can sleep on the couch, if you don't mind."

"Just tell me," Gene says. "Did he leave a number? To call him back?"

"No," Karen says. She doesn't look at him. "He just said he'd see you soon."

He thinks that he will stay up all night. He doesn't even wash up, or brush his teeth, or get into his bedtime clothes. He just sits there on the couch, in his uniform and stocking feet, watching television with the sound turned low, listening. Midnight. One A.M.

He goes upstairs to check on Frankie, but everything is okay. Frankie is asleep with his mouth open, the covers thrown off. Gene stands in the doorway, alert for movement, but everything seems to be in place. Frankie's turtle sits motionless on its rock, the books are lined up in neat rows, the toys put away. Frankie's face tightens and untightens as he dreams.

Two A.M. Back on the couch, Gene startles, half asleep as an ambulance passes in the distance, and then there is only the sound of crickets and cicadas. Awake for a moment, he blinks heavily at a rerun of *Bewitched* and flips through channels. Here is some jewelry for sale. Here is someone performing an autopsy.

In the dream, DJ is older. He looks to be nineteen or twenty, and he walks into a bar where Gene is hunched on a stool, sipping a glass of beer. Gene recognizes him right away — his posture, those thin shoulders, those large eyes. But now DJ's arms are long and muscular, tattooed. There is a hooded, unpleasant look on his face as he ambles up to the bar, pressing in next to Gene. DJ orders a shot of Jim Beam — Gene's old favorite.

"I've been thinking about you a lot, ever since I died," DJ murmurs. He doesn't look at Gene as he says this, but Gene knows who he is talking to, and his hands are shaky as he takes a sip of beer.

"I've been looking for you for a long time," DJ says softly, and the air is hot and thick. Gene puts a trembly cigarette to his mouth and breathes on it, choking on the taste. He wants to say, I'm sorry. Forgive me.

But he can't breathe. DJ shows his small, crooked teeth, staring at Gene as he gulps for air.

"I know how to hurt you," DJ whispers.

Gene opens his eyes, and the room is full of smoke. He sits up, disoriented: for a second he is still in the bar with DJ before he realizes that he's in his own house.

There is a fire somewhere: he can hear it. People say that fire "crackles," but in fact it seems like the amplified sound of tiny creatures eating, little wet mandibles, thousands and thousands of them, and then a heavy, whispered *whoof* as the fire finds another pocket of oxygen.

He can hear this even as he chokes blindly in the smoky air. The living room has a filmy haze over it, as if it is atomizing, fading away, and when he tries to stand up it disappears completely. There is a thick membrane of smoke above him, and he drops again to his hands and knees, gagging and coughing, a thin line of vomit trickling onto the rug in front of the still chattering television.

He has the presence of mind to keep low, crawling on his knees and elbows underneath the thick, billowing fumes. "Karen!" he calls. "Frankie!" But his voice is swallowed into the white noise of diligently licking flame. "Ach," he chokes, meaning to utter their names.

When he reaches the edge of the stairs he sees only flames and darkness above him. He puts his hands and knees on the bottom steps, but the heat pushes him back. He feels one of Frankie's action figures underneath his palm, the melting plastic adhering to his skin, and he shakes it away as another bright burst of flame reaches out of Frankie's bedroom for a moment. At the top of the stairs, through the curling fog, he can see the figure of a child watching him grimly, hunched there, its face lit and flickering. Gene cries out, lunging into the heat, crawling his way up the stairs to where the bedrooms are. He tries to call to them again, but instead he vomits.

There is another burst that covers the image that he thinks is a child. He can feel his hair and eyebrows shrinking and sizzling against his skin as the upstairs breathes out a concussion of sparks. He is aware that there are hot, floating bits of substance in the air, glowing orange and then winking out, turning to ash. The air is thick with angry buzzing, and that is all he can hear as he slips, turning end over end down the stairs, the humming and his own voice, a long vowel wheeling and echoing as the house spins into a blur.

And then he is lying on the grass. Red lights tick across his opened eyes in a steady, circling rhythm, and a woman, a paramedic, lifts her lips up from his. He draws in a long, desperate breath.

"Shhhhh," she says softly, and passes her hand along his eyes. "Don't look," she says.

But he does. He sees, off to the side, the long black plastic sleeping bag, with a strand of Karen's blond hair hanging out from the top. He sees the blackened, shriveled body of a child, curled into a fetal position. They place the corpse into the spread, zippered plastic opening of the body bag, and he can see the mouth, frozen, calcified, into an oval. A scream.

KEVIN BROCKMEIER

Space

FROM THE GEORGIA REVIEW

A TALL WHITE CANDLESTICK burns beside me, its wick an orange comma in the center of its flame. The light fades into darkness by slow degrees, and beyond it I see almost nothing — not
the stiles of the fence, not the spines of nearby rooftops, not power
lines roping to the ground — only headlights swaying on far road-
ways and barbed white stars hovering in the sky. It is as if the city
itself has wandered into sleep, fastening its lids over windows and
streetlamps and neon signs. The candle flame slants in the breeze
with a muffled flutter, the sound of an old filmstrip as its tail slips
from the projector. Eric, our son — fifteen now, Della — reaches
to settle it, then presses a finger to the rim of his wristwatch.
He crooks his arm, exposing the lucent blue pool of a faceplate.
"Two hours," he complains, filling each word with breath. He re-
clines into the straps of his porch chair. There is the light of the
stars, the light of the candle, and between them the steady arctic
glow of his watch — dimmer than the others, less hungry, more
remote.

The insects are circling in specks around the candle. The stars
are wavering in the sky.

Two hours ago I lay in the bathtub, submerging my hands in the
bubbles and watching them poke like little buoys to the surface.
The water dimpled at my chest each time they rose, then flattened
again as they fell. I was searching for a word — what is it, the name
of that force which holds a curve of water above a glass? — when
the lights went out with a soft abrupt tick. As I stood and reached
blindly for the towel rod, I could hear a skin of bathwater trickling
from my body into the tub, though I could not hear much else: the

refrigerator humming in the kitchen, the mutter and throb of the television, the sigh of cool air through the ceiling vents, the purr of electricity behind our floorboards and carpets and walls. Fastening the towel around my waist, I stepped from the bathroom and into the hallway, where the ceiling fan was languishing to a halt.

In the living room, Eric sat in an armchair before the blank face of the television, pecking at the buttons of a remote control. *Damn,* he kept whispering. *Damn. Damn. Damn.*

"What happened?" I asked.

He tapped once more at the keypad of the remote before placing it on a table. I heard sipping, swallowing, the click of ice cubes in a glass. "Power's down," he said.

"Where?" I said. "Just here?"

"How should I know?" He bit into an ice cube, punctuating the thought. "Look outside."

Standing in the doorway, I gazed out at the stars. They were everywhere, dangling from the arm of the Milky Way in dense silver clusters and floating at the far rim of the sky. The moon was invisible — couched, perhaps, behind trees and high buildings, or hidden in the earth's shadow — and the lights of the city had been entirely extinguished. I looked from one star to the next: each seemed to flare brighter and larger, dilating like a bud into flower. A broad-winged katydid gave a whirry leap onto the screen of a nearby window, and the night air resounded with a rich lyric chirring. I could not have told you which I was listening to, the voice of the katydids or the stars. You would have loved this sound, Della.

Now I sit on the back porch, my hands knit together in my lap, drawing in the scent of the grass and the dark summer soil.

"Either the main wire is down," Eric says, "or there was an overload at the power station." He brushes his fingers along his jaw line, scratching at a patch of stubble.

A satellite sweeps through the Northern Cross. I monitor the sky for shooting stars.

"Weather seems fine," I say.

Eric stifles a yawn as he answers. "Maybe somebody fell into the generator," he says, touching his lips. "Some bum or something." I listen for a whiff of laughter, but there is nothing.

"Maybe," I say. Is this what I should say? "But probably not."

*

Three months ago, Della, the city lay hidden beneath a jacket of snow. A flat glacial light was gathered inside the trees and billboards and houses, and heavy clouds slumbered in the gray air. At your funeral, a man with wire-rim spectacles and a black cassock recited a series of verses: Matthew 28:20, John 3:16, Genesis 49:33. The glare of a suspended lamp shone from his lenses, transforming his eyes into vacant white plates. He spoke in a voice like the rustling of leaves, and when he was finished he cleared his throat with a cough. He stepped from the rostrum. He fingered his cross. We filed past you in mute farewell.

In the vestibule, voices hummed and whispered in my ears, and slow willowy hands brushed my arm and my shoulder. I could feel the weight and stillness of the cool quiet space beneath the ceiling. I could see the dim mosaic of the high windows. Our son stood in a side doorway, his head bowed, his chest and stomach giving a few rough heaves. He pressed his hand to his eyes, blotting them dry, then gazed at his fingers. He watched them as if they had returned suddenly from somewhere far away. When I found myself at his side, meeting his eyes through the gaps between his fingers, I did not know what to say.

"She would —" I began. "She was very —" But I couldn't finish.

He touched my coat sleeve and told me not to worry.

In the car, he rested his temple against the window, and his breath made little clouds on the glass. I wondered whether he was watching this, or the flow of the asphalt, or his own reflection. A skin of sleet and snow thaw coated the roadway: arcs of it spurted from beneath spinning tires, spattered from lane to lane, and burst; a spine of it, gone gray with exhaust, wound down the center of the road between streams of traffic. Eric unhitched his seat belt, and its blue sash drew taut beside him. "Are you all right?" I asked. My breath hovered for a few white seconds in the car, then thinned and passed.

"I'm okay," he said, his voice slow and milky. When I placed my hand on his shoulder, he jerked — involuntarily, it seemed to me — and I drew it away.

"You know, Eric, if you need to —"

And suddenly he was yelling at me: "Didn't I tell you I would be okay? Didn't I *just* say that?" He gathered his breath into a long sigh, then said, "Please, Dad. Please. Can't we just stop poking at it for a little while?"

Above the houses and the thin, swooping power lines, a flock of birds dropped silently into the arms of a single bare oak tree. They seemed like a sudden, dense foliage, and as they lifted again I thought of autumn leaves snapping their bulbs and whirling into the sky. "If that's what you want," I said, "I won't say another word."

That night I woke from an oppressive dream. Our bedroom was thick with silence, thick with shadows. I decided to pour myself a glass of water. In the hallway, a cord of light shone from beneath Eric's door. I could hear him behind it: he was sobbing convulsively, gulping for air, and I rested my hand on his doorjamb. A slat of white light covered my socks. "Eric?" I said. He didn't answer. As I stood in the dark — feeling my heart beat in its cage, wondering if he had heard me — he slowly seemed to comfort himself. The spasms of his voice began to ease, and his breathing began to soften. The silence over the next few minutes grew, broken only now and again by a quick, constricted pant. I listened, and brooded, and cared, but I found myself unable to knock.

In the kitchen, water dribbled from a silver faucet into the sink. The glow of a streetlight hazed in through the window. I stood there wondering what I should have done, my nightshirt lifting with each breath.

Outside, the streetlight flickered above the snow. A strong wind piped between the trees, rattling through their dry, weblike branches. It had blown the sky clear while I slept, and I could see the stars pulsing in the night, the eye of the moon rising above the earth.

The candle flame shifts from side to side like a flower petal spun between two fingers. It is yellow from peak to tail and black at its focus, with a horseshoe curve of blue dwindling along its sides. Peering into the dark central pinch of flame, I can see an image of Eric's shoulder and the rim of his chair. When I turn to him, he is leaning in on himself, plucking at his lower lip and staring into the grass. A machine or an animal is making a knocking noise somewhere. It sounds like a woodpecker hammering holes into a tree, louder than the katydids, louder than the cars. Do you remember the day we heard the woodpecker rapping on the oak tree by our driveway, Della? It was our first morning in this house together, our first morning away from the city, and neither of us recognized the sound: you thought it was somebody pounding nails into a board, and I thought it was somebody banging on the front door. Do you remember what you said when our next-door neighbor told us what it really was? You said, "If we have to have holes in our trees, I guess there might as well be birds nesting in them." I think about this all the time.

"Jesus," Eric says. "That's one noisy damned bird."

"I doubt it's a bird. Woodpeckers aren't nocturnal."

"Whatever it is, I feel like it's knocking inside my own head." He mimes firing a shot from a rifle. "What I wouldn't give for a gun right now."

A katydid springs into the candlelight, landing on a yellow dandelion head.

"Your mother —" I say, and Eric twitches up, leaning toward me. I can feel something inside him — someplace dense and wary and hidden — becoming white-hot with brief attention, but it falters before I can speak. "When she was a little girl," I say, "she kept a flashlight by her bed. She told me that she would stand by her window and point it into the sky at night. She would find a spot without stars and shine it there until she went to bed. She thought that the light would reach a planet one day, someplace without a sun. The people there wouldn't be able to see where they were going and suddenly — light. She wanted to help. She told me that."

Wisps of grass cast twitching black shadows in the candlelight. "Where?" asks Eric.

"What?"

"Where? Where were you when she told you that?"

The punctilio of a headlamp swerves at the horizon. I can't remember.

"It's been a long time," I say. "I'm sorry. I can't remember."

"Right," says Eric, loosing another broad yawn. "Okay," he says. Then he turns away, pinches to a center, draws in on himself like a tight, snarled knot.

I am afraid, Della, that as I climb from the well of this time into days of habit and quiet persistence, into weekends and birthdays and sudden new seasons, the things that I know of you will slip quietly away from me. I am afraid that as the glass of my life falls away, I will forget you, and what I believed of you, and what I loved of you. I will sit on the porch steps one brisk fall morning, watching the scissoring legs of the dawn joggers, listening to the warble and peck of the birds, and I will try to call you to mind, and I will fail. I will walk into the living room and find that your face has become just a photograph on the mantel, your name a signature on a yellowed envelope. I will sweep my fingers along the hallway walls and feel them skip against a lappet in the wallpaper, and I will sit at the foot of my bed and gaze into the carpet. I will not remember the timbre of your voice or the cast of your body. I will not remember the breadth and measure of your stride. I will not remember the hunch of your shoulders as you walked against the wind or the set of your elbows as you knotted a scarf. That one smoky winter day you sat in an armchair and leaned into the heat swell of the fire, unbuckling the buckles of your boots, and that afterward you stood with a foot raised to the hearthstone, drew back the mesh of the fire screen, and spurred the fire, then settled in beside me as the sparks raged white and yellow up the chimney — it's a small thing, Della, but this too I will not remember. I will not remember the disposition of your mind and heart toward myself or the world or any one thing. I will forget it all, everything that matters: your laughter, the contour of your face, the tuck of your lip as you arrested a yawn. The triple drum rhythm of your hand and wrist — one-two, pause, three — as you rapped on a door or sounded a car horn. I will forget that you browsed forever at corner newsstands and answered jingling pay phones, that you counted during storms the seconds between lightning flash and thunder crack, that you held our son to your chest and let him cry the day a circus clown fuzzed him with blue confetti. The manner in which I knew you, the moment of our acquaintance, whether you were gracious or severe, soulful or sharp, hopeful or frail with regret: all these things I will not remember.

What I will remember is this: that there was a Della. That in a place now gone dark, within some vale or crimp of lost time, I knew her. And that something of her life passed into and through my own, effecting a conversion. My memory of you will be like the envelope of a bubble — rising out of sight from the collar of its wand, transporting the breath of me to some far place.

My memory of you, Della, will be like the last, quiet pulse of an echo: were I to follow it, I could not say what toward.

I took our son last week, you know, to see the fireworks. From the shelf of a low hill, we watched people stroll from the car park and settle in beside us. Families clustered around ice chests and blankets, around collapsible chairs and coal-orange grills. Wiry adolescents threw Frisbees and packed-foam footballs. As night fell, the heat that billowed from the ground made a chain of lens-shaped clouds over the lake. The first two fireworks were launched from their cannons with a deep bass *whoompf*, erupting above us in showers of red and white. The next one descended in shimmering blue scarves, and another sprayed out from its axis like the leaves of a green palm tree.

Eric sat beside me, teasing a blade of grass into dozens of separate fibers. "I keep thinking," he said, "about that time when the spark almost hit me."

For the first time in weeks he was volunteering to talk, and I almost couldn't believe it. I swallowed before I spoke. "I'm surprised you remember that," I said. "You couldn't have been older than three or four."

"I do, though," he said. He let the grass fall to the ground. "You were holding me on your shoulders. We were watching the fireworks and something went wrong with one of them."

"It exploded too soon."

"Right. What I remember is the sparks. They were raining down into the trees and the lake, and then one must have caught the wind. It fell right beside us. When I looked down, the grass was on fire."

"Just a tuft," I said. I smiled and found myself laughing.

Eric's lips spread into a thin smile. "I was terrified. I didn't calm down until you poured your drink on the fire."

"I remember," I said. The grass had been brown and withered, and it had extinguished with a sound like the flurry of a cymbal. "That wasn't me, though, actually. With the soda. It was a man with a ball cap and a mustache. I didn't know him."

"Oh," said Eric, and his voice died a little. He lifted a finger to his temple. "Strange that I thought it was you." A firework leapt from the shaft of a cannon with a lurid shriek, and he gave a start. A shiver snaked its way along his shoulders. The sky shone green for a moment — I could see it flashing from his cheek — and behind us a small girl began to clap.

Eric pressed a hand to his chest. "Where was Mom?" he asked after a moment. "When the grass caught fire."

"She was sitting on top of the ice chest," I said. "The spark couldn't have fallen more than a few feet behind her, but she didn't notice. When I tried to tell her about it afterward, she wouldn't believe me. You had fallen asleep by the time we packed the car, and she carried you home in her lap."

"Hmm." Eric eased himself into the grass and propped his head upon his transposed wrist. A firework burst above us, and I watched its flares reflect from the surface of the lake, cascading through the water like a school of luminescent fish. Another shattered into sharp blue lines that gleamed from the bellies of two low clouds.

"It looks like lightning," Eric said. He lay gazing into the night, his free hand twisting the wing of his shirt. "What do you call it — you know — the kind that doesn't strike ground?"

"Search me," I said.

"We've been studying it in science class." He closed his eyes for a minute. "Cloud-to-cloud. That's it. There's cloud-to-cloud and cloud-to-ground."

"What's the difference?"

I could see him frowning in the yellow light of a firework. "What do *you* think?" he said. "Cloud-to-ground is the kind that sets trees and houses on fire. You know, that zigzag shape. Cloud-to-cloud is just a flash in the sky."

"Interesting," I said.

He sighed. "To you it's interesting. To me it's just work. Do we really have to talk about science class?"

"We can talk about anything you want."

"Good," he said. "What I want is not to talk at all, Dad. Can we do that?" He lifted himself onto his elbows. "Let's just watch the explosions for a while."

It is a week later now, and all the lights are out. Eric sits in his porch chair and pivots his head to follow something above me — the wind or the stars or the stray smoke of some inward vision. An expression slips into his eyes, timid and wistful, like a fish or a turtle come to surface in a well. "Forty-eight," he says, skittering a hand through his hair.

I turn toward him. "Forty-eight?" I ask. I don't understand.

"The katydids," he says. "You count the times they shrill in twenty seconds: forty-eight. Then you add thirty-nine and it gives you the temperature." He taps his finger on his wrist, calculating. "Which would be eighty-seven, I think."

"Like lightning," I say, trying to listen. "You count the seconds between the lightning and thunder, then divide by five. That's how far away it is." The candlestick burns quietly above a pool of setting wax. I am speaking for a moment as if I were elsewhere, without weight, form, or presence. "The lightning," I say. "In miles," I say. "Your mom taught me that." Then I attempt a joke: "But you don't like to talk about lightning, do you? I forget."

Eric shuts his eyes. He doesn't laugh, but I can tell he is listening. "Dad?" he says.

"Yeah?"

He twiddles at the ruptured plastic tag of his shoelace, then scratches his cheek.

A moment later he says it again: "Dad?"

"What is it, Eric?"

It is then that the power flickers on. We notice it first from a distance. All of a sudden we can see the shape of the city on the land: all the streetlamps and buildings and windows. It is as if the earth and the sky are reaching into one another, exchanging their lights, like clasped hands interthreading fingers. I can hear a rattling sound coming from the air conditioner, and from the living room the voice of a television commercial: *Isn't it time you considered training for a career as a medical assistant?* "Yes!" says Eric, and he hops to his feet and claps his hands. I have not seen such a clear display of emotion from him in months. "Thank you, God!" he says. "Finally!" A light from inside the house sends the shadow of his body slanting in a long line over the lawn. Then, just as suddenly as it returned, the current shuts down and the million lights of the city vanish. The fan in the air conditioner whirs to a slow stop.

I shrug and clap my leg. "Looks like a false alarm."

Eric gives a soft *goddamnit.* "I am so sick of all this," he says. He sits down again, shifting in his chair, and the candlestick hides his face from my view.

"Eric?" I prompt.

"Why can't I just watch TV?" he snaps. "Is that too much to ask?" He leans forward and jerks his head, then punches himself in the arm, a tiny thudding sound muffled by his shirt. It rises in me, the instinct to say, "Don't hit yourself" — but I know better. He would squeeze shut like a snare. Instead I ask, "Are you okay?" and he gives a strangled laugh. "I'm okay when I don't have to think about it," he says.

"I know," I say. "God, I know. Sometimes I wake up at night, and I feel — peaceful. I feel peaceful, and so I think that it must not have happened yet. Isn't that crazy?"

"Not crazy." He shakes his head. "The same thing happened to me the first few weeks, but then it stopped all of a sudden. It won't last forever." He sighs. "But to tell you the truth, I liked it better before it stopped. I just want something to be easy for a change."

One star, more brilliant than all the others, hangs like an ornament at the horizon, swelling brighter and then dimming, swelling brighter and then dimming.

"And it's easy to watch TV?" I say.

"It's easy to watch TV," he agrees.

The katydids are out there calling their names.

The tiny red light of an airplane passes through the sky. It soars past a low cloud, the North Star, the bold white W of Cassiopeia — vanishing and reappearing, winking in a long ellipsis. Inside, its passengers read glossy periodicals, summon flight attendants, and unhitch the frames of their safety belts. They gaze from the panes of double windows and float away in a tight red arc.

"Two hours, twenty minutes," says Eric, illuminating his watch face. He stretches and gives a deep yawn, then throws back his head, tightens his lips, and another shudders through him like a ripple through a pond. "Look, I'm going to turn in," he says, standing. "Nothing to do out here anyway." He excavates a particle of dirt from beneath his thumbnail.

I watch him tuck his hands into the big loose bowls of his pockets — they swallow him up to his forearms — and dig soil from the lawn with the toe of his boot. After a while, he stops short.

"Well," he says, and his chin gives a little jerk. "Good night."

"Good night," I respond.

He steps to the door and it whispers open. Do you need the candle? I think. Can you see your way? But the door slides shut behind him.

A katydid is perched at the edge of the porch, shrilling its drums and fanning its wings, mirroring the candle in its small black eyes. The wind is shivering through the grass and the stars are guttering in the sky. Sometimes, Della, it feels as if I am living inside a mirage. Sometimes it feels as if I myself am the illusion — a wavering in the air, an apparition in a weave of bodies. The pulse of your flashlight is thirty years gone. Such a long time it's been sailing past moons and planets, past stars and dark matter and stray comets. It's been coursing through the gulf of space, its beam like a long silver road. It passed Alpha Centauri as you dressed for your first dance, Sirius as you left home for college. It passed the faint white globe of Tau Ceti as you lifted your veil, touched me with a kiss, and braided your fingers through mine.

It's going, Della. It's on its way.

One fine day, it will burst through the sky of a black world, flashing from trees and houses and lakes. Doorknobs and fence posts will cast thin sharp shadows. Turtles will poke from their shells and bears will stumble from the mouths of caves. Men and women will throw open their windows, trembling and blinking as they step through the doors. On that day there will be banquets and celebrations. The people will dress in their finest robes. The feast will be grand, the conversation merry, and everyone will watch the sky.

DOROTHY ALLISON

Compassion

FROM TIN HOUSE

IN THE LAST DAYS Mama's mouth cracked and bled. Pearly blisters spread down her chin to her throat. The nurses moved her to a room with a sink by the bed and a stern command to wash up every time you touched her.

"Herpes," Mavis, the floor nurse, told me. "Contagious at this stage."

I held Mama's free hand anyway, stepping away every time the doctor came in to wash with the soap the hospital provided. Mavis let me have a bottle of her own lotion when my fingers began to dry and the skin along my thumbs split.

"Aloe vera and olive oil," she told me. "Use it on your mama, too."

I took the bottle over to rub it into the paper-thin skin on the backs of Mama's hands. She barely seemed to notice, though a couple of her veins had leaked enough to make swollen, blue-black blotches. Mama's eyes tracked past me, and even as I rubbed one hand, the fingers of the other reached for the morphine pump. That drip, that precious drip. Mama no longer hissed and gasped with every breath. Now she murmured and whispered, sang a little, even said recognizable names sometimes — my sisters, her sisters, and people long dead. Every once in a while, her voice would startle, the words suddenly clear and outraged. "Goddamn!" loud in the room. Then, "Get me a cigarette, get me a cigarette," as she came awake. Angry and begging at the same time, she cursed, "Goddamn it, just one," before the morphine swept in and took her down again.

That was not our mama. Our mama never begged, never backed up, never whined, moaned, and thrashed in her sheets. My sister Jo and I stared at her. This mama was eating us alive. Every time she started it again, that litany of curses and pleas, I hunkered down further in my seat. Jo rocked in her chair, arms hugging her shoulders and head down. Arlene, the youngest of us, had wrung her hands and wiped her eyes and finally, deciding she was no use, headed on home. Jo and I had stayed, unspeaking, miserable, and desperate.

On the third night after they gave her the pump, Mama hit some limit the nurses seemed determined to ignore. Her thumb beat time, but the pump lagged behind and the curses returned. The pleas became so heartbroken I expected the paint to start peeling off the walls. The curses became mewling growls. Finally Jo gave me a sharp look and we stood up as one. She went over to try to force the window open, pounding the window frame till it came loose. I dug around in Jo's purse, found her Marlboros, lit one, and held it to Mama's lips. Jo went and stood guard at the door.

Mama coughed, sucked, and smiled gratefully. "Baby," she whispered. "Baby," and fell asleep with ashes on her neck.

Jo walked over and took the cigarette I still held. "Stupid damn rules," she said bitterly.

Mavis came in then, sniffed loudly, and shook her head at us. "You know you can't do that."

"Do what?" Jo had disappeared the smoke as if it had never been.

Mavis crossed her arms. Jo shrugged and leaned over to pull the thin blanket further up Mama's bruised shoulders. In her sleep Mama said softly, "Please." Then, in a murmur so soft it could have been a blessing, "Goddamn, goddamn."

I reached past Jo and took Mama's free hand in mine. "It's okay. It's okay," I said. Mama's face smoothed. Her mouth went soft, but her fingers in mine clutched tightly.

"That window isn't supposed to be open," Mavis said suddenly. "You get it shut."

Jo and I just looked at her.

Mama's first diagnosis came when I was seventeen. Back then, I couldn't even say the word "cancer." Mama said it and so did Jo, but I did not. "This thing," I would say. "This damn thing." Twenty-five years later, I still called it that, though there was not much else I hesitated to say. That was my role. I did the talking and carried all the insurance records. Jack blinked. Jo argued. Arlene showed up late, got a sick headache, and left. In the early years it was Jack who argued, and that just made things harder. Now he never said much at all. For that I was deeply grateful. It let us seem like all the other families in the hospital corridors — only occasionally louder and a little more careful of each other than anyone at MacArthur Hospital could understand.

"Who do they think we are?" Jo asked me once.

"They don't care who we are." What I did not say is that was right. Mama was the one the medical folk were supposed to watch. The rest of us were incidental, annoying, and, whenever possible, meant to be ignored.

"I like your mama," Mavis told me the first week Mama was on the ward. "But your daddy makes me nervous."

"It's a talent he has," I said.

"Uh-huh." Mavis looked a little confused, but I didn't want to explain.

The fact is he never hit her. In the thirty years since they married, Jack never once laid a hand on her. His trick was to threaten. He screamed and cursed and cried into his fists. He would come right up on Mama, close enough to spray spittle on her cheeks. Pounding his hands together, he would shout, "*Motherfuckers,* assholes, sonsabitches." All the while, Mama's face remained expressionless. Her eyes stared right back into his. Only her hands trembled, the yellow-stained fingertips vibrating incessantly.

Gently, I covered the bruises on Mama's arm with my fingers. Jo scowled and turned away.

"They should be here."

"Better they're not."

Jo shoved until the window was again closed. When she turned back to me, her face was the mask Mama wore most of our childhood. She gestured at Mama's bruises. "Look at that. You see what he did."

"He didn't mean to," I said.

"Didn't mean to? Didn't care. Didn't notice. Man's the same he always was."

"He never hit her."

"He never had to hit her. She beat herself up enough. And every time the son of a bitch hit us, he was hitting her. He beat us like we were dogs. He treated her like her ass was gold. And she always talked about leaving him, you know. She never did, did she?"

"What do you want?"

"I want somebody to do something." Jo slammed her fist into the window frame. "I want somebody to finally goddamn do something."

I shook my head, gently stroking Mama's cool clammy skin. There was nothing I could say to Jo. We always wanted somebody to do something and no one ever did, but what had we ever asked anyone to do? I watched Jo rub her neck and thought about the pins that held her elbow and shoulder together. There was my shattered coccyx and broken collarbones, and Arlene's insomnia. At thirty, Arlene had a little girl's shadowed frightened face and the omnipresent stink of whiskey on her skin. I had been eight when Mama married Jack, Jo five, but Arlene had been still a baby, less than a year old and fragile as a sparrow in the air.

"What is it you want to do? Talk? Huh?" Jo rolled her shoulders back and rubbed her upper arms. "Want to talk about what a tower of strength Mama was? Or why she had to be?"

My shrug was automatic, inconsequential.

A flush spread up from Jo's cleavage. It made the skin of her neck look rough and pebbly. Deep lines scored the corners of her eyes and curved back from her mouth. In the last few years, Jo had become scary thin. The skin that always pulled tight on her bones seemed to have grown loose. Now it wrinkled and hung. I looked away, surprised and angry. Neither of us had expected to live long enough to get old.

For all that we fight, Jo is the one I get along with, and I always try to stay with her when I visit. Arlene and I barely speak, though we talk to each other more easily than she and Jo. There have been years I don't think the two of them have spoken half a dozen words. In the ten weeks since Mama's collapse, their conversations have been hurt-filled bursts of whispered recrimination. At first, I stayed with Arlene, and that seemed to help, but when Jo and I insisted that Mama had to check in to MacArthur, Arlene blew up and told me to go ahead and move over to Jo's place.

"You and Jo — you think you know it all," Arlene said when she was dropping me off at Jo's. "But she's my mama too, and I know something. I know she's not ready to give up and die."

"We're not giving up. We're putting Mama where she can get the best care."

"Two miles from Jo's place and forty from mine." Arlene had shaken her head. "All the way across town from Jack and her stuff. I know what you are doing."

"Arlene . . ."

"Don't. Just don't." She popped the clutch on her VW bug and backed up before I could get the door closed. "Someday you're gonna be sorry. That's the one thing I am sure of, you're gonna be sorry for all you've done." She swung the car sharply to the side, making the door swing shut. If it would have helped, I would have told her I was sorry already.

Jo put me in the room where her daughter, Pammy, stashes all the gear she will not let Jo give away or destroy — shelves of books, racks of dusty music tapes, and mounted posters on the wall over the daybed. I fell asleep under posters of prepubescent boy bands and woke up dry-mouthed and headachy.

Jo laughed when I asked about the bands. "Don't ask me," she said. "Some maudlin shit no one could dance to — whey-faced girls and anorexic boys. All of it sounds alike, whiny voices all scratchy and droning. Girl has no ear, no ear at all."

Pammy had been picking out chords on the old piano Jo took in trade for her wrecked Chevy. She spoke without looking up. "You know what Mama does?" she asked in her peculiar Florida twang. "Mama sits up late smoking dope and listening to Black Sabbath on the headphones. Acts like she's seventeen and nothing's changed in the world at all."

Jo snorted, though I saw the quick grin she suppressed. She kicked her boot heels together, knocking dried mud on the Astroturf carpet. That carpet was her prize. She'd had her boyfriend Jaybird install it throughout the house. "She's eleven now," she said, nodding in Pammy's direction. "What you think? Should I shoot her or just cut my own throat?"

I shook my head, looking back and forth from one of them to the other. They were so alike it startled me — thick brown hair,

black eyes, and the exact same way of sneering so that the right side
of the mouth drew up and back.

"Hang on," I told Jo. "She gets to be thirty or so, you might
like her."

"Ha!" Jo slapped her hands together. "If I live that long."

Pammy banged the piano closed and swept out of the room. My
sister and I grinned at each other. Pammy we both believed would
redeem us all. The child was fearless.

"We need to talk," I told Arlene when she came to the hospital the
day after I moved in with Jo. Arlene was standing just inside the
smoking lounge off the side of the cafeteria, waiting for Jack to
arrive.

"She's looking better, don't you think?" Arlene popped a Tic Tac
in her mouth.

"No, she an't." I tried to catch Arlene's hand, but she hugged her
elbows in tight and just looked at me. "Arlene, she's not going to
get any better. She's going to get worse. If the tumor on her lung
doesn't kill her, then the ones in her head will."

Arlene's pale face darkened. When she spoke, her words all ran
together. "They don't know what that stuff was. That could have
been dust in the machine. I read about this case where that was
what happened — dust and fingerprints on X-rays." She tore at a
pack of Salems, ripping one cigarette in half before she could get
another out intact.

"God, Arlene."

"Don't start."

"Look, we have to make some decisions." I was thinking if I could
speak quietly enough, Arlene would hear what I was saying.

"We have to take care of Mama, not talk about stuff that's going
to get in the way of that." Arlene's voice was as loud as mine had
been soft. "Mama needs our support, not you going on about death
and doom."

Sympathetic magic, Jaybird called it. Arlene believed in the
power of positive thinking the way some people believed in saints'
medals or a Santeria's sacrificed chicken. Stopping us talking about
dying was the thing she believed she was supposed to do.

I dropped into one of the plastic chairs. Arlene's head kept jerk-
ing restlessly, but she managed not to look into my face. This is how

she always behaved. "Mama's gonna beat this thing," she'd announced when I had first come home, as if saying it firmly enough would make it so. She was the reason Mama had gone to Mac-Arthur in the first place. Jo and I had wanted the hospice that Mama's oncologist had recommended. But Arlene had refused to discuss the hospice or to look at the results of the brain scan. Those little starbursts scattered over Mama's cranium were not something Arlene could acknowledge.

"We could keep Mama at home," she'd told the hospital chaplain. "We could all move back home and take care of her till she's better."

"Lord God!" I had imagined Jo's response to that. "Move back home? Has she gone completely damn crazy?"

The chaplain told Arlene that some people did indeed take care of family at home, and if that was what she wanted, he would help her. I had watched Arlene's face as he spoke, the struggle that moved across her flattened features. "It might not work," she had said. She had looked at me once, then dropped her head. "She might need more care than we could give, all of us working, you know." She had dropped her face into her hands.

I signed off on the bills where the insurance didn't apply. For the rental on a wheelchair and a television, I used a credit card. Jo laughed at me when she saw them.

"You are a pure fool," she said. "Send back the wheelchair, but let's keep the TV. It'll give us something to watch when Arlene starts going on about how *good* Mama's doing."

Mama had had three years of pretty good health before this last illness. It was a remission that we almost convinced ourselves was a cure. The only thing she complained about was the ulcer that kept her from ever really putting back on any weight. Then, when she was in seeing the doctor about the ulcer, he had put his hand on her neck and palpated a lump the two of them could feel.

"This is it," Mama had told me on the phone that weekend last spring. "I'm not going back into chemo again."

She had been serious, but Jo and I steamrolled her back into treatment. There were a few bad weeks when we wondered if what we were doing was right, but Mama had come through strong. I convinced myself we had done the right thing. Still, when afterward Mama was so weak and slow to recover, guilt had pushed me to take a leave from my job and go stay at the old tract house near the Frito-Lay plant.

"We'll get some real time together," Mama said when I arrived.

"You need rest," I told her. "We'll rest." But that was not what Mama had in mind. The first morning she got me up to drink watery coffee and plan what we would do. There was one stop at the new doctor's office, but after that, she swore, we would have fun.

For three days Mama dragged me around. We walked through the big malls in the acrid air conditioning in the mornings and spent the afternoons over at the jai alai fronton watching the athletes with their long lobster-claw devices on their arms thrusting the tiny white balls high up into the air and catching them as easily as if those claws were catcher's mitts. I watched close but could not figure out how the game was meant to be played. Mama just bet on her favorites — boys with tight silk shirts and flashing white smiles.

"They all know who I am," Mama told me. I nodded as if I believed her, but then a beautiful young man came up and paused by Mama's seat to squeeze her wrist.

"Rafael," Mama said immediately. "This is my oldest daughter." "Cannot be," Rafael said. He never lifted his eyes to me, just leaned in to whisper into Mama's ear. I was watching her neck as his lips hovered at her hairline. I almost missed the bill she pressed into his palm.

"You give him money?" I said after he had wandered back down the steeply pitched stairs.

"Nothing much." Mama looked briefly embarrassed. She wiped her neck and turned her head away from me. "I've known him since he started here. He's the whole support of his family."

I looked down at the young men. They were like racehorses tossing their heads about, their thick hair cut short or tied back in clubs at their napes. Once the game started they were suddenly running and leaping, bouncing off the net walls and barely avoiding the fast-moving balls. All around me gray-headed women with solid bodies shrieked and jumped in excitement. They called out vaguely Spanish-sounding names, and crowed when their champions made a score. Now and again one of the young men would wave a hand in acknowledgment.

I turned to watch Mama. Her eyes were on the boys. Her face was bright with pleasure. What did I know? Where else could she spend twenty dollars and look that happy?

When later Rafael jumped and scored, I nudged Mama's side. "He's the best," I said. She blushed like a girl.

Mama was not supposed to drive, so I steered her old Lincoln Town Car around Orlando.

"You are terrible," Mama said to me every time we pulled into another parking space. It was an act. She played as if I were dragging her out, but every time I suggested we go back to the house, she pouted.

"I can nap anytime. When you've gone, I'll do nothing but rest. Let me do what I want while I can."

It was part of being sick. She wasn't sleeping, even though she was tired all the time. She'd lie on the couch awake at night with the television playing low. Every time I woke in the night I could hear it, and her, stirring restlessly out in the front room.

It was awkward sleeping in Jack's house. The last time I had lain in that bed, I had been twenty-two and back only for a week before taking a job in Louisville. Every day of that week burned in my memory. Mama had been sick then too, recovering from a hysterectomy her doctor swore would end all her troubles. Jo was in her own place over in Kissimmee, an apartment she got as soon as she graduated from high school. Only Arlene's stuff had remained in the stuffy bedroom; she herself was never there. At dawn, I would watch her stumble in to shower and change for school. She spent her nights baby-sitting for one of Mama's friends from the Winn-Dixie. A change-of-life baby had turned out to be triplets, and Arlene spent her nights rocking one or the other while the woman curled up in her bed and wept as if she were dying.

"They are in shock over there," Mama had told me. "Don't know whether to shit or go blind."

"Blind," Arlene said. The woman, Arlene told us, was drunk more often than sober. Still, her troubles were the making of Arlene, who not only got paid good money, she no longer had to spend her nights dodging Jack's curses or sudden drunken slaps.

"I'm getting out of here, and I'm never coming back," she told me the first morning of that week. By the end of the week, she had done it, though the apartment was half a mile up the highway, and even smaller than Jo's. I saw it only once, a place devoid of furniture or grace, but built like a fortress.

"Mine," Arlene had said, a world of rage compressed into the word.

Lying on the old narrow Hollywood bed again, I remembered the look on Arlene's face. It was identical to the expression I had seen on Jo when I was packing my boxes to drive to Louisville.

"We'll never see your ass again," Jo had said. Her mouth pulled down in a mock frown, then crooked up into a grin.

"Not in this lifetime."

All these years later I could look back and it was exactly as if I were watching a movie of it, a scene that closed in on Jo's black eyes and the bitter pleasure she took in saying "your ass." I know my mouth had twisted to match hers. We had thought ourselves free, finally away and gone. But none of it had come out the way we had thought it would. I hadn't lasted two years in Louisville, and Arlene had never gotten more than three miles from the Frito-Lay plant. Twenty years after we had left so fierce and proud, we were all right back where we had started, yoked to each other and the same old drama.

"Take me shopping," Mama begged me every afternoon, as if no time at all had passed. I had looked at her neck and seen how gray and sweaty the skin had gone and known in that moment that the chemo had not worked out as we had hoped.

"Tomorrow," I had promised Mama, and talked her into lying down early. Then gone back to curl up in bed and pretend to read so that I could be left alone. Every night for the two weeks I stayed there I would listen to Jack's hacking through the bedroom wall. Every time he coughed, my back pulled tight. I tried to shut him out, listening past him for Mama lying on the couch in the living room. She talked to herself once she thought we were asleep. It sounded as if she were retelling stories. Little snatches would drift down the hall. "Oh James, God that James . . ." Her voice went soft. I listened to unintelligible whispers till she said, "When Arlene was born . . ." Then she faded out again. In the background, Jack's snoring grated low and steady. I curled my fists under the sheets until I fell asleep.

When she took me shopping, Mama bought me things she said I needed. She made me go to Jordan Marsh to buy Estée Lauder skin potions. "It's time," she said. Her tone implied it was the last possible day I could put off buying moisturizer. I submitted. It was easier to let her tell me what to buy than to argue, and kind of fun to let her boss around the salesladies. I even found myself telling an insistent young woman that no, we would not try the Clinique, we were there for Estée Lauder. Afterward we went upstairs to do what we both enjoyed the most — rummage through the sale bins.

"I need new underwear," Mama said. "Briefs. Let's find me some briefs. No bikinis, can't wear those anymore. They irritate my scar." She gestured to her belly, not specifying if she meant the old zipper from her navel to her pubis, or the more recent horizontal patches to either side. I sorted the more garish patterns out of the way, turning up a few baby-blue briefs in size seven.

"Five now," Mama muttered. "Find me some fives, and none of those all-cotton ones. I want the nylon. Nylon hugs me right, and I hate the way cotton looks after a while. Dirty, you know?"

Sevens and eights and sixes. I kept digging.

"Excuse me." The two women at Mama's sleeve looked familiar.

"Mam," the first one said, pushing into the bin. "Excuse me." She reached around Mama's elbow to snag a pair of blue-green briefs. "Excuse me," she said again.

The accent was even more familiar than her flat grayish features and tight blond cap of hair. Her drawl was more pronounced than Mama's, more honeyed than the usual Orlando matrons'. It was a Carolina accent, and a Carolina polite hesitation, too. The other woman reached for a pair of yellow cotton panties, size seven. Mama moved aside.

"So I told him what he was going to have to do," the first woman said to her friend, continuing what was obviously an ongoing conversation. "No standing between me and the Lord, I told him. We've all got a role in God's plan. You know?"

Her friend nodded. Mama looked to the side, her eyes drifting over the woman's figure, the pale white hands sorting underwear, the dull gold jewelry and the loose shirtwaist dress. That old glint appeared in Mama's eyes, and a little electrical shock went up my neck. I moved around the corner of the bin to get between them, but Mama had already turned to the woman.

"I know what you mean." Mama's tone was pleasant, her face open and friendly. The woman turned to her, a momentary look of confusion on her face.

"You do?"

"Oh yes, there is no fighting what is meant. When God puts his hand on you, well . . ." Mama shrugged as if there were no need to say more.

The woman hesitated, and then nodded. "Yes. God has a plan for us all."

"Yes." Mama nodded. "Yes." She reached over and put both hands on the woman's clasped palms. "Bless you." Mama beamed. This time the woman did frown. She didn't know whether Mama was making fun of her, but she knew something was wrong. Her friend looked nervous.

"Just let me ask you something." Mama pulled the woman's hands toward her own midriff, drawing the woman slightly off balance and making her reach across the pile of underpants.

"Have you had cancer yet?" The words were spoken in the softest matron's drawl, but they cut the air like a razor.

"Oh!" the woman said.

Mama smiled. Her smile relaxed, full of enjoyment. "It an't good news. But it is definite. You know something after, how everything can change in an instant."

The woman's eyes were fixed and dilated. "Oh! God is a rock," she whispered.

"Yes." Mama's smile was too wide. "And Demerol." She paused while the woman's mouth worked as if she were going to protest but could not. "And sleep." Mama added that as if it had just occurred to her. She nodded again. "Yes. God is Demerol and sleep and not vomiting when that's all you've done for days. Oh, yes. God is more than I think you have yet imagined. It's not like we get to choose what comes, after all."

"Mama," I said. "Please, Mama."

Mama leaned over so that her face was close to the woman's chin and spoke in a tightly parsed whisper. "God is your daughter holding your hand when you can't stand the smell of your own body. God is your husband not yelling, your insurance check coming when they said it would." She leaned so close to the woman's face, it looked as if she were about to kiss her, still holding on to both the woman's hands. "God is any minute pain is not eating you up alive, any breath that doesn't come out in a wheeze."

The woman's eyes were wide, still unblinking; the determined mouth clamped shut.

"I know God." Mama assumed her old soft drawl. "I know God and the devil and everything in between. Oh yes. Yes." The last word was fierce, not angry but final.

When she let go, I watched the woman fall back against her friend. The two of them turned to walk fast and straight away from us, leaving their selections on the table. I felt almost sorry for them. Then Mama sighed and settled back. With an easy motion, she snatched up a set of blue nylon briefs, size five. She turned her face to me with a wide happy smile. "God! I do *love* shopping."

"Wasn't she from Louisville, that woman had the sports car? The one with those boots I liked so much?" Jo and I were folding sheets. We had cleared about a month of laundry off the bed, shifting sheets and towels up onto shelves and stacking the T-shirts, socks, and underwear in baskets. Jo's rules for housekeeping were simple: she did the least she could. All underpants, T-shirts, and socks in her house were white. Nothing was sorted by anything but size — when it was sorted at all. If I wanted to sleep, I had to get it all off the bed.

"No," I said. "Met her after I moved to Brooklyn."

"Sure had a lot of attitude. And Lord God! Those boots. What happened to her, anyway?"

"Got a job in Chicago working for a news show."

"Oh, so not the one, huh?" Jo made a rude gesture with her right hand. "You talked like she had your heart in her hands."

"For a while." I shook out a sheet and began to refold it more neatly. "But when I moved in with her, things changed. Turned out she had Jack's temper and Arlene's talent for seeing what she wanted to see."

"That's a shock." There was a sardonic drawl in Jo's tone. "Didn't think there was another like Arlene in the world."

"There's a world of Arlenes," I said. "World of Jacks too, and a lifetime of scary women just waiting for me to drag them here so you can talk them out of their boots."

"Well, those were damn fine boots."

Jaybird came in then, dragging his feet across the doorsill to knock loose the sand. Jo waved him over. "You remember the red boots I bought in Atlanta that time?"

"They hurt your feet." Jay took a quick nibble on Jo's earlobe and gave me a welcome grin.

"Just about crippled me. But you sure liked the way they looked when I crossed my legs at the bar that weekend."

"You look good anyway, woman," Jay said. "You come in covered in dog shit and grass seed, I'll still want to suck on your neck. You sit back in shiny red high-heeled boots and I'll do just about anything you want."

"You will, huh?" She snagged one of his belt loops and tugged it possessively.

"You know I will."

"Uh-huh."

They kissed like I was not in the room, so I pretended I was not, folding sheets while the kiss turned to giggles and then pinches and another kiss. Jo and Jaybird have been together almost nine years. I liked Jay more than any other guy Jo ever brought around. He was older than the type she used to chase. Jo wouldn't say, but Mama swore Pammy's daddy was a kid barely out of junior high. "Your sister likes them young," she complained. "Too young."

Jay was a vet. He had an ugly scar under his chin and a gruff voice. Mostly he didn't talk. He worked at the garage, making do with hand gestures and a stern open face. Only with Jo did he let himself relax. He didn't drink except for twice a year — each time he asked Jo to marry him, and every time she said no. Then Jay went and got seriously drunk. Jo didn't let anyone say a word against him, but she also refused to admit he was little Beth's daddy, though they were as alike as two puppies from the same litter.

"To hell with boots," Jo joked at me over Jay's shoulder. "Old Jaybird's all I really need." She gave him another kiss and a fast tug on his dark blond hair. He wiggled against her happily. I hugged the worn cotton sheet in my arms. I'd hate it if Jo ran Jay off, but maybe she wouldn't. Sometimes Jo was as tender with Jay as if she intended to keep him around forever.

Arlene lived at Castle Estates, an apartment complex off Highway 50 on the way out to the airport. It looked to me like Kentucky Ridge, where she was two years ago, and Dunbarton Gardens five years before that. Squat identical two-story structures, dotted with upstairs decks and imitation wood beams set in fields of parking spaces and low unrecognizable blue-green hedges. Castle Estates was known for its big corner turrets and ersatz iron gate decorated with mock silver horse heads. It gleamed like malachite in the Florida sunshine.

When I visited last spring, I went over for a day and joked that if I wanted to take a walk, I'd have to leave a trail of breadcrumbs to find my way back. Arlene didn't think it was funny.

"What are you talking about? No one walks anywhere in central Florida. You want to drown in your own sweat?"

In Arlene's apartments, the air conditioner was always set on high and all the windows sealed. The few times I stayed with her, I'd huddle in her spare room, tucked under her old *Bewitched* sleeping bag, my fingers clutching the fabric under Elizabeth Montgomery's pink-and-cream chin. Out in the front room the television droned nondenominational rock and roll on the VH-1 music channel. Beneath the backbeat, I heard the steady thunk of the mechanical ratchets on the stair-stepper. Since she turned thirty, Arlene spends her insomniac nights climbing endlessly to music she hated when it was first released.

The night before we moved Mama into MacArthur, the thunking refrain went on too long. I made myself lie still as long as I could, but eventually I sneaked out to check on Arlene. The lights were dimmed way down and the television set provided most of the illumination. The stair-stepper was set up close to the TV, and my mouth went dry when I saw my little sister. She was braced between the side rails, arms extended rigidly and head hanging down between her arms. I watched her legs as they trembled and lifted steadily, up and up and up. A shiver went through me. I tried to think of something to say, some way to get her off those steps.

Arlene's head lifted, and I saw her face. Cheeks flushed red; eyes squeezed shut. Her open mouth gasped at the cold filtered air. She was crying, but inaudibly, her features rigid with strain and tightened to a grotesque mask. She looked like some animal in a trap, tearing herself and going on — up and up and up. I watched her mouth working, curses visible on the dry cracked lips. With a low grunt, she picked up her speed and dropped her head again. I stepped back into the darkened doorway. I did not want to have to speak, did not want to have to excuse seeing her like that. It was bad enough to have seen. But I have never understood my little sister more than I did in that moment — never before realized how much alike we really were.

*

Jack has been sober for more than a decade, something Jo and I found increasingly hard to believe. Mama boasted of how proud she was of him. Her Jack didn't go to AA or do any of those programs people talk about. Her Jack did it on his own.

"Those AA people — they ask forgiveness," Jo said once. "They make amends." She cackled at the idea, and I smiled. Jack asking forgiveness was about as hard to imagine as him staying sober. For years we teased each other, "You think it will last?" Then in unison, we would go, "Naaa!"

Neither of us can figure out how it has lasted, but Jack has stayed sober, never drinking. Of course, he also never made amends.

"For what?" he said. For what?

"I did the best I could with all those girls," Jack told the doctor the night Arlene was carried into the emergency room raving and kicking. It was the third and last time she mixed vodka and sleeping pills, and only a year or so after Jack first got sober, the same year I was working up in Atlanta and could fly down on short notice. Jo called me from the emergency room and said, "Get here fast, looks like she an't gonna make it this time."

Jo was wrong about that, though as it turned out we were both grateful she got me to come. Arlene came close to putting out the eye of the orderly who tried to help the nurses strap her down. She did break his nose, and chipped two teeth that belonged to the rent-a-cop who came over to play hero. The nurses fared better, getting away with only a few scratches and one moderately unpleasant bite mark.

"I'll kill you," Arlene kept screaming. "I'll fucking kill you all!" Then, after a while, "You're killing me. You're killing me!"

It was Jo who had found Arlene. Baby sister had barely been breathing, her face and hair sour with vomit. Jo called the ambulance and then poured cold water all over Arlene's head and shoulders until she became conscious enough to scream. For a day and a half, Jo told me, Arlene was finally who she should have been from the beginning. She cursed with outrage and flailed with wild conviction. "You should have seen it," Jo told me.

By the time I got there, Arlene was going in and out — one minute sobbing and weak and the next minute rearing up to shout. The conviction was just about gone. When she was quiet for a little while, I looked in at her, but I couldn't bring myself to speak. Every breath Arlene drew seemed to suck oxygen out of the room. Then Jack came in the door and it was as if she caught fire at the sight of him. For the first and only time in her life she called him a son of a bitch to his face.

"You, you," she screamed. "You are killing me! Get out. Get out. I'll rip your dick off if you don't get the hell out of here."

"She's gone completely crazy," Jack told everyone, but it sounded like sanity to me.

The psychiatric nurse kept pushing for sedation, but Jo and I fought them on that. Let her scream it out, we insisted. By some miracle they listened to us, and left her alone. We stayed in the hall outside the room, listening to Arlene as she slowly wound herself down.

"I did the best I could," Jack kept saying to the doctor. "You can see what it was like. I just never knew what to do."

Jo and I kept our distance. Neither of us said a word.

By the third morning, Arlene was gray-faced and repentant. When we went in to check on her, her eyes would not rise to meet ours.

"I'm all right," she said in a thick hoarse whisper. "And I won't ever let that happen again."

"Damn pity," Jo told me later. "That was just about the only time I've ever really liked her. Crazy out of her mind, she made sense. Sane, I don't understand her at all."

"What do you think happens after death?" Mama asked me.

She and I were sitting alone waiting for the doctor to come back. They were giving her IV fluids and oral medicines to help her with the nausea, but she was sick to her stomach all the time and trying hard not to show it. "Come on, tell me," she said.

I looked at Mama's temples where the skin had begun to sink in. A fine gray shadow was slowly widening and deepening. Her closed eyes were like marbles under a sheet. I rubbed my neck. I was too tired to lie to her.

"You close your eyes," I said. "Then you open them, start over."

"God!" Mama shuddered. "I hope not."

Jo was a breeder, Ridgebacks and Rottweilers. A third of every litter had to be put down. Jo always had it done at the vet's office, while she held them in her arms and sobbed. She kept their birth dates and names in lists under the glass top of her coffee table, christening them all for rock-and-rollers, even the ones she had to kill.

"Axl is getting kind of old," she told me on the phone before I came last spring. "But you should see Bon Jovi the Third. We're gonna get a dynasty out of her."

After her daughter Beth was born, Jo had her own tubes tied. Still she hated to fix her bitches, and found homes for every dog born on her place. "Only humans should be stopped from breeding," she told me once. "Dogs know when to eat their runts. Humans don't know shit."

Four years ago Jo was arrested for breaking into a greyhound puppy farm up near Apopka. Mama was healthy back then, but didn't have a dime to spare. Jaybird called me to help them find a lawyer and get Jo out on bail. It was expensive. Jo had blown up the incinerator at the farm. The police insisted she had used stolen dynamite, but Jo refused to talk about that. What she wanted to talk about was what she had heard, that hundreds of dogs had been burned in that cinderblock fire pit.

"Alive. Alive," she told the judge. "Three different people told me. Those monsters get drunk, stoke up the fire, and throw in all the puppies they can't sell. Alive, the sonsabitches! Don't even care if anyone hears them scream." From the back of the courtroom, I could hear the hysteria in her voice.

"Imagine it. Little puppies, starved in cages and then caught up and tossed in the fire." Jo shook her head. Gray streaks shone against the black. The judge grimaced.

I wondered if she was getting to him.

"And then" — she glared across the courtroom — "they sell the ash and bone for fertilizer." Beside me Jaybird wiggled uncomfortably.

Jo got a suspended sentence, but only after her lawyer proved the puppy farmers had a history of citations from Animal Protection. Jo had to pay the cost of the incinerator, which was made easier when people started writing her and sending checks. The newspaper had made her a Joan of Arc of dogs. It got so bad the farm closed up the dog business and shifted over to pigs.

"I don't give a rat's ass about pigs," Jo promised the man when she wrote him his check.

"Well, I can appreciate that." He grinned at us. "Almost nobody does."

"How'd you get that dynamite?" I asked Jo when we were driving away in Jay's truck. It was the one thing she had dodged throughout the trial.

"Didn't use no dynamite." She nudged Jaybird's shoulder. "Old Bird here gave me a grenade he'd brought back from the army. Didn't think it would work. I just promised I'd get rid of it for him. But it was a fuck-up." She frowned. "It just blew the back wall out of that incinerator. They got all that money off me under false pretenses."

Every time Jack came to the hospital, he brought food, greasy bags of hamburgers and fries from the Checker Inn, melted milkshakes from the diner on the highway, and half-eaten boxes of chocolate. Mama ate nothing, just watched him. The bones of her face stood out like the girders of a bridge.

Jo and I went down to the coffee shop. Arlene, who had come in with Jack, stayed up with them. "He wants her to get up and come home," she reported to us when she came down an hour later.

Jo laughed and blew smoke over Arlene's head in a long thin stream. "Right," she barked, and offered Arlene one of her Marlboros.

"I can't smoke that shit," Arlene said. She pulled out her alligator case and lit a Salem with a little silver lighter. When Jo said nothing, Arlene relaxed a little and opened the bag of potato chips we had saved for her. "He's lost the checkbook again," she said in my direction. "Says he wants to know where we put her box of Barr Dollars so he can buy gas for the Buick."

"He's gonna lose everything as soon as she's gone." Jo pushed her short boots off with her toes and put her feet up on another seat. "He's sending the bills back marked 'deceased.' The mortgage payment, for God's sake." She shook her head and took a potato chip from Arlene's bag.

"He'll be living on the street in no time." Her voice was awful with anticipation.

Arlene turned to me. "Where are the Barr Dollars?"

I shook my head. Last I knew, Mama had stashed in her wallet exactly five one-dollar bills signed by Joseph W. Barr — crisp dollar bills she was sure would be worth money someday, though I had no idea why she thought so.

"Girls."

Jack stood in the doorway. He looked uncomfortable with the three of us sitting together. "She's looking better," he said diffidently.

Arlene nodded. Jo let blue smoke trail slowly out of her nose. I said nothing. I could feel my cheeks go stiff. I looked at the way Jack's hairline was receding, the gray bush of his military haircut thinning out and slowly exposing the bony structure of his head.

"Well." Jack's left hand gripped the doorframe. He let go and flexed his fingers in the air. When the hand came down again, it gripped so hard the fingertips went white. My eyes were drawn there, unable to look away from the knuckles standing out knobby and hard. Beside me Jo tore her empty potato chip bag in half, spilling crumbs on the linoleum tabletop. Arlene shifted in her chair. I heard the elevator gears grind out in the hall.

"I was gonna go home," Jack said. He let go of the doorjamb.

"Good night, Daddy," Arlene called after him. He waved a hand and walked away.

Jo twisted around in her chair. "You are such a suck-ass," she said.

Arlene's cheeks flushed. "You don't have to be mean."

"I can't even say his name. You call him Daddy." Jo shook her head. "Daddy."

"He's the only father I've ever known." Arlene's face was becoming a brighter and brighter pink. She fumbled with her cigarette case, then shoved it into her bag. "And I don't see any reason to make this thing any worse."

"Worse?" Jo twisted further in her chair. She leaned over and put her hand on Arlene's forearm. "Tell me the truth," she said. "Didn't you ever just want to kill the son of a bitch?"

Arlene jerked her arm free, but Jo caught the belt of her dress. "He an't got shit. He an't gonna give you no money, and he can't hurt you no more. You don't have to suck up to him. You could tell him to go to hell."

Arlene slapped Jo's hand away and grabbed her bag. "Don't you tell me what to do." She looked over at me as if daring me to say something. "Don't you tell me nothing."

Jo dropped back in her seat and lifted her hands in mock surrender. "Me, you can say no to. Him, you run after like some little brokenhearted puppy."

"Don't, don't . . ." For a moment it was as if Arlene were going to say something. The look on her face reminded me of the night she had screamed and kicked. Do it, I wanted to say. Do it. But whatever Arlene wanted to say, she swallowed.

"Just don't!" She was out the door in a rush.

I took a drink of cold coffee and watched Jo. Her eyes were red-veined and her hair hung limp. She shook her head. "I hate her, I swear I do," she said.

I looked away. "None of us have ever much liked each other," I said.

Jo lit another cigarette and rubbed under her eyes. "You an't that bad." She pulled out a Kleenex, dampened it with a little of my black coffee, and wiped carefully under each eye. "Not now, anyway. You were mean as a snake when you were little."

"That was you."

Jo's hand stopped. An angry glare came into her eyes, but instead of shouting, she laughed. I hesitated, and she pushed her hair back and laughed some more.

"Well," she said, "I suppose it was. Yeah." She nodded, the laughter softening to a smile. "You just stayed gone all the time."

"Saved my life." I laced my fingers together on the table, remembering all those interminable black nights, Jo pinching me awake and the two of us hauling Arlene into the back yard to hide behind the garage. Bleak days, shame omnipresent as fear, and by the time I was twelve, I stayed gone every minute I could.

"You were the smart one." Jo looked toward the door. I watched how her eyes focused on the jamb where his hand had rested.

"You were smart, I was fast, and Arlene learned to suck ass so hard she swallowed her own soul."

I kept quiet. There was nothing to say to that.

"I dreamed you killed him." Mama's voice was rough, shaped around the tube in her nose.

"How?" I kept my voice impartial, relaxed. This was not what I wanted to talk about, but it was easier when Mama talked. I hated the hours when she just lay there staring up at the ceiling with awful anticipation on her face.

"All kinds of ways." Mama waved the hand that wasn't strapped down for the IV. She looked over at me slyly.

"You know I used to dream about it all the time. Dreamed it for years. Mostly it was you, but sometimes Jo would do it. Every once in a while it would be Arlene."

She paused, closed her eyes, and breathed for a while.

"I'd wake up just terrified, but sometimes almost glad. Relieved to have it over and done, I think. Bad times I would get up and walk around awhile, remind myself what was real, what wasn't. Listen to him snore awhile, then go make sure you girls were all right."

She looked at me with dulled eyes. I couldn't think what to say.

"Don't do it," she whispered.

I wanted to laugh, but didn't. I watched Mama's shadowy face. Her expression stunned me. Her mouth was drawn up in a big painful smile, not at all sincere.

"Did you want to kill him?"

I turned away from the black window, expecting Jo. But it was Arlene, her eyes huge with smeared mascara.

"Sure," I told her. "Still do."

She nodded and wiped her nose with the back of her hand.

"But you won't."

"Probably not."

We stood still. I waited.

"I didn't think like that." She spoke slowly. "Like you and Jo. You two were always fighting. I felt like I had to be the peacemaker. And I . . ." She paused, bringing her hands up in the air as if she were lifting something.

"I just didn't want to be a hateful person. I wanted it to be all right. I wanted us all to love each other." She dropped her hands. "Now you just hate me. You and Jo, you hate me worse than him."

"No." I spoke in a whisper. "Never. It's hard sometimes to believe, I know. But I love you. Always have. Even when you made me so mad."

She looked at me. When she spoke, her voice was tiny. "I used to dream about it," she whispered. "Not killing him, but him dying. Him being dead."

I smiled at her. "Easier that way," I said.

Arlene nodded. "Yeah," she said. "Yeah."

That evening Mavis stopped me in the hall. She had a stack of papers in one hand and an expression that bordered on outrage.

"This an't been signed," she said. Her hand shook the papers. I looked at them as she stepped in close to me. She pulled one off the bottom.

"This is from Mrs. Crawford, that woman was in the room next to your mama. Look at this. Look at it close."

The printing was dark and bold. "Do not resuscitate." "No extraordinary measures to be taken."

I looked up at Mavis, and she shook her head at me. "Don't tell me you don't know what I mean. You been on this road a long time. You know what's coming, and your mother needs you to take care of it."

She pressed a sheaf of forms into my hand. "You go in there and take another good long look at your mother, and then you get these papers done right."

Later that evening I was holding a damp washrag to my eyes over the little sink in the entry to Mama's room. I could hear Mama whispering to Jo on the other side of the curtain around the bed.

"What do you think happens after death?" Mama asked. Her voice was hoarse.

I brought the rag down to cover my mouth. "Oh hell, Mama," Jo said. "I don't know."

"No, tell me."

There was a long pause. Then Jo gave a harsh sigh and said it again. "Oh hell." Her chair slid forward on the linoleum floor. "You know what I really think?" Her voice was a careful whisper. "I'll tell you the truth, Mama. But don't you laugh. I think you come back as a dog."

I heard Mama's indrawn breath.

"I said don't laugh. I'm telling you what I really believe."

I lifted my head. Jo sounded so sincere. I could almost feel Mama leaning toward her.

"What I think is, if you were good to the people in your life, well then, you come back as a big dog. And . . ." Jo paused and tapped a finger on the bed frame. "If you were some evil son of a bitch, then you gonna come back some nasty little Pekingese."

Jo laughed then, a quick bark of a laugh. Mama joined in weakly. Then they were giggling together. "A Pekingese," Mama said. "Oh yes."

I put my forehead against the mirror over the sink and listened. It was good to hear. When they settled down, I started to step past the curtain. But then Mama spoke and I paused. Her voice was soft, but firm. "I just want to go to sleep," she said. "Just sleep. I never want to wake up again."

The next morning, Mama could not move her legs. She could barely breathe. There was a pain in her side, she said. Sweat shone on her forehead when she tried to talk. The blisters on her mouth had spread to her chin.

"I'm afraid." She gripped my hand so tightly I could feel the bones of my fingers rubbing together.

"I know," I told her. "But I'm here. I won't go anywhere. I'll stay right here."

Jo came in the afternoon. The doctor had already come and gone, leaving Mama's left arm bound to a plastic frame and that tiny machine pumping more morphine. Mama seemed to be floating, only coming to the surface now and then. Every time her eyes opened, she jerked as if she had just realized she was still alive.

"What did he say?" Jo demanded. I could barely look at her.

"It was a stroke." I cleared my throat. I spoke carefully, softly. "A little one in the night. He thinks there will be more, lots more. One of them might kill her, but it might not. She might go on a long time. They don't know."

I watched Jo's right hand search her jacket pockets until she found the pack of cigarettes. She put one in her mouth, but didn't light it. She just looked at me while I looked back at her.

"We have to make some decisions," I said. Jo nodded.

"I don't want them to . . ." She lifted her hands and shook them. Her eyes were glittering in the fluorescent lighting. "To hurt her."

"Yeah." I nodded gratefully. I could never have fought Jo if she had disagreed with me. "I told them we didn't want them to do anything."

"Anything?" Jo's eyes beamed into mine like searchlights. I nodded again. I pulled out the forms Mavis had given me.

"We'll have to get Jack to sign these."

Jo took the papers and looked through them. "Isn't that the way it always is?" Her voice was sour and strained. The cigarette was still clenched between her teeth. "Isn't that just the way it always is?"

"Mama's pissed herself," Arlene told me when I came back from dinner. I was surprised to see her. Her hair was pushed behind her ears and her face scrubbed clean. She was sponging Mama's hips and thighs. Mama's face was red. Her eyes were closed. Arlene's expression was unreadable. I picked up the towel by Mama's feet and wiped behind Arlene's sponge. Jo came in, dragging an extra chair. Arlene did not look up, she just shifted Mama's left leg and carefully sponged the furry mat of Mama's mound.

"Jo talked to me." Arlene's voice was low. Without mascara she seemed young again, her cheeks pearly in the frosty light that outlined the bed. Behind me, Jo positioned the chair and sat down heavily. There was a pause while the two of them looked at each other. Then Mama opened her eyes, and we all turned to her. The white of her left eye was bloody and the pupil an enormous black hole.

"Baby?" Mama whispered. I reached for her free hand. "Baby?" she kept whispering. "Baby?" Her voice was thin and raspy. Her thumb was working the pump, but it seemed to have lost its ability to help. Her good eye was wide and terrified. Arlene made a sound in her throat. Jo stood up. None of us said a thing. The door opened behind me. Jack's face was pale and too close. His left hand clutched a big greasy bag.

"Honey?" Jack said. "Honey?"

I looked away, my throat closing up. Jo's hands clamped down on the foot of the bed. Arlene's hands curled into fists at her waist. I looked at her. She looked at me and then over to Jo.

"Honey?" Jack said again. His voice sounded high and cracked, like a young boy too scared to believe what he was seeing. Arlene's pupils were almost as big as Mama's. I saw her tongue pressing her teeth, her lips pulled thin with strain. She saw me looking at her, shook her head, and stepped back from the bed.

"Daddy," she said softly. "Daddy, we have to talk."

Arlene took Jack's arm and led him to the door. He let her take him out of the room.

I looked over at Jo. Her hands were wringing the bar at the foot of the bed like a wet towel. She continued to do it as the door swung closed behind Arlene and Jack. She continued even as Mama's mouth opened and closed and opened again.

Mama was whimpering. "Ba . . . ba . . . ba . . . ba . . . ba . . . ba."

I took Mama's hand and held it tight, then stood there watching Jo doing the only thing she could do, blistering the skin off her palms.

When Arlene came back, her face was gray, but her mouth had smoothed out.

"He signed it," she said.

She stepped around me and took her place on the other side of the bed. Jo dropped her head forward. I let my breath out slowly. Mama's hand in mine was loose. Her mouth had gone slack, though it seemed to quiver now and then, and when it did I felt the movement in her fingers.

Across from me Arlene put her right hand on Mama's shoulder. She didn't flinch when Mama's bloody left eye rolled to the side. The good eye stared straight up, wide with profound terror. Arlene began a soft humming then, as if she were starting some lullaby. Mama's terrified eye blinked and then blinked again. In the depths of that pupil I seemed to see little starbursts, tiny desperate explosions of light.

Arlene's hum never paused. She ran her hand down and took Mama's fingers into her own. Slowly, some of the terror in Mama's face eased. The straining muscles of her neck softened. Arlene's hum dropped to a lower register. It resounded off the top of her hollow throat like an oboe or a French horn shaped entirely of flesh. No, I thought. Arlene is what she has always wanted to be, the one we dare not hate. I wanted Arlene's song to go on forever, I wanted to be part of it. I leaned forward and opened my mouth, but the sound that came out of me was ugly and fell back into my throat. Arlene never even looked over at me. She kept her eyes on Mama's bloody pupil.

I knew then. Arlene would go on as long as it took, making that sound in her throat like some bird creature, the one that comes to sing hope when there is no hope left. Strength was in Arlene's song, peace its meter, love the bass note. Mama's eye swung in lazy accompaniment to that song — from me to Jo, and around again to Arlene. Her hands gripped ours, while her mouth hung open. From the base of the bed, Jo reached up and laid her hands on

Mama's legs. Mama looked down once, then the good eye turned back to our bird and clung there. My eyes followed hers. I watched the thrush that beat in Arlene's breast. I heard its stubborn tuneless song.

Mama's whole attention remained fixed on that song until the pupil of the right eye finally filled up with blood and blacked out. Even then, we held on. We held Mama's stilled shape between us. We held her until she set us free.

Contributors' Notes

100 Other Distinguished Stories of 2002

Editorial Addresses

Contributors' Notes

DOROTHY ALLISON was born in Greenville, South Carolina, and still dreams of that landscape, though these days she lives just outside Guerneville, California, with her partner, Alix Layman, and ten-year-old son, Wolf Michael. Her novels include *Bastard Out of Carolina* (1992) and *Cavedweller* (1997). In addition she has published a book of essays, *Skin: Talking About Sex, Class and Literature,* and a book of poetry, *The Women Who Hate Me.* Her collection of short stories, *Trash,* which includes "Compassion," was recently republished in a new edition. Allison is working on a novel, a few stories, and a collection of really bad poems.

▪ I started trying to write "Compassion" after my mother died in the fall of 1991, but it took me years to get a version down on the page. I wanted to find a way to talk about how embattled families occasionally act with unexpected grace — as my own sisters and I had managed in the long months of my mother's last illness. Reading to an audience has always been a way I can hear what works and does not in a piece of fiction. So I read "Compassion" all over the country, trying to figure out the full story of how those girls could and could not help each other. After two years I had more than a dozen different versions, none of which worked as I had intended. It's a failure, I told myself. I put the drafts in a file and went back to work on a novel about a runaway mother in north Georgia. There was nowhere those girls down in Florida had anything to do with that family up in Georgia. Delia and Cissy and the novel, *Cavedweller,* took over and almost compensated for what had not worked in that short story. Then an odd thing happened. I would be somewhere, visiting a friend or teaching a workshop, and inevitably someone would come up to me and ask me about that story — the one they had heard me read about those sisters. Had it been published? Where could they read it? Sometimes they would repeat to me the mother's question "What do you think happens after you die?" Sometimes they wanted to know if my sister actually raised dogs. No, I had to say. I am the one who has dogs. And no, that story has never been published. I've never quite gotten it right. Then for a couple of days afterward, I would find myself dreaming of Arlene and Jo and that Florida landscape, working my way through anger and grief and how sometimes you dare not forgive but have to behave as if you have. They wore me down, those people. Every time I would give up on my story, they would drive me back to it. I pulled the draft out of the filing cabinet. There were half a dozen different versions of the ending — one so sentimental it made my teeth hurt. That wasn't right. These were not sentimental women. I started all over. What if Arlene was not as pitiful as I had first imagined her? What if Jo were not nearly so strong? What if I didn't try to tie it up all neat at the end? Ten years after I started, I finally got a version I could stand. I wanted to put it back in a file and let it cook another decade, but I was getting ready to do a program in Chicago at Columbia's Story Week. There I was supposed to read with Sherman Alexie, and I knew that a friend who had already asked me about "Compassion" was also going be there. Just finish the thing, I scolded myself. I turned off the part of my brain that kept worrying at what didn't work and packed a new draft to read.

Stubbornly, I didn't let myself think about the story until I stood up to read it for a large welcoming audience. One more time it caught me up — all those pages pulling me along, the mother, that father, those girls who were no longer girls. Then I turned to read the last two pages — and they were not there. I looked up. The audience was leaning forward. The mother was dying. Arlene had left the room. She came back. I saw a woman in the second row put her hand over her mouth. Oh Lord. I lifted my eyes to the back of the room. I let myself unfocus, opened my mouth, and spoke the story's voice. It took me up and carried me through, finished itself the only way it could. As I was leaving, my friend came up and said, "That was perfect. You finally did it." I smiled and asked if anyone had taped the reading. No one had. They had broadcast the program, but there was no tape. In the bathroom I put cold water on my neck and wrote what I remembered. She set us free. That voice, unwavering, knew what I should have known all along. It was not what the girls did, singing or not, begging or not, forgiving or not. It was what death did — held her and set them free. If anyone tells you there is a different ending, there is.

KEVIN BROCKMEIER is the author of the novel *The Truth About Celia*, the story collection *Things That Fall from the Sky*, and the children's novel *City of Names*. His stories have appeared in the *Chicago Tribune*, the *Georgia Review*, *McSweeney's*, *The Year's Best Fantasy and Horror*, and two volumes of the

O. Henry prize stories anthology, as well as other publications. He lives in Little Rock, Arkansas, where he was raised.

▪ I wrote "Space" seven years ago, in the fall of 1996, when I was a student in graduate school. The story began with the passage about Della training her flashlight into the sky. When I was eight or nine years old, I imagined, as she does, that the beam from my flashlight would create an artificial sun for some distant planet. It's an idea that I never forgot. Perhaps its persistence had something to do with my early feelings of nostalgia, that sense of connection I had with a world I could no longer touch but still continued to care about. (On my fourth birthday somebody asked me how I had enjoyed being three years old, and I am reported to have answered that it was okay, but not as good as two had been.) Or perhaps the notion stayed with me because of my love for the idea that there might be life on other planets, an enthusiasm that lasted well into my adolescence, and, I suppose, into my adulthood.

My stories often grow out of some particular image that seems to me to have symbolic implications (a ceiling, a turtle, a Ferris wheel), and in the case of "Space," the flashlight was what I had to start with — that and a last line, "How I wish you and I could be there as well," which does not appear in the story's magazine publication. There is little other autobiography in the story. I was interested while I was writing it in memory and the failures of memory, in the contest between natural and artificial light, and in the difficulty people of deep feeling often have in communicating with each other, and I wanted the narrator's voice to have a sort of cradling effect on the reader.

Now it's late winter 2003. I'm writing this note from inside Little Rock's first (and probably only) snowstorm of the season. Apparently there is a nursery school in town called Hope for the Future Childcare, and last night, during the ten o'clock news, when the list of school closings scrolled across the bottom of the screen, the following notice appeared:

HOPE FOR THE FUTURE — CANCELED

Well, at least they told us, I thought. I imagine that if "Space" had been written today, and if it had been set in a snowstorm rather than a heat wave, that's what Eric might have seen before the television went blank. "Hope for the Future — Canceled."

I owe thanks to Jenny Minton and T. R. Hummer for helping me work through some of the problems "Space" presented me with, and to Frank Conroy and Jonathan Blum for early encouragement.

DAN CHAON is the author of two collections of short fiction, *Fitting Ends*, recently reissued, and *Among the Missing*, which was a finalist for the National Book Award. His stories have appeared in numerous anthologies, including *The Best American Short Stories 1996; The Pushcart Prize 2000, 2002, and 2003;* and *Prize Stories 2001: The O. Henry Awards.* His first novel, *You Remind Me of Me,* is scheduled to be published next summer. Chaon lives with his wife and two sons in Cleveland and teaches at Oberlin College.

▪ Michael Chabon is a very nice person who once selected a story of mine for a prize. One day in the summer of 2002, he e-mailed to ask me if I'd be interested in contributing to an issue of *McSweeney's* that he was guest editing, which was to be what he called an "all-genre" issue. He asked if I would be interested in writing a science fiction, horror, adventure, western, etc., story. I thought it sounded like fun. Chabon spoke of how he had grown kind of tired of what he called "the contemporary, quotidian, plotless, moment-of-truth revelatory story," and I was interested in what he had to say about trying to challenge the boundaries that have been erected between "literary" and "genre" fiction. As a teenager, I was very drawn to books of dark fantasy and horror — Ray Bradbury's *The Illustrated Man* and *Dark Carnival,* Peter Straub's *Ghost Story* and *Shadowlands,* Shirley Jackson's *The Haunting of Hill House,* Daphne du Maurier's *Don't Look Now* — and I have recently grown more aware of the way in which those writers have deeply influenced my own work. I was excited to try to write a story that held a conversation with those old friends.

The first couple of pages of this story had already been written — a fragment of narrative that I'd ended up abandoning, the title stolen from a song by the rock band Belly, the mood drawn from the sad, sinister, raspy songs of Tom Waits. But with the idea of horror and the supernatural in mind, I saw potential in the premise that I hadn't before. I had originally conceived it as a melancholy piece about lost connections and guilt, but the mission to create a horror story gave me a new insight into the subject matter. It gave me the freedom to plunge the story into more extreme corners of loss and resentment that I might not have dared venture into otherwise. I was also helped along by the memory of a story by Raymond Carver called "The Compartment," about a recovering alcoholic father who couldn't bring himself to forgive his son. Years ago, that story bothered me in a way that I never got over, and my conflicted feelings about it came back to me as I was working on this story. I guess you could say that "The Bees" is both a loving and a furious response to the impression "The Compartment" left on me.

RAND RICHARDS COOPER is the author of two books of stories, *The Last to Go* and *Big as Life.* He has taught at Amherst College and Emerson College; his fiction has appeared in *Harper's Magazine,* the *Atlantic Monthly, Esquire,* and many other magazines. Cooper is a contributing editor for *Bon Appétit* and the film critic for *Commonweal.*

• In July 1988 I was in Washington, D.C., apartment hunting during the last century's worst North American heat wave. I'd been living for two years in cool, cloudy Germany, so the heat felt even more brutal. My car lacked air conditioning, and I spent my days rushing from 7-Eleven to Big Y to anywhere else I could borrow someone else's cold air. "Johnny Hamburger" began in a memory of that summer and the wish to write a story in which heat would be a force, almost a character — a story that would resolve itself in terms of heat and its opposite.

The other elements of "Johnny Hamburger" came together as usual, from here, there, and everywhere: a college summer spent working on a dock-building crew; a car accident my sister witnessed; a favorite hometown burger joint; a story someone told me about a golf-ball–sized hailstone; a boyhood ritual of swimming with my father. And a song. I first heard Tracy Chapman's 1988 pop hit, "Fast Car," in a room full of Germans who sat listening in solemn admiration. Something obscurely irritating in the memory of that solemnity made me want to create a character who couldn't stand "Fast Car." Imagining someone who hates what you like is one of fiction's pleasing tricks of sympathy; I myself rather liked "Fast Car," but through Johnny Hamburger's eyes, it seemed eminently hateable. A fiction editor I sent the story to — someone who didn't know me — told me she guessed the story was autobiographical, that Johnny's life was more or less my own. I took that as high praise, since it couldn't be further from the truth.

EDWIDGE DANTICAT is the author of *Breath, Eyes, Memory; Krik? Krak!; The Faming of Bones; Behind the Mountains,* a young adult novel; and *After the Dance: A Walk Through Carnival in Jacmel, Haiti.* She is also the editor of *The Butterfly's Way: Voices from the Haitian Dyaspora in the United States* and *The Beacon Best of 2000.*

• "Night Talkers" started out as an essay, which I wrote a few years ago, after a visit to Beausejour, a village in the mountains of northern Haiti, where my father was born. I had often spent summers in Beausejour as a child, with my aunt Ilyana, who was still living there. Soon after that visit my aunt Ilyana died, and I was unable to attend the funeral because by the time the news reached the capital and made its way to my family in Brooklyn, she had already been buried. One of the things that Aunt Ilyana and I have (had) in common is that we both talk(ed) very loudly and expressively in our sleep, which inspired her to create a special term for us, *palannits* — an expression derived from the Creole word *pisannit,* or people who wet their beds. I was very sorry that I didn't get to attend my aunt's funeral and spent many nights lying awake imagining how it must have been. The desire to recreate a mourning period for Aunt Ilyana, one that I could be part of — if only on paper — was the genesis for this story. As with most of my stories, other concerns intruded; political violence and deportations also found themselves in the piece. But in the end, "Night Talkers" is a tribute to Aunt Ilyana, who made me feel at ease in her house by allowing me to "wet my bed" with words.

E. L. DOCTOROW'S work has been published in thirty languages. His novels include *Welcome to Hard Times, The Book of Daniel, Ragtime, Loon Lake, Lives of the Poets, World's Fair, Billy Bathgate, The Waterworks,* and *City of God.* Among his honors are the National Book Award, two National Book Critics Circle Awards, the PEN/Faulkner Award, the Edith Wharton Citation for Fiction, the William Dean Howells Medal of the American Academy of Arts and Letters, and the National Humanities Medal (conferred by the president). He lives and works in New York.

• Some years ago, in southern California, I saw a young woman in a long paisley dress walking barefoot on the Coast Highway. She was carrying a bouquet of flowers. Why I've made her into Karen Robileaux, the kidnapper of a newborn, I have no idea. Perhaps only a woman in love with Lester Romanowski would do this desperate thing. Not to condone her actions, but I must have decided that while a man would kidnap a child for ransom, a woman kidnapper would want the child for herself.

ANTHONY DOERR'S debut collection of stories, *The Shell Collector,* won the New York Public Library's 2003 Young Lions Award and Barnes & Noble's 2003 Discover Award. His fiction has appeared in *The O. Henry Awards: Prize Stories,* the *Paris Review, Zoetrope: All-Story,* and the *Atlantic Monthly.* He is currently a Hodder fellow at Princeton University, where he is completing a novel.

• Every spring, growing up, my mom and dad used to drive us back to Ohio from Florida in our big, rusty Suburban, and in the back seat my brothers and I would keep watch over all sorts of sea bounty for my brother's aquarium: anemones in gallon jugs of seawater, octopi in sloshing pails. One year we brought back a stone crab, I remember, maybe the size of a C battery, and within days it had taken over the entire tank, reaching up and hauling down fish one by one and tearing them in half. It lived for years, brazenly, not even bothering to hide among the rocks, and it grew eventually to about the size of a pack of cards. A few times it even escaped from the aquarium and went scrambling off toward the kitchen and hid under the woodstove. We were all slightly afraid of it.

Probably much of my amazement at the determination of small marine creatures started with that crab: it'd be roaming around our family room and outside it would be *snowing.* When you get stung by something, especially, whether it's a jellyfish or fire coral, you can feel it too: despite the pain, *because* of the pain, you have to admire the creature's tenacity. Mollusks and crustaceans and echinoderms have been around so much longer than we have, and they'll be around after all of us are gone. The story of the shell collector was in many ways an excuse to explore that.

This story owes a substantial debt to Kenneth Brower's essay "On the Reef, Darkly," and to other profiles of the blind physical scientist Geerat Vermeij, who more than demonstrates that a sightless observer can contribute significantly to the study of mollusks.

Curiously, a year after I wrote the story, I learned that a biotech company in Silicon Valley designed an analgesic pain drug called Ziconotide from cone venom. With a few alterations, the drug, rather than blocking specific neural pathways in the brain, merely inhibits them, not shutting down brain cells but "muting their excitability." In trials, Ziconotide has successfully controlled the severe chronic pain caused by cancer and AIDS, and it is expected to be on the market by the end of 2003.

It seems that every year the membrane between what can harm us and what can help us grows thinner. A huge thanks to everyone who worked on this story with me.

LOUISE ERDRICH grew up in North Dakota and is enrolled in the Turtle Mountain Band of Ojibwe. She is the author of eight novels, including *Love Medicine,* which won the National Book Critics Circle Award, and *The Last Report on the Miracles at Little No Horse,* which was a finalist for the National Book Award. She has also published children's books, poetry, and a memoir of early motherhood, *The Blue Jay's Dance.* Her short fiction has won the National Magazine Award and appears in the O. Henry and Best American short story collections. She lives in Minnesota with her children and runs a small independent bookstore, the Birchbark.

- An Ojibwe man who grew up in a very traditional world told me that as a child, he knew an old man named Shamengwa whose arm was withered and folded up. I just could not stop thinking about Shamengwa, the Monarch butterfly. On a car trip, my mother told me about a boy she'd known of in the Turtle Mountains of North Dakota, who had hidden his fiddle-playing from his strictly religious parents. From then on, the story almost wrote itself. I let it accumulate over years, piece by piece. When it was done, I had the peculiar feeling that it had all really happened. I want to thank Shamengwa.

RYAN HARTY'S collection of stories, *Bring Me Your Saddest Arizona,* won the 2003 John Simmons Award for Short Fiction and will be published this fall. Harty lives in San Francisco with his wife, Julie Orringer, who is also a writer. He teaches creative writing at Stanford University and is working on a novel.

- This story began with the image of a boy splayed out on a hill. At first

I didn't know what to make of the image; the boy's arm, for reasons I couldn't comprehend, seemed to have become detached from his body. Multicolored wires curled out of the torn end. Was this science fiction? I'd never written a science fiction story and was reluctant to try. But I felt I understood something about the story's narrator — a distraught father who had learned to deal with difficult situations and make them easier for his son. I knew I wanted this man to share some of the qualities of my own father, who had died less than a year before I began writing the story.

It took a month or so to get through a draft and more than four years to come up with an ending I liked. I'd work on the story for a few weeks at a time, then put it aside to tend to other projects. Each time I came back, I was sure I'd read through it quickly and know just how to end it. But I never did. At issue for me was meaning: what was I trying to say about love and relationships? Was the father, with his ability to love his son beyond all reason, a heroic figure or a tragic one? During the years I struggled with the ending I vacillated between the two possibilities. When I finally saw that they were equally true, the ending came quite naturally.

ADAM HASLETT is the author of *You Are Not a Stranger Here*, which was nominated for the National Book Award and received the L. L. Winship PEN/New England Award and the New York Magazine Fiction Award. He is a graduate of the Iowa Writers' Workshop and the Yale Law School. He lives in New York City.

▪ Though I've spent most of my life in the United States, I'm half English, went to school there as a child, and visit a certain amount. Some of that country's habits of mind and rhythms of speech are very much a part of me. As a result, there are times when I find it easier to set stories in Britain. Certain kinds of emotional reserve are more plausible over there. "Devotion" is first and foremost a story about reserve and its effects on love. It's also about the safety of remaining the same. In an earlier draft the former lover actually appeared for the dinner, but after reading this I realized the story wasn't chiefly about the brother and sister's relationship to him but about their relationship to each other. So, mindful of what in some moods I think of as the short story writer's duty to try to distill a narrative down to its emotional core, I rewrote, leaving just his conversation on the phone. It's a sad story in many ways. My only hope is that it approaches some honest apprehension of the characters' moral life.

NICOLE KRAUSS'S first novel, *Man Walks into a Room*, was published in 2002 and was a finalist for the Los Angeles Times First Fiction Prize. Her poems and essays have appeared in the *Paris Review, Ploughshares, Modern*

Painters, Partisan Review, and the *New York Times,* and on the BBC. She lives in Brooklyn, where she is working on a new novel.

• "Future Emergencies" was the first short story I published. I started writing fiction a couple of years ago, when I began *Man Walks into a Room.* Two weeks before September 11, I handed in the final draft. At the time I was living in an apartment with windows from 1950, ten floors above the FDR Drive in New York, and I'd gotten used to, had even come to depend on, the noise of cars and the wail of sirens. Occasionally I'd pause to think about the sound of other people's emergencies. But mostly I thought about the noise only when it was absent, when the FDR was closed for the president's motorcade or a foreign dignitary going to the UN. At those times, a feeling of loneliness would come over me, and I would look up from my work to try to figure out what had suddenly changed. I think that phrase — "other people's emergencies" — is somewhere in *Man Walks into a Room.* I thought of it often during the year I was living there and writing that book. But future emergencies — an inevitable declension, the sound of other people's emergencies portending one that might one day be your own — was just a title in my head, waiting for a story that either would come one day or wouldn't.

For me, the morning of September 11 began, like so many other mornings, with the sound of sirens. According to the file on my computer, I wrote the first two pages of "Future Emergencies" on September 24. The rest I wrote a month later. But I didn't think I was writing a response to any particular event. What deeply struck me then, and continues to move me, is how people adapt. It might be the most sophisticated and the most animal part of us at once: the ability to get used to almost anything in order to preserve a sense of normalcy. When I wrote "Future Emergencies," that's what I must have been thinking about — how gifted we are at adjusting to our circumstances in order to survive, and subsequently, how difficult it is to listen to the dissenting voice in us that says, *There must be some other way.* It's March 31, 2003, as I write this. Occasionally I wonder how long we can continue to adapt before we become another species entirely.

ZZ PACKER was raised in Atlanta, Georgia, and Louisville, Kentucky. Her stories have appeared in *The New Yorker, Harper's Magazine, Story, Plough-shares, Zoetrope: All-Story,* and *The Best American Short Stories 2000.* Her collection of short stories, *Drinking Coffee Elsewhere,* was published in March 2003.

• "Every Tongue Shall Confess" started as a need; I grew up in a southern black Pentecostal church, and I wanted — needed — to portray its vibrancy without judging it. My prior attempts at this story, however, ended up too cartoonish, too flip, too something.

Previously, the story was *Rashomon*-like in structure, showing three different viewpoints during slightly overlapping moments of time. When I went to revise the story, I saw that I was asking the structure to do the work that only strength of character could accomplish (in short, it wasn't working). I began to reevaluate Clareese and decided that her viewpoint was the all-important one: she watches (mostly without observing), she does her duty, she sits back down in her choir mistress's seat, she goes to work.

I know so many women like Clareese, in and outside the world of the Pentecostal church — women who must keep moving and doing because reflection for them is tantamount to idleness. I am drawn to these lonely, soldierly women like Clareese, whose unwavering sense of rectitude is the fount of both comedy and tragedy in the story — or so I hope.

DEAN PASCHAL, originally from Albany, Georgia, now lives in New Orleans, where he works as an emergency room physician. He has undergraduate degrees in zoology and electronic engineering. He recently went back to school to become certified in tropical medicine. His first book, *By the Light of the Jukebox,* which includes the story "Moriya," was published in May 2002.

• How did I come to write "Moriya"? Weakness, I suppose. I tried desperately *not* to write "Moriya." I had other things I was working on, specifically, the revisions of two novels. I was happy doing that, didn't want to be doing anything else, when suddenly this beautiful mechanical doll began entering my mind. Wherever I went, she would follow; not an hour passed that I didn't see or hear something new about her. I had to carry paper in my pocket, fiddle with sentences while at work, at restaurants, in taverns and bars, or while waking up, fumbling for the light, trying desperately to find paper and pen. Finally I had such a critical mass of information that it became necessary to set every other thing aside and put her story together. It was virtually effortless, came together in about a month, which is very fast for me.

There is something else, though, about "Moriya," which is peripheral yet may be of interest to readers. This "something else" may not be absolutely unique in the long history of this series, but my guess is that it would have to be extremely rare. I have been writing for years — decades, actually — and though I currently have other things in print, even a book of short stories, not one syllable of my fiction had ever been accepted or published prior to the acceptance of "Moriya" by the *Ontario Review*. So it is particularly pleasing to find that she is going to be in *The Best American Short Stories.* I suppose one would have to say that that little doll has gone the distance on those heartbreaking mechanical legs. Pretty amazing. She did it on her own, too. I was just watching.

MARILENE PHIPPS is a writer and a painter who was born and grew up in Haiti. She is a Guggenheim fellow and has also won fellowships at Harvard University's Center for the Study of World Religions, Bunting Institute, and W.E.B. DuBois Institute. Her poetry has earned her the 1993 Grolier Poetry Prize and has been anthologized in *The Beacon Best of 1999*. Her poetry collection *Crossroads and Unholy Water* won the 1999 Crab Orchard Review Poetry Prize. Her fiction has appeared in *Transition, Callaloo,* and *Crab Orchard Review*. She is putting finishing touches to a collection of interconnected short stories under the working title "Remember the Mountain."

- I once had the privilege of listening to the real-life account of a Haitian man's failed journey at sea. The story "Marie-Ange's Ginen" was inspired by his account. The characters in my fictional version of a classic boat-people exodus are all invented. Yet writing "Marie-Ange's Ginen" helped me give a meaningful shape to a time of separation and loss in my own life.

SHARON POMERANTZ is a 2002 graduate of the University of Michigan M.F.A. program. Her short fiction has appeared in the *Black Warrior Review, Colorado Review, Massachusetts Review, Michigan Quarterly Review,* and *Ploughshares*. In 1998 her story "Shoes" was broadcast on National Public Radio's Selected Shorts program. She lives in Ann Arbor and is currently at work on a novel.

- Last year a friend called me in distress about several new tropical fish he'd bought for his tank. They were Ghost Knife fish and they kept disappearing — he feared his other fish were eating them. When I asked him what a Ghost Knife was, he described it in much the same language I use in my story, "blind and dependent on sonar," so that the fish travels hesitantly and moves sideways as much as forward. To me, it sounded like he was describing a dysfunctional relationship more than a fish, and when I got off the phone I wrote down what he'd said for future use (an occupational hazard, I think).

About six months later, Aric Knuth, a writer who uses natural landscape beautifully in his fiction, challenged me to write a landscape-oriented story. We were then in Nick Delbanco's graduate fiction workshop at the University of Michigan. Aric's challenge was a bit tongue-in-cheek: my stories are generally urban, and my characters don't care much about nature. But I thought of an experience that I'd once had taking a train from Manhattan to Schenectady. We traveled into an electrical storm and had to sit on the tracks in pitch blackness for over an hour. Huge lightning bolts lit the sky like something out of a horror movie, and the rain and winds were so powerful that our train suddenly felt fragile, but the atmosphere was very romantic. I put these two things — the fish and being trapped on the train — together and came to this upstate/downstate story of dysfunctional love. As is so often the case, in the editing process much of the description of the storm came out. I guess I'm still not a landscape writer.

EMILY ISHEM RABOTEAU was born in 1976 and grew up in Princeton, New Jersey. She has a B.A. from Yale and a recent M.F.A. from New York University, where she was a *New York Times* fellow. Her short stories have appeared in *Tin House, Transition, African Voices,* and *Callaloo.* The *Chicago Tribune* gave her the Nelson Algren Award for Short Fiction in 2001, and her first book will be published in 2004.

• The first line of this story came to me in a dream about colored glass. I copied it in a book I keep by my bed at night, and when I woke up the next morning, I wrote the first draft. The relationship between the newlywed couple is based on a friendship between two of my college classmates, both of whom were first-generation immigrants but from wildly different cultures. These two had a lot in common. They were both exoticized. They both grew up in Long Island. They were similarly driven to succeed by overbearing parents who came here with the American dream. They were both premed, and they even sort of looked alike. But in spite of the fact that she had a painful crush on him, he wouldn't go out with her, because she wasn't Muslim. I tried to imagine what their life might have been like if they'd gotten married. "Kavita Through Glass" was rejected by almost thirty journals.

JESS ROW's first collection of stories will be published in 2004. His work has appeared in *Ploughshares, Ontario Review, Harvard Review, Threepenny Review,* and other journals, and his story "The Secrets of Bats" was selected for *The Best American Short Stories 2001.* Row lived in Hong Kong from 1997 to 1999, working as an English teacher at the Chinese University of Hong Kong, and received his M.F.A. at the University of Michigan in 2001. He lives with his wife, Sonya Posmentier, in New York City, and is an assistant professor of English at Montclair State University in Upper Montclair, New Jersey.

• During the two years I lived in Hong Kong, one of my closest friends was a young philosophy professor at my university named Youru Wang. We met every week in his office to talk about Buddhist and Chinese philosophy; I needed a guide to the treacherous depths of Nagarjuna and Candrakirti, and he wanted to keep up his conversational English, since he hoped eventually to get a teaching job in the United States. (He now teaches at Rowan University in New Jersey.) After our meetings we would adjourn to the faculty dining hall and eat dim sum. Over rice crepes and *xiao long bao* and *dan taat* pastries he told me, in bits and pieces, the long story of how he left Shanghai to study in America in the late 1980s and spent eight years struggling to finish his doctorate, piecing together scholarships, work-study jobs, and illegal side work to survive. "We Chinese have a joke," he told me with a mischievous smile. "Ph.D. means 'Pizza Hut Delivery.'" He spent one summer delivering Chinese food by bicycle in New York and was robbed by a group of kids posing as customers; this was a common experience, he told me, and he was lucky to have escaped unharmed. (Last October, in fact, a deliveryman named Jian Chun Lin was murdered in Brooklyn in very similar circumstances.) Dr. Wang never described his experience to me in any detail; the circumstances I invented in "Heaven Lake" are entirely my own invention. But I want to give him credit for inspiring the story simply by being who he is.

The "story" that Liu tells the unfortunate Willie in "Heaven Lake" is a paraphrase from a chapter of the Taoist philosophical text called the Zhuangzi, or, as most English readers know it, the Chuang-tzu. Like much of the Zhuangzi, this chapter (usually translated as "Free and Easy Wandering") gives the reader a vertiginous sense of wandering in a universe whose boundaries and laws are not fixed; it challenges us to face a world of ceaseless flux, in which, as Zen master Hongren put it, *beihuan jiaoji*, "grief and joy are intertwined." "Heaven Lake" was written with the spirit of Zhuangzi in mind, if only in the sense that while writing it I kept bumping up against my own limitations, like the cicada who looks up to see the great bird headed south and says, "If I try my hardest, I can just make it up to the branch of that elm tree. How is that *he* can fly ninety thousand miles?"

If any readers are interested in learning more, there are excellent translations of "Free and Easy Wandering" in Burton Watson's *Chuang Tzu: Basic Writings* and David Hinton's *Chuang Tzu: The Inner Chapters.*

MONA SIMPSON is the author of *Anywhere But Here, The Lost Father, A Regular Guy,* and *Off Keck Road.*

- "Coins" was the first piece I wrote of what has become a book I've now worked on for six years and counting. The book, called *My Hollywood,* is drenched with Los Angeles, the city that claimed a large share of my growing up and proved the setting for my life's greatest failures and losses.

All of this work is built out of the resonant (for me, at least) ironies of having been a helpless anonymous kid baby-sitter in mansions and returning here again to hire an immigrant nanny in what must seem to her another such house, only because I am a woman who wants to work.

SUSAN STRAIGHT has published five novels; the most recent, *Highwire Moon,* was a finalist for the National Book Award in 2001. Her stories and essays have appeared in numerous magazines and journals, including *Harper's Magazine, Salon,* the *New York Times Magazine,* and others. She was born in Riverside, California, where she lives with her three daughters.

• I have many female relatives and friends who work as correctional officers, and I also have many relatives and friends who are incarcerated. Having given writing workshops at prisons for ten years, and having seen all those faces inside, both working and waiting, I could only write a story. Then I was afraid to send it anywhere, and I am immensely grateful to have been introduced to Tamara Straus at *Zoetrope: All-Story*, who treated the story so well.

MARY YUKARI WATERS is half Japanese and half Irish-American. Her short stories have appeared in *The Best American Short Stories; The O. Henry Awards: Prize Stories; The Pushcart Book of Short Stories: The Best Short Stories from a Quarter-Century of the Pushcart Prize;* and *Francis Ford Coppola's Zoetrope: All-Story 2*. She is the recipient of an NEA literature grant. Her first collection of short stories, *The Laws of Evening*, was published in May 2003 and chosen for Barnes & Noble's Summer 2003 Discover Great New Writers program. She lives in Los Angeles.

• I first wrote "Rationing" about six years ago. But it never really came together, even after a lot of revisions and a lot of different titles. I finally gave up. The story stayed in my computer for several years, forgotten, until I chanced across it one day when I was cleaning out my files. After so long, it was like reading a story written by someone else. My mistakes, in hindsight, seemed so obvious and simple that suddenly I couldn't wait to sit down at my desk and give it another try. The final rewrite was relatively fast — I'd had a six-year head start, after all — and this time everything somehow fell into place. Perhaps because this story has taken so long to reach maturity, against all the odds, it remains one of my personal favorites.

100 Other Distinguished Stories of 2002

SELECTED BY KATRINA KENISON

Editorial Addresses of American and Canadian Magazines Publishing Short Stories

Ache
P.O. Box 50065
Minneapolis, MN 55405
www.achemagazine.com
$25, Brian Bieber

African American Review
Shannon Hall 119
St. Louis University
220 N. Grand Union Boulevard
St. Louis, MO 63103-2007
web.indstate.edu/artsci/AAR
$38, Joe Weixlmann

Agni Review
Boston University Writing Program
236 Bay State Road
Boston, MA 02115
agni@bu.edu
$15, Sven Birkerts

Alabama Literary Review
272 Smith Hall
Troy State University
Troy, AL 36082
$10, Donald Noble

Alaska Quarterly Review
University of Alaska, Anchorage
3211 Providence Drive
Anchorage, AK 99508
ayaqr@uaa.alaska.edu
$10, Ronald Spatz

American Letters and Commentary
850 Park Avenue, Suite 5b
New York, NY 10021
www.amletters.org
$8, Anna Rabinowitz

American Literary Review
University of North Texas
P.O. Box 311307
Denton, TX 76203-1307
www.engl.unt.edu/alr
$10, Barbara Rodman

Another Chicago Magazine
Left Field Press
3709 North Kenmore
Chicago, Il 60613
$8, Sharon Solwitz

Antioch Review
Antioch University
150 East South College Street

Yellow Springs, OH 45387
$35, Robert S. Fogarty

Appalachian Heritage
Berea College
Berea, KY 40404
$18, James Gage

Arkansas Review
Department of English and
Philosophy
P.O. Box 1890
Arkansas State University
State University, AR 72467
$20, William Clements

Ascent
English Department
Concordia College
901 Eighth Street
Moorhead, MN 56562
olsen@cord.edu
$12, W. Scott Olsen

Atlantic Monthly
77 North Washington Street
Boston, MA 02114
www.theatlantic.com
$14.95, C. Michael Curtis

Baffler
P.O. Box 378293
Chicago, IL 60637
thebaffler.com
$24, Thomas Frank

Bamboo Ridge
P.O. Box 61781
Honolulu, HI 96839-1781
brinfo@bambooridge.com
$35, Eric Chock and Darrell H. Y. Lum

Bellevue Literary Review
Department of Medicine
New York University School of
Medicine
550 First Avenue
New York, NY 10016
www.BLReview.org
$12, Danielle Ofri

Bellingham Review
MS-9053
Western Washington University
Bellingham, WA 98225
$14, Brenda Miller

Bellowing Ark
P.O. Box 55564
Shoreline, WA 98155
$15, Robert Ward

Berkshire Review
P.O. Box 23
Richmond, VA 01254-0023
$8.95, Vivan Dorsel

Black Warrior Review
P.O. Box 862936
Tuscaloosa, AL 35486-0027
www.webdelsol.com/bwr
$14, Matt Maki

Blackbird
Department of English
Virginia Commonwealth University
P.O. Box 843082
Richmond, VA 23284-3082
Gregory Donovan

Bomb
New Art Publications
594 Broadway, 10th floor
New York, NY 10012
www.bombsite.com
$18, Betsy Sussler

Book
252 W. 37th St., 5th floor
New York, NY 10018
$19.95, Jerome V. Kramer

Border Crossings
500-70 Arthur Street
Winnipeg, Manitoba R3B 167
$27, Meeka Walsh

Boston Review
Building E 53, Room 407 MIT
Cambridge, MA 02139

www.bostonreview.mit.edu
$17, Joshua Cohen

Boulevard
PMB 325
6614 Clayton Road
Richmond Heights, MO 63117
$15, Richard Burgin

Brain, Child: The Magazine for
Thinking Mothers
P.O. Box 1161
Harrisonburg, VA 22801
www.brainchildmag.com
*$18, Jennifer Niesslein, Stephanie
Wilkinson*

Briar Cliff Review
3303 Rebecca Street
P.O. Box 2100
Sioux City, IA 51104-2100
$10, Phil Hey

Bridge
119 North Peoria, #3D
Chicago, IL 60607
$30, Mike Newirth

Bridges
P.O. Box 24839
Eugene, OR 97402
$15, Clare Kinberg

Callaloo
Department of English
Texas A&M University
4227 TAMU
College Station, TX 77843-4227
$37, Charles H. Rowell

Calyx
P.O. Box B
Corvallis, OR 97339
calyx@proaxis.com
$19.50, Margarita Donnelly

Capilano Review
Capilano College
2055 Purcell Way
North Vancouver

British Columbia V7J 3H5
$25, Sharon Thesen

Carolina Quarterly
Greenlaw Hall 066A
University of North Carolina
Chapel Hill, NC 27514
$12, Clare Douglass

Carve Fiction Writers Association
SAO Box 187
University of Washington Box 352238
Seattle, WA 98195
www.carvezine.com
Melvin Sterne

Chariton Review
Truman State University
Kirksville, MO 63501
$9, Jim Barnes

Chattahoochee Review
Georgia Perimeter College
2101 Womack Road
Dunwoody, GA 30338-4497
$16, Lawrence Hetrick

Chelsea
P.O. Box 773
Cooper Station
New York, NY 10276
$13, Alfredo de Palchi

Chicago Quarterly Review
517 Sherman Avenue
Evanston, IL 60202
*$10, S. Afzal Haider, Jane Lawrence,
Elizabeth McKenzie, Brian Skinner*

Chicago Review
5801 South Kenwood
University of Chicago
Chicago, IL 60637
www.humanities.uchicago.edu/review
$18, Eirik Steinhoff

Cimarron Review
205 Morrill Hall
Oklahoma State University
Stillwater, OK 74078-0135

www.cimmaronreview.okstate.edu
$16, E. P. Walkiewicz

Colere
Coe College
1220 1st Avenue NE
Cedar Rapids, IA 52402
Laura Farmer

Colorado Review
Department of English
Colorado State University
Fort Collins, CO 80523
creview@vines.colostate.edu
$24, David Milofsky

Columbia
2960 Broadway
415 Dodge Hall
Columbia University
New York, NY 10027
$10, J. Manuel Gonzales

Comfusion / Lotus Foundation
304 South Third Street
San Jose, CA 95112
auer@comfusion.com
Victoria Auer

Confrontation
English Department
C. W. Post College of Long Island
University
Greenvale, NY 11548
$8, Martin Tucker

Conjunctions
21 E. 10th Street, #3-E
New York, NY 10003
$18, Bradford Morrow

Connecticut Review
English Department
Southern Connecticut State University
501 Crescent Street
New Haven, CT 06515
Vivian Shipley

Crab Creek Review
P.O. Box 840

Vashon Island, WA 98070
$10, editorial group

Crab Orchard Review
Department of English
Southern Illinois University at
Carbondale
Carbondale, IL 62901
www.siu.edu/~crborchd
$15, Richard Peterson

Crazyhorse
Department of English
College of Charleston
66 George Street
Charleston, SC 29424
$15, Bret Lott, Paul Allen, Carol Ann Davis

CrossConnect
P.O. Box 2317
Philadelphia, PA 19103
David Deifer

Crucible
Barton College
P.O. Box 5000
Wilson, NC 27893-7000
Terrence L. Grimes

CutBank
Department of English
University of Montana
Missoula, MT 59812
cutbank@selway.umt.edu
$12, Siobhan Scarry

Daedalus
136 Irving Street, Suite 100
Cambridge, MA 02138
$33, James Miller

Denver Quarterly
University of Denver
Denver, CO 80208
$20, Bin Ramke

Descant
P.O. Box 314
Station P
Toronto, Ontario M5S 2S8

www.descant.on.ca
$25, Karen Mulhallen

Descant
TCU
Box 297270
Fort Worth, TX 76129
$12, Lynn Risser, David Kuhne

DoubleTake
55 Davis Square
Somerville, MA 02144
www.doubletakemagazine.org
$32, R. J. McGill

Elle
1633 Broadway
New York, NY 10019
$14, Ben Dickinson

Epoch
251 Goldwin Smith Hall
Cornell University
Ithaca, NY 14853-3201
$11, Michael Koch

Esquire
250 West 55th Street
New York, NY 10019
www.esquire.com
$17.94, Adrienne Miller

Eureka Literary Magazine
Eureka College
300 East College Avenue
Eureka, IL 61530-1500
$15, Loren Logsdon

Event
Douglas College
P.O. Box 2503
New Westminster
British Columbia V3L 5B2
$22, Christine Dewar

Fantasy & Science Fiction
P.O. Box 3447
Hoboken, NJ 07030
GordonFSF@aol.com
$38.97, Gordon Van Gelder

Fiction
Department of English
The City College of New York
Convent Avenue at 138th Street
New York, NY 10031
www.ccny.cuny.edu/Fiction/fiction.htm
$7, Mark Mirsky

Fiction International
Department of English and
Comparative Literature
San Diego State University
San Diego, CA 92182
$12, Harold Jaffe, Larry McCaffery

Fiddlehead
UNB P.O. Box 4400
Fredericton
New Brunswick E3B 5A3
$20, Mark Anthony Jarman

Five Points
Georgia State University
Department of English
University Plaza
Atlanta, GA 30303-3083
$15, Pam Durban, David Bottoms

Florida Review
Department of English, Box 25000
University of Central Florida
Orlando, FL 32816
www.pegasus.cc.ucf.edu/~english/
floridareview/home.htm
$10, Pat Rushin

Flyway
206 Ross Hall
Department of English
Iowa State University
Ames, IA 50011
$18, Sam Pritchard

Folio
Department of Literature
The American University
Washington, DC 20016
$12, Geoffrey D. Witham

Gargoyle
Paycock Press
c/o Atticus Books & Music
1508 U Street NW
Washington, DC 20009
$20, Richard Peabody, Lucinda Ebersole

Georgia Review
University of Georgia
Athens, GA 30602
www.uga.edu/garev
$24, T. R. Hummer

Gettysburg Review
Gettysburg College
Gettysburg, PA 17325
$24, Peter Stitt

Glimmer Train Stories
710 SW Madison Street
Suite 504
Portland, OR 97205
*$32, Susan Burmeister-Brown,
Linda Swanson-Davies*

GQ
4 Times Square, 9th floor
New York, NY 10036
$19.97, Walter Kirn

Grain
Box 1154
Regina, Saskatchewan S4P 3B4
www.grain.mag@sk.sympatico.ca
$26.95, Elizabeth Philips

Grand Street
214 Sullivan Street, #6C
New York, NY 10012
$25, Jean Stein

Granta
1755 Broadway, 5th floor
New York, NY 10019-3780
$32, Ian Jack

Great River Review
Anderson Center for Interdisciplinary
Studies
P.O. Box 406

Red Wing, MN 55066
$12, Richard Broderick, Robert Hedin

Green Hills Literary Lantern
North Central Missouri College
Box 375
Trenton, MO 64683
$7, Sara King

Green Mountains Review
Box A58
Johnson State College
Johnson, VT 05656
$15, Tony Whedon

Greensboro Review
Department of English
University of North Carolina
Greensboro, NC 27412
www.uncg.edu/eng
$10, Jim Clark

Gulf Coast
Department of English
University of Houston
4800 Calhoun Road
Houston, TX 77204-3012
$22, Mark Doty

Gulf Stream
English Department
Florida International University
3000 NE 151st Street
North Miami, FL 33181
$9, John Dufresne

Harper's Magazine
666 Broadway
New York, NY 10012
$16, Lewis Lapham

Harpur Palate
Department of English
Binghamton University
P.O. Box 6000
Binghamton, NY 13902
$16.66, Toiya Kristen Finley

Harvard Review
Poetry Room
Harvard College Library

Cambridge, MA 02138
$16, Christina Thompson

Hawaii Pacific Review
1060 Bishop Street, LB 402
Honolulu, HI 96813
hpreview@hpu.edu
Patrice Wilson

Hawaii Review
University of Hawaii
Department of English
1733 Donaghho Road
Honolulu, HI 96822
$20, Michael Puleloa

Hayden's Ferry Review
Box 871502
Arizona State University
Tempe, AZ 85287-1502
www.haydensferryreview.org
$10, Julie Hensley, Bill Martin

High Plains Literary Review
180 Adams Street, Suite 250
Denver, CO 80206
$20, Robert O. Greer, Jr.

Hudson Review
684 Park Avenue
New York, NY 10021
$24, Paula Deitz, Frederick Morgan

Idaho Review
Boise State University
Department of English
1910 University Drive
Boise, ID 83725
$9.95, Mitch Wieland

Image
323 South Broad Street
P.O. Box 674
Kennett Square, PA 19348
www.imagejournal.org
$36, Gregory Wolfe

Inkwell
Manhattanville College
2900 Purchose Street

Purchose, NY 10577
$10.50, Karen Sirabian

Iowa Review
Department of English
University of Iowa
308 EPB
Iowa City, IA 52242
www.uiowa.edu/~iareview
$18, David Hamilton

Iris
Women's Center
Box 323 HSC
University of Virginia
Charlottesville, VA 22908
$9, Virginia Moran

Italian Americana
University of Rhode Island
Providence Campus
80 Washington Street
Providence, RI 02903
$20, Carol Bonomo Albright

J&L Illustrated
P.O. Box 723991
Atlanta, GA 31139
Jason Fulford

Jewish Currents
22 East 17th Street
New York, NY 10003
$20, editorial board

The Journal
Department of English
Ohio State University
164 West 17th Avenue
Columbus, OH 43210
$12, Kathy Fagan, Michelle Herman

Kalliope
Florida Community College
3939 Roosevelt Boulevard
Jacksonville, FL 32205
$12.50, Mary Sue Koeppel

Kenyon Review
Kenyon College
Gambier, OH 43022

www.kenyonreview.org
$25, David H. Lynn

Lake Affect
P.O. Box 10116
Rochester, NY 14610
$12, Michelle Cardulla

Lilith
250 West 57th Street
New York, NY 10107
lilithmag@aol.com
$18, Susan Weidman Schneider

Literal Latte
61 East 8th Street, Suite 240
New York, NY 10003
litlatte@aol.com
$11, Jenine Gordon Bockman

Literary Imagination
Department of Classics
221 Park Hall
University of Georgia
Athens, GA 30602-6203
$25, Sarah Spence

Literary Review
Fairleigh Dickinson University
285 Madison Avenue
Madison, NJ 07940
www.theliteraryreview.org
$18, Rene Steinke

Louisiana Literature
Box 792
Southeastern Louisiana University
Hammond, LA 70402
$12, Jack B. Bedell

Louisville Review
Spalding University
851 S. Fourth Stret
Louisville, KY 40203
$14, Sena Jeter Naslund

Lynx Eye
ScribbleFest Literary Group
542 Mitchell Drive
Los Osnos, CA 93402
$25, Pam McCully, Kathryn Morrison

The MacGuffin
Schoolcraft College
18600 Haggerty Road
Livonia, MI 48152
$15, Arthur J. Lindenberg

Madison Review
University of Wisconsin
Department of English
H. C. White Hall
600 North Park Street
Madison, WI 53706
$15, Jessica Agneessens, Meaghan Walker

Manoa
English Department
University of Hawaii
Honolulu, HI 96822
$22, Frank Stewart

Massachusetts Review
South College
Box 37140
University of Massachusetts
Amherst, MA 01003
www.massreview.com
$22, David Lenson, Mary Heath, Paul Jenkins

Matrix
1455 de Maisonneuve Boulevard West
Suite LB-514-8
Montreal, Quebec H3G IM8
matrix@alcor.concordia.ca
$18, R.E.N. Allen

McSweeney's
826 Valencia Street
San Francisco, CA 94110
submissions@mcsweeneys.net
$36, Dave Eggers

Meridian
Department of English
P.O. Box 400145
University of Virginia
Charlottesville, VA 22904-4145
$10, Paula Younger

Michigan Quarterly Review
3032 Rackham Building
915 East Washington Street
University of Michigan
Ann Arbor, MI 48109
$25, Laurence Goldstein

Mid-American Review
Department of English
Bowling Green State University
Bowling Green, OH 48109
www.bgsu.edu/midamericanreview
$12, Michael Czyzniejewski

Midnight Mind
P.O. Box 1131
New York, NY 10003
$10, Brett Van Ernst

Minnesota Review
Department of English
East Carolina University
Greenville, NC 27858
$45, Jeffrey Williams

Mississippi Review
University of Southern Mississippi
Southern Station, Box 5144
Hattiesburg, MS 39406-5144
www.sushi.st.usm.edu/mrw
$15, Frederick Barthelme

Missouri Review
1507 Hillcrest Hall
University of Missouri
Columbia, MO 65211
www.missourireview.org
$19, Speer Morgan

Moment
4710 41st Street NW
Washington, DC 20016
editor@momentmag.com
$14.97, Herschel Shanks

Mondo Greco
34R South Russell Street, Suite 2B
Boston, MA 02114-3936
mondogreco@att.net
$19, Barbara Fields

Natural Bridge
Department of English
University of Missouri, St. Louis
8001 Natural Bridge Road
St. Louis, MO 63121-4499
www.umsl.edu/~natural/index.htm
$15, Ryan Stone

Nebraska Review
Writers Workshop
WFAB 212
University of Nebraska at Omaha
Omaha, NE 68182-0324
$15, James Reed

New England Review
Middlebury College
Middlebury, VT 05753
NEReview@middlebury.edu
$23, Stephen Donadio

New Letters
University of Missouri
5100 Rockhill Road
Kansas City, MO 64110
$17, James McKinley

New Orleans Review
P.O. Box 195
Loyola University
New Orleans, LA 70118
$12, Christopher Chambers

New Orphic Review
706 Mill Street
Nelson, British Columbia V1L 4S5
$25, Ernest Hekkanen

New Quarterly
English Language Proficiency
Programme
Saint Jerome's University
200 University Avenue West
Waterloo, Ontario N2L 3G3
$36, Peter Hinchcliffe, Kim Jernigan

New Renaissance
26 Heath Road, #11
Arlington, MA 02474

wmichaud@gwi.net
$11.50, Louise T. Reynolds

New Yorker
4 Times Square
New York, NY 10036
$46, Deborah Treisman

New York Stories
English Department
La Guardia Community College
31-10 Thomson Avenue
Long Island City, NY 11101
$13.40, Daniel Lynch

Night Rally
P.O. Box 1707
Philadelphia, PA 19105
www.nightrally.org/interlo.htm
$21, Amber Dorko Stopper

Night Train
85 Orchard Street
Somerville, MA 02144
www.nighttrainmagazine.com
$17.95, Rusty Barnes

Nimrod
Arts and Humanities Council of Tulsa
600 South College Avenue
Tulsa, OK 74104
nimrod@utulsa.edu
$17.50, Francine Ringold

Noon
1369 Madison Avenue
PMB 298
New York, NY 10128
noonannual@yahoo.com
$9, Diane Williams

North American Review
University of Northern Iowa
1222 West 27th Street
Cedar Falls, IA 50614
NAR@uni.edu
$22, Vince Gotera

North Carolina Literary Review
Department of English
2201 Bate Building

East Carolina University
Greenville, NC 27858-4353
Margaret Bauer

North Dakota Quarterly
University of North Dakota
P.O. Box 8237
Grand Forks, ND 58202
ndq@sage.und.nodak.edu
$25, Robert Lewis

North Stone Review
Box 14098
Minneapolis, MN 55414-0098
$25, James Naiden

Northwest Review
369 PLC
University of Oregon
Eugene, OR 97403
$20, John Witte

Notre Dame Review
Department of English
356 O'Shag
University of Notre Dame
Notre Dame, IN 46556-5639
$15, John Matthias, William O'Rourke

Oasis
P.O. Box 626
Largo, FL 34649-0626
$20, Neal Storrs

Oklahoma Today
15 North Robinson, Suite 100
P.O. Box 53384
Oklahoma City, OK 73102
$16.95, Louisa McCune

One Story
P.O. Box 1326
New York, NY 10156
$21, Hannah Tinti, Maribeth Batcha

Ontario Review
9 Honey Brook Drive
Princeton, NJ 08540
www.ontarioreviewpress.com
$16, Raymond J. Smith

Open City
225 Lafayette Street
Suite 1114
New York, NY 10012
editors@opencity.org
$32, Thomas Beller, Daniel Pinchbeck

Orchid
3096 Williamsburg
Ann Arbor, MI 48108-2026
$16, Keith Hood

Other Voices
University of Illinois at Chicago
Department of English, M/C 162
601 South Morgan Street
Chicago, IL 60607-7120
www.othervoicesmagazine.org
$24, Lois Hauselman

Oxford American
P.O. Box 1156
404 South 11th Street
Oxford, MS 38655
www.oxfordamericanmag.com
$24.95, Marc Smirnoff

Oxygen
537 Jones Street, PMB 999
San Francisco, CA 94102
oxygen@slip.net
$14, Richard Hack

Oyster Boy Review
P.O. Box 77842
San Francisco, CA 94107
www.oysterboyreview.com
$20, Damon Sauve

Pangolin Papers
Turtle Press
P.O. Box 241
Norlond, WA 98358
$20, Pat Britt

Paris Review
541 East 72nd Street
New York, NY 10021
$34, George Plimpton

Parting Gifts
3413 Wilshire Drive
Greensboro, NC 27408-2923
Robert Bixby

Partisan Review
236 Bay State Road
Boston, MA 02215
www.partisanreview.org
$25, William Phillips

Penny Dreadful: Tales & Poems
P.O. Box 719
Radio City Station
New York, NY 10101-0719
mpendragon@aol.com
$12

Phantasmagoria
English Department
Century Community and Technical
College
3300 Century Avenue North
White Bear Lake, MN 55110
$15, Abigail Allen

Playboy
Playboy Building
919 North Michigan Avenue
Chicago, IL 60611
$29.97, Christopher Napolitano

Pleiades
Department of English and
Philosophy, 5069
Central Missouri State University
P.O. Box 800
Warrensburg, MO 64093
$12, R. M. Kinder, Susan Steinberg

Ploughshares
Emerson College
120 Boylston Street
Boston, MA 02116
www.emerson.edu/ploughshares
$22, Don Lee

PMS poem/memoir/story
Department of English
University of Alabama at Birmingham
HB 217, 1530 3rd Avenue South
Birmingham, AL 35294-1260
$7, Linda Frost

Porcupine
P.O. Box 259
Cedarburg, WI 53012
ppine259@aol.com
$15.95, group

Post Road
P.O. Box 590663
Newton Center, MA 02459
$16, Catherine Parnell

Potomac Review
P.O. Box 354
Port Tobacco, MD 20677
elilv@juno.com
$20, Eli Flam

Potpourri
P.O. Box 8278
Prairie Village, KS 66208
potpourripub@aol.com
$16, Polly W. Swafford

Prairie Fire
423-100 Arthur Street
Winnipeg, Manitoba R3B 1H3
prfire@escape.ca
$25, Andris Taskans

Prairie Schooner
201 Andrews Hall
University of Nebraska
Lincoln, NE 68588-0334
www.unl.edu/schooner/psmain.htm
$26, Hilda Raz

Prism International
Department of Creative Writing
University of British Columbia
Vancouver, British Columbia V6T 1W5
prism@interchange.ubc.ca
$18, Billeh Nickerson

Provincetown Arts
650 Commercial Street
Provincetown, MA 02657
$10, Ivy Meeropol

Puerto del Sol
Department of English
Box 3E
New Mexico State University
Las Cruces, NM 88003
$10, Kevin McIlvoy

Quarry Magazine
P.O. Box 74
Kingston, Ontario K7L 4V6
goldfishpree@hotmail.com
$15, Alice Terry

Quarterly West
312 Olpin Union
University of Utah
Salt Lake City, UT 84112
$14, Stephen Tuttle

Rain Crow
2127 W. Pierce Avenue, #2B
Chicago, IL 60622-1824
http://rain-crow.com/
$15, Michael Manley

Ralph
Box 7272
San Diego, CA 92167
$10, A. W. Allworthy

Reading Room
Great Marsh Press
P.O. Box 2144
Lenox Hill Station
New York, NY 10021
www.greatmarshpress.com
$65, Barbara Probst Solomon

REAL
School of Liberal Arts
Stephen F. Austin State University
Nacogdoches, TX 75962
$15, Dale Hearell

Red Rock Review
English Department, J2A

Community College of Southern
Nevada
3200 East Cheyenne Avenue
North Las Vegas, NV 89030
$9.50, Richard Logsdon

Red Wheelbarrow
De Anza College
21250 Stevens Creek Boulevard
Cupertino, CA 95014-5702
www.deanza.fhda.edu/redwheelbarrow
$5, Randolph Splitter

Republic of Letters
120 Cushing Avenue
Boston, MA 02125-2033
rangoni@bu.edu
$25, Keith Botsford

River City
Department of English
University of Memphis
Memphis, TN 38152
$12, Tom Carlson

River Oak Review
734 Noyes Street, #M3
Evanston, IL 60201
maryleemock@mindspring.com
$12, Mary Lee MacDonald

River Sedge
Department of English
University of Texas
1201 W. University Drive, CAS 266
Edinburg, TX 78539-2999
$12, Dorey Schmidt

River Styx
Big River Association
634 N. Grand Boulevard, 12th floor
St. Louis, MO 63103-1002
$20, Richard Newman

Room of One's Own
P.O. Box 46160
Station D
Vancouver, British Columbia V6J 5G5
www.islandnet.com/Room/enter
$25, collective

Salmagundi
Skidmore College
Saratoga Springs, NY 12866
$18, Robert Boyers

Salt Hill
English Department
Syracuse University
Syracuse, NY 13244
salthill@cas.syr.edu
$15, Ellen Litman

Santa Monica Review
1900 Pico Boulevard
Santa Monica, CA 90405
$12, Andrew Tonkovich

Seventeen
850 Third Avenue
New York, NY 10022
$14.95, Patrice G. Adcroft

Sewanee Review
University of the South
Sewanee, TN 37375-4009
$20, George Core

Shenandoah
Troubador Theater, 2nd floor
Washington and Lee University
Lexington, VA 24450-0303
www.wlu.edu/~shenando
$15, R. T. Smith

Slow Trains Literary Journal
P.O. Box 4741
Englewood, CO 80155
$14.95, Susannah Indigo

Songs of Innocence
Pendragon Publications
P.O. Box 719
Radio City Station
New York, NY 10101-0719
mpendragon@aol.com
$12, Michael M. Pendragon

Sonora Review
Department of English
University of Arizona

Tucson, AZ 85721
$12, Linda Copeland

South Carolina Review
Department of English
Clemson University
Strode Tower, Box 340523
Clemson, SC 29634-1503
$10, Wayne Chapman, Donna Haisty Winchell

Southeast Review
Department of English
Florida State University
Talahassee, FL 32306-1036
southeastreview@english.fsu.edu
$10, Tony R. Morris

Southern Exposure
P.O. Box 531
Durham, NC 27702
southern_exposure@i4south.org
$24, Chris Kromm

Southern Humanities Review
9088 Haley Center
Auburn University
Auburn, AL 36849
www.auburn.edu/english/shr/
home.htm
$15, Dan R. Latimer, Virginia M. Kouidis

Southern Review
43 Allen Hall
Louisiana State University
Baton Rouge, LA 70803
$25, James Olney, Dave Smith

Southwest Review
Southern Methodist University
P.O. Box 4374
Dallas, TX 75275
$24, Willard Spiegelman

Story Quarterly
431 Sheridan Road
Kenilworth, IL 60043-1220
storyquarterly@hotmail.com
$12, M.M.M. Hayes

Sun
107 North Roberson Street
Chapel Hill, NC 27516
$34, Sy Safransky

Sycamore Review
Department of English
1356 Heavilon Hall
Purdue University
West Lafayette, IN 47907
www.sla.purdue.edu/academic/engl/
sycamore/
$12, Barbara Lawhorn-Haroun

Talking River Review
Division of Literature and Languages
Lewis-Clark State College
500 Eighth Avenue
Lewiston, ID 83501
$14, Nikki Allen, Eldy Schultz

Tampa Review
University of Tampa
401 West Kennedy Boulevard
Tampa, FL 33606-1490
$15, Richard Mathews

Thin Air
P.O. Box 23549
Flagstaff, AZ 86002
www.nau.edu/english/thinair
$9, A. Vaughn Wagner

Third Coast
Department of English
Western Michigan University
Kalamazoo, MI 49008-5092
$11, Adam Schuitema, Jason Skipper

Thought
P.O. Box 117098
Burlingame, CA 94011-7098
$10, Kevin Feeney

Threepenny Review
P.O. Box 9131
Berkeley, CA 94709
$16, Wendy Lesser

Timber Creek Review
8969 UNCG Station

Greensboro, NC 27413
timber_creek_review@hoopsmail.com
$15, John Freiermuth

Tin House
P.O. Box 10500
Portland, OR 97296-0500
$39.80, Rob Spillman

Transition
69 Dunster Street
Harvard University
Cambridge, MA 02138
transition@fas.harvard.edu
*$27, Kwame Anthony Appiah, Henry
Louis Gates, Jr., Michael Vazquez*

TriQuarterly
2020 Ridge Avenue
Northwestern University
Evanston, IL 60208
$24, Susan Firestone Hahn

Turnrow
English Department
The University of Louisiana at Monroe
700 University Avenue
Monroe, LA 71209
$7, Jack Heflin, William Ryan

Two Rivers Review
P.O. Box 158
Clinton, NY 13323
Phil Memmer

Virginia Adversaria
Empire Publishing, P.O. Box 2349
Poquoson, VA 23662
Empirepub@hotmail.com
Bill Glose

Virginia Quarterly Review
One West Range
Charlottesville, VA 22903
$18, Staige D. Blackford

War, Literature, and the Arts
Department of English and Fine Arts
2354 Fairchild Drive, Suite 6D45
USAF Academy, CO 80840-6242

donald.anderson@usafa.af.mil
Donald Anderson

Wascana Review
English Department
University of Regina
Regina, Saskatchewan
$10, Marcel DeCoste

Washington Square
Creative Writing Program
New York University
19 University Place, 2nd floor
New York, NY 10003-4556
washington.square.journal@nyu.edu
$6, James Pritchard

Weber Studies
Weber State University
Ogden, UT 84408
$20, Brad Roghaar

West Branch
Bucknell Hall
Bucknell University
Lewisburg, PA 17837
$10, Paula Closson Buck

Western Humanities Review
University of Utah
255 South Central Campus Drive
Room 3500
Salt Lake City, UT 84112
$14, Barry Weller

Willow Springs
Eastern Washington University
705 West 1st Avenue
Spokane, WA 99201
$11.50, Jennifer S. Davis

Wind
Wind Publications
P.O. Box 24548
Lexington, KY 40524
www.wind-wind.org
$15, Chris Green

Windsor Review
Department of English
University of Windsor

Windsor, Ontario N9B 3P4
$29.95, Alistair MacLeod

Witness
Oakland Community College
Orchard Ridge Campus
27055 Orchard Lake Road
Farmington Hills, MI 48334
www.witnessmagazine.com
$15, Peter Stine

Wordwrights!
Argonne Hotel
1620 Argonne Place NW
Washington, DC 20009
$25, Ronald Douglas Baker

Yale Review
P.O. Box 208243
New Haven, CT 06520-8243
$27, J. D. McClatchy

Yankee
Yankee Publishing, Inc.
Dublin, NH 03444
www.newengland.com
$22, Judson D. Hale

Zoetrope
The Sentinel Building
916 Kearney Street
San Francisco, CA 94133
www.all-story.com
$20, Tamara Straus

Zyzzyva
P.O. Box 590069
San Francisco, CA 94104
editor@zyzzyva.org
$28, Howard Junker

THE B·E·S·T AMERICAN SERIES ™

THE BEST AMERICAN SHORT STORIES® 2003
Walter Mosley, guest editor • Katrina Kenison, series editor

"Story for story, readers can't beat the *Best American Short Stories* series" (*Chicago Tribune*). This year's most beloved short fiction anthology is edited by the award-winning author Walter Mosley and includes stories by Dorothy Allison, Mona Simpson, Anthony Doerr, Dan Chaon, and Louise Erdrich, among others.

0-618-19733-8 PA $13.00 / 0-618-19732-X CL $27.50
0-618-19748-6 CASS $26.00 / 0-618-19752-4 CD $35.00

THE BEST AMERICAN ESSAYS® 2003
Anne Fadiman, guest editor • Robert Atwan, series editor

Since 1986, the *Best American Essays* series has gathered the best non-fiction writing of the year and established itself as the best anthology of its kind. Edited by Anne Fadiman, author of *Ex Libris* and editor of the *American Scholar*, this year's volume features writing by Edward Hoagland, Adam Gopnik, Michael Pollan, Susan Sontag, John Edgar Wideman, and others.

0-618-34161-7 PA $13.00 / 0-618-34160-9 CL $27.50

THE BEST AMERICAN MYSTERY STORIES™ 2003
Michael Connelly, guest editor • Otto Penzler, series editor

Our perennially popular anthology is a favorite of mystery buffs and general readers alike. This year's volume is edited by the best-selling author Michael Connelly and offers pieces by Elmore Leonard, Joyce Carol Oates, Brendan DuBois, Walter Mosley, and others.

0-618-32965-X PA $13.00 / 0-618-32966-8 CL $27.50
0-618-39072-3 CD $35.00

THE BEST AMERICAN SPORTS WRITING™ 2003
Buzz Bissinger, guest editor • Glenn Stout, series editor

This series has garnered wide acclaim for its stellar sports writing and top-notch editors. Now Buzz Bissinger, the Pulitzer Prize–winning journalist and author of the classic *Friday Night Lights,* continues that tradition with pieces by Mark Kram Jr., Elizabeth Gilbert, Bill Plaschke, S. L. Price, and others.

0-618-25132-4 PA $13.00 / 0-618-25130-8 CL $27.50

THE B·E·S·T AMERICAN SERIES ™

THE BEST AMERICAN TRAVEL WRITING 2003
Ian Frazier, guest editor • Jason Wilson, series editor

The Best American Travel Writing 2003 is edited by Ian Frazier, the author of *Great Plains* and *On the Rez*. Giving new life to armchair travel this year are William T. Vollmann, Geoff Dyer, Christopher Hitchens, and many others.

0-618-11881-0 PA $13.00 / 0-618-11881-0 CL $27.50
0-618-39074-X CD $35.00

THE BEST AMERICAN SCIENCE AND NATURE WRITING 2003
Richard Dawkins, guest editor • Tim Folger, series editor

This year's edition promises to be another "eclectic, provocative collection" (*Entertainment Weekly*). Edited by Richard Dawkins, the eminent scientist and distinguished author, it features work by Bill McKibben, Steve Olson, Natalie Angier, Steven Pinker, Oliver Sacks, and others.

0-618-17892-9 PA $13.00 / 0-618-17891-0 CL $27.50

THE BEST AMERICAN RECIPES 2003–2004
Edited by Fran McCullough and Molly Stevens

"The cream of the crop . . . McCullough's selections form an eclectic, unfussy mix" (*People*). Offering the very best of what America is cooking, as well as the latest trends, time-saving tips, and techniques, this year's edition includes a foreword by Alan Richman, award-winning columnist for *GQ*.

0-618-27384-0 CL $26.00

THE BEST AMERICAN NONREQUIRED READING 2003
Edited by Dave Eggers • Introduction by Zadie Smith

Edited by Dave Eggers, the author of *A Heartbreaking Work of Staggering Genius* and *You Shall Know Our Velocity*, this genre-busting volume draws the finest, most interesting, and least expected fiction, nonfiction, humor, alternative comics, and more from publications large, small, and on-line. *The Best American Nonrequired Reading 2003* features writing by David Sedaris, ZZ Packer, Jonathan Safran Foer, Andrea Lee, and others.

0-618-24696-7 $13.00 PA / 0-618-24696-7 $27.50 CL
0-618-39073-1 $35.00 CD

HOUGHTON MIFFLIN COMPANY   www.houghtonmifflinbooks.com